AF489719

Fiona Quinn Seal of Approval

(Not issued lightly, but always with a heaping of love)

Content:

Fiction. Music. Friends. Grief. And just a touch of time travel.

Language:

Pretty clean: nothing to make you blush or hide from your nan.

Violence and Sex:

Nope. This isn't that kind of story.

Music:

Total fire. You might even find some that shouldn't exist.

Emotions:

You might laugh. You might cry. Possibly at the same time.

Tolerance:

Everyone is invited to the table. Come as you are.

Warning: If you happen to find a tachyon solution, please don't mix it with your music.

Your results may vary.

This story explores themes of loss and healing. Please take care as you read.

Ena Quinn-Baker

In

Keeping Time

A Sound Logic Journey

D.P. Sheil

Berets & Ascots Publishing

Keeping Time

Is dedicated to my wife, Amanda

Takes someone special to support

A hare-brained idea written by a scatter brain

Love You!

Music in this Book:

Sing along, we know you want to

Keeping Time Playlist
All songs mentioned in the book
http://bit.ly/4esUVem

Keeping Time Chapter Titles
The songs behind the chapter titles
https://bit.ly/44tyUaI

Fiona & Ena's Playlist
Dive deeper into Fiona and Ena's
shared vibe https://bit.ly/4eurn01

Train Playlist
You'll know when you know.
https://bit.ly/4kl7lGK

Lost to Time Album
The Fin Whales
https://bit.ly/4liABhI

Swell Time Single
The Fin Whales
https://bit.ly/46WCIo1

Fast Train Lost Name
Sound Logic
https://bit.ly/42GmMmA

A note from the narrator:

Readers, it is an honor to bring the world of Ena Quinn Baker to you. I have done my best to tell this story as accurately and authentically possible. Ena's life sings with energy, drive, and unapologetic brilliance. My deepest hope is that I did her justice and that you find joy in the following pages.

If you dig Ena's vibe and want to keep up with what else is going on with Ena and her friends, visit us at the website or follow us on socials. We'd love to hear from you.

For hidden extras, puzzles, and bonus material, visit
https://enaquinnbaker.com/

Substack: https://enaquinnbaker.substack.com/

Bluesky: @EnaQB

Instagram: @EnaQB

TikTok: @enaQB

Acknowledgments

This story wouldn't exist without a chorus of voices.

To **Amanda**, my partner in life. Thank you for believing in me when this was just an idea born by nostalgia in a bar listening to a 90s song. Your patience, support, and sense of humor gave this book room to breathe.

To **Mom and Dad**. Thank you for raising someone willing to take the plunge and picking me up after the frequent wipeouts.

To **Zuri**. Our long walks helped me figure out so much. Thanks for pulling me away from the computer to grab the leash.

To **Kris**. Your insight and guidance at the very beginning of my writing and publishing journey meant more than I can say.

To **Val M. Mathews**. For the indispensable editing and coaching that brought this story to the next level.

To **Dylan**. Your time was invaluable. Thanks for helping me understand a different generation a tad better.

To the beta readers: **Annika, Camille, Ella, Erika, Francie, Lance, Lynn,** and **Suz**. You bravely walked into this story, and your feedback made it better.

To the **music**. Real and imagined. It has the power to heal, to bring us together, and to take us back and move us forward. It kept the beat, and it kept me going.

And finally, to you, **dear reader**. Thank you for your time and attention. I hope this story is worthy of both.

DRIVE

Ena sat in the passenger seat of her grandmother's old blue Subaru Outback, the faded paint a testament to years of loyal service. A CD played softly—"New Slang" by The Shins—blurring into the quiet whir of her fidget spinner. She stared out the window, feigning calm, but her fingers betrayed her. First days were never easy.

The past year had been a whirlwind. Her family had uprooted from fast-paced, no-nonsense Boston to laid-back Portland, Oregon. Moving was hard enough, but starting eighth grade in a new school? That was a different level of impossible.

Ena stood out, whether she wanted to or not. Shoulder-length pale blonde hair, steel-blue eyes flickering with wry intelligence, and a half-smile revealing a mischievous right dimple. This combination of looks, intelligence, and energy made people curious. In Boston, she'd found her groove; it worked for her. In Portland, she wasn't sure where she fit.

Her grandmother, Fiona, had insisted on driving her. Ena had expected her dad to take her, but he had relented when Fiona, his mother-in-law and an undeniable force of nature, said she wanted the job. Ena wasn't sure why; they'd never spent much time alone together before.

Fiona wasn't the grandmotherly type. She made it clear she was Fiona or Fi, not Grandma or anything close. She knew exactly what she liked, making her effortlessly cool. Short platinum hair, chic glasses, and a black leather jacket over a band tee from a group Ena had never heard of. She had once run an independent rock magazine that prided itself on discovering artists before they climbed the charts. She'd long since moved on from her chain-smoking days but still indulged in the occasional cigarette. Her voice carried the gravelly rasp of someone who had spent decades inhaling nicotine and music.

Ena had seen her only a handful of times growing up—family visits full of sing-alongs, noise, and too many people talking at once. Even then, Fiona had always watched her with a kind of quiet intensity, as if she unearthed a quality in her that Ena hadn't figured out yet. Fiona's intensity and vibrance had intimidated Ena during those visits.

Fiona reached over, resting her hand on Ena's fidget spinner, stilling it. "Kiddo," she said, her voice softer than usual, "I know the first day at a new school, especially at your age, is tough. It's unsettling. But what you do in the next few days will set things in motion that could ripple through the rest of your life."

Ena was caught off guard. She hadn't expected a speech.

"You're smart," Fiona continued. "And beautiful."

Ena made a face. Compliments always made her squirm. Was she supposed to say thank you? Deflect? Compliments from Fiona felt different from those from teachers or friends' parents—simple facts, not platitudes.

"That combination will open a lot of doors for you," Fiona said with a knowing smile. "But the easy doors? The ones that swing wide open? They're usually the least interesting. And the ones you have to shove open, or better yet, the windows you barely notice? You know, like the ones cracked just enough to squeeze through. Those lead to the real adventures."

Ena turned the words over in her mind, unsure of what to say.

Fiona leaned back, stealing a quick glance at her. "You're going to face choices, Ena. Use your intelligence. Listen to your heart. And look for the people who challenge you, who inspire you, who stand by you when things get tough."

Ena frowned. She wasn't thrilled about starting over somewhere new with no friends, no clue what the school would be like. "Fi, you make it sound so serious. Like I'm about to start running the country or something. It's just eighth grade."

"Fair." Fiona chuckled, her gravelly voice lightening. "I don't mean to make it sound like a burden. You should have fun, enjoy being young. But even the small choices matter. They build. And they can open doors you don't even see yet."

Ena wasn't sure how to respond. There was meaning beneath her grandmother's words, an unspoken gem, but she couldn't quite grasp it. It seemed like Fiona sensed Ena's need for space and reached for the radio, turning the volume back up as they pulled up to the school.

"Ena, you're going to do great today," Fiona said. "Don't let an old lady's musings get in your head. Go have some fun."

Ena cracked a small smile. She opened the door and slid out, the warm summer air hitting her face.

The school loomed ahead: big, unfamiliar, indifferent. Around her, clusters of kids chattered, laughing, reuniting after summer break. Their voices blurred together, an electric hum of excitement and nerves.

In Boston, she'd be with her friends, swapping stories about summer break like everyone else. Here, she was just…alone. A weird mix of dread and intrigue buzzed through her, like her feet were wired into the concrete beneath her. *Guess I'd better figure this place out.* Ena took a deep breath, gripping the straps of her backpack.

Here goes nothing.

WALLS

Ena pulled out her phone and slipped in her earbuds. The song "Believer" filled her ears, the pounding beat pressing confidence into her spine. One last hitch of her backpack. And into the wildness of eighth grade.

She stepped forward, dropping into the chaos of middle school. Lockers slammed, laughter shrieked, and someone was already crying near the office. Clusters of kids clogged the hallways, laughing, jostling, staking their claims. Friends gathered at lockers. Others sprinted in frantic chases. Two boys stood off, trading open-palmed slaps to prove who was tougher.

A voice floated down, cutting through the noise. "Excuse me."

Ena barely had time to react before a frumpy administrator materialized in front of her, barring the way like an overzealous mall cop.

"No phones."

Ena sighed, pulling out her earbuds and wrapping them around her phone. Just as she was about to shove it in her backpack, the administrator stuck out a hand—a greedy, waiting hand.

"You can have it back at the end of the day. Come to the principal's office before you leave."

Ena's hands balled into fists. *Wait, what?*

"I'm new here. I didn't know…"

The administrator's finger jabbed toward a sign on the wall. A cellphone circled in red with a slash through it. Beneath, a pithy slogan: *If you use it, you lose it.*

"Sorry, honey." No warmth. No sympathy. Just the brittle satisfaction of bureaucracy at work. "How else are you going to learn?"

Ena's stomach dropped. First day. First five minutes. And she'd already screwed up. She hadn't been the model student at her old school; she knew how to push the rules without getting burned.

Her hands trembled as she surrendered the phone, watching helplessly as the administrator turned, already scanning the crowd for more victims.

"Brutal. Ms. Anderson got you before you even made it five steps."

Ena turned toward the voice. The speaker was a lanky girl, all elbows and knees, dark hair barely tamed by a braided ponytail and slightly smudged rectangular metal-rimmed glasses. Behind them, dark, intelligent eyes held a hint of amusement.

Before Ena could respond, the girl disappeared into the crowd, swallowed by the middle school current.

Ena stood frozen, her world tilting slightly off its axis.

No friends. No phone. No clue how to survive this. She wished her best friend from Boston, Silvia, were here. She would definitely mock her for getting busted, but somehow, Ena knew it would feel easier with her around.

She forced herself forward, but without the armor of her phone, her music, every step left her more exposed. Nothing about this was how she'd imagined it. If she was honest with herself, she thought she'd stroll in like a boss—effortless, cool, unbothered. She kept her eyes down, focusing on her feet, occasionally glancing up to search for her first class.

English. Room 112 according to her schedule.

She spotted the room and stepped inside. A PowerPoint slide glowed on the whiteboard, displaying a seating chart. A cluster of kids crowded around it, groaning, swapping complaints.

An overdramatic voice cut through the chatter. "Ugh, seriously? I have to sit next to Skyler…again?"

Ena turned toward the voice. The speaker, Ashley Douglas, according to the chart, was all polished effort. A too-tight ponytail, lip gloss layered on like a second skin, and an Abercrombie T-shirt that had peaked last spring. Ena knew the type—someone trying just a little too hard to hold onto their place in the social order.

Ena found her seat, centered in the second-to-last row. She slid into the chair. Every part of this scraped against her nerves. Like she'd been dropped into a world with no map and no way to be sure of her footing.

The classroom continued to fill. Then, the girl who didn't have to try walked in. Tall, long straight black hair so shiny it shimmered, and a perfect smile. Her entire aesthetic said: I don't have to work to look like this.

Ashley perked up in her seat instantly. "Hi, Madison!" she chirped, just a little too eagerly.

"Ashley." Madison's response was flat, an acknowledgment so lukewarm it shouldn't have been satisfying, but Ashley still beamed, like it was a win.

Madison made her way toward Ena. The power of her gaze hit like a spotlight, a critical assessment that didn't feel cruel, just calculating.

"New?" Madison asked as she passed, not dismissive, just curious.

Ena froze. Was that directed at her?

"Yeah? Moved from Boston," she answered.

Madison took the seat directly behind Ena. As she did, the quiet but undeniable pull of attention shifted to Ena, reassessing. Madison's approval, however small, signaled to the class to take Ena seriously.

The teacher, in her mid-thirties, neatly dressed yet comfortably casual, stood up from behind her desk and smiled. Her shoulder-length sandy-blonde hair framed a face that exuded the easy confidence of someone who knew exactly who she was.

"Good morning, everyone. I'm Ms. Nikola. This summer, my partner and I got hooked on classic arcade games at Ground Kontrol. We went almost every weekend, and I'm proud to say we almost beat Dragon's Lair, which, if you don't know, is basically an animated medieval torture chamber designed to eat your quarters."

She crossed her arms, smiled playfully. "Also, I hold the high score on Tron, and I don't expect any of you to come close anytime soon."

A few students chuckled. Ena liked her already.

"Now that you know a little about me, we're going to be spending plenty of time together this year. So, let's take a few minutes to get to know each other." Ms. Nikola scanned her seating chart. "Mateo Alvarez, we'll start with you."

A boy in the front row straightened up. "Mateo Alvarez. This summer I went to basketball camp and learned to dunk."

From across the room, someone snorted. "You capping, bruh. That was a seven-foot hoop."

Mateo scoffed. "I didn't see you dunk."

Ena sighed to herself. If they were going to argue over every introduction, this would take forever. Maybe long enough that she could just skip the awkward look-at-me moment altogether.

A few more students rattled off their names, most mentioning sports camps, music camps, or family vacations. Then it was the smallest kid in the room's turn.

"I'm Skyler Duval, my pronouns are they/them. I spent a week at a silent retreat on Mount Shasta. My energy felt centered when I returned." Skyler was dressed in what resembled a cream-colored monastic robe, sitting with perfect posture, hands resting gently on their desk. Straight black hair hung to mid-neck, framing a thoughtful face and brown eyes that seemed to perceive more than was readily visible.

A few kids exchanged glances, some chuckled. Ena wasn't sure how to react, but the quiet confidence in Skyler's voice made her curious.

Behind her, a voice floated just loud enough for Ena to hear. "He's always so weird."

Ena tensed. Clearly, Madison was not a fan.

When it was her turn, Ena took a deep breath.

"Ena Quinn-Bakah." Her nerves slammed her straight into her exaggerated Boston accent. "This summah, I moved from Bawston to Pahtland, 'cause my mom and dad wanted to move back."

A voice drifted from behind her. "Nice accent."

Ena couldn't tell if Madison meant it or was just amused. Either way, all she wanted to do was to crawl under her desk after letting that stupid accent slip.

A few more students rattled off their names. Then…

"Madison Sloane, as you all know. I spent six weeks with my family in Italy." Madison delivered it with the enthusiasm of someone reciting a math problem, like jetting off to Italy was as routine as a trip to the grocery store.

The introductions wrapped up. A few students shifted in their seats, some already zoning out, others sneaking glances at the clock.

Ms. Nikola straightened. "Thank you for those introductions. Now, let's get to work."

She stepped toward the whiteboard and picked up a dry-erase marker.

"For tomorrow, your first assignment: Read Robert Frost's 'Neither Out Far Nor In Deep.' We'll discuss what you think it means."

A few students groaned softly. Ena just scribbled the title in her notebook. She'd barely survived the first day's introductions. Tomorrow, she did not want to look foolish. Again.

INTO THE WILD

The morning classes blurred together, a steady stream of introductions, seating charts, and teachers rattling off expectations. By lunch, Ena had picked up on a few clues about the amorphous social hierarchy, who seemed to draw the most attention, who was quick to acknowledge whom.

She barely had time to scan the cafeteria when Madison appeared at her side.

"Hey, why don't you eat with us?" Not a question. An expectation. A gift.

"Sure," Ena said, uncertainty blooming beneath her skin. Fiona had pushed her to make her own choices this morning. Now she was letting herself be pulled by the current, not charting her own path. The day had started so rough, easy felt good.

Ena trailed behind Madison to a long cafeteria table, the kind with blue plastic stools bolted to the frame. One seat, dead center, had been strategically left open. Another, at the far edge, sat conspicuously unclaimed. Without hesitation, Madison slid into the center like the seat had been pre-warmed for her. Ena hesitated just a beat, then made her way to the edge, perching like a satellite trying to find the right orbit.

The conversation barely skipped a beat.

"Oh. My. God. Mateo grew like six inches over the summer," one girl said, her voice pitched high enough to carry, like she hoped someone overheard.

"And his hair is, like, almost hot now," Ashley chimed in, twirling her ponytail like it had a direct line to her brain.

Ena kept her face neutral, unpacking her lunch slowly, hoping no one noticed how out of sync she was next to their glossy rhythm.

Madison piped in. "And Skyler didn't grow an inch. His ego's the only thing that did."

Giggles rippled across the table.

Ena said softly, "I thought they said their pronouns were they/them."

Madison rolled her eyes. "You'll learn. That's just Skyler trying to stand out. He's always looking for attention."

All eyes turned to Ena, watching, waiting. What would she do?

She didn't know Skyler. She didn't know anyone. *Maybe Madison was right. Maybe it was performative. But even if it was, that was their choice, right?*

Madison broke the silence.

"Anyway, Boston? What do you think of Portland?"

There was a test embedded in that simple question.

"Portland's pretty cool," Ena said. "We moved a few weeks ago, so I'm still figuring things out. I love seeing Mt. Hood pop into view. It's like it just shows up when you least expect it."

That seemed to pass. The table returned to their regularly scheduled programming: who grew, who didn't, who wore the wrong thing, who was obsessed with which YouTuber. Ena listened, but it was more like she was an observer behind glass.

It was all so…easy. She looked around the table and saw the rhymes to her old life—jokes, stories, the same pecking order. But it all sounded just slightly off, like a guitar that hadn't been tuned quite right.

And Fiona's voice echoed in her mind: Easy doors are the least interesting. The words hit differently now, casting a strange shadow.

Lunch was divided into two segments. The first twenty minutes for eating, the next twenty spent outside. A chime sounded.

"Time to walk the yard," Madison said, as the girls stood and dropped their trash in the bins on their way out.

Ena followed them into the courtyard. They drifted toward the basketball courts, where Mateo and the other boy from English, Adrian, were already midway through a jumping contest on the short rim. As more boys filtered onto the court, the contest melted into a game.

Ena's interest in watching evaporated. She drifted toward the edges.

That's when she saw her again, leaning against the wall, the girl from the hallway. The one who'd clocked her phone getting confiscated. Ena realized she'd been in her math class too. She walked toward her.

"Hi, I'm Ena." It came out a little awkward. She scrambled for anything to hold onto and spotted the girl's messenger bag.

"Cool bag. I like that patch."

The girl cast a quick glance down at the stitched corner of her bag: *404: Not Found.*

"Piney. Uh, thanks."

Silence lingered. Piney didn't seem interested in going further.

"So, I guess you saw me get busted for my phone this morning."

"Yeah. Miss Anderson lives for that stuff. Let a million things slide, but phones? Nope. You gotta learn the tricks."

Piney's tone was flat, her eyes already drifting elsewhere.

Ena hesitated. She could drift off, pretend she was just passing through.

That would be easy. But Fiona's voice echoed again: *windows cracked just a bit.*

Ena glanced down at the patch.

"So…are you into computers?"

Piney's gaze flicked toward her. She scoffed.

"You might say that." She let it hang for a beat. "You need me to remove you from a no-fly list or something?"

Ena squinted. *Was that a joke?* She wasn't totally sure.

Piney jutted her chin toward the basketball court. "You best not ignore the Queen Bee. She's beckoning."

Ena looked over her shoulder. The basketball game was in full swing. Madison caught her eye and sent a tight glare. Apparently, she wasn't supposed to be this far out of Madison's orbit.

Ena hesitated. The conversation appeared to be over. Piney had made sure of that.

But the idea of drifting back to the "cool" kids made her stomach twist.

"I think I just want to walk around a bit," Ena said. "It's been a crap day."

Piney eyed her. Not warm. Not cold. Just…studying.

I'M WITH YOU

By the end of the day, Ena felt wrung out. She hadn't expected it to be this hard. Every little thing reminded her of what she'd left behind. Her old school, her friends; all of it felt very far away.

She trudged alone to the principal's office to pick up her phone. Ms. Anderson stood behind the counter like a troll guarding a hoard of confiscated electronics, her hands resting on a cardboard box full of phones.

Ena asked, avoiding eye contact, "Can I have my phone back?"

"Is this the one?" Ms. Anderson asked, holding it up, headphones neatly coiled around it, as if humiliation needed to be gift-wrapped. "I hope you learned something."

Yeah, but not what you think. Next time, she'd need to be more careful with her phone.

She pushed through the front doors, bracing for the awkward scan of unfamiliar faces and minivans. But then she spotted Fiona.

Leaning against her well-worn Subaru, Fiona could've been plucked from the liner notes of a forgotten 1980's record. One boot crossed over the other. Aviators on. Reading a paperback, held loosely in one hand. Like waiting was an art form and she'd mastered it.

She was older than the parents waiting for their kids, decades older. But that only made her cooler. They looked like they were playing dress-up in adulting. Fiona had invented it and then tossed it aside to chase more interesting opportunities.

"Hey, baby girl," Fiona said, slipping the book into her jacket as she popped open the passenger door. Somehow, when she said it, the nickname didn't sting.

"How'd it go?" Fiona asked, circling to the driver's side.

Ena missed Boston. Friends who got her. Teachers who lit up at her name. The comfort of knowing where she stood.

"Sucked." One word. The only one that fit.

Here, she was no one. Just another new kid lost in the blur. No history, no context, no one to catch her if she slipped. She missed her best friend, Silvia. It had only been a few weeks, but already the miles felt like a wedge. Texts slowed. Video chats got harder to time. Their snap streak dangled by a thread.

Fiona let out a low, gravelly chuckle. "Yeah. That sounds about right. Eighth grade, new school? Total chaos."

The tension in Ena's shoulders eased. No empty promises, no clichés. No "give it time" or "you'll make new friends." Just truth. It made her feel seen like someone had finally read the same script she was stuck inside.

As they pulled away from the school, Fiona rolled down her window and took a slow drag from her cigarette. Smoke curled out into the late afternoon.

"So," she said, exhaling, "what are you gonna do to make tomorrow better?"

Ena slouched in her seat. *Make it better? How about survival?*

That wasn't the question she expected. Not "what happened?" Not "how are you feeling?" But "what are you going to do?"

It felt weirdly empowering. And also, impossible.

"I don't know," Ena said softly as thoughts raced through her brain. *Madison? Friend or foe? Piney? More to her than meets the eye, easily the most interesting student she met today. Who to trust? Who is worth the effort?*

Fiona nodded, like that was a perfectly valid answer. "It ain't easy," she said. "But think about the moments that felt the least terrible today. The ones that had even a flicker of something good. How do you make more of that?"

"Well," Ena hesitated. "There was this one girl. She seemed, I don't know, comfortable in her own skin. Like she knew who she was. But I don't think she likes me."

Fiona's lips curled into an almost smile. "If she doesn't like you, she doesn't know you."

Fiona stated it as fact.

"Look for the bridge. Look for what connects you two. Maybe you'll build a friendship, maybe you won't. But there's value in the effort."

That was the thing about Fiona; her advice never sounded like orders. No blueprints, no commands. Just choices. Possibilities. Agency.

And yet sometimes Ena wished Fiona would just tell her what to do.

Ena shifted the conversation, nodding to the book tucked in the drink holder. "What are you reading?"

"*Time's Rhythm*. I'm just starting it, but I love how they **stuck Spotify playlists into that little section** before the story kicks in. Easy to miss, but it's cool being able to follow along with the songs as they come up."

Fiona pulled up in front of Ena's house.

"Thanks for the ride, Fiona."

"Ena, you have a fan. I think you're awesome," Fiona said with a grin, "in ways you will see in time. If you are willing to talk to an old lady, I am here anytime for anything. Love you, baby girl."

The words threw Ena for a loop, leaving her uncertain how to respond. "Thanks. Love you too," she said, stumbling over the words. She opened the car door and climbed the front steps to her house.

HARD PLACE

Ena, drained from the day, headed straight to her room, her safe haven. She dropped her bag beside the desk without a thought. Above her bed, a Fin Whales poster dominated the wall: Eva Kinsella, mid-strum, caught in a moment of raw energy. She looked out at the crowd, but it always felt like she was looking straight at Ena.

The Fin Whales were everything Ena loved: powerful, honest, and never playing by anyone else's rules. Fiona had helped launch them; she reviewed their first album, *Lost to Time*, before anyone else had heard it. The band had blown open the doors in the mid-'80s. Then, just like that, they were gone. A bus crash on the way home from a gig. Music timeline cut.

Ena crossed to her guitar stand and lifted her candy apple red Squier Jaguar electric guitar with practiced care. Her parents offered it as a peace offering when they announced they were moving back to Portland to start her mom's company. She plugged in her headset, settled on the edge of the bed, and let her fingers find the opening chords of LP's *Lost on You*. Silvia's favorite song.

She'd been working on the song for weeks, smoothing the transitions, nailing the dynamics, feeling the emotion behind every chord shift. It demanded more than technique, it demanded focus. And that's what made it perfect for today.

The day had left her raw, being the new girl in a sea of unfamiliar faces.

Everyone around her seemed locked in place, knowing exactly where they stood and who their people were. Ena felt off-kilter, like she'd only just glimpsed the edges of the puzzle she was supposed to fit into.

The melody rose up around her, aching and defiant. Each note steadied her breath. Each chord gave shape to everything she couldn't say out loud.

She didn't need anyone to understand. She just needed the music. Where everything else faded into the background. Time blurred. Ena barely noticed the minutes slipping past until her phone buzzed beside her.

Text from Dad: *Dinner in 10.*

She slowly let out her breath and gently returned her guitar to its stand, giving it a quick glance, a silent thank-you, then headed downstairs.

She spotted his broad shoulders at the stove. The smell of his stir fry filled the air, a perfect swirl of sweet and tangy, garlic and heat, giving Ena a sense of home. "Hey, Dad."

He looked back with a warm smile. "How'd it go, kiddo? Did you kill it at school?"

"More like it killed me," she said, sighing, and dropped into a chair.

Her dad, Jason, turned from the stove, brow furrowed, his soft brown eyes searching her face. "That bad? I'm sure it'll get better."

He still had the build of a former baseball player—broad-shouldered and solid—though now there was a hint of middle-aged softness that his shirt didn't quite hide. His once-dark brown hair was fully salt-and-pepper, a mix of silver and brown, with a single rogue curl that flopped onto his forehead no matter how many times he brushed it back.

His baseball nickname was "Popeye," and with forearms like small tree trunks, it still fit. The way his sleeves stretched slightly when he lifted the frying pan made Ena smile.

He was still strong. Just…dad strong.

She loved him for it. He was corny, often embarrassing, but unquestionably hers. The kind of dad whose love was loud and constant, even when his timing wasn't perfect.

"How about helping your old man set the table?"

Ena grabbed four plates and the usual forks and knives from the cabinets. As she started setting the table, her little brother Byron bounced into the room like a tightly coiled spring finally released. His brown eyes matched Jason's, and his hair was a wild nest of tangles and curls that looked like they'd never once met a comb.

At nine, Byron had the energy of a small sun. Just being near him felt like standing in a solar storm—constant disruption, invisible but impossible to ignore.

"How'd it go, big guy?" Jason asked, flipping the last of the stir fry.

"It was awesome! We played kickball, and I scored like four times. And I met this kid, Xander, who likes frogs almost as much as I do!"

"Well, that does sound awesome," Jason said, smiling as he transferred the stir fry into a serving dish. He set it on the table alongside a bowl of rice just as Tara walked in, sharp green eyes behind rimless glasses, looking like she was halfway through solving a quantum equation.

She lifted her glasses and glanced at her daughter, a faint red mark crossing the bridge of her nose where her glasses had pressed too long. Her phone buzzed once in her back pocket before she silenced it with a quick tap. She brushed a strand of her brown hair streaked with blonde highlights behind her ear, gave Jason's arm a squeeze as she passed, and took her seat at the table.

The family settled into their usual spots and began passing dishes around.

"How were your days, kids?" Tara asked, her voice a little distant, like she hadn't fully come down from whatever she'd been working on.

Byron relaunched into his day's highlights, talking faster than an over-caffeinated mouse on a sugar rush. Tara smiled, clearly amused by her son's boundless energy and excitement, her fingers absently tracing the rim of her water glass as she listened.

When he finally paused for breath, Tara turned to Ena. "And you?"

"It was fine, I guess. What you'd expect." Ena shrugged.

Jason raised an eyebrow and exchanged a quick glance with Tara. Tara's gaze lingered on Ena, soft yet steady, as if she were trying to read between the lines, but she didn't push. She simply nodded and reached for the serving spoon.

Ena doubted her mom would get it and didn't really feel like explaining. Tara was always busy, and when she wasn't, she tried to fix everything. Ena didn't want a pep talk or a generic "it'll be fine" speech.

Jason noticed the suspicious lack of green on Byron's plate. "I think you might be missing something, buddy." He heaped a generous spoonful of stir-fried vegetables in front of Byron.

"But they're gross," Byron whined.

"Gross?" Jason grinned, signaling an incoming dad joke. "Not even close. You're about 134 short. That's only ten pieces of veggies."

Byron's expression fell flat.

"Really?" Ena arched a brow. "Math jokes at dinner? You're such a dinosaur."

Jason remained smug. "I'm expanding minds and palates over here."

Ena rolled her eyes. Classic Dad. Some things never changed.

They finished dinner with little fuss. Tara thanked her husband and eyed her children meaningfully. "That was delicious, wasn't it?"

"Thanks, Dad," Ena said, offering him a small but genuine smile.

"At least the rice was good. Thanks, Dad," Byron said as he pushed back from the table.

Ena stood and took her plate to the sink. She still had a poem to read for English.

And maybe, if there was time, she'd run through the bridge of the song one more time.

Come as You Are

Ena's plan was simple: stay off the radar as much as she could, get a sense of the social terrain, and avoid any attention. That lasted all of five minutes.

Ms. Nikola started English class. "Yesterday, I assigned 'Neither Out Far Nor In Deep.' So, let's begin discussing it. Ena, would you like to start us off?"

"Er…Well, I think Robert Frost is saying that people waste time watching things that don't really matter instead of actually living. Like, they avoid stuff that challenges them or makes them think deeper."

"Good, Ena," Ms. Nikola said, giving her a nod of approval. "Would anyone else like to add a perspective?"

Skyler raised their hand.

"Skyler?"

"I think Ena's take really gets what Frost is trying to say. People do avoid going deep. They stay on the surface, just staring out. That hits home.

"But the imagery doesn't totally work for me. I mean, he uses the sea to show how people aren't looking beyond their own noses, but the beach is where you can see the farthest.

Where else do you even get a horizon like that? If everyone just turned around and looked away from the ocean, they literally wouldn't be able to see as far."

A few quiet snickers from nearby desks barely registered.

"And the ocean? You can't see into it. Kinda feels unfair to call people out for not doing the impossible. And that thin line we call the horizon? That's magic. We've all imagined what's beneath the surface, sharks, whales, shipwrecks, and then just beyond it, that's where imagination meets what's just out of reach."

Ena wasn't sure what to make of Skyler's answer, but their presence was inviting in a way she hadn't experienced before.

Skyler continued. "Honestly, if Frost were writing today, he'd probably be talking about people staring at their phones instead of actually living. That imagery lands for me. But the ocean metaphor? It doesn't fit."

Ena turned toward Skyler, seated near the front. Their voice had been calm, thoughtful like they weren't trying to prove anything, just stating things as they distinctly saw it. Somehow, Ena felt both completely validated and invited to look again. Not corrected, not dismissed, just…expanded. Skyler's words didn't undo her answer. They unfolded it.

"Well, Skyler," Ms. Nikola said, a little surprised. "Thank you. That was a unique interpretation of the poem. Anyone else?"

Adrian raised his hand and didn't wait to be called on. "I don't know about all that deep ocean stuff," he said, cracking a grin, "but I think surfers are cool."

Laughter rolled through the room, and even Ms. Nikola let out a sigh-smile as she moved on.

♪ ♫ ♪

When lunch rolled around, Ena walked into the cafeteria.

"Hey Ena, you're sitting with us, right?" Ashley called from just behind her.

Ena looked over at Madison's table, where she was holding court. Back in Boston, she had her spot at the same table every day, one just like Madison's. Popularity wasn't something she chased; it just came with the territory. Now, looking at that table, it still felt easy, safe, comfortable.

But not today. She wanted—no, felt compelled—to find Skyler.

"I don't think so. Maybe tomorrow," Ena replied.

Ashley raised an eyebrow. "I don't know about where you come from, but some damage around here can't be undone."

Ena nodded, but her eyes were already scanning the cafeteria. She spotted Skyler at a table near the windows, every seat around them empty.

She walked over. "Mind if I sit here?"

Skyler's eyes drifted up to meet hers, as if they resurfaced from a distant thought. "Of course not."

"Thanks." Ena slid into the seat across from them, setting her lunch bag down. From here, she could see the whole cafeteria. "What you said about the poem earlier was really interesting. I hadn't thought about it that way."

Skyler tilted their head. "I thought your take was really good. I hope I didn't step on it."

"No, not at all."

There was a pause. Skyler picked at the edge of their sandwich.

"Can I be honest with you, Ena?" they said, voice light but direct. "You're torching your social currency by sitting with me. I'm persona non grata around here."

Ena bit her inner lip and said, "Well, I don't know about that, but I think I can handle it. Sounds like a them problem, not a me problem."

Skyler let out a soft chuckle. Ena couldn't tell if it was amusement, acceptance, or something else entirely. She scanned out over the cafeteria, Madison was glaring. Skyler's warning echoed in her head. The stakes felt unfairly high. Like one conversation could blow up whatever fragile footing she had at this new school. Madison seemed to make it a choice: her or Skyler. But all Ena wanted was to talk to someone who made her think about something other than survival.

And somehow, Skyler's calm, steady presence made Ena feel not just comfortable but ready to explore what lay beneath. "Do you have any idea why you're persona non grata?" she asked.

Skyler paused, looking at her with a careful, thoughtful gaze. They weren't used to such direct questions, but they didn't seem to mind it.

"I can only speak from my side," they said. "But I think it goes back about two years. It was summer...I was at a swimming hole nearby. I got stuck underwater. By the time my mom pulled me out, I wasn't breathing. No pulse. She did CPR until the paramedics arrived."

Ena's breath caught.

"I know it sounds strange," Skyler continued, "but something happened while they were trying to save me. It wasn't a dream. It wasn't like passing out. It was an experience. Ineffable."

Ena shot a quizzical look "Ineffable?"

"Yeah, those times words fail to describe something. But it changed me, every part of me. I felt like I traveled back in time and met the first humans, or maybe possibly older. They didn't speak like we do, but I understood them. They told me: We are one. We were one. We will be one."

Skyler's words weren't dramatic or forced. They were calm, almost casual, which made them even more compelling for Ena.

"And I felt it. In my bones. That all the divisions we make between people are made up. Lies we tell ourselves so the world doesn't feel like too much. Those divisions keep us from what we could be. From becoming something beautiful together. After that, I couldn't go back. I couldn't pretend I didn't know. It became part of me. And not a lot of kids are comfortable with that. So here I am, living my truth. Persona non grata."

Ena was quiet and still, trying to absorb it all.

"You're released," their voice gentle. "If that was too weird."

Ena didn't respond, but she didn't move either.

The silence sat between them, charged but not uncomfortable. Skyler leaned back, gazing past her. "Most people do move. I'm used to that."

Ena looked at them for a long moment. "I'm not most people."

Somewhere inside her, she could almost hear Fiona's voice: *And look for the people who challenge you, who inspire you.* Skyler definitely qualified as someone who challenges people, and Ena was beginning to feel the wisdom of Fiona's words.

The bell rang, signaling the halfway point. Around them, trays clattered and chairs scraped as kids packed up for mandatory outside time. Ena stood, slinging her bag over one shoulder. "Time for mandatory sun exposure," she said.

"A daily reminder we're still animals," Skyler replied, rising with unhurried ease.

They moved toward the doors together, cafeteria noise trailing behind them.

The air outside was thick with late summer heat, hotter than normal. The sun refused to fade just yet. Skyler walked as if they had nowhere to be. Ena followed, unsure where they were going, only that she wasn't ready for the conversation to end.

The silence wasn't awkward. It had space in it, like breathing room neither of them knew they needed. They began circling the yard, falling into an easy rhythm.

"So," Skyler said, glancing over. "What about you?"

"Well, I grew up in Boston. Just moved to Portland."

Skyler shook their head gently. "No, I mean what matters to you? What's the thing that makes you you?"

"Music," she said, without hesitation. "I mean, I love it like it's a limb. A vital organ. Without it, I'm not me."

She flicked her eyes toward Skyler, who was listening, really listening. With Skyler, Ena felt free in a way she hadn't yesterday at the table with Madison and her minions.

"My grandmother published this music magazine for decades, *True Notes*. She knows everything. Like the deep history. She doesn't just love the songs; she loves the artists who make them. I guess it's in my genes. Now I can't imagine life without it. It's how I see the world."

Skyler's eyes lit up. "Really? I love percussion. It's like…I'm not creating music, I'm revealing it. Like the rhythm was already there, and I'm just bringing it to the surface."

"Maybe we should play together sometime," Ena said. "I love my guitar. Could be fun to see what kind of music we can *reveal*." She delivered the word with a sly half-smile, just enough to show her right dimple and let Skyler in on the tease.

The bell sounded again, calling them back to the grind of classes.

STAND BY ME

The next few weeks ticked by, and Ena and Skyler were fast becoming friends. They spent weekends playing music, sometimes talking for hours, sometimes not at all. They didn't even have to try to keep their Snapstreak alive. Ena had never met anyone like Skyler, curious, calm, quietly intense, and insanely smart. In them, Ena found a friendship with a foundation deep and solid, a friendship that could survive the storms. It surprised her how quickly and naturally it all settled into place, as if it had always been waiting there.

Life in Boston had started to fade into the background of Ena's thoughts. She still liked her friends and missed them, but they never challenged her in all the best ways while leaving judgment out.

She'd talked to Fiona about Skyler once. Fiona had smiled, one of those quiet, knowing smiles that meant she'd already seen the shape of it. "These are the people who make life interesting," she'd said. "As long as your journeys overlap, however long that is, enjoy it fully. Don't hold back." At the time, Ena hadn't realized how much Fiona's words echoed the lyrics of "Season of Love," that emotional Fin Whales ballad, one of Ena's favorite songs—a song about not knowing how long a love will last, only that while it does, you owe it your whole heart. The echo of the song in Fiona's words was comforting. A little haunting in how love and friendship can be both beautiful and fragile. Ena thought of Silvia, left behind in Boston. She didn't mean to drift away. It just happened. Their closeness had once felt so natural, but now it felt distant, like a memory from a different timeline.

Ena had been spending more time with Fiona lately. Since moving to Portland, Ena had found Fiona more approachable, and every conversation felt like a warm embrace and an open invitation to go deeper when Ena was ready. The awe, bordering on fear, that she'd felt at first had started to shift. Fiona was often the first person she thought of when anything significant happened. Fiona never treated Ena like a kid, always respected her thoughts, but never let her off the hook, either. Fiona challenged her, believed in her, and pushed her. And for the first time, Ena felt empowered in a way no other adult had allowed.

♪ ♫ ♪

One day in the hallway at school, Madison approached Ena with a smug half-smile.

"So, I see you have a thing for freakshows?"

Ena scoffed. "Madison, if you took two seconds to actually talk to Skyler, you'd see you have them all wrong."

Madison rolled her eyes. "He's weird and just wants to show off his big brain."

Ena met her gaze, steady and unflinching. "It's *they*. Skyler isn't putting on a show, they're just being themselves. You should try accepting that."

"Whatever, you made your choice." Madison's expression turned colder. "You could've had a seat at the table, Ena. Don't pretend like I didn't offer."

" 'Neither Out Far Nor In Deep' must have been written for you, Madison." Ena laughed quietly. "I guess I learned something in English already."

Madison didn't flinch. She just turned and walked the other way, as if she hadn't heard, sneakers squeaking on the linoleum.

♪ ♫ ♪

As Ena worked her way past the door after Math class that day, she heard, "Hey Boston, hold up."

Piney appeared by her side.

"I heard you went a couple of rounds with Madison this morning."

"Yeah, that bridge is now officially burnt," Ena replied.

"Props. People are talking. You held your own." Piney held out a fist for a bump. "I thought you were just another cheerleader type. You've got guts, I'll give you that."

"I've never had a friend like Skyler," Ena said. "I couldn't let it slide. Skyler acts like it doesn't get to them, but me? I can't just stand there while someone goes after my friend."

"Skyler's still weird. But you? Maybe you're not basic after all."

Piney drifted toward her next class, her head shaking like she'd just encountered a sudoku she couldn't solve. Why had Piney even talked to her today? She'd barely acknowledged Ena's existence since the first day of school, and now, suddenly, she reached out. Was it just to hand out props? Or was there more?

It *felt* like more. Piney was hard to read.

♪ ♫ ♪

By lunch, Ena needed a break. It had been a morning: the confrontation with Madison, the conversation with Piney, the fact that people were *talking*. Ena was ready to get off the ride for a minute. She sat down across from Skyler and let out a long sigh.

"I heard about Madison," Skyler said, their tone calm and even, without a trace of accusation. "You know you don't have to defend me, right?"

"Skyler, she attacked you. I can't just stand by and let my best friend get torn apart."

Skyler tilted their head slightly, as if considering a deeper truth. "When Madison strikes to hurt, she's ultimately hurting herself. When we hurt others, we hurt ourselves. I know it sounds like I stole it from a poster in a guidance counselor's office, but..." They paused in thought and then added, "I've made it mine."

Skyler had said it like a mantra, and Ena wondered who Skyler might've been if the near-drowning had never happened. If they had walked a different path, who would they be now.

The two sat in silence for a moment, and then Skyler said, "Best friend, huh? You have no idea what it means to hear that."

PEOPLE ARE STRANGE

Ena didn't know what to say to that. So instead, she switched gears. "Do you know Piney Kapoor?" she asked, taking a bite of her sandwich.

"Piney? She's brilliant. Her real name's Anaya, but she totally owns 'Piney.' She's obsessed with computers. But definitely one of the hardest people to read." Skyler paused, then added, "She can reduce someone to emotional jelly with a single sentence."

"Huh," Ena said. Skyler's words reaffirmed what Ena had believed. She still felt intrigued by Piney but unsure if she could solve that puzzle.

♪ ♫ ♪

The cafeteria speaker chimed, signaling the forced outside time. Ena and Skyler headed out for their usual walking laps around the yard, while most kids gathered around the basketball court to battle for their place in the social hierarchy.

As they passed Piney, sitting alone, back against the wall, notebook open, pen flying across the page, a jolt ran through Ena's nerves, but she pushed past it. Maybe it was her friendship with Skyler, maybe it was Fiona's inspiration, or maybe she was just bolder now than in her previous life. She would never have reached out to an apparent loner like this.

"Hey, Piney!" she called, projecting more confidence than she felt.

Piney lifted her gaze. "What's up, Boston?" Then, with a polite nod: "Skyler."

"Wanna join us?" Ena asked.

Piney didn't answer right away. She clicked her pen closed, studying them with a squint like she was completing an equation in her head.

"Why not? I wasn't getting anywhere with this anyway." She stood, slid the notebook into her messenger bag, and fell into step beside them like she'd always been there.

After a few strides, Ena turned to her. "What were you working on?"

"Lyrics," Piney said, as if it wasn't a big deal. But she didn't offer more.

Skyler piped up, "Did you know Ena is kind of a music genius? Her grandmother used to run an indie music magazine."

"Really?" Piney's curiosity outpaced her skepticism for a moment.

"Yeah, I mean, I love music. My guitar's basically part of my family. Skyler is being generous with the 'genius' part. Do you play an instrument?"

"I have been known to tickle the keys on a keyboard." Piney seemed to be trying to regain her upper hand in the conversation.

"Cool," Ena said.

As they finished a lap around the yard, Piney veered off back to her spot. "Later" is all she said.

"Huh, that was interesting," Skyler said. "I just learned more about Piney than I have in the past two years."

"Interesting indeed," Ena replied.

She didn't know for sure, but it seemed like she'd cracked the surface and been rewarded for it. That tug she'd sensed earlier? It had only gotten stronger.

U.N.I.T.Y.

One evening while Ena was working on homework at her desk in her room, her phone dinged.

Her Snapchat app: *Piney Kapoor sent you a friend request.*

Ena was a bit surprised; Piney had reluctantly walked with her during lunch once but hadn't reengaged since. Ena hit accept.

Immediately, a message popped up.

PINEY: *You have to see this.*

ENA: *What?*

PINEY: *Madison's doing a poll on her Private Story.*

PINEY: *Skyler's winning "Most Pretentious" and "Most Likely to Date a Chimp."*

PINEY: *It's rigged. She's being a total snake.*

Another message pinged.

PINEY: *Someone from math class AirDropped it to me. Probably thought I'd find it funny.*

Two screenshots followed.

The first showed a poll in pink text over a picture of a dangling monkey: *Most Likely to Date a Chimp. Skyler: 82%.*

The second: *Most Pretentious.* Skyler again.

Small text underneath: 15 people voted.

ENA: *Madison has gone too far. I don't know how, but I'll get her for this.*

PINEY: *What you got in mind?*

ENA: *idk*

ENA: yet.

ENA: *We can't tell Skyler, it would kill them.*

PINEY: *[Mouth zippered emoji.]*

ENA: *Meet me at Skyler's locker tomorrow before class.*

♪ ♫ ♪

Ena had a restless night, turning over plans and discarding each one. Madison was going to pay, somehow.

Ena and Piney met at Skyler's locker. Already taped to it were two printed screenshots from Madison's Snapchat story polls:

"Most Likely to Date a Chimp."

"Most Pretentious."

And right underneath, in that cruel flourish:

Your fans have spoken.

Ena grabbed the paper and tore it down just as Skyler was walking up.

"What was that?"

"Oh, nothing."

"Ena, it clearly wasn't nothing. What was it?"

The sudden firmness in Skyler's voice caught Ena off guard. She had never heard them sound so direct, so forceful.

She hesitated, then slowly unfolded the paper and handed it over, heart pounding. She hated the idea of being the one to deliver pain. This was the closest she'd ever come to the receiving end of this kind of cruelty. She had never bullied anyone, but she'd never stepped in, either.

Skyler read it silently. Their eyes shimmered, glassy with hurt. They closed them and took five painfully slow, deliberate breaths.

Piney and Ena stood frozen, unsure what to do, unsure what to say.

"When we hurt others," Skyler said quietly, repeating their mantra, "we hurt ourselves."

"Skyler, this isn't okay. I'm not letting it go. We're going to get even," Ena said, her voice sharp enough to cut steel.

"Ena, I appreciate that," Skyler replied gently. "But there's no such thing as getting even. More damage doesn't undo damage."

"I do not care!" Ena snapped. "Someone is going to pay."

She thought about Luke from her old school and how everyone laughed at him, how she'd stayed silent. She hadn't helped then. But she could now. Guilt for Luke and a fierce need to protect Skyler pushed her forward.

Her eyes flicked across the hall and landed on a poster taped to the wall:

MADISON SLOANE

FOR

Student Body President

A vote for Madison is a vote for class.

A glimmer of an idea began to spark.

♪ ♫ ♪

After school, Ena lay on her bed, schoolbooks open but forgotten. Her thumbs hovered over her phone as she and Piney plotted quietly and carefully through a string of disappearing Snapchat messages.

ENA: *I think I have a plan for Madison.*

PINEY: *Intriguing. What kind of plan?*

ENA: *The less you know, the better.*

ENA: *But I need your help. You in?*

PINEY: *Always. What do you need?*

ENA: *Access to the admin Wi-Fi.*

ENA: *And. An app. Something custom.*

They messaged back and forth all afternoon and deep into the night, Ena careful with her words, Piney precise with her code.

♪ ♫ ♪

A few days later, after school, Piney led Ena to her house. Ena was silent, coiled tight with nervous energy.

The front door creaked open before they even reached it.

A voice called from behind it: "Shoes off, Piney!"

"Hey, Grams," Piney called back.

They stepped inside. The smell of turmeric and lavender hung in the air. Ena hadn't known what to expect, colder, more high-tech maybe, but this felt lived-in. Soft. Smart. Old and new, tangled together.

Piney dropped her backpack and started toward her room.

"Not quite, sweetheart," came the voice again.

Piney spun around and grinned, then threw her arms around her grandmother.

"And who might this be?" her step-grandmother asked, turning to Ena with kind, inquisitive eyes.

"Ena Quinn-Baker. School project," Piney said, already half-turned toward the hallway.

"Well, Ena Quinn-Baker, it is a pleasure to meet you. You may call me Josephine."

"Nice to meet you, Josephine," Ena said, taking in the tall, elegant woman, her chestnut skin framed by short, tightly curled gray hair.

Piney led her to a room off the hall, part bedroom, part command center.

"Okay, Quinn-Baker," she said, settling into her chair. "You absolutely sure about this?"

"Yes," Ena said. "One hundred."

"Then give me your phone."

Ena handed it over. Piney got to work—lines of code, a flash drive, a connection cable, the quiet hum of a plan coming together. A few minutes later, she held the phone back up. "Done."

A new icon had appeared on the home screen: a matte gray circle with a hammer in the center. U.T.I.L.I.T.Y. was spelled out underneath in clean block letters.

"U.T.I.L.I.T.Y.?" Ena asked, raising an eyebrow.

"Let's just say…inspired by the Queen herself," Piney said, not looking up.

Ena quipped with a sly smile. "You're such a nerd."

"A dangerous one," Piney responded with a wink and a smile. "When it's go time, tap it once. When it's over, tap it again. It'll wipe itself completely. No logs. No traces."

Ena stared at the icon. Her heart pounded, equal parts fear, thrill, and resolve.

She wasn't just going to get even.

She was going to make Madison feel it.

Heads Will Roll

The next day, Ena walked into English class, rubbing her temples. She hoped Ms. Nikola bought it. She needed the excuse to sneak her phone out during the speeches.

"Headache, Ena?" Ms. Nikola asked, not unkindly.

"Yeah. I don't feel great," Ena muttered. "Okay if I just rest my head during announcements?"

Ms. Nikola gave her a quick once-over, then nodded. "Sure. Just don't fall asleep."

Ena slid into her seat and set her backpack on the floor beside her chair, already unzipped. She dropped into her desk with a sigh, then, while no one was looking, slipped her phone from her pocket into her lap and folded her arms on the desk.

The overhead speakers crackled to life.

"Today we'll be hearing speeches from your student government candidates."

Ena didn't lift her head. Her thumb hovered over the screen, watching and waiting.

Two other student body president speeches came and went. She barely heard them. Her focus was locked on the moment she'd planned for.

"And now, running for president, Madison Sloane."

Ena tapped the U.T.I.L.I.T.Y. icon.

Right on cue, as Madison's voice—clear, confident, smug—rang through the speakers, the bright snap of drums and a crisp guitar riff slid in underneath.

Paramore's "Ain't It Fun" hummed beneath Madison's words, each line landing like a counterpoint to her campaign promises.

Ena stayed perfectly still, head down, face hidden.

Madison kept talking, oblivious to the background audio threading through her big moment for all to hear.

Laughter rippled across the room. Someone actually snorted. Madison didn't stop.

"Oh my god. Someone just showed her we don't all revolve around her," Ena heard whispered.

Ena didn't lift her head. Her heart thudded in her chest, but her face stayed pressed to her arm. Everything was going to plan. Just the dim glow of her phone screen. Her thumb, hovering, ready.

Madison droned on, completely unaware that her speech had become a duet.

As it ended, Ena tapped the icon again. The song vanished, as did the icon on her phone.

She kept her head down, exhaled silently, dropped the phone back into her backpack, and zipped it closed like nothing had happened. Her teacher didn't say anything. Ena doubted Ms. Nikola saw anything.

Ten minutes later, Ms. Anderson walked into the classroom, her face unreadable. She leaned in to speak quietly to Ms. Nikola for a full minute.

"Ena," Ms. Nikola said, her voice missing its usual warmth. "Principal Gump would like to see you. Please go with Ms. Anderson."

Ena stood, keeping her expression neutral. Her heart pounded, but her mind was steady. *They've got nothing. Piney's app left no trace. No proof, no consequences.* Ena had never pulled anything like this before, but she was smart enough to cover her tracks. She was pretty sure.

She followed Ms. Anderson down the hall, rehearsing her lines. The moment she stepped into the principal's office, her breath caught. Madison was still there, red-eyed, mascara smudged, a tissue clutched in one hand.

That landed better than expected. A flicker of triumph surged through Ena. Madison had started it with that smug little poll. This? This was just balance. Fair is fair.

Principal Gump cleared his throat.

"Ms. Quinn-Baker," he said, peering over wire-rimmed glasses, bent, slightly askew, like the rest of him. "Do you have anything to say?"

Ena hesitated.

Looked at Madison.

Then back at Gump.

"I don't know," she said, tilting her head. "Nice speech, Madison."

"Don't even, Ena. I know it was you," Madison snapped.

Ena didn't flinch. "Not sure what you're talking about. I've had a headache all morning." She shrugged just enough to sell it. "What exactly are you accusing me of?"

Principal Gump cut in. "Thank you, Madison. That was a great speech. I need to speak with Ena alone."

Madison stood with a sigh and shot Ena a look that could have lit a fire. This wasn't over.

Once the door clicked shut, Gump turned back to Ena. "It's pretty obvious you were involved. Ms. Nikola said you were acting strangely this morning, and she saw you sneak your phone back into your bag right after Madison's speech. You didn't pull this off alone. The only question is, who helped you?"

Ena sat up straighter. "I really don't know why you think I did anything. Aren't I innocent until proven guilty?"

"Schools don't have to operate that way," Gump said. "We already have grounds for suspension; I just haven't decided for how long."

Ena crossed her arms. "Then just suspend me. I don't see why I'm here if the decision has already been made."

"Well, that depends. Who helped you? Was it Anaya?"

"You mean Piney?" Ena let out a soft laugh. "I'm sure she had nothing to do with anything."

"Should I bring her in to discuss this?"

Ena tilted her head. "*If* I were responsible, why are you so sure I couldn't have done it alone?"

"Because this wasn't some low-effort prank. It took planning. It took skill."

"I don't know. Maybe whoever did it used YouTube." Ena shrugged. "But as far as I know, Piney's got no beef with Madison. None. She wouldn't waste her time."

She paused, then leaned in slightly.

"You're right, I don't like Madison. But when she put up that gross little poll about Skyler? Nothing. Not a word from the school. Total radio silence."

She met Gump's eyes.

"But someone embarrasses the Queen Bee, and suddenly it's all hands on deck. Heads must roll, right?"

A beat.

"Hypocritical much?"

Gump narrowed his eyes. "Young lady, you need to watch that tone. At this point, we're talking about how long, not if, you'll be suspended." This was new territory for Ena. She had always managed to stay off the radar of her old school's administration.

Ena folded her arms. "Then suspend me. I plead the fifth."

He sighed. "I see we're at an impasse. You can think this over for the rest of the week—at home. We'll call your parents to pick you up."

"My parents are at work. Can you call my grandmother, Fiona?"

Gump typed into his computer, waited, then nodded. "She's listed as a backup. We'll contact her."

DON'T LET ME DOWN

Ena waited on the front steps of the school, arms crossed, phone in hand. She messaged Skyler and Piney: "Suspended. See you next week."

Fiona's blue Subaru rolled up with a soft crunch of gravel. The Fin Whales were already playing. The dreamy swell of "Voices of Whales" drifted through the open window:

> *I don't know what's coming, can't divine*
> *There's something here I cannot find.*

Ena slid into the passenger seat, shutting the door like it was any other Tuesday. "Hi, Fiona." She tried to sound casual, like this was no big deal.

Fiona shifted into drive. Her voice was calm but carried a little extra gravel. "Well, baby girl. Got yourself suspended, huh?"

Ena's shoulders sagged. "I guess so. I mean, they just accused me. No proof. Nothing. I can't believe they can do that."

"Mmm." That low hum meant she heard more than just the words.

They drove in silence for a moment. The Fin Whales continued to swell through the speakers, bassline heavy, raw, and urgent.

"You know why I love The Fin Whales so much?" Fiona asked, tapping the steering wheel in rhythm.

Ena shrugged. "I don't know. They're awesome?"

With a broad smile, Fiona said, "They are. But there's more to it. We helped shine a light on them with our zine. *True Notes* didn't make them great, they already were. But we helped people see it. Lifted them out of obscurity. Gave them a little push toward becoming, well, a force."

Ena nodded. "Right. You've always had a great ear. You know what's good."

At the stoplight, Fiona watched her thoughtfully. Ena wasn't quite catching the deeper meaning. "That was our whole ethos for *True Notes*, you know. Shine the light. We didn't do takedowns. Never ran stories calling people sellouts. We figured if someone made it in music, good for them, however they got there. We lifted people up. Not tore them down."

Ena leaned her head against the window. "Yeah, but that's different. You were helping people who deserved it."

Fiona nodded, it did not seem to be in agreement, just acknowledgment. She didn't press further. She'd said what she needed to say, and now she let it hang in the air, trusting that when Ena was ready, the words would strike the chord she intended.

♪ ♫ ♪

When Tara got home from work, Ena was summoned to the living room. Tara and Jason sat together on the couch. The loveseat was left for Ena, alone, under scrutiny.

Jason spoke first. "Ena, we're really disappointed in you."

His voice was calm, but the look on his face, like his heart had cracked, made Ena want to shrivel up. She'd never seen that expression before. Not on her dad.

"This is so unfair," she said. "I'm being punished, and there's no proof."

"Stop it. Just stop." Tara's voice cut through the room, sharp enough to make Ena flinch. "We didn't raise you to do things like this."

"I didn't do anything!" Ena snapped. "And even if I did, Madison deserved it."

"Ena! Enough!" Tara's voice rose higher than Ena had ever heard it, tight, almost shaking. "No one deserves to be treated like that." Ena had not been in this level of trouble before and was not expecting this. She knew she would get grounded, but her mother seemed out of control for a prank where no one got hurt.

"You don't know what she did to Skyler," Ena shot back. "She deserved it. Props to whoever pulled it off."

Jason's voice was softer, but the disappointment hit harder. "Your mom's right. That's not how we treat people. That's not who you are. Or at least—I thought it wasn't."

That one stung.

Ena pushed up from her seat. "Well, you clearly don't believe me either!"

"Where do you think you're going?" Tara snapped. "Sit down."

Ena dropped back into the loveseat with a heavy sigh and crossed arms.

"Are you seriously still pretending you're innocent?" Tara's voice didn't waver. "You're not just guilty, Ena. You're a disappointment."

Ena froze. Her mom just went too far. Ena didn't blink. For a second, she wasn't even sure she remembered how to breathe. *Mom has seriously lost it.*

Jason stepped in; his voice measured. "Two weeks. No phone. No screens. No friends. Laptop for school only. Home, school, and your grandparents, nothing else."

Ena rolled her eyes. "This is ridiculous." Ena still felt justified. Madison got what she deserved, but Fiona's words rang. *We didn't do take-downs.* She had never seen her parents this disappointed in her, and it hurt.

"Is that all?" she added flatly.

"No, that is not all," Tara said. "Two weeks is the minimum, if this attitude doesn't change, expect a longer sentence."

"Whatever." Ena's voice was flat as she got up and fled to the sanctuary of her room.

She grabbed the first notebook she could find and started scribbling words without structure, just heat: Skyler. Madison. Fiona. Mom. A whole page of *NO ONE GETS IT* over and over until the pen bled through the paper.

She flipped the page and kept going, her hand slower now, the fire giving way to heavier emotions and thoughts.

Skyler didn't deserve it. Madison deserved it.

Skyler didn't deserve it. Madison deserved it.

The rhythm faded. Her writing slowed as anger drained into exhaustion.

Then, almost without realizing it, she wrote: *But would Skyler have wanted it?*

Ena stared at the words, unsure where they came from. Unsure how to answer them.

CONFESSION

The alarm jolted Ena awake the next morning. She'd forgotten to turn it off the night before. For one blissful second, she thought it was a normal day.

Then it hit her: Suspended.

Ena bargained with the universe: *please just roll back time.* She wasn't even sure she'd do it differently, but the punishment felt bigger than the crime. She let her head fall back onto the pillow. No reason to get up.

A knock at the door.

"Time to get up," Jason said through the wood.

"I'm suspended, in case you forgot."

"Ena, no one forgot. You're not staying here alone. I'm dropping you off at your grandparents' on my way to work. Twenty minutes. Downstairs."

Ughh. Can't I just sleep in?

Ena groaned to herself as she dragged her body out of bed.

♪ ♫ ♪

Ena's grandparents' home was intimidatingly large, fourteen windows stretched across the front, a wide, covered porch that ran the full length of the house. A porch swing and two Adirondack chairs sat at one end, and at the other, a bamboo table with four mismatched chairs. Standing squarely in the center, a light blue front door with a stained-glass panel in the top third—swirling vines and golden leaves curling toward each other in a shape that almost suggested an hourglass. A set of broad wooden steps led up to it like an invitation.

In the yard, a towering maple stood guard, its leaves already began to signal the coming fall. Streaks of yellow, orange, and red glowed in the morning sun, foretelling the season's change.

Ena climbed the steps and rang the doorbell.

The door opened with a warm creak.

"Well, if it isn't our little miss troublemaker," her grandfather said in that soft, inoffensive, grandparently way that made it impossible to get mad.

"Hi, Granddad," Ena replied, her voice sounding inadequate and awkward, at least to herself.

Graeme Quinn was tall and lean, with wispy gray hair and sharp, intelligent walnut eyes. Everything about him seemed quietly observant, like he was always one thought away from an invention or a joke.

He led her through the wide front hallway toward the back of the house. A well-worn wooden table in the breakfast nook was wedged beneath a trio of windows, with a built-in bench along two sides and a simple oak chair at the head of the table.

Fiona sat on the outer edge of the bench, a ceramic mug of coffee cradled in both hands, steam curling up toward her face. Her short silver hair was a bit spikier than usual, but in typical Fiona fashion, she pulled it off like it was entirely intentional.

She smiled when she saw Ena. "Hey, kiddo. So, the real punishment begins—a whole day with your grandparents."

The joke helped release some of the tension from Ena's shoulders.

Fiona's hand drifted absentmindedly to the little gold eighth note pendant at her collarbone, tugging gently at the delicate chain for a moment.

"Love, careful," Graeme said lightheartedly, "I don't want to have to fix that chain again."

"Well, old man," Fiona said with a wink, "gotta keep you on your toes somehow."

"Speaking of staying on our toes," Graeme added, glancing at Ena, "what do we have on the docket for our houseguest-slash-inmate?"

His dry humor didn't quite hit the mark. Ena just stared at him.

"It's a beautiful day," Fiona said, "and the garden's calling. Why don't we start out there?"

"Perfect," Graeme agreed. "The roses need deadheading."

Ena's eyes darted between them. *Wait. They're serious?*

"Um, I'm wearing my best jeans," she said, trying to sound casual. "Might not be the best time to ruin them."

Fiona didn't miss a beat.

"Funny thing about this enormous old house," she said, rising with her mug in hand. "Somewhere in here, I'm almost certain we have something to protect denim."

"Yes, if only we had something that could...oh, I don't know...could go over everything." Graeme tapped his chin. "Hmm. What would you call a thing like that? It's right on the tip of my tongue...over...hmm...all...That's it! Overalls!" He chuckled, pleased with himself.

Ena did not find the joke nearly as amusing.

♩ ♫ ♩

Ena stood in the backyard in too-big beige overalls, clearly borrowed from someone taller and wider. The pant legs were rolled several times but still grazed the tops of her sneakers. The shoulder straps refused to stay snug.

She looked like a reluctant scarecrow in training.

Graeme crouched beside a rose bush along the back fence, gently snipping below a wilted bloom and dropping it into the yard debris bin.

After demonstrating a couple more times, he handed the shears to Ena. "Your turn."

She snipped a bloom just like Graeme had done and tossed it in the debris bin.

"Good, I think you've got it," Graeme said with a nod, gesturing down the long row of bushes. "Now, have at it."

This was not what Ena had pictured when she imagined being suspended from school. She'd told herself it might be boring days, some extra guitar practice, and time inching by like an unmotivated sloth. Instead, it was forced labor in a floppy beige costume.

The three of them worked in separate pockets of the yard. Fiona was weeding around the raised beds, her movements easy and familiar. Graeme drifted between pruning and repairing tools, humming to himself. Ena, meanwhile, found herself locked into the repetitive, scratchy, slightly-stabby task of deadheading.

At first, she clipped the blooms with just a touch too much force. Anger simmered beneath the surface: anger at getting caught, at a punishment that felt way over the line, at having no say in how she spent her time. But little by little, her hands settled into a rhythm. The silence shifted from awkward to peaceful. Her thoughts faded into the background.

Time slipped past, unnoticed.

Just as she finished the final bush, Fiona's voice floated from across the yard. "Well, I'd call that a productive morning. Who's up for lunch?"

♪ ♫ ♪

After lunch, Fiona led Ena into her study. The room had warm oak floors and walls lined with floor-to-ceiling mahogany bookshelves, every shelf crowded with books, zines, and artifacts of a life well-lived.

"I think it's time we rearranged the LPs," Fiona said, gesturing toward three long shelves packed with vinyl and eyeing them with a mix of fondness and frustration. "I put them in alphabetical order once, but it just feels wrong to have Nirvana sitting next to Ricky Nelson."

"Ricky who?" Ena asked.

Fiona arched an eyebrow.

"Ricky Nelson. A cleaner-cut version of Elvis in the '50s and '60s. But without him?" She pulled out an album. "Rock 'n' roll might never have had a seat at the table."

Fiona slid a big black vinyl disc from its sleeve. Gently placing it on the turntable, she started it. The Cowboy Junkies' "Mining for Gold" filled the room, the lead singer's voice razor-soft, a haunting acapella. "Let's arrange them by genre and release date. Each genre gets its own milk crate. Once we are done, we can reshelve them."

Fiona pointed to the corner of the room next to the bay window bench. "Can you grab those milk crates in the corner?"

Ena turned, spotted the stacked wooden crates, and hauled them over, spreading them across the study floor. Fiona grabbed a few records from the shelf and began placing them into their proper milk crate.

Ena followed her lead, crouching beside the scattered crates, sleeves of albums in her lap.

They worked in quiet rhythm for a while, Fiona humming now and then, Ena asking questions about genres or unfamiliar artists as they sorted.

Eventually, Fiona slowed, her fingers resting lightly on the edge of a record sleeve.

"So, Ena," she said casually, not looking up, "why'd you do it?"

Ena froze.

"Do what?" she asked, still clinging to the last thread of plausible deniability.

Fiona glanced over, one brow raised.

"Baby girl, I'm too old to be fooled by weak deflection. You know what I mean."

Ena's shoulders sagged. Fiona had seen right through her.

"You should've seen what Madison did to Skyler," Ena said, her voice tight. "It crushed them."

Fiona turned fully toward her now, her tone gentle but steady. "What did she do?"

"She made this awful poll on Snapchat and then taped the results to Skyler's locker so they couldn't miss it." Ena swallowed hard. "Most likely to date a monkey. Most pretentious."

Fiona whistled out a long breath, puffing her cheeks before exhaling. "That's cruel. And it shouldn't have happened."

Ena nodded, her voice rising with the memory.

"Skyler tried to hide it, but it really hurt them. And no one did anything! It was all on Snapchat, so it disappeared. The printouts didn't have names. People took screenshots, but… nothing. No consequences."

Fiona tilted her head, not unkindly. "That you know about."

"Something should have been done," Ena said, almost ignoring Fiona's last comment. "Madison needed to be knocked off her high horse."

Fiona's eyes softened. "And you figured you were the one to do it?"

Ena held her gaze. "They're my best friend. I couldn't let it go."

Fiona was quiet for a moment, then nodded. "That part is admirable, Ena. That loyalty, however misdirected in this case, is very special." Fiona's voice softened, but not too much. "But did Skyler want this? Did they ask you to get involved?"

Ena faltered. "Hmm, no," she said, her confidence slipping. "I kept it from them on purpose. They don't retaliate."

Fiona let out a thoughtful "Hmmmm," allowing Ena's last words to linger in the air like an echo down a long hallway.

She gave Ena a moment to sit with it, then asked gently: "How do you think Skyler feels about the prank?"

Ena's eyes dropped to her hands in her lap. Fiona's questions landed harder than any of the accusations she'd faced over the past two days.

"I don't know," she admitted, trying to summon some piece of her earlier conviction. "And I can't find out. Suspended and grounded, remember?"

Fiona let the sharpness pass without a blink.

"Well," Fiona said gently, "maybe when you get the chance, you'll want to."

Fiona reached for another album, Judith Hill, *Back in Time*, but didn't slide it into a crate. Instead, her eyes met Ena's, steady. "If I swear to keep this between us," Fiona said, "can I ask you something?"

"I guess," Ena replied, unsure what was coming next.

"You didn't pull this off all by yourself, did you?"

The way Fiona asked, calm and certain, made Ena's stomach flip.

"You swear? You won't tell anyone?"

Fiona nodded. "Promise."

"A girl helped me. The one I told you about after my first day. Piney." Ena took a breath. "It was still my idea. I made the plan. I'm the one who's responsible. She shouldn't get in trouble."

Fiona was quiet for a beat, then nodded taking in Ena's words.

"Well, I don't know about that, but a promise is a promise," Fiona said, sealing the promise. "Do you know if she got in trouble?"

"No, I won't until I see Piney next. No screens. No way to text." Ena was resigned to her fate.

"Hmmm," Fiona said, like she understood more than what had been said.

"What, Fi?"

"There had to have been suspicion. You protected her. That's rare, kiddo. Loyalty like that doesn't come around every day."

Fiona had pulled thoughts to the surface Ena wasn't sure she was ready to face. She had never felt the burden of loyalty this way before. Now she felt she owed it to Skyler and Piney. And that made her smile. But had she been loyal to Skyler? She had left them out of the prank because Ena knew they wouldn't approve.

Ena returned to sorting the albums while also sorting through the conversation. She was unsure of what came next.

But one thing was clear to Ena. Fiona didn't just admire loyalty; she lived it. And she saw that loyalty in Ena. And she offered it back.

In that moment, Ena knew it deep in her bones: Fiona would always be there.

WRECKING BALL

The days of Ena's suspension ticked by. Mornings were spent with Fiona and Graeme, mostly doing chores, but never without purpose. In the afternoons, Fiona seemed to craft quiet opportunities to grow closer, and their bond deepened. Fiona was more than a grandmother; she was an adviser, a confessor. A friend.

One afternoon, they gathered around the piano. Graeme played almost any song Ena could throw at him, with Fiona and Ena singing along, laughter bubbling up between verses. Music, for a moment, made everything else fade.

At night, Ena retreated to her room, guitar in hand, headphones on, determined to nail the trickiest riffs of her favorite songs. Suspension still carried the weight of a punishment, but in the quiet, in the rhythm, Ena found a kind of peace.

Ena's parents had scheduled a date night for Friday, so Byron came over after school. He was glued to a game on his iPad at the kitchen table while Ena and Graeme sipped water.

"Yes!" Byron suddenly yelled. "I finally unlocked Krux!"

Graeme glanced over, amused. "Krux? That sounds impressive. What is it?"

Byron didn't look up. "He's a Time Twin. Only the best character in the game. He can freeze time or rewind it to fix your mistakes."

Graeme rubbed his chin, intrigued. "Rewind time, fix mistakes. Playing with dangerous concepts, wouldn't you say, Ena?"

Ena had been half-tuned out but perked up at that. "Sounds pretty wild," she said with a small grin.

Byron had already sunk back into the game, lost to the world.

Graeme leaned in just a bit, lowering his voice. "If you could go back in time, where would you go?"

Ena tilted her head. "I dunno. Maybe hear The Fin Whales live. Maybe see Elvis before he was famous. That'd be wild. What about you?"

Graeme nodded slowly. "Good picks. Me? I wouldn't risk it."

"Why not?"

"Because I'd be terrified of breaking something," Graeme said softly. "One little change. Maybe Fiona and I never meet. Maybe your parents don't end up together. I love this life too much to roll those dice."

Ena turned that over in her head, suddenly more aware of how fragile good things could be.

♪ ♫ ♪

Monday finally rolled around.

That peace she had settled into during her suspension shattered almost as soon as Ena stepped foot in school.

Madison stepped in front of Ena, cutting off any easy escape.

"Ena Quinn. Or should I say *Anakin?* Why don't you go back to the dark side?"

The words came out too loud, too stiff—too rehearsed. Ena figured Madison must have planned every detail, the busiest stretch of the hallway, the perfect moment, the line she'd practiced so many times it should have been effortless.

Instead of landing with effortless sting, the line just sat there.

Ena didn't even flinch. "Okay, Stormtrooper. No aim, no originality, no impact. Missed again."

Passing by, Dylan, one of Ena's classmates, caught the exchange and grinned. He slowed just enough to grab a bottle of water from his bag, handing it to Madison. "You might need this for that burn."

With a quick nod to Ena, he kept walking, a silent approval.

Madison's whole body visibly tightened, and she let out an exaggerated sigh, flicking her hair over her shoulder. "Ugh, whatever. I don't have time for your little nerd debates."

She turned on her heel, already scanning the hallway, not for an exit, but for validation from someone, anyone. Her eyes landed on Ashley, always aware of her precarious position with the cool kids. Madison scoffed. "She's such a freak."

Ashley hesitated for a beat too long, then nodded. "Yeah. I mean, yours was way better."

Not the hype Madison was hoping for, but enough to save face. With another dramatic hair flip, she strutted off like the whole thing had gone exactly as planned.

But Ena caught it, that tiny flicker of frustration Madison couldn't quite hide.

"Damn, EQB," came a familiar voice from behind her. "Wasting no time. That was vicious."

Ena turned around to see Piney's grinning face.

"Remind me never to get on your *dark* side," Piney said, her tone low and satisfied.

She fell into step beside Ena without waiting for an invite, like it was the most natural thing in the world.

"Missed you too, Piney," Ena said with a chuckle.

"How was your vacation?"

"Well, sun, sand, surf, what more can a girl ask for?" Ena grinned.

"That was a sick prank you pulled," Piney said, her voice lighter now. "All by yourself."

"You never know what one girl can pull off with *YOU*tube."

They both laughed as they neared Skyler's locker. Piney wasn't just being nice; a comfort and ease grew between them. Ena felt like she had aced a test she didn't even know she was taking.

"Morning, sunshine," Ena said.

"Good morning, Ena," Skyler replied. Flat. Cold.

The smile slid from Ena's face. "Everything okay?"

Skyler didn't answer. "We're going to be late," they said, already turning toward English class.

Ena stood frozen for a beat, then turned to Piney. "What was that?"

Piney shrugged. "No clue. But yeah, that was weird."

♪ ♫ ♪

Lunch finally arrived. Ena hadn't stopped thinking about Skyler.

Piney fell in step next to Ena, like they had always had lunch together. Ena was conflicted. She wanted Piney to know she was invited, but just not today.

She didn't say anything. Inertia won.

The three of them ate together, awkward silence filling the spaces between even more awkward attempts at conversation. Skyler barely spoke. Ena's heart wobbled off-kilter, like she was playing the wrong chords in a song she used to know by heart.

When the mid-lunch chime rang, Ena turned to Piney. "I need to talk to Skyler. Alone. Okay?"

Piney gave her a quick nod. "I get it. Catch you later."

Ena jogged after Skyler. "Hey, wait up."

Skyler didn't stop walking.

"What's wrong?" Ena asked.

Skyler finally turned, their expression unreadable. "You ask what's wrong?"

"I don't know, Skyler. I swear. I thought—"

"That you could fight my battles for me? That you could decide how justice gets served without me?" Skyler shook their head. "You didn't think about the fallout. About how it would land on me."

"I was trying to protect you," Ena said quietly. "You're my best friend. I couldn't let Madison get away with it."

"And I'm telling you, you could have. You should have."

Skyler's voice cracked just slightly. "Dropping to her level doesn't make you better. It just adds more hurt to the world. And this time, that hurt came back on me."

Ena's shoulders crashed down, throat tight. "I didn't mean to—"

"The worst part?" Skyler said, eyes locked on hers. "You and Piney, yeah we all know, worked on it together. And you kept it from me. Deliberately. That broke something. That hurt more than Madison ever has. Or ever could."

Ena's voice dropped to barely a whisper. "You're right. About all of it. I messed up. I'd take it back in a second if I could. I'm so, so sorry."

A long silence hung between them.

"Can you forgive me?" Ena finally asked.

Skyler didn't answer immediately. Then a simple "Why?"

Ena knew what they were asking. She stared at the ground, nudging a loose stone with her toe. "Because I knew you wouldn't be okay with it. You'd say we're better than that, and you're right. But I was so mad, like stupid mad. And I wanted her to get a taste of what she's been serving up. I just…didn't want to let you talk me out of it. So, I didn't give you the chance."

"I can forgive you, Ena, but I can't unfeel the hurt. That, that will take time."

"I'll take that. I am so, so sorry. I did not mean to hurt you. I messed up big time."

Skyler looked at Ena, nodded once, then turned and walked on, alone.

Ena didn't follow. She just stood there, wrecked, watching the space grow as Skyler left her behind. Distance that felt permanent.

START AGAIN

Ena walked through the rest of the school day in a daze. She needed to talk to someone.

After the final bell, she headed to the one place she could still go while grounded, the only place that didn't feel like a punishment: her grandparents' house.

She rang the bell, and Fiona opened the door, a soft smile already forming until she saw Ena's face.

Ena didn't say a word. She rushed forward and wrapped her arms around her grandmother like Fiona was a rock in the middle of a raging river. She clung to her, sobbing hard now, not caring how it sounded. For the first time since the prank, she let it all go.

Fiona held her without question, without words, just gently stroking her hair.

When the sobs finally slowed to gulps of air, Fiona whispered, "Oh, baby girl. Come in. We're here. Tell us everything."

Inside, they sat in the living room, Ena sinking into the couch where just days ago, she and her grandparents had been singing, laughing, trying to stump Graeme on the piano. That version of her life felt light years away, like it belonged to someone else entirely.

She told them every detail of the fallout with Skyler.

"I didn't mean to," Ena said, voice hoarse, "and now I lost my best friend. The best friend I've ever had."

Fiona was quiet for a moment, then said, "Maybe. Maybe not. Skyler is sharp. But Skyler is hurt, deeply hurt. They might get over it."

Graeme leaned forward, elbows on knees. "They might just need a little space. Doesn't mean they've stopped caring."

Ena was unconvinced. "I don't know, it felt like I broke something. No clue how to make it better. I just wish I could go back in time and undo this."

Fiona slid her golden eighth note pendant back and forth on its chain. "I know someone who's great at fixing things."

"But I don't even know where to start," Ena said.

Graeme leaned back in his chair, his hand thoughtfully rubbing his chin. "To fix a thing, we need to know how it broke."

"Well, Skyler's mad at me because I went behind their back to hurt Madison."

"Hmm, let's break that down a little more," Graeme said, his scientific mind taking the driver's seat. "What I am hearing is that they felt excluded. That stings for sure. Hmmm. What else do you think, Ena?"

"Skyler is big about when we hurt others, we hurt ourselves." Ena reflected for a moment. "Well, I guess I just proved their point."

Fiona said, "That sounds interesting. There is truth there. What could we do with that?"

Ena bit her lower lip in thought. After a moment, she said, "I don't know. But they talk about how it's destructive. They use that word a lot."

Graeme leaned back, eyes narrowing, not in judgment, but in focus. A glimmer sparked behind his glasses. He didn't say a word.

Fiona noticed too. "Oh no," she said lightly, nudging him with her elbow. "He's got that look again."

"What look?" Ena asked, frowning.

Graeme just smiled. "The kind that takes a little time to explain."

Ena gave a quiet, confused laugh. For the first time that day, her shoulders loosened a little.

A flicker of uncertainty tugged at Ena's thoughts. Graeme and Fiona seemed to have more answers than they were giving right now. But it was getting late and Ena needed to be home for dinner.

♪ ♫ ♪

After dinner, Ena went up to her bedroom. In her notebook, she wrote two words:

DESTRUCTION,

EXCLUSION.

She wrote them a few more times, pondering those wonders and trying to feel the meanings more fully than she had before.

She then wrote, *Creation? Inclusion?*

Then again, in all caps—*CREATION*—tall enough to span four lines. Underneath that, similarly, *INCLUSION.*

Ena flipped the page and started drawing.

♪ ♫ ♪

The next day at school, Ena saw Skyler.

"Morning, Skyler?"

"Good morning, Ena," Skyler replied just as coolly as the day before.

That stung Ena, but she was committed to giving Skyler the space they wanted.

During lunch, Ena shared her drawing with Piney.

"Love it, 100 in," Piney said. "But we need a name for this mission. What do you think of Project Bang and Boom?"

Ena shook her head. "Too obvious. Skyler's more, I don't know, artsy but precise. Like when they explained their weird music term, Klangfarben. They said it was like coloring with sound."

Piney grinned. "Yeah, that feels more Skyler."

Ena smiled. "Operation Klangfarben."

"Done," Piney said. "Operation Klangfarben it is."

♪ ♫ ♪

After school, Ena rushed to her grandparents' house, her sketch folded carefully in her backpack as if it were made of glass. She didn't even take off her shoes before pulling it out.

Fiona took one look and smiled like she'd been expecting it. "That's my girl. Creation as an instrument."

Graeme's eyes lit up. He grinned like a kid in a candy store. "Now that's a solution I'd be proud of. I think we can help get you started."

He clapped his hands and stood. "Let's see what we can find."

He led her out to the backyard, stopping in front of his workshop, the birthplace of many of his strangest, most brilliant ideas.

With a mischievous glint in his eyes, he let out three low whistles. A small door above the workshop creaked open, and a narrow ladder folded down with a soft clank. *Of course, Granddad rigged the attic to respond to a whistle.* She was constantly amazed by the things he dreamed up.

Ena had never been invited into Graeme's workshop before, and for a moment, she thought today might be the day. But instead of the lab itself, he led her to the attic above it. Still, it was the closest she'd ever gotten. But this *was* Graeme's storage space. *What kind of discoveries might be waiting inside?*

"Come on," Graeme said, already climbing. "You're about to see my treasure trove."

Ena followed him up into the attic above the workshop. The air smelled like old wood, metal, and possibility. Every inch of space had been maximized; bins and racks lined the walls, filled with carefully sorted scraps of wood, metal, and plastic. Pipes were bundled by size. Shelves were labeled in Graeme's precise handwriting: *Curved Connectors, Hollow Tubes, Gears, Wheels*—raw material waiting to be transformed.

What would be junk in most garages clearly held value here.

Ena stood in awe. "This is amazing." It felt like stepping inside Graeme's mind, with every odd part and forgotten gadget carefully arranged, seeing potential where others saw scrap, and leaving space for creativity to take hold. She couldn't shake the feeling that Graeme wasn't just letting her explore a workshop; he was offering her a glimpse into something sacred.

Graeme beamed. "It's not junk if you know what you're looking for and where to find it."

He guided her to a section stacked with metal pipes. "Take whatever you think might work."

Ena combed through the pipes, feeling like a scavenger in *The Walking Dead*. She pulled out a few metal pipes of various lengths, shapes, and sizes.

"I think that's a great start," Graeme said.

He climbed down first. Ena handed the pipes to him, one by one. Then she followed, back to earth, as if she had returned from a trip to another world.

"We'll keep them here for now," Graeme said, chuckling. "Once you're paroled, we'll bring them over to Piney's." The gentle ribbing landed just right.

Three sharp whistles from Graeme, the ladder folded up, and the attic door closed.

The treasure trove was sealed, but the spark it lit was just getting started.

LET'S BUILD A FIRE

The week passed slowly. Ena's world was small—only school and home—but with ideas and plans rattling around her brain, it had suddenly grown much bigger. Her mind buzzed with sketches, modifications, and wild ideas. Every free moment was spent imagining what this gift for Skyler could become. At lunch, she and Piney volleyed ideas back and forth like they were scheming a heist.

Hope grew.

So did excitement.

Each day, Ena tried to reach out to Skyler, offering small kindnesses, jokes, quiet invitations. Skyler wasn't ready. But that didn't change Ena's determination. This was for them. Not to fix anything, not to prove anything. Just to show them, without words, what they meant to her.

She wasn't even excited to get ungrounded. What mattered most was the chance to complete the project for Skyler. A gift weird and joyful. A gift only they would fully understand.

Sunday night, over dinner, she finally asked, "So, tomorrow's two weeks. Do I get ungrounded?"

Tara didn't answer immediately. "You know, Ena," she started, the edge in her voice not completely gone, "I talked to your grandparents. They think you've grown a lot from this. But honestly? I'm not sure."

Ena still didn't fully understand why her mom had been so mad. But now wasn't the time to argue.

Jason reached across the table and supportively touched Tara's hand. "Why do you think we should lift the grounding?" he asked, turning to Ena.

"Well, for one," Ena said, "I didn't try to break any rules. Model prisoner. And two, Fiona really helped me think through everything. I'm sorry. Truly. I just—" Her voice caught. "I just want to make something right."

Jason looked at Tara. "Hon?"

Tara let out a long breath. "Fine. We can unground her." Then she turned, locking eyes with Ena. Tara's eyes glistened. "But if you ever do anything like that again, you might be grounded into your thirties. We are not raising bullies."

Bully. The word landed sharp in Ena's ears. *But I was fighting a bully, wasn't I?* At her old school, she'd always been near the top. Not mean, but she hadn't exactly stood up for anyone, either. When kids got picked on, she just stayed out of it.

And now here she was getting called a bully for finally standing up for Skyler. Her chest tightened. That wasn't fair. Was it?

She nodded anyway. It didn't matter what she had intended anymore. What mattered was what she'd do next.

♩ ♫ ♩

Monday morning, Jason handed Ena her phone as she came downstairs.

She didn't even check her notifications. Her thumb moved on instinct.

Group chat: Piney and Skyler.

She tapped it, dropped a single link no caption: *[YouTube link to "I'm Free" by the Soup Dragons.]*

A beat later, she added a grinning selfie, peace sign up, poorly backlit, but she didn't care.

Then she noticed it, her snap streaks with Piney and Skyler? Gone. Zero.

She fought back the lump in her throat. One more thing to rebuild.

Piney DM'd Ena immediately.

PINEY: *Operation Klangfarben full go?*

ENA: *100.*

ENA: *My granddad will bring everything over, cool?*

PINEY: *Let's do this.*

Ena watched the group chat. She waited.

A few minutes later, Skyler opened the Snap.

No reply. No emoji. Just seen. It stung.

Ena had to get to school. The day passed like any other, slow, ordinary. But underneath, she buzzed with anticipation.

When the final bell rang, she bolted.

Out front, Piney was already waiting. Graeme rolled up in his aged beige Ford Ranger, the kind of truck that had seen things, weathered, well-maintained, and clearly loved. A blue tarp bulged up from the bed like it was hiding treasure.

Ena and Piney squeezed into the front seat, shoulder to shoulder. Graeme dropped it into gear without a word, just a knowing smile, and headed for Piney's house.

In the driveway, he backed in carefully. Then, with a bit of theatrical flair, he hopped out, lifted the tarp, and pulled down a small ramp. He rolled out what looked like the base of a sit-stand desk, but knowing Graeme, it was much more than that.

"Girls," he said, brushing off his hands. "I hope you don't mind, but I couldn't help myself. Thought you might like a little head start."

Ena's eyes lit up. "This is perfect!"

She threw her arms around him. "Thank you!"

"I wasn't exactly sure of the dimensions you'd need, so…"

He pressed a button on the crossbar. It rose with a quiet whir. Another button, and arms extended smoothly outward from the center.

Graeme couldn't hide the grin stretching across his face.

Piney let out a gasp. "Oh my God. That. Is. Fire."

Ena's mouth hung open. Her grandfather had done this for them. They wouldn't have been able to build a base like that, and it was perfect.

"Thank you so much." She looked at Graeme.

Those four words were more than enough for Graeme.

Graeme helped them unload all of Ena's pipes. He gave them a plastic box with lots of tiny drawers filled with various screws, washers, bolts, wires, and various other bits and bobs. He handed them each a drill. "I think this is enough to make you dangerous," he said with a wink.

As he drove away, Piney turned to Ena and whispered, "Project Klangfarben, from idea to reality. Let's do this thing!"

Every day after school, Piney and Ena worked. Experimenting with placement, which pipes fit in the right places.

At one point, they were stumped by a problem. Two pipes sat in what seemed like the exact right spots, but they kept clanging against each other. It had the right appearance but sounded wrong. Ena and Piney swapped ideas, moving effortlessly from words to drawings and back. Eventually, they threaded a piece of wire through just the right way.

Solution found.

By Friday evening, they put the final bolt in place. They stepped back.

They didn't say a word. They just stared.

"Creation." She let the word hang there, weighty with new meaning.

Creation does feel good. Monday, this didn't exist. And now, here it was.

Real. Tangible. Done.

For now.

CLOSER TO FINE

Phase 2 of Operation Klangfarben had officially begun.

"So, the big question, how do we get them to even come over to see this glorious creation?" Ena asked as she and Piney admired their creation.

"Skyler and I have been keeping our Snapstreak alive. Not super active, but still going," Piney said. "Maybe we just send a mystery message. Something to get them curious enough so they can't resist."

"Like 'Existential Calamity. Need help! 10:00 a.m.?' " Ena offered.

"I like it. Close. How about, 'The universe asked. Answer at my house. Tomorrow, 10:00 a.m.' "

"Let's send it."

Piney opened her phone:

PINEY: *Universe asked. Answer at my house. Tomorrow. 10 a.m.*

SKYLER: *Questions clearer than answers.*

"What do you think that means?" Ena asked, looking over Piney's shoulder.

"Skyler being Skyler. We'll find out soon enough."

"I guess I'll see you in the morning. Whatever happens, we crushed it," Ena said, offering a fist bump to Piney.

♪ ♫ ♪

Ena woke up at 6:00 a.m. after a night of fitful sleep. Going back to sleep wasn't an option. The house was silent, so Ena picked up her electric guitar, plugged in her headphones, and played "Riptide" by Vance Joy. Her stress melted away as she was absorbed in the music, the chords, the finger movements. For that moment, it was just Ena and the music.

Eventually, the house started to wake up. Ena headed downstairs for breakfast. Her dad, rocking some serious bedhead, was in the kitchen starting the coffee maker.

"Hey, there's my girl. Are you and Piney still working on your project today?" Jason asked.

"We finished our project. Today is the big reveal. I hope Skyler comes over. It's for them." Ena's voice trembled on the final words.

"A peace offering, eh?" Jason asked.

"Nah, not really a peace offering. More like a gift. No strings, no expectations. If they love it and still can't be friends…I don't know, it'll hurt, but I'll live. I'll know I gave it my best."

Jason grinned. "You know, Ena, you really have grown through all of this. And I am proud of you."

Her dad's comment left a warm spot in Ena's chest. After the turmoil of the past few weeks, those words settled over her with unanticipated grace, more than she expected. She gave him a small smile, eyes dropping to the counter, words stuck behind her teeth.

"Do you need a ride over to Piney's?"

"We told Skyler 10:00 a.m., and there's plenty of time. I might just walk, if that's okay?"

"Sure, of course. Byron probably has three soccer games today, so I'm sure he'll keep us busy."

Ena sat down at the table, bowl of cereal in hand.

Jason said with a twinkle in his eye, "Hey Ena, knock knock."

Ena sighed. "Who's there?"

"Lettuce."

"Lettuce who?"

"Lettuce know how it goes with Skyler."

"OMG, Dad! They get worse every time!" A quiet laugh escaped her lips. Her dad's love came wrapped in a corny joke, supporting her in his own way.

♪ ♫ ♪

Around 9:00 a.m., Ena grabbed her guitar case and made her way to Piney's. As she walked, her phone dinged with a text.

GRAEME: *Today's the big reveal?*

ENA: *Yep. [Fingers crossed emoji.]*

GRAEME: *Any chance you'd let an old man come by for it?*

ENA: *Sure.*

Ena arrived at Piney's just a few minutes before Graeme. Despite his age, he had the giddy energy of a kid at Christmas. "Can I see it?"

"Nope," Piney said. "The garage door doesn't open until Skyler arrives."

"*If* Skyler arrives," Ena added, uncertainty slipping into her voice.

Ten in the morning came and went. Then, 10:15…still no Skyler.

"They're not coming," Ena said, dejected.

Each passing minute pulled Ena deeper into doubt. She worried she'd broken Skyler's trust beyond repair. She wished she could turn back time—not for Madison's sake, but because losing Skyler over this wasn't worth it. Not even close.

Graeme's hand rested gently on her shoulder. No words, just warmth. And somehow, a sliver of hope.

Piney peered down the street. "Look!"

Skyler had just turned the corner, heading toward the house.

Ena's heart raced. Hope, uncertainty, and fear collided in her chest.

Skyler, eyes squinting, stared at Piney and then Ena.

"Wait! Is this an ambush? Because that's not cool."

"Skyler, this is just for you," Ena said. "No expectations. Just an attempt to say: I really *hear* you."

Skyler froze, looking unsure if they should stay or leave.

"Don't you want to know what the universe asked?" Piney added.

Skyler squinted their eyes. "What?"

"The question was," Piney said, walking toward the garage door, "What is something 100% Skyler?"

She pressed the garage door button.

Graeme raised his phone to record.

As the door rose, a cluster of pipes attached to Graeme's stand came into view. A mallet with an oversized white plastic head hung from a hook.

Skyler's mouth dropped. Words failed them.

When the door was fully open, Skyler stepped forward, picked up the mallet, and struck one of the largest pipes. A deep, resonant note rang out.

The note hung in the air, round and rich, like a breath held too long finally being released.

"You did this for me?" they asked, eyes bouncing between Piney and Ena.

"It was mostly Ena," Piney said. "I helped a bit, but it was her idea, her design. She did this for you."

Skyler gazed at the instrument, then at Ena. Their eyes glistened. "For me?"

"Skyler, you're my best friend. I just—" Ena hesitated, her voice shaky, "I wanted you to know how much you mean to me. That I really heard you. We made this so you could create music. And maybe, when you want, with me. With us. If or when you're ready."

Skyler sat down on the nearby stool, picked up the mallet again, and tested the instrument. Striking pipe after pipe, exploring its tones.

"Ena, Piney, no one has ever done anything like this. It's like you looked out far and in deep, and saw the real me. It would be my honor to create music with you."

The tension—inside Ena, among the trio—vanished.

Graeme slid his phone back into his pocket, smiling.

He stepped closer, running a hand along the pipes. "Girls, you've exceeded all my expectations."

"Skyler, my granddad helped with the build. He made the frame adjustable. Check this out." Ena pushed a button to extend the arms. "There's space for you to add more. Change it. Make it yours."

Ena watched as Skyler's eyes shot wide open, scanning each pipe and element of the instrument. She could tell Skyler wasn't just seeing what it was but imagining what it could become.

Graeme stepped back. "I imagine the three of you would like to test it out."

As he turned to leave, Ena ran up and hugged him. "Thank you, Granddad. I love you."

"Love you too, Ena."

Once he was gone, Ena brought out her guitar, Piney set up her keyboard, and Skyler settled behind their new percussion rig.

For the rest of the morning, the three of them played, improvising, experimenting, listening.

Their rhythms intertwined, not always pretty, but their joy was undeniable.

A warm glow embraced Ena: Skyler hadn't just loved the gift; they'd understood exactly what it meant.

A statement of friendship. A statement of love.

HOME

The leaves shifted from green to fire-bright reds, oranges, and yellows before tumbling to the ground. Piney, Skyler, and Ena had become inseparable, bonded through jam sessions at Piney's, endless Snapchat streaks, shared school projects, and memes that stitched inside jokes into something deeper. Friendships were repaired. Trust, rebuilt.

Thanksgiving break arrived with a hush. The city lay still under a blanket of snow, the roads nearly empty. Ena's mom drove without hesitation, her reflexes honed over a decade of Boston winters.

"So, you've made some good friends with Skyler and Piney, huh?" Tara asked.

"Yeah. They get me," Ena replied. She intended those words to sting, and by the grimace on Tara's face, her words had done their job. Her mom still saw her as a little kid, not who she was becoming. Tara seemed too wrapped up in work to even notice Ena wasn't a girl anymore. She wasn't really trying to hurt her, just trying to wake her up, to make her see the real Ena.

"I guess—" Tara paused. "That's great, Ena."

"Yeah, they are pretty great."

The gulf between them stretched wide, as cold as the frigid streets outside. Ena sensed her mother wanted to say more, ask more, but every time she tried, Ena turned her face toward the window, sliding further away. They drove in silence the rest of the way.

When they pulled up in front of Piney's house, Tara said, "I'll pick you up. Do you know what time?"

"Can't I just text you when we're winding down?"

"Sure, honey. Love you."

"Yeah. Love you too." Ena said it with all the enthusiasm of a tired sloth.

♪ ♫ ♪

Ena, with her guitar strapped on her back, knocked on the front door. Mrs. Lanier, Piney's step-grandmother, opened it.

"Hey, little porcupine, your friend is here," she called over her shoulder, her melodic voice carrying like a jazz riff, loud but never sharp. "Come on in, Ena. It's freezing out there."

Inside, the house smelled like cardamom tea and cinnamon rolls. Piney's moms were seated at the breakfast bar, coffee mugs in hand, mid-conversation. Ena didn't get to see them together that often. Both were doctors at the nearby hospital and worked long, unpredictable hours.

Dr. Kapoor, Piney's biological mom, had the sharper edges: intensely focused, quick to listen, quicker to move. Her dark hair was pulled into a no-nonsense bun, but her eyes were warm when they landed on Ena.

Dr. Lanier, who Piney simply called Mom, had a slower rhythm. Her hair was pulled back with a wide headband, and she wore an oversized cardigan that looked like it had lived a good life. She had the kind of voice that made people feel calmer just by hearing it.

Together, they were a study in contrasts, precision and patience, but the ease between them was unmistakable. Piney's house had a sense Ena couldn't quite name; the warmth of a second home, a sense that understood the word "welcome" in every way that mattered.

"Good morning, Ena," Dr. Kapoor said, setting her mug down. "Glad you survived Thanksgiving."

"Come sit. I think Piney's setting out in the garage," Dr. Lanier said with a smile. "You want some tea?"

"No thanks, Dr. Lanier."

"How was your Thanksgiving?" she asked.

"You know, the usual. Turkey, mashed potatoes, green bean casserole. It was pretty quiet. My uncles were with their partners' families, so it was just my grandparents and us."

"Well, that's nice," Mrs. Lanier said, warmly nodding.

Piney came in from the garage. "Hey, you made it through the snow!"

"Ya know, Bahston. This isn't even a flah-ry," Ena said in an exaggerated Boston accent.

Soft laughter filled the room.

"I've got the heaters going in the garage. Once Skyler gets here, it should be warm enough," Piney said.

The adults drifted into a conversation about weekend plans while Ena and Piney started talking through a possible playlist. A few minutes later, Skyler arrived, stomping snow from their boots on the doormat before coming in.

The trio shuffled into Piney's detached garage, the cold nipping at their heels. Ena tugged the side door shut with a soft thud.

"Your moms are so cool," she said, pulling her guitar out of its case. "I feel like they actually get us."

"Maybe," Piney replied, her voice flatter than Ena expected.

Ena dropped her bag onto a beanbag chair. "I don't know, my mom just doesn't get it. Like she has no clue that we aren't little kids anymore."

"I hear you," Piney said, fiddling with the dials on her keyboard. "But sometimes? My moms are relentless. An A-minus might as well be an F."

"Parents are hard," Skyler added, settling behind their pipe-percussion monstrosity. "My dad, no bad vibes, but he gets my pronouns right, like, ten percent of the time. Tops."

"My dad made us watch *Back to the Future*." Ena said. "He laughed at 1955 awkwardness until I pointed out the movie came out closer to 1955 than to today. That quieted him down."

Skyler's eyes sparkled. "Ooh, Time travel. I love thinking about all the paradoxes. I've read a little about theories on how time travel might work. Makes my head hurt, but immensely interesting."

Piney rolled her eyes. "We don't have time to walk through all the anomalies and ripples of time travel. We're here to make some noise, so let's do it."

Skyler tapped a pipe. "Fair."

Piney assessed Skyler's setup. The instrument had evolved since its debut back in October. More pipes. A couple metal pans. Even a wind chime now dangled from one arm.

"You ever gonna give that thing a proper name?" Piney asked.

Skyler fidgeted. "I was thinking…maybe Korakama?"

"Korakama?" Piney echoed curiously, not judging. "What's the story?"

"Well, kora is an African stringed instrument," Skyler said. "But it also reminds me of corazón, heart. Music connects us. It's emotional. It can reach back through time and cross boundaries."

"And kama," Piney added. "As in the Purusharthas, life goals? Kama: love, connection, belonging."

Ena raised an eyebrow.

"What?" Piney said. "Grandmother Kapoor. She teaches me stuff when I visit my dad."

Skyler lit up. "Piney, you nailed it."

"Korakama. I love it," Ena said. "Now let's hear Korakama sing. Start with 'Electric Feel' by MGMT?"

Piney grinned. "Perfect. Let's get this party started."

"Count us in, Skyler," Ena said.

Skyler counted them in with two soft taps on a copper pipe. Ena launched into the opening riff of "Electric Feel," her fingers steady and sure. Piney layered in an ambient synth wash that shimmered like light on ice.

Korakama clattered to life, part rhythm, part chaos, and somehow perfectly in time. The garage filled with music that was a little too loud for the space, but none of them cared.

"Okay, this actually slaps," Piney said, nodding to the beat.

"Right?" Ena tilted her head, smiling as she sang the chorus, her voice bright and loose.

Skyler didn't just keep rhythm. They orchestrated it, weaving in clinks and clangs with wild precision, like a conductor made of elbows and instinct. They hit the last note with a clatter of pipes and a fading synth echo.

"That was so not the original tempo," Piney said.

"Creative license," Skyler said, spinning a metal spoon between their fingers.

"It's so totally us," Ena added. "Honor the music but add our own twists."

"Ena, you're starting to sound like Skyler. We need to split you two up," Piney teased.

They laughed, a laughter that filled the room with more than friendship. It was kinship.

Outside, the cold pressed in. But inside, warmth radiated not just from the hum of the electric heaters, but from a feeling harder to name.

A feeling that lived somewhere between friendship and freedom.

Between music and meaning.

GOLDEN BROWN

Darkness seemed to wrap around Portland; the days were short, and even when the sun showed up, it mostly lurked behind a blanket of gray. Ena and Fiona were in the kitchen the Saturday before Christmas. The entire house was steeped in the scent of melting butter, warm chocolate, and cookies just starting to turn golden, a scent that wrapped around her like comfort made real. A little Bluetooth speaker played softly from the counter, their shared Spotify playlist filling her grandmother's kitchen with the soundtrack of their bond.

They'd been baking all morning: mixing doughs, sifting flour, frosting cooled batches. Fiona always made more cookies and more types of cookies than anyone could reasonably eat. This was the first year Ena had been part of the ritual. Fiona never fit anyone's mold. Some might not expect this of her, but Christmas cookies were a fully Fiona-owned and approved tradition.

"Baby girl, it's been a heck of a year for you, hasn't it?" Fiona asked.

"Fi, yeah. It's kind of been crazy. But I don't know, I really feel like I found my place. Piney and Skyler, they're so different in a lot of ways, but they click where it means something. It's like they're my second family. I can't imagine not knowing them."

Fiona gently stroked the back of Ena's hair. "It's weird how that happens. Strangers can become family so quickly. When we're lucky. Or when we make our own luck."

Ena met her gaze. Fiona had a way of making things feel more real, like she could name the thoughts Ena hadn't yet found words for.

"It's special," Fiona nodded. "The strange thing I've learned is, the tighter I try to hold on to moments like that, the more easily they slip away. Like trying to grasp water. Open hands will hold it. But tighten your grip—"

"And it's gone." Ena's eyes dropped back to the cookie sheet in front of her. She kept spooning dough onto the tray, Fiona's words still rattling around in her brain, trying to land in the right place.

Fiona broke the silence. "So, you three have been playing together a lot. Are you officially a band?"

"No, we just like to jam."

Fiona raised an eyebrow. "That's too bad. You three are so smart and talented. Could be something special."

Those words didn't come cheaply. Fiona wouldn't say talented unless she meant it, and she knew what she was talking about.

They spent the afternoon finishing the cookies. There was an easy comfort between them, mutual respect, love, and joy. They talked about things that mattered, laughed at misshapen cookies, swapped jokes and silly stories. Time with Fiona always flew too fast.

Fiona made Ena feel seen for who she was becoming, while Tara was stuck seeing her as the little kid she'd been.

"Echo Beach" by Martha and the Muffins started on the speaker. Fiona closed her eyes and hummed along. The chorus wound through the doldrums of work to the longing for another time and returning to a favorite beach. Opening her eyes, Fiona looked at Ena and said, "You know, some songs are like magic. They do more than just remind you of a memory. It's like you're almost there, reliving a special moment. This is one of those songs for me."

"Really? Where does this song take you?"

"Oh, just someplace meaningful. A night and a conversation that never really left me."

"It's kind of cool how music can let you time travel like that."

The playlist continued on in the background. Ena wiped flour from her hands and glanced around the cozy, sugar-dusted kitchen, surveying the mountains of cookies she and Fiona had baked.

As they were cleaning up, Ena laughed. "Fi, you remember how I told you I was kind of afraid of you that first day of school? I can't believe I ever felt like that."

Fiona let out a loud cackle. "Some people mistake me for a tiger, but I'm just a gentle pussycat."

"With sharp claws when you need them." They both burst into laughter.

♪ ♫ ♪

That night, back in her room, Ena opened the group chat with Piney and Skyler.

ENA: *I think Fi wants us to start a real band.*

PINEY: *[Surprise emoji.]*

SKYLER: *If we do that, we need a name?*

ENA: *IDEAS?*

PINEY: *Piney & Her Followers.*

SKYLER: *[Face Palm emoji.]*

SKYLER: *Pretentious Pretenders?*

ENA: *Silly Soundfactory?*

PINEY: *Music Delusions.*

SKYLER: *The Treble Rebels.*

ENA: *oof. That's like a dad band name.*

PINEY: *Cacophony & Friends.*

SKYLER: *Weirdos in Harmony.*

ENA: *Kinda Loud, Kinda Lost.*

PINEY: *404: Band Not Found.*

SKYLER: *I'd actually wear that on a hoodie.*

ENA: *SAME.*

PINEY: *New rule: we can't pick a name until we've jammed enough to deserve one.*

SKYLER: *agreed. That's sound logic.*

ENA: *Wait. Is that it?*

SKYLER: *?*

ENA: *Sound Logic? Band name.*

PINEY: *Huh! Not sure, but it does have a ring to it.*

SKYLER: *I kind of like it.*

ENA: *We can always change it but it fits us.*

ENA: *For now at least.*

TO THE MOON AND BACK

The short Portland winter days were finally starting to stretch, their edges smudging into early evening light as February came to a close.

Fiona, ever the force of nature, had insisted on attending today's Sound Logic rehearsal. If Ena was honest with herself, she was afraid to have Fiona there, but at the same time, she was excited to play for her.

Fiona's cup of herbal tea steamed nearby, but her full attention was on the kids. She nestled deep down into the old bean bag chair, worn and lopsided from the years of kids crashing there before her.

Piney, Skyler, and Ena huddled near their makeshift setup, exchanging nervous glances. They opened with Modest Mouse's "Float On," a bold choice. The intro was rough, chords clashing slightly, rhythm loose. All three were painfully aware of Fiona's presence. To them, she wasn't just Ena's grandmother. She was a walking music encyclopedia, a living legend with indie cred older than they were.

But then something shifted.

The music began to carry them. The tension melted, and the trio started listening, really listening, to each other. Piney adjusted her tempo. Skyler found a thread of chaos and bent it into beautiful sound. Ena locked into the groove. They weren't just playing notes anymore; they were playing together.

They'd come a long way since October. For three thirteen-year-olds, they were actually kind of incredible. And Ena could sense Fiona was seeing and feeling it.

As they worked through their playlist, Fiona clapped when the music spoke to her, sometimes off the beat just to throw them playful shade. Other times she closed her eyes, letting the music ripple through her, her head gently swaying as if communing with the rhythm itself.

When the final song faded out, Fiona pushed herself up from the bean bag chair with surprising energy and gave them a standing ovation. "Color me impressed," she said, her voice rich with pride. "You all have come a long way in a really short time."

The kids exchanged wide-eyed grins, flushed with the kind of pride only earned in front of someone who really knows.

"Started off a little nervous, eh?" Fiona added, her tone teasing but kind.

"Yeah," Ena admitted, rubbing the back of her neck.

"It's a good thing," Fiona said. "Means you cared. Means you were trying to give your best to your audience. But the real magic? It happens when you're playing for them while almost forgetting they're there."

The band nodded slowly, the idea sinking in like a challenge they were eager to rise to.

Fiona turned to Skyler. "That contraption of yours creates some wild sounds. You've got a knack for pushing right up to the edge of chaos. But not falling in. Brilliant."

"Thanks, Mrs. Quinn," Skyler said, beaming.

Fiona gave a mock frown. "Graeme's mother is long gone. I'm Fiona." She winked.

Then to Piney: "You're advanced on those keys. How long have you been playing?"

"I started pretty young," Piney replied. "My parents read some study that said early music lessons boost intelligence, so, yeah."

Fiona laughed, low and warm. "Well, whatever the reason, it's working."

She turned to Ena, her eyes sharp with pride. "And you, you've been practicing. You hit a few notes I didn't even know were in your range. And you barely looked at your guitar while you sang."

Ena flushed. Compliments from Fiona weren't casual. They were earned.

"Fi, we've been working. I'm glad it's showing." Ena nodded at Skyler and Piney, still packing up. "Means a ton coming from you."

She slung her guitar into its case and gave her bandmates quick hugs. "Later, legends."

Outside, the cold air held on tight, delaying the promise of spring. Ena slipped her guitar into the back seat of Fiona's car and dropped into the passenger seat. Fiona was already in, a cigarette glowing between her fingers.

"You know, baby girl," Fiona said and blew smoke out the cracked window. "You three are actually good. Not Moda Center good—not yet—but closer than you think."

"Thanks, Fi." She wanted to say more, but the words jammed up in her throat.

Fiona turned to her, eyes bright. "You've done some amazing things in a short time, baby girl. I'm really proud of you."

Ena stared at her hands. "Fiona, it's all you. You got me going. That first day of school, your old woman ramblings about doors and windows." She glanced up at her grandmother, a big grin on her face.

Fiona elbowed her lightly. "Watch it."

"I mean it. Every talk we've had, every random thing you've said. It's like you always knew what I needed to hear."

Fiona gave a quiet smile. "That's sweet, but I'll only take a little credit. The rest? That's on you. You made the choices. You built the band. You opened the doors. And believe it or not, you've taught this old dog a few tricks too."

Ena glanced sideways. "Maybe I could teach you one more."

She nodded toward the cigarette in Fiona's hand.

Fiona let out a long sigh. "Oh, baby girl. I wish. I've quit a million times. But it never sticks."

It rattled Ena. Fiona had always seemed unstoppable, fierce, free, fully herself. It hadn't occurred to her that there were things Fiona couldn't beat.

"Well, maybe quit number one million and one. Who knows? It might be the one."

Fiona looked at the cigarette, then flicked ash out the window. "Maybe. Or maybe I'm just too old a dog to unlearn this trick."

Ena leaned her head back against the seat. "I love you, Fi."

Fiona smiled without looking away from the road. "To the moon and back, kiddo. Love you too."

They turned onto Ena's street. Fiona eased the car to the curb. Ena climbed out, grabbed her guitar, and shut the door gently behind her.

As she reached the top of the front steps, she turned back.

Fiona was already pulling away, a wisp of exhaust curling behind her.

Ena stood still for a moment, the cold barely registering. She wrapped her arms around herself, not from the chill, but from a warmer place: family, Fiona, someone who now meant more to her than she ever expected. Her grandmother was so uniquely Fiona. So fiercely Fiona.

And Ena loved her for it.

Hospital Beds

Ena stared out the window during math class, watching the rare March sunlight spill across the schoolyard. She wondered how much longer the class would drag on, her mind drifting to how much time she wasted listening to lessons about things she already understood.

Her thoughts were interrupted when the principal's assistant, Miss Anderson, entered the room. Miss Anderson was always pale and frumpy, her ill-fitting navy-blue pantsuit making her look even more out of place. But today, she seemed paler than usual. She flicked her eyes toward Ena before quickly shifting her attention to Ms. Johnson, the math teacher.

An expression passed over Ms. Johnson's normally stoic face, its meaning Ena couldn't quite place. Horror? Disgust? Whatever it was, it sent a shiver down Ena's spine. And for some reason, Ena had the sinking feeling that the look was meant for her.

Ms. Johnson cleared her throat. "Ena, could you please go to the principal's office with Miss Anderson? Take all your things."

A ripple of murmurs spread through the class as Ena slung her backpack over her shoulder. She caught a few quizzical stares from her classmates, but none as pointed as Madison's. Seated in the front row, Madison shot her a smug, condescending look that said everything without a single word. *Finally caught again, huh?*

Miss Anderson, uncharacteristically tenser than normal, avoided Ena's gaze as she hurried her out of the room. The stiffness of her posture, the way she walked a little too quickly, made the unease in Ena's stomach grow.

Ena asked uncertainly, "Miss Anderson, can you at least tell me what this is about?"

"I don't think I'm the one to say." Miss Anderson's voice was softer than usual, none of the usual sharpness, none of the clipped, impatient edge she used when calling students to the office. And that scared Ena more than anything else.

Ena's mind raced as they walked, running through every possible thing she could have done to get called to the office like this. Nothing added up.

As they reached the principal's office, Ena's anxiety spiked. She froze at the sight of her mom standing there, pale, near tears, next to Principal Gump. *If Mom is already here, whatever they think I did must be really bad.* Her stomach twisted.

"Mom!" Ena's voice came out in a rush, panic bubbling up. "I swear, I don't know what they think I did, but I didn't do it!"

Tara moved toward Ena quickly, her expression crumbling. "Oh, Ena, you did nothing."

Her voice wavered, and Ena watched in stunned silence as she tried to hold back tears.

"I don't know how to say this," Tara continued, her hands shaking. "It's Fiona. She had a heart attack this morning. She's at the hospital, and things aren't looking good."

Ena's breath caught in her throat.

"She's asking for you," Tara said, blinking back tears. "Your dad is picking up your brother. We're meeting them at the hospital."

Ena was unsteady, like the floor had been ripped out from under her. Her gaze swept the room: Miss Anderson, Principal Gump, her mother. No one seemed to know what to say. *Aren't they adults? Aren't they supposed to have the right words?*

Tara pulled her into a hug. "We have to go."

Ena let herself be led out of the office, her mind reeling. *This can't be right. They must have it wrong. Fiona is too much of a badass, too much of a fighter for this.* Over the past eight months, she had grown so close to Fiona, and the thought of seeing her strong, fiercely independent grandmother weak and vulnerable in a hospital bed made her stomach churn.

Tara had parked illegally right in front of the school. As they descended the school's imposing granite steps toward the car, Tara was in full all-business mode: shoving everything else aside, focusing only on the next step. It wasn't completely natural, but Ena reached for her mother's hand, the urge rising before she could second-guess it. A small gesture of comfort that broke the moment.

Her mother let out a shaky breath, barely holding back tears. She smiled faintly at Ena, pulled her into a tight embrace, and whispered, "Thank you. I love you." Then, just as quickly, she slipped back into her composed, determined state and strode toward the car.

The ride to the hospital was tense and silent. Ena wanted to say something, anything, to ease the tension, but every thought and question could not find a strong enough foothold. The only sound was the hum of the engine as it cycled through gears. Tara tightly clenched her fingers around the steering wheel. The way her mom stared straight ahead, rigid and unblinking, told Ena just how close to the edge she was.

Ena's mind raced back over the time she had spent with Fiona, the bond they had built. Fiona had an unwavering belief in her, one that made Ena feel empowered, capable, seen. Was she really going to lose that?

They pulled into the hospital parking garage, and Tara drove briskly past the first few levels, searching for a spot. Every time she turned the wheel, the tires let out a high-pitched squeal. Ena had the fleeting thought: *Why do they design garages so that even the slightest turn sounds like you're on a racetrack?* Then she immediately scolded herself. *How can I think about something so trivial right now?*

Her mom found a spot and was out of the car in a flash. Ena hurried after her as they crossed the skybridge and navigated their way to the intensive care unit.

Her father and brother hadn't arrived yet. Inside the room, Graeme sat beside Fiona, gently stroking her hair, his hand wrapped around hers. Fiona was barely recognizable beneath the wires and tubes, a stark contrast to the force of nature Ena had admired.

Seeing them, Fiona's lips curled into a faint smile. "There are my girls," she rasped. Her voice was weaker but still carried the familiar grit of a lifetime of living a life on her own terms. She placed her free hand over Graeme's. "Love, can you give me a moment with Ena?"

Graeme hesitated. He kissed the top of Fiona's hand, lingering as if trying to make the moment stretch longer. When he finally rose, his eyes glistened with unshed tears. He offered Ena a weak smile and a nod before stepping past her to embrace her mother. Then, together, he and Tara left the room.

Ena took the seat Graeme had vacated, her fingers carefully lacing through Fiona's frail ones. She had never really noticed the fine wrinkles or the faint yellow tinge in Fiona's fingers. It was overwhelming—the sterile scent of antiseptic, the neutral-colored walls, the relentless beeping of monitors. Ena had never been in a hospital room. Everything was too bright, too exposed, too…wrong.

Fiona's grip on Ena's hand tightened slightly. "Kiddo, things don't look good for me," she said, her gravelly voice weaker, barely recognizable. "I've cherished these past months, getting to know you, seeing what an amazing, strong person you're becoming. I love you, Ena, more than words can say. And if this is my coda, I want you to know that no matter what, I'll always be with you. In your heart, in your mind, in ways you will only discover with time."

Ena sniffled, struggling to keep her composure. "I love you too, Fi. You inspired me long before we moved here, and you've taught me so much since. I don't want to lose you."

Fiona let out a weary chuckle. "Baby girl, that's not up to me. And it's certainly not up to you, either. I won't go without a fight, but this might be one I can't win."

She paused to catch her breath, each word now an effort.

"I've lived one heck of a life. Maybe I smoked too many cigarettes, drank a little too much, pushed a little too hard. And now, maybe the bill is coming due."

Ena squeezed Fiona's hand, her tears now falling freely. "Can I admit something to you, Fi?"

Fiona gave a slight nod, her tired eyes studying Ena with quiet curiosity.

"I didn't get it, why you were so insistent on driving me to my first day of school. I thought it was kind of weird." Ena let out a shaky breath, half a laugh. "But I'm so glad you did. What you told me in the car. It made all the difference. I don't think I would've had the guts to sit with Skyler at lunch. And Piney? She would've just scared me off."

Ena smiled through her tears.

"They're the best friends I could ask for," Ena continued. "And you helped me find them."

Fiona lightly chuckled. "You, my dear, are extraordinary. And you will do extraordinary things. If I could give you a gift, it would be the confidence I have in you. I don't want you to live a life defined by the false boundaries we place on ourselves."

Ena wiped her tears and nodded. "Fi, I want to live up to that. I don't know how yet, but I'll try. When I have a choice to make, I'll think—what would Fiona do? And I won't go for the wide-open door first. I'll look for the obscure window I can wriggle through instead." Ena's small, sly half-smile emerged, her right dimple appearing.

Fiona's eyes softened. "You *were* listening." Her voice was barely more than a whisper now. "I love you, baby girl. Can you send in your mother?"

Ena leaned in and kissed Fiona's cheek. "I love you more."

She gently laid Fiona's hand back on her stomach, took a deep breath, and stood.

Outside, her mother and grandfather sat silently in the hallway, hands clasped together. Tara's head rested on Graeme's shoulder, and Graeme's head leaned against hers.

Down the hall, Ena spotted her father and brother approaching.

Ena gently placed a hand on her mother's shoulder. "Mom, Fi wants to talk to you."

Ena closed the distance between her and her father in an instant, throwing her arms around him and holding on as tightly as she could. The moment his steady presence grounded her, the dam inside her broke. She sobbed uncontrollably into his chest, the magnitude of everything crashing down at once.

Her father said nothing, he simply held her, his arms strong and steady, his hand gently stroking her hair. He didn't try to hush her or offer empty reassurances. He just let her be.

For a few precious moments, she let herself sink into the safe harbor of his embrace. But then, the thought crept in, *he needs space too.* There were others who needed him, pain that he also had to bear.

Reluctantly, Ena loosened her grip, although part of her wished she didn't have to let go.

Everything was happening both too quickly and unbearably slowly. Jason had been on the phone for what seemed like hours: relaying updates to Ena's uncles, coordinating their travel to Portland, trying to piece together the logistics for such a difficult situation.

Fiona had been clear; she wanted time with each person individually. Byron went in after Tara, his usual energy dimmed by the significance of the moment. When he emerged, he was quiet, his face pale, his usual bounce gone. Jason's time with Fiona lasted longer. When he finally stepped out, he said nothing. The depth of those conversations lingered in the air, heavy and unspoken, as if each exchange was meant to remain sacred.

No one quite knew what to do. Tara returned to Fiona's room to check on her. Jason, unable to sit still, kept offering to run to the cafeteria for food, even though no one had an appetite. His restlessness was palpable, as if he needed an outlet, some excuse to move, to *do* anything.

After Tara left Fiona's room, the doctor arrived for a check-in. He asked for a moment alone with Fiona. The door closed, and time stretched unbearably. Ena watched, nerves thrumming, as the minutes ticked by. Tara wrapped her arms around Jason and stared at the door to Fiona's room as the doctor continued his check-in.

When the doctor finally emerged, he sought out Tara and Graeme, his expression carefully measured. He was a shorter, stout man with metal-rimmed glasses and kind, steady brown eyes, the sort of eyes that softened even the hardest news. His voice dropped to a hushed tone. Her mother and grandfather reacted almost in unison, their right hands rising to cover their mouths as they absorbed the meaning of the doctor's words.

Ena couldn't make much of what he said. She strained to listen, only catching "…make her as comfortable as possible."

Graeme and Tara returned to the family gathered outside Fiona's room. Tara met Jason's eyes and said, "It's getting late. Why don't you take the kids home and get dinner ready? Dad and I will stay a while longer. We'll call if anything changes."

Ena wanted to protest, to insist on staying, but the quiet resolve in her mother's voice and the subtle shake of her father's head told her this wasn't a discussion. This was how it had to be.

The drive home was silent, except for the occasional tap and swipe of Byron's fingers on his iPad. Ena clenched her jaw, irritation bubbling up as he played *Fruit Ninja.*

How can he be slicing fruits right now?

THE PARTING GLASS

Back home, Jason moved straight to the kitchen, pulling out ingredients for a simple pasta dinner. After dinner, Ena, feeling untethered, drifted to her room. She lay on her bed, staring at the ceiling, her thoughts swirling. *Fiona was healthy and vibrant this morning. How can everything change so fast? Are we really going to lose her?*

She had never been this close to a serious illness before. She understood it in an abstract way, like a fact you read in a book. But she had never expected it to feel like this—a storm of conflicting, confusing, and unexpected emotions.

Waking from a difficult night, Ena opened her eyes and immediately regretted it. The ache in her chest, the knot in her stomach, *Yep, still there*. Yesterday hadn't been a dream. It had been worse.

When she walked into the kitchen, the note on the island confirmed it all:

> *Kids, off to the airport to pick up Uncle Mike. Back around 7:30. Your mom's already at the hospital. I'll grab some Annie's Donuts on the way home.*
> *—Dad*

Ena lingered over the note, unsure what to do with herself. She went upstairs and peeked into Byron's room. He was still curled up, clutching his extra pillow like the teddy bears he swore he had outgrown.

Not knowing what else to do, Ena wandered back into the kitchen and started making coffee, mimicking the routine she had watched her parents go through so many times. She wasn't planning on drinking any of it—well, maybe just a sip—she figured her dad and Uncle Mike might appreciate it. The familiar steps of measuring grounds and pouring water gave her hands purpose. It felt normal, a physical action in a morning where everything was completely wrong.

A few minutes later, the front door opened. Her dad walked in first, carrying a large, plain white box from Annie's Donuts. Right behind him was Uncle Mike, pushing his rolling suitcase inside.

If Fiona had a presence that filled the room, Uncle Mike had inherited it in both size and spirit. He was taller and broader than Jason, his deep, booming voice carrying an effortless warmth. Mike had started going bald relatively young, but he had embraced it fully, the top of his head now completely smooth and shiny. His sharp blue eyes sparkled behind wire-rimmed glasses, always brimming with mischief and kindness.

"Ena! You're growing up so fast. Come over here and give your *favorite* uncle a hug. I won't tell Uncle Brandon," he added with a chuckle.

The warm smile and his attempt at lightheartedness were both comforting and heartbreaking. Ena managed a small smile as she stepped into his embrace, breathing in the familiar fresh scent of his eucalyptus soap, the same one he'd been using for years.

"I made coffee, thought you two might want some with the donuts."

Mike poured himself a mug and one for Jason.

Jason set the donut box down on the counter and ran a hand through his hair with a sigh before taking the mug from Mike. "Alright, Brandon lands at 9:15. I'll head to the airport in about an hour to grab him. Mike, you staying here with the kids, or do you want to come with me?"

Mike took a sip of his coffee, nodding approvingly at Ena before answering. "I'll tag along. Gives Brandon and me a chance to talk on the way back."

His voice was light, but Ena recognized that tone, the kind adults used when they had things to discuss that kids weren't meant to overhear. What he really meant was that he and Brandon needed to have a serious conversation before they got to the hospital.

Jason gave a small nod of understanding. "Sounds good. We'll swing by the hospital right after. Tara said she'd call if anything changes, but for now, Fiona's still holding steady."

Ena stayed quiet, watching the back-and-forth. It was strange, how life kept moving even when everything screamed that it should stop. Her dad was making plans, her uncle was drinking coffee like it was any other morning, and yet, in the back of her mind, all she could think about was Fiona in that hospital bed.

"Do we have to wait for Uncle Brandon?" she asked, her voice small. "Can't you drop me off at the hospital now?"

Jason hesitated, his expression softening as he looked at her. "I know you want to be there, Ena. But there's going to be a lot of coming and going today. Let's eat something first, and then we'll head over after we pick up Brandon. That way, we're all together."

Ena bit her lip but nodded. It wasn't the answer she wanted, but she didn't argue. Instead, she reached for a donut, although her stomach was too tight for food. She hesitated for a moment, then took a bite of a peanut butter chocolate butterfly. The rich, sugary sweetness melted on her tongue, offering an odd but fleeting sense of comfort.

Ena spent the next couple of hours in her room, listening to the Spotify playlist she and Fiona had created earlier that year. Each song carried a memory, a conversation, a shared laugh. When "Someone Great" by LCD Soundsystem came on, Ena froze. The lyrics landed differently now, their once-catchy cadence turning sharp and raw. A song they used to sing along to without really paying attention was suddenly devastating, every beat echoing the ache of what she might be about to lose. It made her feel closer to Fiona, grounding her in the familiar as she waited anxiously for her dad to return with Uncle Brandon.

When she finally heard the front door open, she bolted down the stairs, eager to leave for the hospital as soon as possible.

Uncle Brandon stood just inside, looking a little travel-worn but familiar all the same. In so many ways, he was the opposite of Uncle Mike. Where Mike was broad and commanding, Brandon was lean and understated. His brown hair, streaked with gray, was a perpetual mess, as if he had run his fingers through it one too many times. He was quiet, often saying something awkward, but his kindness was the same as his brother's, his soft brown eyes holding the same warmth.

"Hey, Ena," Brandon said with a hesitant smile. "Oh boy, you're getting big, I mean, growing up."

Ena gave a small smile. She hadn't seen him since a family gathering two years ago, and even now, he still had that awkward-but-genuine way about him.

Jason clapped a hand on Brandon's shoulder. "You want some coffee or anything?"

Brandon shook his head. "I'm sure I'm keeping everyone from seeing Mom. Let's just get to the hospital."

That was exactly the response Ena had been hoping for.

Jason nodded and turned to her. "Can you grab your brother and tell him to get ready?"

Byron had been in the backyard for the past hour, burning off some of his endless energy on the trampoline. Ena stepped outside and yelled, "Byron! Time to go! Get inside and get ready."

Byron came running in, flushed from exertion, and came to screeching halt when he spotted Uncle Mike and Uncle Brandon standing near the doorway. "Hey, Uncle Mike! Hey, Uncle Brandon!" he said cheerfully as he tugged on his jacket.

Jason took one look at him and sighed. "You're a mess. Go change. You have five minutes."

Byron groaned but dashed upstairs, emerging moments later in a chaotic mix of mismatched clothes. Jason rolled his eyes. "Good enough. In the car, everyone."

They all piled into the family's dark blue minivan, its interior still clean but lived-in, loose receipts tucked into the cup holders, and a faint scent of Tara's peppermint breath mints lingering in the air. With a low hum of the engine, they set off for the hospital.

When they arrived, they made their way to Fiona's room. The moment her sons walked in, her weak eyes brightened.

"Mikey and Brandon, you made it!" she said, her voice hoarse but full of warmth.

Mike and Brandon went straight to her bedside, taking her hands, their voices a blend of relief and quiet concern as they caught up with Fiona and Graeme.

Jason placed the remaining donuts on a small table in the corner, and Tara immediately grabbed one before giving Jason a knowing look.

"Come on," she said, nudging him toward the door. "Let's take the kids for a walk."

Jason gave a small nod, and they ushered Ena and Byron out of the room.

"I could use a little air," Tara admitted as they stepped into the stairwell at the end of the hallway. They descended the four floors to the main level, weaving through the corridors in a slow, looping walk through the hospital.

For thirty minutes, they wandered, stretching their legs, giving Fiona, Graeme, and her sons space, and letting the reality of the day settle in. Ena stayed quiet, lost in thought. Ena had had an unwavering faith in Fiona's strength, an unwavering faith in doctors to fix things. Now, it was like someone had yanked that rug out from under her and she was uncertain where to place any faith. If only she could go back in time—to that moment in the car, convince Fiona to quit smoking—maybe things would be different. Maybe Fiona would still be safe at home.

When they returned to Fiona's room, she greeted them with a weak but signature mischievous smile. "You know, a family that sings together stays together. How about indulging an old woman with a song? Let's do 'Love Cats' by The Cure."

Ena's heart swelled at the request. She reached for her phone, pulled up her karaoke app, and found the track. She checked around the room, nodded at everyone, then hit play.

As the bouncy, unmistakable beat filled the room, Uncle Mike immediately started slapping a steady rhythm against his broad chest, effortlessly syncing with the bassline. The energy shifted. Lighter, as if the music itself had cracked open a window to the past.

Brandon's eyes drifted shut, his head swaying gently in time, fully lost in the groove. Tara, always so composed, let her all-business exterior soften as she allowed the music to wash over her.

Jason, lacking the Quinn family's natural musical instincts, hung back with an amused smile. He quietly mumbled the lyrics under his breath, his foot bouncing instinctively to the beat, unable to not be caught up in that moment.

As they sang, the tension that had been hanging thick in the air seemed to dissolve. Smiles emerged while they sang, and for a few moments, they were all present in this moment, like this was just another family gathering.

As the last notes faded, Mike clapped his hands together. "Ena, can you pull up 'Swell Time' by The Fin Whales on that thing?"

Ena grinned and cued up the song. "One, two, three…" She held up four fingers, then pressed play.

Mike pointed to Tara, and she picked up the lyrics:

"*Boardwalk Dreams, seagull screams…*"

After a few lines, the whole room joined in, their voices blending together, rising and falling with the melody. Throughout the song, Mike kept pointing at different family members, handing them verses and lines. When he pointed at Ena, she grinned and ad-libbed, "*Fiona made her own rules…*" instead of the original "*But we made our own rules.*"

Mike's face broke into a wide smile; that was exactly what he had been hoping for.

As the song came to a close, Fiona let out a small clap, her eyes twinkling with gratitude. "My family, so much joy you've given me, now and through the years. That was special. Wonderful. Beautiful."

She squeezed Graeme's hand. "Thank you for indulging me."

Then, with a playful smile, she continued, "And now, if you'll indulge me one more time—everyone out. I want to spend some time with the love of my life without you all gawking about."

A few chuckles rippled through the room as she tugged Graeme's hand closer.

Mike let out a mock gasp. "You mean we're *not* your greatest loves?"

Fiona shot him a playful look. "Not even close, kid."

With that, the family smiled, exchanged glances, and quietly filed out, leaving Fiona and Graeme in the quiet, intimate space they deserved. As they filed out, Mike gave Ena a fist bump to acknowledge Ena's perfectly executed ad lib.

Later that night, Ena bolted upright from a deep sleep, her heart pounding, a sudden, inexplicable wave of dread washed over her. No one could say for certain, but later, Ena swore it was exactly when Fiona had her second and fatal heart attack. For Ena, that moment was more than a coincidence. It was Fiona's final goodbye.

JUST BEFORE

The evening after Fiona passed, Ena lay in bed, numb with disbelief.

She was just here.
She can't really be gone…can she?

She had been listening to the Fin Whales' only album, *Lost to Time*, when their grief-filled ballad, "Just Before," came on.

The words crushed her.

As the final chorus played, Ena imagined that Fiona was reaching through the music, speaking to her directly:

> *Just before*
> *You left me behind*
> *Your touch said I'd be fine*
> *Just before*
> *Our final embrace*
> *Your smile, a final grace*
> *Your words erased the score*

Eva Kinsella's wavering voice, the delicate fingerpicked melody, it killed. But sweetly. Painfully honest. So true to everything Ena was feeling.

Tears streamed down her face. She didn't sob. She didn't wail. She just let go.

She replayed the song again.

I wasn't ready to take it in
Your fading smile, paper-thin

Truth in those words unfolded, quiet and undeniable. She wasn't ready, she would never have been ready. Fiona was a force of nature, like the wind. *How can she be gone?*

Her mind drifted to the little things that would never happen again. No unexpected texts. No surprise pickups from school. No whispered truths in crowded rooms.

Fiona had that gift. The way she spoke truth with a certainty that made Ena *want* to hear it. Her belief in Ena had never wavered. She didn't push. She didn't decide. She simply held the lantern, steady and sure, lighting the next few steps so Ena could walk them herself.

Fiona had seen her truly. Not the version she hoped for. Not only who Ena was. But who she could become.

Fiona was so unapologetically Fiona. She loved deeply, she fought vigorously, she laughed easily. She carved a path that Ena could only hope to come close to walking.

And now she was gone.

But that song. That voice. Those lyrics. Fiona had been part of The Fin Whales' story of making it big, and now the band was returning the favor.

Fiona, using *their* words as one last message. A final gift.

Ena would recover. The pain was real, and for now, *that* was enough.

In her mind's eye, she could see it: Fiona, still holding the lantern. Lighting the way forward through the grief. No pressure. No expectations. Just presence.

WISH YOU WERE HERE

The days and weeks after Fiona passed were a whirlwind of emotions: grief, outbursts, and the constant coming and going of family and friends. Fiona had requested, though in the world of Fiona, *insisted,* on a natural burial, so the burial had to happen quickly. In the days after Fiona passed, Mike and Brandon's family arrived. They all were staying in Graeme and Fiona's large, but not quite large enough, house.

Graeme, quietly overwhelmed by loss, leaned on Jason to help navigate the logistics. Jason, ever the steadying force, handled the details with quiet efficiency, ensuring everything unfolded as seamlessly as possible.

The natural burial was an intimate family affair, set in a serene meadow surrounded by Oregon's ever-present evergreens, their towering forms obscuring the horizon. The soft rustling of the wind through the trees was the only sound as the family gathered, their shared grief woven into the stillness of the moment.

Before anyone spoke, Ena scanned the faces around her and realized just how much of Fiona lived on in her children; in their own ways, they each carried a piece of her spirit. Fiona had never wanted anyone to be constrained by the expectations of others, and now, in this moment, Ena could see how deeply that belief had shaped her family.

Her gaze landed on Mike and his husband, Geoffrey. Geoffrey was average height and build, with dark hair, dark eyes, and a neatly trimmed beard, where flecks of gray had begun to show at the corners of his chin. He and Mike were a perfect match. Geoffrey was always generous in giving Mike the spotlight he thrived in yet never losing his own presence. Between them stood their five-year-old daughter, Vivian, clutching their hands tightly.

Nearby, Brandon and his wife, Nia, stood together, their fingers laced in silent support. Nia was strikingly beautiful, tall and graceful. She carried herself with quiet strength, unashamed in her grief, tears spilling freely down her cheeks. Their three sons—Zane, Marcus, and Ellis, ranging in age from fourteen to nineteen—stood beside her in a line, tallest to shortest, their expressions solemn and stoic.

Ena shifted her gaze to her right, where her mother stood. For perhaps the first time, it truly dawned on Ena that Tara, in her own way, had honored Fiona's spirit all along. A leader in AI research, an entrepreneur who had forged her own path. Her mother had never conformed to the comfortable or expected. She, too, had refused to be bound by anyone else's rules.

Fiona's legacy wasn't just in the music she loved, the words she spoke, or the fire she carried; it was in all of them, in the way they lived, the choices they made, the quiet defiance they each held in their own way. Ena had never been more grateful for this wild and perfectly imperfect family.

A few days after the burial, the family gathered for a celebration of life in Fiona's honor. They drove a little way out of town to a friend's vineyard, where a big barn stood open and welcoming. It was exactly the kind of gathering Fiona would have wanted, free of pomp and formality, filled instead with music, laughter, and the kind of people she had collected in her orbit over the years.

Ena was both astounded and unsurprised by the sheer number of people who came. But more than that, she was struck by the diversity of the crowd. Young and old, button-down shirts and leather jackets. Faces tattooed and pierced. Mohawks, ponytails, and everything in between. People of all colors, from all walks of life, even a few famous musicians. All there for the same reason: to celebrate someone who had left a mark on them. In that crowd of strangers, Ena felt steadier knowing Piney and Skyler were there. Her people, in the middle of Fiona's people.

After some time, Graeme stepped up to the microphone. His voice was steady, although his eyes glistened. "Thank you all for coming. Words won't do justice to what it means to see each and every one of you here. Fiona would hate it if we let this become somber, so let's have fun and enjoy each other the best we can. If you feel like it, the mic is open. Anyone is welcome to come up and share a story, a thought, or whatever compels you."

At first, only a few people trickled up to speak, sharing brief anecdotes, funny memories, and heartfelt words. Ena sat between her parents, words and feelings swirled through her, a need to share building until she thought she might burst. She looked at her mom, then at her dad.

Jason caught the look, saw the unspoken question, and nodded. "She'd love to hear it," he said softly.

Ena took a deep breath and walked up to the mic. She scanned the crowd, a sea of faces, some familiar, most strangers, all here because of Fiona. She swallowed and cleared her throat. Ena almost believed the thumping of her heart was being amplified through the mic. She had never spoken to such a large crowd.

Her first words came out weaker than she wanted. "Fiona was my guide. When I needed someone to hold the lantern, to light up the next few steps. She was there."

She paused, inhaling deeply. In that moment, she swore she could feel Fiona beside her. Grounding her. Strengthening her. She straightened her posture, and when she spoke again, her voice was clear, steady, strong.

"And looking around this room, I know I'm not alone in that. A lot of you, probably all of you, felt her light. She made things better, clearer."

Her gaze drifted across the crowd, finding her uncles, her grandfather, her mother.

"I didn't really know Fiona very well until we moved here last August. But in such a short time, she changed how I see things. She changed what's possible."

She let the words settle, letting herself feel them.

"I'm gonna miss her so much. But I know she's still with me. Her voice in my ear, her light in the dark, that steady hand when I need it most. She'll always walk beside me."

She paused, steadying herself. Then, one last time, she let Fiona's name rest on her tongue, honoring her.

"Thank you, Fi. I was lucky to call you my grandmother."

A hush settled over the crowd as she stepped away from the microphone. Then, warm applause. Not just polite, but heartfelt. She made her way over to Skyler and Piney.

Skyler blinked back a tear. "You really do have Fiona's spirit in you. That was beautiful."

Piney gave her a crooked smile. "Yeah, E. I was like...one line away from crying. Almost."

The remembrances continued. Mike, Brandon, and Tara sang one of Fiona's favorite songs, "This Town Ain't Big Enough for Both of Us," from their childhood family music nights. Others shared tributes in the form of songs, poems, and words. Each one a testament to Fiona's impact.

She was loved. And she would be missed.

In the days that followed, family and friends gradually drifted back to their daily lives.

Tara frequently went over to check in on Graeme, and Ena invited herself most of the time. The distance that had been forming between Ena and her mother over the months before Fiona's passing had started to shrink. Tara saw the way Ena had matured through this experience, and in turn, she began treating her less like a child and more like the young adult she was becoming.

Ena cherished these quiet moments, sitting with her mother and grandfather in the breakfast nook of Graeme's house, sipping tea, reminiscing about Fiona. For the first time, she truly felt invited to the table, not as a child but as an equal. Her thoughts, her memories, her contributions weren't dismissed as frivolous or naive. She belonged. She loved the way their conversations wove between laughter and tears. One moment, sharing a story so absurd they couldn't help but laugh so hard, sometimes a bit harder than warranted; the next, sitting in reflective silence, tears sliding down their cheeks, reflecting on one of so many stories demonstrating Fiona's generous and loving spirit.

One afternoon, when Tara and Ena arrived at Graeme's house, they found him sitting at the piano, his fingers trailing over the keys as he played "I Will Follow You Into the Dark" by Death Cab for Cutie. The soft, melancholy notes filled the quiet space, wrapping around them like a living memory.

As the last chord faded, Graeme exhaled slowly and looked up, first at Tara, then at Ena. His gaze drifted across the living room as if seeing the shadows of his life with Fiona. He shook his head. "This house. It's just too big. Too quiet. Too empty without her."

He rubbed a hand over his face.

"It feels silly to hold onto it. It feels wrong to let it go. Every part of this house has Fi's fingerprints on it." His voice was thick with emotion.

Without hesitation, Tara walked over to the piano bench and wrapped an arm around his shoulders, pressing a gentle kiss to the top of his head. "You don't have to do anything right now, Dad. But if it would help, maybe Ena and I could start going through some things together. Just a little at a time. Maybe the closets? Or the attic?"

Graeme sat still for a moment, his hands resting on the keys, before giving a slow nod. "Yeah. Yeah, maybe something small like the attic is a good place to start."

WALKMAN

Ena was thrilled. She had never been in the attic before. It wasn't forbidden exactly, but it always seemed like it carried an invisible "Do Not Enter" sign.

She and her mom climbed to the top floor of the house, where Tara reached for a cord dangling from the ceiling. With a firm tug, the attic door creaked open, revealing a fold-out wooden ladder. A musty breath of air drifted down.

Ena followed Tara up, her heart pounding with anticipation.

The attic was huge. She had always imagined a cramped, dusty space, but instead, it stretched the entire length of the house, tall enough to stand in. Wooden beams reached up from each side, meeting at the roofline.

Graeme's scientific mind was on full display. Every few feet, support beams framed neat rows of storage. Unlike the chaotic, cobweb-filled attic Ena had envisioned, this one was meticulously organized, each section carefully labeled by family member, with Fiona and Graeme's belongings further sorted by category.

Still, there was so much stuff. Ena had no idea how she and her mom could tackle it all.

"Mom, it doesn't smell old and dusty like I thought it would."

"That's dad," Tara said with a twinkle in her eye. "He rigged up a homemade contraption to keep the air moving and the attic cool all year. Said if we were going to store a bunch of stuff up here, it shouldn't just rot away."

A narrow path cut through the center, flanked by decades of family keepsakes stacked in orderly rows with three bare lightbulbs dangling from the roofline. Tara let out a chuckle, shaking her head.

" 'Start small,' he said. 'Just the attic,' he said. Yeah, right." She sighed, rolling up her sleeves. "Alright, let's get to work."

Tara pulled out the first box from her section, her childhood, packed away in cardboard. Ena crouched beside her, fascinated.

One by one, Tara unearthed forgotten relics from her school years, elementary drawings, high school notebooks, old clothes. Some made her laugh, others made her shake her head, "I'm astonished that Mom kept these for all these years."

She paused on a picture for a moment.

"Okay," she said, brushing dust off her hands. "Four piles: toss, donate, keep, and things Granddad might want. He gets the final say, but we can start sorting."

She reached into another box and pulled out a tangled mess of old electronics.

"Ena, can you run downstairs and ask Granddad for some batteries? All the common kinds. Oh, and see if he has any Febreze. I hate the smell of musty old things."

Ena darted off and was back in minutes, carrying a bowl full of batteries, AA, AAA, C, D, and even a few obscure sizes, and a bottle of Febreze. But when she returned, it wasn't the piles of things her mother had sorted that caught her attention.

Her mother had pulled out a denim jacket, old, faded from black to gray, its elbows worn soft, almost white from years of wear. It wasn't threadbare, but it had clearly had a history without words to tell it.

"Oh, cool!" Ena grabbed the jacket, gave it a quick spritz of Febreze, and shrugged it on, pushing her arms through the sleeves. It felt broken in, perfectly soft. She grinned wide.

Tara rolled her eyes, but a small smile tugged at her lips. "That was from when I was just getting into my goth phase. It used to be black, but after years of daily wear and frequent washing. It started to fade. I totally forgot about it."

"What do you think?" Ena asked, her shoulders confidently slouched. "It works with my T-shirt, don't ya think?" Ena was wearing a retro Replacements T-shirt, the bandmates sprawled on a rooftop, big hair catching the light in a washed-out blue print.

Tara paused, tilting her head. "If I squint, I swear I could be looking at a kid from the '80s."

As they continued sorting through Tara's past, the attic became more cramped, forcing Ena to do more of the excavating. She pulled out what looked like a two-sided gray briefcase.

Curious, she flipped the latches and opened one side. To her delight, it was packed with cassette tapes. Row after row of albums filled the case, their spines flashing familiar and unfamiliar band names. She skimmed through them, her fingers brushing over plastic covers and faded stickers. She flipped it over and scanned the other side, nearly one hundred tapes in total. Some she recognized. Many she didn't. She snapped the case shut and promptly carried it to the "Keep" pile.

Tara, watching, let out an exasperated sigh. "What are we going to do with those? No one even has a tape player anymore."

Ena's eyes gleamed mischievously as they landed on a treasure in the yet-to-be-explored part of Tara's old things, a big boom box, complete with a microphone. Two tape decks between two speakers, the long black rectangle seemed to have more buttons and knobs than necessary. "I have some ideas."

Tara followed her gaze, and the second she spotted the boom box, her face softened with nostalgia. "Oh my gosh. I spent *so much* time singing into that microphone growing up. No matter how mad I was—at Fiona, at school, at life—recording myself always made me feel better."

Tara had not spoken much about growing up. Her words reminded Ena that her mother had truly been a kid once. A kid who could get mad at Fiona. Ena grinned at the thought of a young version of her mother. "Can we see if it still works?"

Tara chuckled. "We can try, but tapes could degrade and become unplayable over time."

"How about this?" Ena pulled an unopened the Fin Whales cassette from the carrying case. "It's never even been opened."

Tara tilted her head. "I forgot about that. For some reason, Mom gave that to me 'just in case' I wore out the other one. I always thought that was weird since I didn't play my other copy that much."

"Fi knew how awesome they were, maybe she thought you listened to them more."

Tara shrugged and flipped the boom box over. "Do we have four D batteries over there?"

Ena rummaged through the bowl of batteries and handed her mom a handful of the oversized batteries. Tara snapped them into place and flipped the boom box upright. Ena unwrapped the cellophane from The Fin Whales' cassette.

Ena hesitated. "Not exactly sure what to do with this."

Tara half-grinned, took the tape, and slid it in like second nature. She pressed play. For a moment, silence. Then a fuzzy crackle. And suddenly, music burst through the speakers along with the undertone of the whir of the gears moving the tape through the machine. It still worked. After all these years.

Ena's half-smiled, giving her mom the look that always meant *I told you so*, without her ever needing to say the words. She continued rummaging through the unsorted cassettes, pulling out an old cardboard box labeled "Blank Cassettes."

Her expression turned mischievous as she held it up.

"Um, Mom, look what I found. Wanna record something on your old boom box for old time's sake?"

Tara hesitated, glancing at the cluttered attic, the past spread out around them in piles of memories. "Okay. But we have to sing the 'Quinn-Baker Family Anthem.'"

Ena felt her cheeks turn bright red. She had written a silly song when she was eight. She had outgrown it and was embarrassed by its simplicity, but she said, "Okay."

Ena watched Tara work the old boom box. It was a true relic. Tara had to push both the record and play buttons to start the recording. She was amused at how mechanical it was to record a song.

They sang the lyrics together, Ena singing high and Tara singing an octave lower:

> *We are the Quinn-Bakers*
> *We are singers and makers*
> *We are a family of fun*
> *Quick to a pun*
> *Rest assured we aren't fakers!*
>
> *The youngest is Byron*
> *He's as loud as a siren*
> *A bundle of energy*

Bouncing off walls
Crazy as a brother can be!

Then there's Ena. Hey, that's me!
I sing so beautifully!
Sometimes I'm wild
A little bit sly
Trouble just comes naturally!

Jason is the dad
With jokes that are bad
He might be a jock
But he still loves a rock
And his dancing is kinda sad!

My mom is Tara
She's tough as a bear-a
She builds and she schemes
Chasing big dreams
Her brain's beyond compare-a!

We are the Quinn-Bakers
We are singers and makers
We dance, we play, we rock all day
We are the dream-chasers!

We are the Quinn-Bakers,
We sing and we play
Now Dad has a joke
Oh no, run away!

Ena did her best imitation of her dad's deep voice.

Why don't skeletons sing?
They don't have the guts.

After watching Tara handle the boombox like an old pro, Ena quickly rewound the tape, pushed eject, and popped the freshly recorded tape into the chest pocket of the denim jacket she was still wearing—making sure her mom could not get her hands on it and ensuring no one ever would hear it.

"OK, Ena, we really need to focus."

Ena surveyed the four piles of stuff they had made and what was still left in just Tara's section. It was a huge job. The "Toss" pile was by far the largest. It was full of broken toys, no longer working electronics, and clothing that was not even worth donating. The "Donate" pile was the second largest and piled high with clothing that someone might want for an authentic vintage look. A handful of awards, recognitions, and mementos sat in the "Granddad Decides" pile. In the "Keep" pile stood just the boombox and cassette carrying case, in essence, Ena's pile.

Ena continued to dig through Tara's old stuff. As she was pulling out a yellow Walkman from under a pile of clothes, the headset cord got wrapped around some science stuff in Graeme's adjacent discarded experiment section. With a final tug, the Walkman came out, pulling a glass beaker with it. Ena was quick to act and was able to keep the beaker from falling and breaking, but the topper popped off and splashed a clear liquid on the Walkman still in Ena's hand.

"Ehm, Mom? Nothing bad happened, but I spilled something on this Walkman, the situation is fully contained, but I am going to run downstairs and dry it off, OK?"

"Sure, honey."

Ena grabbed a couple of double AA batteries and The Fin Whales cassette and carefully descended the fold-out ladder. She went to the guest bedroom's bathroom to dry off the Walkman. Strangely, it was already fully dry. She popped the batteries in, then the cassette tape, and pressed play.

As the song, "Fight, No Flight," started to play, a dot appeared in front of her face. It was blacker than anything she had ever seen. The matte black trucks she would occasionally see in parking lots looked like shining stars compared to this blackness. The complete absence of light in this dot was no bigger than a dime.

Ena wondered if it was a weird eye floater.

She reached out her finger toward the dot and—

PASTIME PARADISE

Ena's world squeezed and stretched all at once, like time and gravity had turned inside out. The song kept playing in her ears. Suddenly, she was in a recording studio, and The Fin Whales were on the other side of the glass, singing the very song that had just been playing through the now-silent Walkman.

Ena had never been so disoriented. *Did I faint? Fall asleep?* It seemed too real to be a dream. But it had to be. The Fin Whales had all died in that tragic bus crash so long ago.

The song finished up. The sound engineer spoke into the mic. "Great take. Let's take a 15-minute lunch break, and then we can get to work on 'Midnight Current.'"

Ena quickly slid on her belly and hid under the orange pleather sofa in the back of the studio. Lead singer Eva Kinsella walked into the sound room and discussed some of the logistics with the sound engineer. Ena stared at her. Eva Kinsella. *THE* Eva Kinsella. She couldn't believe it, so young, so undeniably alive. Ena did not want this dream to end.

After a few minutes, everyone had cleared out of the sound room, their voices fading down the hall. Ena waited, listening. Then, cautiously, she slid out from beneath the couch, her heart hammering. Curiosity got the better of her.

This had to be a dream, so nothing bad could really happen.

She ran her hands lightly over the mixing board, feeling the cool metal and plastic, the rows of dials and switches beneath her fingertips. She didn't press buttons or slide any levers, but just being this close to it, touching things that had recorded real music, was strangely thrilling. *This dream is so weird. I never remember feeling things in dreams.*

Her gaze drifted to the scattered papers on the desk: set lists, handwritten notes, track sheets. Nothing particularly interesting, at least, not compared to the fact that she was here, in a moment that shouldn't exist. Then, a sparkle caught her eye. To her right, on the table where Eva had been standing, lay a small, shimmering triangle. Ena reached for it, turning it over in her palm. It was a guitar pick, well-worn and smooth from years of use. Made of celluloid, its marbleized, pearlescent finish caught the light just right, swirling with deep blues and purples. She held it closer. In the center, a faded logo, barely legible.

She rolled it between her fingers, tracing the softened edges, wondering how many songs had been played with it, how many hands had held it before hers.

Her breath hitched. Footsteps in the hallway. They were coming back. Ena's stomach lurched as she scrambled back under the couch, pressing herself into the shadows. The door creaked open. The sound engineer strode back in, resuming his spot behind the mixing board as if he'd never left.

It wasn't until she shifted that Ena felt the pick still in her hand. She clenched her jaw. Too late to put it back. Panic flashed through her. She hadn't meant to take it. With as little movement as possible, she slipped it into her back pocket.

Eva's voice rang out, sharp and rising, "Okay, this isn't funny. Who took it?"

The sound engineer turned. "What are you looking for?"

"My lucky pick," Eva snapped. "I put it *right here.*"

A wave of guilt hit Ena hard. But what could she possibly do? She didn't even know where she was or even if this was real, or just some vivid, impossible dream. Frozen, breath shallow, Ena stayed hidden.

Eva kept looking, checking the floor, the table, her pockets. Ena silently begged Eva not to turn around and see her under the couch.

"Time is money, Eva," the sound engineer said, "and it ain't cheap around here. Let's go."

A wave of exhaustion slammed into her. Ena's vision blurred at the edges, her limbs suddenly heavy, as if the pick had drained the energy from her fingertips. She fought to keep her eyes open, to stay alert, but before she could even process what was happening, her body went slack. She didn't just fall asleep. She plunged into unconsciousness.

Deep.

Silent.

Dreamless.

LOST IN THE SUPERMARKET

When Ena awoke, she was engulfed in darkness and silence. The recording room around her was eerily still, the air thick with the scent of stale cigarettes and old equipment. For a brief moment, she wondered if she was still dreaming. But everything was off-kilter in a way that sent panic clawing up her throat.

Everything was so vivid, so bizarre, but it had to be impossible. The Fin Whales died not too long after the release of their album. It was impossible that she time-traveled, but she somehow was here. Uncertain. Afraid. Lost. Hoping there was some way to wake herself up. To learn that this was only a dream.

For the first time in her life, she was completely alone. No parents. No Fiona. No friends to call for help. If she had Skyler and Piney, they could hatch a plan. But now, Ena had to figure out what to do.

She instinctively reached for her phone, only to realize she had left it on a box back in the attic. Not that it would have been useful. Even if she had it, there was no Wi-Fi, no cell service, just a useless piece of plastic and glass in an era where it didn't belong.

Swallowing hard, Ena slid out from under the couch, brushing dust from her jacket. She crept toward the door, slipping into the dimly lit hallway. Her heart pounded as she hurried down the corridor, past the empty reception desk, and out onto the street.

She came to an abrupt stop.

The street was both vaguely familiar and completely alien.

The recording studio was on Southwest Stark Avenue; she knew exactly where she was in Portland, but everything else was wrong.

The first thing that struck her was the cars. They were boxy, full of unnecessary sharp angles, gleaming with chrome, their colors far bolder than anything in 2019. Wood-paneled station wagons rolled past, their enormous chrome bumpers practically flashing in the sunlight. A blue Volvo with squared-off headlights. A brown and gold Oldsmobile creeping down the street. Unlike the muted grayscale of modern cars, these were red, gold, light blue, deep forest green.

And yet, despite the color, the city itself was grittier, dirtier, and rougher around the edges, carrying a life unfamiliar to Ena.

The smell of cigarettes hit her next. It was everywhere.

Everywhere.

She passed a phonebooth, where a guy with a green mohawk, a leather jacket covered in metal studs, and a dangling cigarette spoke into the receiver, his voice sharp and animated. The phonebooth itself was plastered with concert flyers, bright neon colors screaming out "THE WIPERS LIVE AT SATYRICON" and "NAPALM BEACH FRIDAY NIGHT!"

Ena kept walking, her sneakers scuffing against the uneven pavement, her senses absorbing the surreal mix of familiar and alien.

Pedestrians brushed past her, completely ignoring her presence. A stark contrast to 2019, where people were more likely to be glued to their phones. Here, no one was looking down at a screen. Instead, businessmen in ill-fitting suits puffed on cigarettes, teenagers loitered on street corners, and an old woman with a shopping cart full of aluminum cans rattled her way past.

And then there were the bumper stickers.

Not only were the cars boxy and hideous, but they were absolutely covered in stickers. A beaten-up Pinto in front of her had a peeling sticker that read: "My Porsche is in the shop."

A light blue Volvo station wagon proclaimed: "Save the Whales." And "Hart for President," its colors fading and corners curling off the bumper.

On the back of a red and white VW Bus was an absolute sticker explosion, so much so that Ena couldn't even see the paint. Unlike the pristine, nostalgia-polished VW Vans Ena occasionally spotted in 2019, this one had lived a tough life. The van's rust-speckled body bore the bruises of time, with stickers not just telling a story but seemingly holding the whole thing together.

"My KARma ran over your DOGma."

"Honk if parts fall off."

"No Nukes!"

There were others so risqué that they made her blush.

She kept moving, following the familiar way toward Burnside Bridge.

Down below, Tom McCall Waterfront Park was different. Cleaner. The grass was lush and untouched, with no worn dirt paths cutting through it. The park wasn't yet the hangout for food carts, cyclists, and runners. The Willamette River ran dark, gritty, grimy. It took on the tone of the rest of the city. A tugboat chugged along, guiding a barge filled with freshly cut logs upriver toward the Columbia.

But Ena wasn't here to admire the scenery. Her mind was spinning with questions she couldn't answer. What had happened? How had she ended up here? How could she get back? She floated, untethered, through a world that wasn't hers.

She wandered east, passing storefronts that looked straight out of a time capsule.

A rental shop advertised, "VHS & BETA MAX MOVIE RENTALS!"

A record store pulsed with Journey's "Girl Can't Help It." Arena-sized riffs spilled from crackling speakers as a kid inside mimed an air guitar solo.

A guy leaned against a gold Trans Am with a massive black bird stenciled across the hood. He wore a pink Izod shirt with the collar flipped up, his blonde hair frozen in a spiky mullet, a cigarette dangling from his fingers. He was a caricature of an '80s movie villain come to life. Ena struggled to keep a straight face.

She was starting to feel the seriousness of it all. To make matters worse, hunger gnawed at her stomach, her throat dry.

A Plaid Pantry convenience store came into view. She hurried inside.

At first glance, it was comfortingly familiar. The layout wasn't so different from the Plaid Pantries in her time. But the inventory and prices told a different story.

The candy aisle threw her for a loop. Snickers and KitKats were still there, but the packaging looked old, off somehow. There were brands she had never seen before: "Bonkers!" (weirdly thick fruit chews), "BarNone" (a peanut-buttery chocolate bar). To her disbelief, Candy Cigarettes sat right next to the gum, their little white sugar sticks pretending to be something more sinister. And she wondered who would eat Garbage Can-dy—literal trash-shaped candy, fish bones, and all—in garbage-can-shaped containers. She grabbed a candy bar and went to grab a SmartWater, except SmartWater didn't exist yet. The only bottled option was Evian. She sighed, grabbed one, and made her way to the counter.

The cashier, a pale, thin woman with jet-black hair styled into an artful mess, rang up her purchase. Ena handed over her twenty-dollar bill. The woman barely glanced at it before laughing. "Kid, I don't know what you're up to, but this is the worst counterfeit I've ever seen."

Ena's stomach dropped. "What?"

The woman pushed the candy and water aside. "Get outta here."

Heat crawled up Ena's neck. Embarrassment. Frustration. Fear. The reality of her situation crashed over her. She was stuck here. Alone. With no money.

Her chin quivered, her eyes welled up. This is going to be really, really hard. Maybe the cashier saw Ena's barely holding it together because she sighed, her voice low and flat. "Look, I don't know what your deal is, but I need to reorganize the cigarettes under the counter. If your stuff *happens* to disappear while I'm down there, that's not my problem."

Ena did a double-take. The woman knelt behind the register. Ena grabbed the water and candy and bolted.

She made her way toward Broadway Avenue; her thoughts tangled in the impossibility of her situation. The hum of Portland at dusk surrounded her: the distant honk of a car, the murmur of people spilling out of a restaurant, the rhythmic click of a walk signal changing. She walked past storefronts, their neon signs flickering to life, until she reached a movie theater, its marquee glowing against the darkening sky.

The blocky, black letters announced the current showings:

Top Gun

Ferris Bueller's Day Off

Now Playing: Aliens

Coming Soon: *Star Trek IV*

Ena slowed, drawn to the colorful posters lining the entrance. A *Top Gun* poster: impossibly young Tom Cruise in a bomber jacket, squinting like the sun was his enemy, Kelly McGillis by his side and an F-14 jet roaring across the top. *Up there with the best of the best*, it read, like the movie was daring her to measure up.

But it was the *Aliens* poster that caught her eye—the cold, shadowed face of Sigourney Weaver, toting a massive gun while cradling a child, her expression caught somewhere between rage and terror. The background was a blur of smoke and steel and danger. Something about it gave her chills, as if even the movies were warning her: This isn't home.

She forced herself to look away. The scent of butter-soaked popcorn drifted from the lobby, but it was no longer comforting. It only made the moment more real. She wasn't in 2019 anymore.

At first, her steps had seemed aimless, but now she realized her subconscious had been guiding her all along. She reached 18th Avenue, and she knew. If she turned left, she'd be heading straight toward her grandparents' house. Lacking any better plan, that's exactly what she did. As she walked, the grit of the city faded behind her, giving way to the leafy streets of the Irvington neighborhood. Yet, even here, it didn't feel entirely like the version she knew. Not all the houses exuded the wealth and care she was used to in 2019. Some were frozen in time, home to aging hippies who had never quite moved on.

Ena passed front yards with BMX bikes carelessly abandoned as if the riders had been beckoned to another adventure. A group of boys played tackle football on the grass, their shouts echoing between the houses. Nearby, a pair of girls whipped long ropes in sync as another girl jumped in perfect rhythm, Double Dutch, her braids bouncing with each hop.

What struck Ena the most, though, was the absence of parents. There were no watchful eyes on porches, no adults hovering nearby. Just kids, completely unsupervised, climbing trees, speeding down sidewalks on bikes without helmets, launching skateboards off rickety ramps made from old boards and stacked bricks. She shook her head. *How did anyone survive childhood like this?*

And yet, despite the recklessness of it all, there was an undeniable freedom about it. No one was worried about being tracked, no one was glued to a screen, no one was being called home via text message. It was just kids being kids, fully immersed in the moment. For the first time since she'd woken up in the recording studio, she felt a glint of hope grow rather than panic that had held tight all day.

DÉJÀ VU

Ena made her way toward her grandparents' house, her heart pounding in her chest. It was familiar, but not.

The large maple tree in the front yard was there, but it wasn't quite as majestic and sprawling as she knew it to be in 2019. The front porch swing still hung at the north end, but instead of the bamboo table and chairs she was used to, there was a set of wrought iron furniture, the kind with intricate curls in the metalwork, softened by cushions in a faded floral print that screamed early '80s.

Her gaze flickered to the front door. In her time, it was pale blue. Now, it was painted a deep red, standing out sharply against the house's muted exterior. But the stained-glass window embedded in the door, the one with the swirling vines and golden leaves, remained the same. That tiny detail sent a strange ache through Ena's chest.

Now that she was actually here, standing in front of the house, she had no idea what to do.

She couldn't just walk up, knock on the door, and say, "Hi, I'm your granddaughter from 2019." That wouldn't go well. She stared at the sidewalk, heart pounding, and kept walking, passing the house entirely. When she reached the end of the block, she turned around, her mind racing.

Maybe she could sneak into the backyard and crash in Graeme's shed, where he kept his larger science projects. If it was unlocked. If she could even make it that far without being seen.

She slowed her pace as she neared the house again, her head down, weighing her options. That's when she saw her. At first, it was just a silhouette in the distance, moving toward her with Fiona's unmistakable purposeful stride, almost a hop in her step.

Ena's breath caught. It was her grandmother's unmistakable walk, her energy, her presence. But as the gap between them shrank, a cold realization settled over Ena like a fog. This wasn't the Fiona she knew. This was Fiona of 1986.

She still wore a black leather jacket, still had that slight frame, but she was so much younger. Her face was softer, her hair darker, glossier, and the lines that marked her wisdom in 2019 were just beginning to emerge.

Ena's feet froze in place. She wasn't ready for this. She turned away, panic curling in her stomach. She didn't have a plan, didn't know what to say, didn't even know if she could trust her own voice.

But Fiona had already spotted her.

"Sweetheart, are you lost?"

Ena's breath hitched.

It was Fiona's voice, but not quite. The gravelly rasp she knew so well was only a hint in this younger version. She swallowed hard, clenched her fists for a second, trying to steel herself. Slowly, she turned back.

"Um, yes. I—I'm really lost."

Fiona frowned slightly, studying her, then gave a warm, reassuring nod.

"Oh, dear. Well, why don't you come with me? We'll get you sorted out."

It wasn't a question. Fiona placed a gentle hand on Ena's shoulder, guiding her toward the house. The kind of touch that made it clear this was not a request.

As they walked, Fiona took her in, her eyes sharp, assessing, just as Ena had seen her do a thousand times before. "So. A fan of the Replacements, huh?" Fiona nodded toward Ena's T-shirt, raising an eyebrow. "You're ahead of the game. Not too many kids your age even know who they are yet, much less wear the merch."

Ena's pulse spiked. She cleared her throat, forcing herself to sound casual.

"Oh, uh, yeah. I just…really like their music. They never cared about playing it safe, and I like that."

Fiona hummed in approval. "Good taste. You might just be alright, kid."

Then, after a beat: "What's your name, sweetheart?"

Ena's mouth opened "En…ah." Her name had already started to slip out before she caught herself. She remembered what Graeme had said about time travel, how he wouldn't risk it because he loved his life too much to mess it up. It felt like a warning. She had to be careful.

She coughed, covering the awkward pause. "Jennifer."

Fiona's eyes narrowed slightly, but then she just shrugged. "Alright, Jennifer."

They reached the house. Before Ena could take in the differences inside, a loud, exasperated voice rang out from the hallway. "Oh, great."

Ena's head snapped up. A girl her own age stood at the other end of the hall, arms crossed, her sandy blonde hair frizzing slightly around her face despite being yanked into a high, slightly messy ponytail. Her thick bangs were just a little too long. Braces flashed as she twisted her lips into a smirk, but the effect was undercut by the faintest hint of insecurity in her expression.

She wore a black T-shirt, faded and slightly too big, as if it had been washed a hundred times to get it just right. The band logo on the front was partially obscured by crossed arms, but Ena could make out jagged white lettering. Paired with dark jeans that had been cut and restitched at the seams, it was the kind of outfit that was supposed to look effortless but took real effort to put together.

She rolled her eyes dramatically before calling out to the entire house, her voice dripping with sarcasm. "Mom's brought home another stray!"

"Manners!" Fiona snapped.

Ena's stomach dropped. The snarky voice had tones that were vaguely familiar. It was her mother. A thirteen-year-old Tara. Ena stared, wide-eyed, as it fully sank in.

Her mom. At her age. In the house she had only known as her grandparents'. This was too weird.

She took in the interior of the house. The exterior had barely changed through the decades. But inside? It was as if someone had drawn her grandparents' house from memory and then exaggerated all the wrong parts. The hallway walls were lined with a bold patterned wallpaper, busy and loud. Mustard-colored wall-to-wall carpeting stretched across the floor, soft but oddly oppressive.

STRANGER IN A STRANGE LAND

Fiona led Ena into the kitchen, and immediately, everything felt wrong. The layout was the same, but the details were jarring. Gone were the muted neutrals and soft yellow accents Ena knew from 2019. Instead, a garish avocado-green refrigerator and dishwasher yelled at Ena that she was in unfamiliar lands. The cabinets, thickly stained with knotty wood, were several shades darker than necessary, making the kitchen feel smaller and more cramped. Her eyes landed on the red plastic wall phone, mounted near the doorway. A bulky rotary dial sat in the center; its numbers faded from years of use. A long, curly, red cord twisted down almost to the floor and coiled back up to the receiver.

Ena steadied herself. *This is real.*

At the breakfast nook, a younger Graeme sat, reading a science magazine, his mustache hovering over his upper lip. His hair was thicker, with more color, his face had fewer wrinkles, but he had the same focused intensity Ena had always known.

Fiona gestured toward the phone. "Do you want to call your mom? I'm sure she's worried sick."

Ena's stomach tightened. She forced herself to nod. "Um, I can try, but I don't think she'll answer."

She hesitated, staring at the phone like it was some ancient artifact unearthed from another civilization. She had seen this done in a YouTube challenge. Slowly, she placed her finger in the plastic hole over the number nine, spun the dial, and let it click back. Then the number seven. She worked her way through her mother's number, painfully aware of Fiona's gaze on her. Her parents had drilled her on memorizing their phone numbers. And yet, the second she held the receiver to her ear, she already knew what would happen.

A hollow *do...do...do* filled the line, followed by a mechanical voice: "We're sorry, the number you have dialed is not in service. Please check the number and dial again."

Ena's fingers clenched around the receiver before she carefully set it back on the hook. Fiona studied her, head tilted slightly, eyes sharp. "Don't know your own mother's number?" she asked lightly. "Seemed like you dialed a few too many digits."

Ena's mind raced. She had to come up with a credible story. Fast. She straightened up, putting on the most casual, matter-of-fact tone she could manage. "Well, we live in a commune down south, and we only have one phone for the whole group. I don't even know if we still keep it running. I wasn't supposed to be in Portland, but I…uh…hitched a ride. Hid under some boxes and supplies in the back of a pickup truck. Sometimes, folks make trips up here to sell goods and buy necessities."

She winced internally. *Was this too much? Too weird?*

"Don't worry," Ena added quickly. "We're not some cringe cult or anything. We don't shun technology. We just…have our own vibe." She shrugged. "Try to keep to ourselves."

Fiona's eyes narrowed. There was a pause, long enough for Ena's heart to hammer against her ribs.

"Mhm," Fiona murmured, clearly not convinced but also not pressing the issue. Finally, she sighed. "Well, I guess you're stuck with us for a little bit while we figure this out."

Ena gasped. This was real. This was happening. She had to be careful. Very careful. Ena remembered talking about Byron's game with Graeme and his words about not wanting to time travel for fear of messing things up.

"Thank you, ma'am," she said, then hesitated before adding, "And sir," as she looked toward Graeme. Ena let out a slow breath, forcing herself to stay composed.

Fiona, meanwhile, softened slightly. "If you're staying with us for now, you might as well call me Fiona."

"And Mr. Quinn," Graeme added flatly, still not looking up from whatever article had captured his attention.

Fiona rolled her eyes.

Ena nodded quickly, unsure what else to say. Fiona rested a hand lightly on Ena's shoulder and gestured toward the hallway. "Why don't you go to the TV room and relax for a bit? My sons, Brandon and Mike, are in there. Could you let Brandon know he's been beckoned? It's his turn to cook, and he needs to get started."

Ena hesitated. She could have found the TV room blindfolded, but Jennifer wouldn't know where it was. And if Fiona was already suspicious, Ena couldn't afford to slip. She tilted her head, playing up the uncertainty. "Um, Fiona. Where is the TV room?"

Fiona's gaze lingered on her for a second longer than Ena was comfortable with. Then she smiled, gesturing toward the hallway. "Down the hall, second door on the left."

Ena forced herself to nod and walk calmly in that direction. Her heart, however, was racing.

Ena *found* the TV room exactly where she knew it would be, but she hesitated for a moment before pushing the door open. Raw, punchy music filtered through the cracks, unmistakably '80s. As she stepped inside, the glow of the television illuminated the room. MTV was on, playing "Walk This Way" by Run-DMC with Aerosmith. Snare cracks and guitar riffs shouted out from the screen as Run-DMC and Steven Tyler burst through a wall of sound and plaster.

Mike, no more than eleven years old, was bouncing rhythmically in that unselfconscious way only a kid could, feet shifting, shoulders moving, lost in his own little world as he stood no more than two feet from the TV.

Sixteen-year-old Brandon, on the other hand, was slouched on the couch, only half-engaged, tapping away at a handheld electronic baseball game. The flickering red LED lights reflected on his face as he pressed buttons, clearly not at all interested in the music video playing in the background.

Ena cleared her throat. "Uh, hi. I'm Jennifer." The name still sounded unnatural in her mouth, but she had a role to play. She turned to Brandon, who barely acknowledged her presence. "Your mom sent me to get you. Said it's your turn to make dinner." She exaggerated an eye roll to sell it. "Her words, not mine. *Beckoned*, actually."

Brandon let out an exaggerated sigh, dramatically shutting off his baseball game. He rolled himself upright, stretching like a guy who had been rudely interrupted from an endeavor far more important than what he was actually doing. Without a word, he shuffled past her and out the door.

As the video ended, Mike finally seemed to register Ena's presence. He spun around, his bright blue eyes locking at her with laser focus.

On the screen, MTV had cut to a commercial break. Two people, lost in their Walkman worlds, wandered down a busy city street. They collided, sending their snacks flying. Chocolate tumbled into peanut butter. Gasps, followed by accusations:

"Hey, you got chocolate in my peanut butter!"

"You got peanut butter on my chocolate!"

The unfamiliar jingle kicked in, a saccharine, irresistible promise of the perfect snack.

Mike launched into interrogation mode. His questions came rapid-fire:

"Where are you from?'

"How long are you staying?"

"Do you like to sing?"

"Who's your favorite band?"

Ena had no time to answer. Mike was practically vibrating with curiosity, his enthusiasm unbridled. Ena tried to keep up. "Uh—" she started, but before she could form a full thought, he fired off another one: "Wait! Did you see the Replacements?"

Ena's mind scrambled. This was young Mike, not the uncle she knew. He was a full-on, excitable, music-obsessed kid, and judging by his expression, she had just earned serious credibility with her Replacements tee.

Ena studied him for a second. Mike-the-eleven-year-old showed no hints of the mountain of a man he would one day become. He was a wiry, hyperactive kid, all uncontrolled limbs and nervous energy, with a mop of brown hair that refused to stay out of his face. His oversized *A-Team* T-shirt, featuring Mr. T pointing sternly with *I Pity the Fool!* emblazoned beneath, nearly engulfed him whole. The hem flapped as he bounced in place, brimming with restless energy. His white socks, striped with thick bands of yellow and blue, had long since given up their battle against gravity, sagging around his ankles as if they, too, were exhausted from trying to keep up with him. If she squinted, it was like seeing her brother Byron in a distortion mirror rather than meeting the eleven-year-old version of Uncle Mike.

This was going to be interesting.

In what seemed like no time, certainly not enough for a full dinner to be made, Mike and "Jennifer" were called to the kitchen. Ena followed him, her curiosity piqued.

She barely managed to keep a straight face when she saw what was waiting on the table in the breakfast nook. In the center sat a large bowl of greasy ground beef, a smaller bowl of shredded cheese, and another filled with iceberg lettuce. The chopped tomatoes were an anemic shade of pink, barely qualifying as ripe. A giant red-and-white bag with a bold blue stripe announced *Nacho Cheese Flavor*, its circular window revealing a mass of unmistakable orange dusted triangular chips.

Six mismatched plates were scattered around the table, barely fitting on the well-worn wooden surface. Brandon, standing at the head of the table, looked pleased with himself, though he tried to play it cool. "Taco Salad," he announced.

Ena almost laughed. *This* was taco salad?

The family piled into their usual spots, squeezing onto the built-in bench. Graeme took his usual chair at the head of the table. Ena hesitated, unsure where to sit, not just physically, but in every sense of the word. Finally, she slid into the last open spot beside Graeme.

Across the table, Fiona and Graeme exchanged a wordless conversation, a silent battle of expressions and faint smiles. Ena imagined the exchange going something like this:

> Graeme: *Really? This is what we're having for dinner?*
> Fiona: *Look, he's proud, and he tried.*
> Graeme: *You're right, like always.*

With barely a pause, Graeme turned to Brandon and said, "Looks delicious. You're becoming quite the chef."

Brandon absorbed the praise, and for the briefest second, his too-cool exterior cracked, revealing just a kid basking in the glow of his father's approval. Ena caught the flicker of emotion on his face, and in that moment, a warm surge of appreciation rose for her grandfather.

Brandon's mask slid back into place just as quickly. "Uh, yeah. You're welcome," he mumbled, shifting uncomfortably. His future self's awkwardness in full display in the boy at the table.

Ena eyed the food warily. This was nothing like the taco salad she knew. But before she could process it, Mike lunged for the bag of Doritos, shaking out a mountain-sized pile onto his plate.

Fiona gave him a sharp look. Graeme, his voice calm but firm, simply said, "Uh-uh. Half of that goes back in the bag."

Mike sighed dramatically but obeyed.

Everyone assembled their plates in their own way. Mike kept his meat and cheese separate from the chips, with only the tiniest nod to vegetables. Most of the others layered everything directly onto the chips. Graeme and Fiona took most of the lettuce and tomato, clearly trying to balance out the meal. Tara and Brandon switched between using their fingers and forks, depending on their mood. Ena copied them as best she could, trying to blend in.

Dinner was a familiar symphony of clinking forks and half-hearted conversation. Fiona and Graeme asked about the kids' days, receiving a series of grunts and one-word responses in return. Then, predictably, Mike broke the rhythm with an animated story about how he and a friend had found an injured bird after school. He rattled through every detail: how they scrambled to find a shoebox, how the bird almost escaped twice, how his friend's dad was a veterinarian and was *definitely* going to save it.

Ena smiled, watching her uncle as a kid. The same boundless enthusiasm, the same inability to tell a story briefly. It was surreal. Then, the conversation turned toward *her*.

Fiona cleared her throat and addressed the family. "So, Jennifer is joining us for a little while as we figure some things out." She kept her voice casual, but Ena could feel Fiona watching her carefully. "We had some challenges getting in touch with her parents, but I'm sure we'll get everything sorted out quickly. In the meantime, Tara, she'll be using your trundle bed."

Tara groaned. "Mom!"

Fiona's tone sharpened instantly. "Tara."

It was one word, but it carried the sting of a full reprimand. Tara huffed, flicking her bangs with an exaggerated breath, but didn't argue further.

Graeme picked up seamlessly. "Your mother and I need to do a little gumshoe work tomorrow, and you know we're approaching the final edits for this month's issue. Time's going to be tight, and we need everyone helping." He turned to Tara, his look leaving no room for negotiation. "Jennifer should go with you to school tomorrow. We'll call the office in the morning and let them know a family friend is visiting."

Tara slouched further but nodded. Ena could feel the tension rolling off her; this was not what Tara wanted. Not at all.

As dinner wrapped up, Graeme set the post-meal expectations. "Chef Brandon, thanks for a great meal. Tara and Mike, you're on dishes."

Tara grumbled under her breath but got up. Mike, in typical fashion, tried to make a break for it, but Fiona's raised eyebrow froze him mid-step. Ena instinctively started gathering plates, intending to help, but before she could take more than a step, Fiona spoke.

"Jennifer?"

Ena kept stacking dishes, only glancing up when she noticed Fiona watching her expectantly. Oh, Jennifer. That was her. She set the stack of plates down and nodded quickly. "Uh, yes?"

Fiona gave her a knowing look. "Would you mind joining me in my study?"

I STILL HAVEN'T FOUND WHAT I'M LOOKING FOR

Ena followed Fiona into her study, a space that was unmistakably hers. Unlike the rest of the house, this room felt like the Fiona she knew. The warm white oak floors gleamed under the dim light, and the towering mahogany bookshelves stretched from floor to ceiling, packed with a mix of records, books, and well-thumbed music magazines. Fiona's sturdy oak desk stood exactly where Ena expected, facing the bay window with its built-in bench, her private perch overlooking the world.

The room connected Ena to the house she had known and, by contrast, made the rest of the house feel even more off.

On the wall behind the desk, a framed cover of *True Notes* first edition of Fiona's music magazine from July 1976, held a place of pride. The artwork reimagined Washington's cherry tree myth; only this time, a mohawked rocker in black swung a guitar like an axe, mid-swing, about to strike the trunk. The image was bold, irreverent, and unmistakably Fiona.

But while the bones of the room were the same, the details reminded Ena just how far she was from home. The pillows and cushions on the bench were different, plush but boldly patterned in geometric shapes, the kind of fabric that screamed late '70s, early '80s. A large rug sprawled in front of Fiona's desk, a bohemian patchwork of deep indigo, burnt orange, and ochre, worn soft by years of foot traffic. The edges were frayed, the patterns reminiscent of a special find collected from a market overseas, vintage but full of life.

Fiona grabbed a pack of cigarettes from the top of her desk, tapped one out with practiced ease, and slipped it between her lips. The flick of her lighter was quick, effortless, as if it had been done a thousand times before. She took a slow, measured inhale, letting the smoke curl around her before exhaling in a long, steady stream. Her eyes fluttered shut for a moment, a small sigh of satisfaction escaping her lips. When she opened her eyes, she caught Ena staring, her expression tight, clearly uncomfortable.

Fiona eyed the cigarette, rolling it between her fingers before giving a small, wry smile. "These are probably going to kill me one day," she said and exhaled another plume of smoke. "But…" She let the sentence hang in the air, unfinished, as if the rest wasn't worth saying.

Fiona gestured to Ena's T-shirt. "So, Jennifer, you're into The Replacements." It was more a statement than a question.

She moved to the bay window and, with practiced ease, pulled the cushions aside, flipping open the bench seat to reveal a hidden compartment. Fiona removed a few old boxes filled with papers and two throw blankets. Fiona then pressed her foot just so against a section of the baseboard.

The soft click triggered a hidden latch, and a false bottom lifted with a gentle whoosh of air, revealing the hidden compartment beneath.

Fiona shot Ena a knowing look. "You have to keep this a secret."

She ran her fingers over the white spines of cassette holders with handwritten labels.

"I love music. I love the artists. But sometimes I can't help myself. When something is truly special, I want to revisit it. These aren't just tapes; they're history. Little moments in time that would otherwise be lost. I always splurge on the good tapes. The music deserves that."

Ena's breath caught in her throat. She thought Fiona was only talking about nostalgia, about capturing fleeting moments.

Fiona grabbed a cassette from the organized rows of cassettes. "This one's from a trip to Minneapolis a couple of years ago."

She crossed the room to her stereo system, a massive silver-faced receiver with glowing dials, a turntable, twin speakers that could probably shake the house if she dared to crank them. The dual cassette deck was nestled between it all, sleek and well-maintained. This wasn't just any stereo; this was an audiophile's system, meant for someone who lived and breathed music.

She pushed the tape in and pressed play. At first, there was only the sound of a crowd and muffled cheers, a burst of feedback, voices echoing in some small club. It was raw and electric, a moment frozen in time. Then came the bright, jangling opening of "I Will Dare," the chords tumbling over each other in their rush to be heard. Westerberg's voice cut through the haze—grinning, defiant, and just a little frayed around the edges.

Goosebumps erupted along Ena's arms as a wave of shock washed over her. The recording wasn't great. Bootleg quality, a little too much treble, the bass slightly distorted. But it was real. Fiona had a secret stash of live recordings.

Fiona settled onto the window seat, replacing the cushions before patting the space beside her. Ena hesitated for a second before sitting down.

"So," Fiona began, her voice casual, but her eyes sharp. "How are we going to get you back to your family?"

Ena's mind raced. Lying to Fiona hit harder than lying to anyone else. But what choice did she have? "I—I haven't left the commune very often," she started, stalling. "In fact, this is the first time I've ever been on my own in the outside world."

She let her imagination take over.

"Our place is deep in the woods, somewhere south of Eugene. I don't know the name of the closest town."

Fiona nodded, considering this. "Alright. I have some friends in Eugene; I'll give them a call, see if anything rings a bell."

Ena forced herself to act normally and said, "Thank you." The gratitude in her voice was real, even if everything else was a lie.

"What are your parents' names?"

Ena blurted out the first thing that came to mind, Skyler's parents' names. "Jean and Ed."

"And a last name?"

She hesitated for just a second too long before answering. "Edison." Ena heard how ridiculous it sounded when said out loud.

Fiona arched an eyebrow but didn't press. "Alright. Jean and Ed Edison. Graeme and I will make some calls in the morning, see if we can track them down."

Great, I just said my fake dad is Ed Edison.

"I'm sorry for being such a mess," Ena said quietly. That, at least, was the truth. "I feel so dumb for creating so much chaos. And for not being super helpful."

She shifted in her seat under Fiona's watchful gaze.

Ena continued, "Well, maybe after school, I can hit the library and see if I can help figure things out."

"Alright, kiddo. Get some rest. Tomorrow's a big day."

Fiona took a beat, ruffling her hair lightly before guiding Ena toward the door, and then added, "Tara can lend you some clothes for tomorrow. She'll show you how to wash your clothes when you get home."

Ena lingered in the doorway, her hand gripping the frame as she hesitated. A fleeting thought made her turn back. Fiona was watching her. She leaned casually against the desk, arms crossed, but there was an intensity behind her gaze, like she was trying to fit together the edges of a puzzle that didn't quite align. Fiona's pose reminded Ena of the end of her first day at school and seeing Fiona leaning against her car. Fiona had helped her find her way then, but now?

A lump formed in Ena's throat. Seeing Fiona alive again was both a gift and a gut punch. Lying to her was a betrayal, but Ena couldn't risk the truth. She didn't want to do anything that could endanger her future or her family. Fiona wouldn't believe her anyway or, worse, she would, and that could change everything. Ena hated twisting the truth, but every option felt dangerous. She chose the lie because it was the least likely to break everything apart.

She thought about her uncles—the hyperactive eleven-year-old Mike and too-cool-for-school Brandon. And her mother (her mother!) an eye-rolling, sullen thirteen-year-old starting to push for independence.

It was all too much.

Despite being surrounded by family, Ena had never been more alone. The gravity of it pressed down on her, a tangle of emotions too big to hold all at once. She wanted to be strong, to keep it together, but the enormity of it all made her feel impossibly small. Ena's fingers itched for her phone to text Skyler and Piney. She felt even more lost without them.

"Thank you, Fiona, and goodnight," Ena said, her voice thin and brittle.

"Night, Jennifer. Don't you worry, we'll figure this out," Fiona said. Her words came easily, instinctively, but beneath the certainty in Fiona's voice, Ena sensed doubt lingering, silent but present. "Go find Tara. She'll show you around."

GAMES WITHOUT FRONTIERS

Ena left Fiona's study and made her way toward the TV room. As she passed through the living room, she spotted Graeme sitting in a deep purple velvet wingback chair, completely engrossed in *The Tao of Physics*. His brow furrowed in concentration, one hand absently rubbing his chin, an action Ena had seen so often before.

To him, she wasn't his granddaughter. She was just a stranger passing through.

And somehow, that stung more than she expected.

When she entered the TV room, she found Mike and Brandon sitting on the floor, hunched over the Atari, playing *Pitfall!* The warm, low hum of the television and the rapid *beep-boop* sounds of the game filled the room. Ena held back a laugh at the simplicity of the graphics, the clunky joystick in Brandon's hands, the single red button that appeared to control the entire world, and the laughably pixelated world.

Without looking up, Brandon deftly maneuvered the character to grab a swinging vine, avoiding crocodile-infested waters. Mike, completely absorbed, bounced on his knees in anticipation.

Ena cleared her throat. "Do you know where Tara is?"

Still glued to the screen, Mike replied without hesitation, "Probably in her room. Like always."

Ena nodded. "Thanks." She turned back toward the stairs, already knowing exactly where to go.

At the second-floor landing, she turned left down the hallway. A door at the end of the hall stood closed, plastered with a handmade warning sign: *ENTER AT YOUR OWN RISK!* Between two holographic skull stickers, the words *KEEP OUT* were scribbled underneath in black marker for extra emphasis.

From inside, the pulsing synths of Berlin's *The Metro* drifted through the door, the distant, detached vocals threading through the air like a warning of their own.

Ena hesitated. This was too weird. Tara clearly didn't want her in there. She clearly didn't want *anyone* in there. And yet, Ena had to go in. She had to keep up the act. She had to be *Jennifer*.

She knocked.

"Who is it?" came a flat, clearly annoyed voice from the other side.

Ena hesitated. "En…Jennifer."

A pause. Then, an exasperated sigh. "Enter if you must."

Ena slowly pushed open the door, peeking in first before stepping inside. She took in the room.

It was a space in transition, much like the girl who occupied it. The walls were still pale yellow, but one side had been claimed by *The Cure* and *Siouxsie Sioux* posters. Moody and dark, it was a stark contrast to the pink curtains with faded rainbows still covering the window. On Tara's dresser, nestled between stacks of cassette tapes and a few dog-eared books, sat a tube of dark lipstick, the deep plum color visible through its clear plastic cap. A *Question Authority* sticker was slapped onto the corner of her mirror.

Ena scanned the bookcase, her eyes drifting over the eclectic mix of books crammed onto the shelves: well-worn Stephen King horrors, a few outgrown *Choose Your Own Adventure* novels, and a thick, white-spined book with *BASIC* emblazoned across it in bold letters.

Sitting there, gleaming under the soft glow of the room's light, was the impossibly familiar boom box. The very same boom box she and her mom had excavated from the attic just this morning.

Was it still this morning if she was now 33 years in the past?

The boom box was brand new, its plastic still carrying that faint chemical scent of fresh electronics, a far cry from the dusty antique she had held only hours, *or decades*, ago.

At her desk, Tara sat hunched over a Commodore 64, fingers flying across the keyboard. A small, flickering 13-inch TV screen displayed lines of monochrome BASIC code as she typed, completely focused.

Ena lingered in the doorway, unsure what to say. This was her mother. *Her mother.* A thirteen-year-old kid, not much different from her. It was impossible to reconcile this version of Tara, the serious, standoffish, tech-savvy girl in front of her. She was a sharp contrast with the woman Ena knew from her own time, the ambitious, no-nonsense entrepreneur who had co-founded her own AI company.

"You have a computer? Cool," Ena said, stepping in.

Tara's fingers lingered for half a second before she shrugged, trying to play it off. "It's whatever."

Ena saw through her mom acting disinterested. She got it, recognizing the same tendency in herself. After all, Ena imagined that being a girl who loved computers in 1986 wasn't exactly a ticket to popularity, but she also sensed a quiet pride in the way her mom straightened up a little. In a way, her 1986 mom reminded her of Piney. She imagined Piney and Tara would've been friends if they were in school together.

"What are you working on?" Ena asked.

Tara shifted in her chair, as if debating whether or not to downplay it. "Oh, uh…just some dumb text-based vampire game. *For school.*" The last part was added quickly, as if she needed an excuse for how much time she was spending on it.

Ena smiled and said, "Right on. That's cool." The conversation was awkward for both of them. Both were hiding their own truths, neither wanting to reveal too much.

Tara turned to look at her, tilting her head. "A *commune*, huh? You probably haven't even seen a computer before." She spun back to the keyboard, fingers flying again. "Want to play a game I wrote?"

Tara typed: *SAVE "VAMPIRE",1* before Ena could say anything.

A line of text flickered on the screen. Tara pressed two buttons on the tape recorder hooked up to the computer. A whirring noise filled the room as the data saved onto the cassette. After a few moments, the screen blinked: *READY.*

Without missing a beat, Tara loaded up another program. *LOAD "SKIING",1,1*

The tape recorder clicked into motion again, reading the data back into the computer. Tara hid a grin and said, "This is one of the first games I wrote." She was clearly proud but trying to act like it wasn't a big deal.

On-screen, a few simple menus appeared before a large *H* popped up in the middle of the screen. To either side, columns of *T*'s formed two vertical paths of varying widths. The screen counted down from three, and then the strings of *T*'s began scrolling upward. Tara tapped the *Z* and *X* keys, shifting the *H* back and forth, keeping it between the moving obstacles.

Then, the inevitable happened. The *H* collided with a *T*. Instantly, the *H* transformed into an *X*. A beat later, a crudely animated snowplow slid onto the screen from the right moving left: *)-o=o*

As the snowplow moved across, it erased the row, pushing the *X* out of view. A moment later, a message popped up: *WIPEOUT.*

The screen cleared and a prompt appeared: *Would you like to play again? (Y/N)*

Tara turned to Ena. "Wanna try?"

Ena was both amused and impressed. The game was *so* simple, but it was Tara's. A thirteen-year-old had coded it, and that was pretty cool. Ena could almost hear Piney mocking the primitive text graphics but secretly admiring the DIY vibe.

"Sure," she said.

Tara slid out of her chair and stepped aside, letting Ena take her place at the desk. Ena settled in. The second the game started, she realized how tricky it actually was. Keeping the *H* between the barriers wasn't quite as simple as it looked.

Tara smirked, clearly enjoying watching someone struggle through her creation.

For a brief moment, the awkwardness between them faded. They were just two kids, playing a game.

TALKING IN YOUR SLEEP

As the night wound down, Tara's passive-aggressiveness came out in full force. Now dressed in a pair of cotton shorts and an old, worn-out T-shirt, she rummaged through her dresser before tossing a frilly pink nightgown at Ena with a smirk. "You can wear this."

Ena caught it, staring at the ruffled sleeves and lace-trimmed collar. The expression on Tara's face made it clear; this wasn't an act of kindness. It was a power move.

Ena bit back a response. *She's thirteen. She doesn't know any better. This isn't my mom, not yet.* Still, it stung, like one of Madison's power moves. Her mom would never treat someone this way, but this version of her mother-to-be?

And it didn't stop there. When it came time to brush their teeth, Tara pulled open a drawer and plucked out a small red toothbrush still in the packaging. She turned it over in her hands, inspecting it like she was debating whether to hand it over, before extending it to Ena.

"Guess you'll need this," she said. The bright *Hot Wheels* logo on the handle made it obvious; it had been meant for Mike.

Ena hesitated before taking it. "Thanks," she mumbled. She told herself that at least it was new. At least Tara was making an effort, minimal as it was.

But the truth was, with every second that passed, she was shrinking away inside herself. She wanted to find the perfect words, but what was there to say? She was stuck here, at the mercy of people who didn't know her. Who couldn't truly know her.

Back in Tara's room, the trundle bed had been pulled out and made up with a simple sheet and blanket. The sight was familiar: Ena and Byron had shared this setup whenever they visited Portland in the past. But tonight, it felt different. She wasn't welcome. She wasn't wanted.

Tara flopped onto her own bed and flicked on the metal gooseneck lamp clamped to her headboard, casting a focused beam of light onto the book in her hands, *The Dark is Rising* by Susan Cooper.

"Night," she said, without emotion, without looking up.

Ena stared at the ceiling. Her chest tightened, doubt creeping in like a fog.

The rhythmic creak of the bedsprings and the soft flip of Tara turning pages were the only sounds in the room. Eventually, Tara clicked off the light, rolled over, and within minutes, her breathing slowed into the steady rhythm of sleep.

Ena, however, lay wide awake, every muscle tense with the impossibility of her situation. This house, this version of her family, the lie she had to keep up, the uncertainty of it all. It was too much. She could barely breathe.

Carefully, she pushed back the blanket and slipped out of bed. The floorboards hardly creaked as she tiptoed down the hall to the bathroom. Closing the door behind her, she perched on the closed toilet lid, elbows resting on her knees, and let her head fall into her arms.

She held it together for exactly five seconds before the first sob escaped. Then another. The dam broke. Ena pressed her sleeve to her mouth, desperate to muffle the sound, but the tears wouldn't stop. The enormity of it all crashed down: the loneliness, the disorientation, the intentional jabs from Tara. It was too much to hold in. Skyler would have known what to say, would have found the words to make it bearable. But Skyler wasn't here. Couldn't be here.

A soft knock came at the door.

"Jennifer?" Tara's voice, quieter than before. Not mocking. Not irritated. Just…there.

Ena stiffened, sniffling hard, but Tara knocked again, lightly. "Jennifer? Can I come in?"

Ena croaked out, "Sure."

The door cracked open, and Tara stepped inside, hesitating for just a second before settling on the edge of the bathtub across from Ena.

"You okay?" Tara asked, although the answer was obvious.

Ena wiped at her tears, but it was useless. She'd been caught. She tried to smile, but it faltered. She just shrugged.

Tara traced the pattern in the linoleum with her toes. "Look, I know I was a jerk," she admitted, her voice unusually soft. "It's not completely on you. It's just—my mom's always bringing home strays. Almost always girls. And I'm just expected to adjust, to share my space, to go along with it. I don't even get a say."

Tara sighed.

"I was like really mad at her. But I took it out on you. That was lame. I guess I owe you an apology."

Ena wiped lingering tears from her face, sniffling. For the first time since she got here, Tara's attitude began to make sense. "Thank you," she whispered.

Then, before she could stop herself, she added, "I'm just really freaked out. No clue how I'm going to get home. I miss my friends and my family. I feel completely lost."

Tara studied her for a second. In an attempt to lighten the mood, she nudged Ena's foot with hers. "Well, my parents have never not found someone's family before. They're kinda miracle workers."

Ena let out a weak, watery chuckle. *Unless they have a time machine, this might be the first time they fail.*

"I hope they have a big miracle up their sleeve," she murmured.

For a while, they just sat there. The bathroom, once just another familiarly unfamiliar space, didn't feel quite so suffocating anymore. The tension between them was melting. And as they talked, about nothing and everything, Ena began to see flickers of someone she recognized. The Tara that was already not overly sentimental, but beneath the sharpness, there was a quiet, protective compassion, like the version of her mom Ena knew.

Tara let out a small sigh and stood up from the edge of the bathtub. "We better get some sleep."

Ena nodded, following her back down the hall. The tension that had been pressing down on her all night wasn't gone, but it had eased, just a little. The magnitude of everything still lingered, but for the first time since she arrived, she didn't feel quite so alone.

When her head hit the pillow, exhaustion finally won. Her eyes closed, and she fell into a deep sleep.

The ice between Tara and Ena had thawed. They were still far from friends, but in that moment, their guards were down, and a fragile connection had formed.

BULLETPROOF

Ena and Tara woke to the gratingly enthusiastic voice of a DJ blasting from the alarm clock radio, announcing a call-in contest for concert tickets. The clock read 6:45 a.m., too early for that level of energy. Both girls groaned, rubbing their bleary eyes after a restless night of poor sleep.

Still half-asleep, Tara tossed Ena a pair of slightly faded jeans, the left knee patched with a red-and-blue plaid iron-on, and a loose-fitting T-shirt with a barely legible band logo, worn soft from repeated washing. It was clear these weren't Tara's favorites, maybe even a hand-me-down from Brandon, but compared to the frilly pink nightgown Ena had been stuck in, it was a truce of sorts.

Downstairs, the smell of fresh-brewed coffee mingled with the sharp scent of cigarette smoke. In the kitchen, a Mr. Coffee machine sat on the counter, its half-full glass pot revealing dark brown liquid. Next to it stood a large red tin of Folgers instant coffee.

Fiona sat at the table, coffee cup in one hand, a cigarette in the other, exhaling smoke like it was as much a part of her morning ritual as breathing. Across from her, Graeme nursed his own coffee, steam curling lazily above the mug as he flipped through the newspaper, eyes skimming headlines before pausing on articles of interest.

Mike was hunched over a big bowl of *Life* cereal, shoveling spoonfuls into his mouth while he read the back of the cereal box with deep concentration, as if it held the secrets of the universe.

Fiona looked up as Tara and Ena entered. She noted Ena's change of clothes and flicked a glance at Tara, an almost imperceptible nod that acknowledged some kind of détente had been reached.

"Morning, ladies," she greeted, voice husky from years of cigarettes.

Mike slurped up the last of his cereal and hopped off his chair. "I'm watching cartoons before school," he announced, already halfway out of the kitchen.

The girls ate quickly, and as they finished up, Brandon came barreling through like a gust of wind. Without breaking stride, he snatched an untouched piece of toast from Fiona's plate, jammed it into his mouth, and slung his backpack over one shoulder before bolting out the door.

Graeme, barely looking up from his paper, announced dryly, "Guess he was running late."

Tara hoisted her overstuffed backpack onto her shoulders. "We better get going. It's a bit of a walk to school."

As they made their way toward school, the unmistakable clickety-clack of a skateboard on pavement caught Ena's attention. She turned her head just as Tara did, spotting a boy weaving smoothly down the sidewalk. His straight sandy-brown hair swooped dramatically over his right eye, forcing him to tilt his head slightly to see past it. He wore a sun-faded red T-shirt with a small Town & Country Surf yin-yang logo stamped over the left chest, baggy shorts, and scuffed black-and-white Vans that slapped rhythmically against the pavement with each kick-push.

With an effortless motion, he popped the tail of his board, sending it up into his hand in a fluid, practiced move. "Hey, Tara!" he called, grinning.

Tara's expression instantly cooled. "Hey," she replied, her tone sounding deliberately neutral.

"What's up?" the boy asked, trying to keep things casual.

"Nothing." Tara's response was clipped, making it clear she had no interest in small talk.

The boy hesitated, shifting awkwardly on his feet. He was trying, Ena could see that, but Tara wasn't making it easy.

Tara finally said, voice edged with a tone sharper than indifference. "I don't know what you're up to, but I'm not falling for a dumb prank."

The boy's face scrunched in confusion. "What? Paranoid much? I was just saying hi. Sheesh."

Tara crossed her arms. "You jocks always think you're so slick, but you only have lame jokes and pranks."

He opened his mouth as if he was about to plant a comeback, but then he sighed and shook his head. "Scouts honor. No pranks. Just saying 'Hi.' "

Tara's eyes flicked toward the ground. "Whatever. Here. Something to remember me by."

Before he could react, she stooped down, grabbed a random rock from the ground, and held it out to him.

"Jason, rocks are for jocks." Her voice was flat, her expression unreadable.

Jason took it and stared at it in his hand. He looked genuinely confused, maybe even a little hurt, but he didn't argue.

Ena watched the exchange, her gaze drifting to the stone resting in Jason's palm. Something about its shape tugged at the edges of her memory, a flicker of familiarity she couldn't quite place. Then her eyes returned to Jason himself. The way his lips pressed into a subtle frown, the slight sag in his posture, the flicker of disappointment in his eyes.

It was a look Ena knew all too well. She had seen it before, on the face of her father when she had let him down.

"Wow," Ena said as they walked away. "That was kinda brutal."

Tara scoffed. "You don't get it. This school isn't some commune where everyone sings 'Kumbaya' and shares their feelings. It's eat or be eaten. The jocks run the show, and they're always up to trouble."

She shot a glance over her shoulder.

"Most of them are idiots, but Jason? He's smart, for a jock, which makes him even more dangerous."

Ena frowned. "Dangerous? He seemed...I don't know, kind of nice?" She pictured the Jason she knew and his terrible dad jokes, easy grin, the quiet way he always made time for her. The words Jason and Dangerous together made no sense. Or maybe that was the problem, Ena never knew *this* Jason.

Tara snorted. "Yeah, that's how they get you."

There was a deeper story here, more that Tara wasn't saying. Ena hesitated.

"Did he ever successfully prank you?" Ena asked.

Tara's jaw tightened. "Let's just say he showed his true colors in fourth grade."

Ena waited, but Tara didn't elaborate. Instead, she quickened her pace, putting distance between them and Jason, as if leaving him behind physically might erase whatever memory still lingered.

Ena frowned. What had happened in fourth grade? What had Jason done to make Tara this guarded, this sharp-edged? And more than that—how did this Tara, the one practically radiating disdain, turn into her mom, the woman who had married *that* Jason?

The pieces didn't fit. It was like looking at a puzzle with half the pieces missing, the gaps too wide to form a clear picture. Ena wasn't just confused. Her head spun as she began to understand more than she ever had a right to know.

As they started up the stairs, two girls with feathered hair and an air of forced confidence stood perched on the ledge beside the steps, like they'd studied a magazine on how to be cool but missed a few key instructions.

"Hey! It's Fart Tearin' Tara."

Tara didn't break stride. "Wasn't funny in fourth grade, still not funny. Sad you peaked so early."

"Nerd."

"Losers," Tara shot back over her shoulder as they reached the top of the steps.

Ena was taken aback. *This was not what she had expected.*

Before she could say anything, Tara waved a hand dismissively. "Ignore Tweedle Dee and Tweedle Dum. Carrie and Eileen tormented me in fourth grade, but now they're nobodies, less than, actually. Trying too hard and getting nowhere." Ena knew the type as her thoughts shifted to Ashley and her desperate bid to hang on.

Ena stole a quick look back at the girls, their laughter sharp and hollow, like they were clinging to a joke that had long since lost its bite. Their smugness was paper-thin, an illusion held together by habit more than power. Tara, on the other hand, didn't even break stride.

This morning was turning into a crash course in things Ena had never known about her mom. She'd never pictured her as someone who had to fight her way through school, always on guard, always ready with a sharp comeback. How many times had she walked into this same battle? How many times had she taken the sting of their words and kept moving?

Tara was hiding it well, but if this was the routine, it had to hurt. It had to cut deep.

Skyler had faced this too: whispers, stares, people who never tried to understand them. But she'd seen them float past it, somehow untouched. Tara didn't float, she fought. Down in the trenches, fists clenched behind her words.

She wanted to hug her mom-to-be. She wanted to hug Skyler. Both had learned how to survive, in such different ways. And right now, both felt completely out of reach.

SUBDIVISIONS

Tara pulled open the heavy front door, and Ena followed her into the school's main lobby.

The chaos hit Ena instantly. The air smelled like pencil shavings, cafeteria grease, and the too-strong scent of Aqua Net hairspray. The halls throbbed with energy, kids shouting to each other over the noise, lockers slamming like drumbeats. A boy punched another kid surprisingly hard. Ena flinched, expecting a fight to break out, but instead, the puncher bolted down the hall, laughing, while the other boy shook it off, calling after him, "Payback's coming!" The surrounding students barely reacted. It was rougher than what Ena was used to, but here, it was just background noise.

The colors hit her next. Everything was louder, the neon posters plastered on the walls, the students themselves. The school was awash in bold pinks, electric blues, and clashing patterns. Girls with gravity-defying bangs and feathered hair leaned against lockers, holding books at their waists. Boys with mullets and shaggy cuts roughhoused in groups, their T-shirts blaring Def Leppard, Van Halen, or bold neon graphics. Acid-washed denim jackets were everywhere.

Ena took it all in, wide-eyed, mouth slightly agape.

"Come on, freak," Tara said barely audibly, grabbing Ena's wrist and tugging her forward. "We have to get to English."

The classroom was filling up by the time they arrived. Tara slid into a seat at the very back of the room, slouching as if to take up as little space as possible. Ena followed suit, keeping close. Tara placed her binder, labeled *Trapper Keeper*, on her desk. Tara wasn't the only one; they were coming out of backpacks all around the room, with bright and splashy designs. Except for Tara's. Her binder was a solid, matte black with a single silver sticker of a crescent moon near the bottom corner.

The bell rang, and their teacher stood up from behind her desk, scanning the room. The nameplate on her desk read, *Mrs. Whitaker*. "Good morning, class."

Her eyes landed on Ena.

"Looks like we have a visitor. Ms. Quinn, would you mind introducing your guest?"

Tara barely lifted her head. "This is my cousin Jennifer."

Mrs. Whitaker nodded expectantly. "Ms.…?"

Ena wanted to shrink down in her seat.

Mrs. Whitaker repeated the question.

Oh, right. "Edison."

"Welcome, Ms. Edison." Mrs. Whitaker said, smiling. "Would you like to stand and add anything?"

Ena hesitated before rising awkwardly to her feet. "Uh, hi. I'm Jennifer Edison." She winced internally. Obviously, they knew that already. "I'm just visiting for a couple of days while my parents, um, figure some things out."

Mrs. Whitaker seemed satisfied. "Thank you, Ms. Edison. You may be seated."

Ena relaxed a little as she sat back down, hoping that was the last time she'd have to address the class.

Mrs. Whitaker grabbed a well-worn paperback from her desk. "Alright, let's dive in. We're continuing our discussion on *1984* by George Orwell. He wrote this in 1949, thirty-seven years ago, and here we are. Clearly, his version of 1984 didn't come to pass."

A small, knowing smile played on her lips.

"But I want to hear your thoughts. What did you think of Orwell's vision of the future? Did anything stand out to you?"

Two hands shot up immediately from the front row. One belonged to a small boy who braced his raised arm with the other, his hand quivering with enthusiasm. The other was a girl sitting with perfect posture, her dark pigtails secured with bright pink barrettes, arm straight and high, fingers wiggling eagerly.

Mrs. Whitaker scanned the room, clearly hoping to call on someone less eager. After a pause, she relented. "Mr. Wormser?"

The boy launched into a rapid recap of the book's key events; his summary thorough but lacking any real insight. He had definitely read it. He just didn't have much to add beyond a detailed retelling.

The girl's hand shot back up before he even finished. Mrs. Whitaker sighed but gave a small nod. "Alright, Ms. Suarez?"

Ms. Suarez straightened. "*1984* is a warning against totalitarian regimes, obviously. Big Brother represents the Communist Party, and Orwell was predicting how dangerous that kind of government control could become."

There was some scattered discussion around the room, some students engaging and others zoning out. Mrs. Whitaker let the conversation run its course before her gaze landed back on Ena.

"Ms. Edison," she said. "I know you may not have read the book, but would you like to add anything?"

Ena startled. She *hadn't* read it. But as she listened to the discussion, a theme had clicked. This book was written thirty-five years before 1984. She was coming from thirty-five years *after* 1984. The class saw Orwell as a man predicting the future. But *she* was the one living in *their* future.

"Well," Ena started, picking her words. "I think Orwell was totally right to warn people about what can happen with too much government control. Like, that kind of stuff is scary. But I don't really think it could happen in the U.S., at least not like in the book. We care a lot about freedom and privacy and all that. It'd take something huge, like a total takeover, for it to really happen."

A few kids nodded. That gave her a little confidence.

"But—" she paused. "I still think spying could be a big deal. Not like Big Brother, with government control. Sneakier. Like, we'll just kind of let it happen without realizing. If technology keeps getting better, people might trade privacy for, I don't know, convenience or games or whatever. And then instead of being forced, we'll sort of…just let it happen. Not by the government, but by companies. And that might end up being just as bad. Maybe even worse."

Silence.

Ena gulped as all eyes stared at her like she was some kind of alien.

Mrs. Whitaker studied Ena with an appraising look. "That's an interesting perspective, Ms. Edison."

Her response earned a death glare from Tara.

Mrs. Whitaker gave a small nod before addressing the class. "So, corporate control versus government control. Which one is more dangerous? Let's discuss."

As the conversation picked up again and attention moved away from where she and Tara sat, Tara shot Ena a sharp look, half disbelief, half exasperation, as if to reprimand her for chumming the waters.

With an audible huff, Tara fluttered her bangs and sank lower in her seat.

Ena winced. She had gone too far.

SCHOOL DAYS

The morning dragged Ena through a series of contradictions, half-familiar and half-baffling. The desks, the bells, the teachers droning through lessons? Easy enough to process. But then there were the little things, tiny details that snagged in her brain like a skipped record.

Math quizzes were handed out, streaked with blurry purple ink that made them barely legible. A few kids lifted the pages to their noses, inhaling like the fumes were some kind of forbidden high.

Ena sniffed hers. The oily, metallic scent left more questions than answers.

In science class, the teacher was wiry and wild-eyed, with a pocket protector crammed full of pens. He scribbled equations across the board with such frantic enthusiasm he nearly vanished into a cloud of his own chalk dust. The shrill scrape of chalk made Ena's spine curl, but no one else seemed to notice.

Lunch was chaotic.

Tara had packed her lunch and sat alone in the farthest corner of the cafeteria, her back to the room, her posture closed off. She wasn't interested in the swirling energy of the cafeteria, the clattering trays, the scrape of chairs against the floor, the overlapping voices bouncing off the tiled walls.

Ena, on the other hand, couldn't stop watching. She had expected lunch tables to be cliquish, but the way they divided was different from what she was used to. The younger kids still clung to same-gender groups, giggling in hushed conversations or launching spitballs across tables. The older ones had begun mixing, but it was awkward and hesitant. Girls sat beside boys without quite talking to them yet, like two separate species still figuring out how to interact. Each table almost claimed its identity, each its own little nation, complete with its own uniform.

One group wore crisp polo shirts, pastel-colored with tiny, embroidered alligators or polo players on their chests, collars popped in casual defiance. Another table, a stark contrast, was dominated by kids in dark shirts with band logos sprawled across the front: Van Halen, Black Sabbath, AC/DC. Some paired their shirts with well-worn denim jackets, the sleeves either rolled up or defiantly cut off. A few tables had kids hunched over chessboards, their striped shirts and too-big glasses signaling a kind of youthful innocence that hadn't yet been chipped away.

Ena could see how someone like Tara, who didn't fit neatly into any group, might have found it easier to just opt out. Or maybe she'd been opted out without even choosing.

She turned back to Tara, who was methodically unwrapping her sandwich, completely uninterested in the social ecosystem unfolding around them. For Tara, lunch wasn't a social event. It was an obligation, just another part of the school day to endure.

It wasn't just the seating arrangements that unsettled Ena. The conversations she overheard were full of jokes that would have gotten someone suspended in 2019. Casual comments reinforced stereotypes, and flippant homophobic remarks were tossed around as punchlines. Ena's stomach turned. She had known things were different back then (back now?), but hearing it firsthand made it all the more real.

"Jennifer," Tara said, her voice low with an edge, "what part of eat or be eaten didn't you understand? Why did you geek out in English class? You'll be gone in a couple of days, but I get to deal with the fallout for weeks."

Ena collected her thoughts. "Tara, I'm really sorry. I wasn't expecting the question, and before I knew it, I just…blurted out my response."

"It was so weird." Tara studied her, suspicious. "Where did that even come from?"

"I don't know," Ena said truthfully. "I just started and couldn't stop."

"Whatever." Tara's tone made it clear the conversation was over.

Long before the bell rang, Tara packed up the remnants of her lunch, tossed them in the trash, and slung her backpack over one shoulder. "Computers are next period. Let's go to the lab now."

The computer lab smelled of overheated circuits and dust.

Mr. Benson, the computer teacher, sat at his desk finishing a slightly bruised banana. He looked up as Tara walked in. He was young, probably in his late twenties, with brown hair neatly parted down the middle and soft, kind eyes that crinkled slightly when he smiled.

"How's my *star pupil?*" he asked, his voice light with amusement.

"Fine," Tara mumbled, her usual sharpness dulled. Ena noted the shift. This was the first time Tara had seemed even remotely uncomfortable all day.

Mr. Benson's gaze moved to Ena. "And who's this?"

"My cousin, Jennifer." Tara's voice was a little too casual, her usual sharp edges softened.

Ena was surprised. That was the nicest introduction Tara had given her all day.

Before Mr. Benson could ask anything else, Tara shoved her hands into her pockets. "Hey, anything I can help with?" The question came too quickly, as if she needed to be useful, needed to justify showing up early.

"Hi, Jennifer," Mr. Benson said, his voice just as warm as his smile. Then, with a glance at Tara, like he understood more than what she had said, he nodded toward the chalkboard. "Actually, yeah. Erasers and blackboard could use some cleaning."

Ena didn't miss the way he balanced kindness with distance, making Tara feel comfortable while keeping their interaction firmly in the realm of teacher and student.

Tara nodded and grabbed a small bucket from the supply shelf. "I'll do the board if *you* take the erasers," she said, already making her way out the door.

Ena eyed the dusty erasers beneath the blackboard, then turned to Mr. Benson, hoping for a signal. Nothing. She looked back at the erasers, hesitating.

"Uh, this might be a stupid question, but how do you actually clean these?"

Mr. Benson chuckled, clearly amused but lacking any mean-spiritedness. "Take two at a time over to the trash can," he said, pointing to the corner of the room. "Clap them together a few times, *gently*, until most of the dust shakes loose."

Ena picked up a pair, their weight oddly more substantial in her hands than the dry erase erasers she was used to. She stepped toward the trash can and, on impulse, smacked them together a little harder than necessary, letting out a small huff of frustration at Tara, at this ridiculous day, at everything.

A thick cloud of white dust exploded into the air, engulfing her instantly. Coughing, she fanned the air uselessly, blinking as the haze settled around her.

"Maybe *not* so hard," Mr. Benson said, biting back a laugh. "And, uh, closer to the trash can next time."

Ena let out a sheepish sigh, giving the erasers a few gentler claps before setting them down, a faint layer of chalk now clinging to her t-shirt. From across the room, Tara returned with a bucket of water and a rag, wiping down the blackboard in smooth, practiced motions. As she worked, the dusty pale green surface darkened to a deep, shining emerald, deleting the faint remnants of past lessons.

Ena brushed off her hands and took in the lab. The computers were nothing like what she was used to. They had bulky beige casings, thick boxy monitors with dark screens that flickered green text when powered on. Each had a clacky mechanical keyboard, and many had two stacked floppy disk drives. A few had external drives connected with thick gray cables, relics of an earlier setup.

She turned to Tara, about to ask if these were compatible with the computer she had at home, but Tara was already at a workstation, turning one on. As the green glow of the screen flickered to life, other kids started to file in.

MESSAGE IN A BOTTLE

The school day continued to fly by, but Ena was less like a student and more like an archeologist trying to decipher the remnants of a lost civilization. Everything was just familiar enough to be disorienting. The rhythm of the day wasn't that different from her own time—bells still rang, teachers still assigned homework—but every classroom experience revealed another strange eccentricity of the past. The overhead projector, with its plastic sheets and smudgy markers, was wielded like a magical artifact. Notes zipped across aisles in expertly folded shapes, passing under the radar of teachers who had clearly developed selective blindness. And then there was social studies, where the discussion of nuclear war wasn't some distant historical fact but a real, looming fear. The way her classmates talked, you'd think Soviet paratroopers might descend onto the football field at any moment.

After school, Tara led Ena to the library. At first glance, it looked like any other: rows of bookshelves, the hum of quiet conversation, the smell of paper and dust. But standing in the middle of it, Ena felt unmoored. Where was she even supposed to start? She needed to figure out how to get home, but what was she supposed to look up? *How to Un-Time Travel?* She chuckled to herself. *Reading about Oregon communes probably isn't going to help.*

"I'm going to play *Oregon Trail,*" Tara said. "Let me know when you find what you're looking for." Tara peeled off toward the corner where two clunky computers sat.

Ena wandered through the aisles, scanning the spines of books without any real plan. When she reached the magazine section, she noticed rows of hardbound volumes, their faded covers lined up like forgotten encyclopedias. *Scientific American* caught her eye. Maybe, just maybe, she could find an article or a book about time travel. Some wild theory that could help her make sense of this. She flipped to the table of contents. Nothing. Another issue. Still nothing. The realization hit hard: *How do you find anything without Google or Wikipedia?*

A voice interrupted her spiral.

"Are you alright, dear?"

Ena turned to see a stout woman in a floral-print dress with a name tag that read *Mrs. Plumlee.*

"I'm a bit lost," Ena admitted. "I'm—doing a research project on time travel. How would I find an article about that?"

Mrs. Plumlee's face lit up with librarianly purpose. She pointed to a long row of pale oak cabinets filled with drawers upon drawers, each with a small metal handle and a label tucked into a brass frame. "Card catalog is just over there."

Ena stared at the cabinets like they were an alien artifact. "Oh," she said blankly.

Mrs. Plumlee's smile didn't falter. "Let me help."

She led Ena to the drawers and pulled one open, fingers dancing over the index cards with practiced ease. Within seconds, she flipped to a card and gently pulled it forward, leaving it exposed among the tightly packed rows. The top read

Time Travel, but the rest was an indecipherable jumble of names, numbers, and call codes that might as well have been hieroglyphics to Ena.

"This tells you where to find the article," Mrs. Plumlee explained, sliding out a narrow wooden writing slab nestled between the upper and lower sections of the cabinet. From a tiny metal box, she plucked out a stubby pencil, the kind Ena had only ever seen at mini-golf courses, and handed it to her. "Write down the details, and I'll show you where to find it."

Ena copied the information. Mrs. Plumlee returned to her desk while Ena flipped through a few more cards, still feeling like she was working through an escape room puzzle rather than a research task. She brought her scribbled notes back to Mrs. Plumlee, who inspected them with a nod.

"Alright," the librarian said. "Let's start with this one. It's on microfiche."

"Micro fish?" Were they about to sift through some kind of tiny underwater archives? Would they need a snorkel?

Mrs. Plumlee, entirely unbothered by Ena's confusion, led her to a wall of metal cabinets and pulled open a drawer, flipping through manila envelopes until she found the right one. She pulled out a few stiff sheets of film, negative-like, but smaller and denser.

She led Ena to a hulking machine with an enormous screen, a small glass tray beneath it. "This is a microfiche reader," she explained, loading the film onto the glass. With the press of a button, the screen flickered to life, and a reverse-image magazine page filled the display.

It was as if Ena's brain was buffering. Instead of scrolling or clicking, she had to *physically maneuver* the film by pushing the glass tray around to change the view. She hesitated, then tried it herself, slowly getting the hang of the awkward mechanics. Piney would not believe this was how people 'googled' in the '80s, and seeing it for herself, Ena still had a hard time believing it.

Every article she found was full of high-level physics, black holes, wormholes, faster-than-light travel. Nothing practical. Nothing useful. But then, one article caught her eye. One of the authors, Dr. P. Docks, was a physics professor associated with the City of Portland University. If Ena could actually talk to him, maybe, just maybe, he could help her figure out a way back.

She was more confused than ever about how she'd ended up in 1986. And even less sure she'd ever find her way back. She had felt a little like a fish out of water when she moved to Portland and started at her new school. Now, she felt like an alien visiting a distant planet. The thought that she may never make it back to her own time and would have figure out how this world actually worked made her whole-body tense up.

LET'S GO TO THE MALL

Tara and Ena walked home through the tree-lined streets, golden sunlight dripping through the green leaves like honey. The air carried the first crisp bite of fall, though summer clung stubbornly, unwilling to fully surrender just yet. Their footsteps fell into an easy rhythm, the silence between them stretching comfortably.

Ena was lost in thought, trying to untangle the emotions the day had stirred. She had spent an entire day in the distant past, uncertain how or even if she would ever get home. The uncertainty of it all sat heavy and unreal. Even Madison's drama would be easier to handle. At least that world made sense. Beside her, Tara seemed relieved by the quiet, her mind elsewhere, sifting through yet another grueling day of middle school. It was a life she longed to outgrow.

When they reached Tara's house, Tara pushed open the backyard gate, letting it swing shut behind them with a soft creak. Two bikes leaned against the back of the house, their tires caked with dried mud. Tara slid her key into the lock and nudged the door open.

A wave of warmth greeted them, carrying the rich, fragrant smell of stew simmering in the crockpot.

Brandon's voice rang out from the hallway, the phone cord stretched taut from the kitchen. "Yeah, let's meet there in a few." He reappeared, returning the receiver to its cradle with a decisive click, then caught sight of them.

"Hey," he said to Tara and Ena, understated as usual. "I'm headed over to the mall. Wanna come?"

"Oh my god, *the mall*," Tara gasped in an exaggerated Valley Girl drawl. "I have *nothing better* to do." She dropped the affectation and slung her backpack onto the kitchen table, her voice flat to mask any excitement. Then, begrudgingly, "We'll have to bring Mike."

"Mike!" Brandon summoned, loud enough to ensure he was heard in all corners of the house. "We're going to the mall, get your butt down here."

A series of thuds and the unmistakable sound of a body crashing into something echoed from upstairs. Then, the hallway erupted with what sounded like a herd of elephants as Mike barreled into the kitchen, breathless with excitement. Ena, well-versed in the chaotic energy of scrawny, hyperactive boys, was at ease. There was a familiarity, almost *too* familiar, in the way Mike moved—an echo of her own little brother, Byron. And yet, she couldn't shake the thought: Will Byron grow up to be anything like the towering, gregarious man she knew Mike would become?

Brandon scribbled a note for their parents and led the way out. The four of them wound through the neighborhood, the tree-lined streets gradually giving way to the buzz of busy commercial roads.

As they approached the mall, Ena stopped short. It was completely wrong.

The long, windowless, three-story building she knew from 2019 was gone. In its place stood a two-story open-air mall, light brick, and concrete planters, with bridges connecting each wing. This version thrived. The parking lot was packed. Mothers wrangled toddlers in and out of station wagons. Kids tore ahead, giddy with freedom. Teenagers loitered on the bridge overlooking the ice rink. They were making sure they would be seen.

Near one of the planters to the right of the entrance to the shopping area, a group of four older teens with long feathered hair occupied more space than seemed necessary. Two perched on the planter's edge, one leaned against it with casual indifference, and the fourth stood facing them, waving a cigarette as he spoke. A thin haze of smoke drifted around them, curling in the late afternoon light. Their jean and leather jackets, paired with black band tees—Pink Floyd, Led Zeppelin, Rush—gave them a uniform look. They all wore dark high-tops, Doc Martens or Converse All-Stars. Girls and boys were nearly indistinguishable from each other, but the easiest way to tell them apart was the presence (or lack) of wispy mustaches.

Ena, Skyler, and Piney knew the modern mall as a dying husk, a place of empty storefronts and halfhearted clearance sales. But here? It hummed with life.

Neon store signs flashed their glowing invitations. The air thrummed with overlapping music spilling from different shops. Teenagers drifted in and out of stores that catered directly to them—skateboard shops, walls of high-top sneakers in a riot of colors, record stores. The crowd pulsed with energy, an entire ecosystem of adolescence in motion.

As they passed a row of payphones, Ena overheard a girl with giant feathered auburn hair, twisting the cord around her finger as she hissed into the receiver, "Allyson, Lincoln is here. I think he's looking for you! You need to get here now!"

Mike turned to Brandon and said, "I'm going to the arcade?" It was more of a question than a statement.

Brandon nodded, already knowing how this would go. "Meet back here at 5:45 sharp." His emphasis wasn't just a warning; it was a prophecy. Mike, already halfway gone, tore off toward the stairs, his pockets jangling with quarters.

Brandon peered at Tara, eyebrows raised.

"5:45. Here. Got it." Tara didn't break stride as she peeled off in the opposite direction, moving with purpose.

Ena followed Tara, passing displays that looked almost alien. A Benetton store, its window bursting with color, every sweater and windbreaker in shades so bold they looked like a crayon box exploded. The mannequins inside were posed mid-stride, as if frozen in the middle of a power walk, dressed in oversized knits, bright corduroy pants, and layered polo shirts with popped collars. Even the logo, *United Colors of Benetton*, looked like it belonged more to an international peace summit than a clothing store. A RadioShack window showcased a home computer, a bulky beige machine with a keyboard attached. Inside, a salesman demonstrated some gadget on a green-on-black screen to a pair of interested dads.

Then, the unmistakable synth opening of A-ha's "Take On Me" spilled into the mall before she even saw the store.

The music store entrance was wide open, an invitation to step straight into a world of music. The store hummed with activity. Pairs and groups of teens flipped through racks of LPs and cassettes, the latter encased in those absurdly long beige anti-theft cases. Ena drifted down the aisle, skimming titles. Some she recognized—Michael Jackson, Madonna, Prince—but others were mysteries, names she might have only half-heard from Fiona. The Psychedelic Furs? Hüsker Dü?

After several minutes of flipping through tapes, it became clear Tara had no intention of buying an album. Eventually, she wandered up to the counter and grabbed a six-pack of 90-minute blank tapes.

The cashier barely looked up as he rang her up. He had the air of someone who had peaked in high school and refused to acknowledge the passing of time, a mullet that had likely seen better days, a Rolling Stones shirt that had long since faded.

"That'll be seven-fifty."

Tara handed over a ten, took her change, and grabbed the thin plastic bag holding the tapes.

Ena, sensing Tara might need a break from her, said, "I'm going to check on Mike at the arcade."

"Cool," Tara said, barely looking up. The sense of relief was palpable.

On her way to the arcade, the smell of fresh roasted nuts and sugary milkshakes wafted out of a store Ena had never heard of: Morrow's Nut House.

The arcade throbbed with noise and light. Machines flashed and beeped, their screens a pixelated riot of color. Groups of kids hovered around the most popular games, quarters lined up neatly along the edges, placeholders for the next challenger.

Ena spotted *Dragon's Lair* and Jason at the same time.

Jason caught her eye and, with a confidence she hadn't seen that morning, walked over.

"Hey. You're Tara's friend, right?"

"Eh...cousin." Ena gave her signature half-smile. "Jennifer. Not sure I've made it to 'friend' status."

"Jason." He stuck out a hand, easy, self-assured.

She hesitated. This is my dad. Thirteen years old, confident, already moving with the unshakable ease of an athlete. Tara had warned her not to trust him, just another junior high school boy, a jock. And yet, standing in front of her, so familiar and yet so removed from the man she knew, she struggled to make the connection.

"That was rough this morning," Ena said carefully, testing.

For the first time, Jason's confidence faltered, and his cheeks reddened. Was he embarrassed that Ena had witnessed that exchange this morning, or was there more?

"Yeah, sorry." He scratched the back of his neck, recovering. "That was…awkward." He didn't stumble over it, but the shrug wasn't as smooth either, like he wasn't used to missteps.

Ena let the silence stretch just long enough to see if he'd say more. He didn't.

Instead, he pivoted. "So, how long are you visiting?"

Ena stiffened. The question shouldn't be hard, but it landed like a punch to the gut.

How long was she visiting? She had no idea. She was stuck in 1986. No way of knowing when, or if, she was getting back. But she could not come close to saying that. Not to Jason. Not to anyone.

She inhaled slowly, keeping her voice level. "A couple of days. Long story." The words came out clipped, half a warning. Don't ask.

"Cool. Well, uh, good seeing you." Jason seemed to pick up on her cue and took half a step back, already disengaging. "I think I'm up next."

He nodded toward *Dragon's Lair*, as if relieved to have an escape route, and turned back toward the game.

Ena was about to move on when a sharp, piercing whistle cut through the arcade noise. Jason.

"I got next." His voice was steady, low, carrying just enough force to make it clear; this wasn't a discussion.

The kid about to play, maybe a year older, broad-shouldered, didn't even look up. "You snooze, you lose," he mumbled, about to slide his quarter toward the slot.

Jason wasn't having it.

With one swift motion, he planted a firm hand against the kid's chest and shoved him back. Not hard enough to start a fight, but not friendly either. The kid stumbled, startled, a flicker of uncertainty flashing across his face.

Jason, completely unfazed, fluid in his movements, stepped into position and, with the confidence of someone who had never doubted the outcome, slotted his quarter into the machine.

The other kid hesitated. He could push back, make a scene, but he didn't. He scoffed under his breath, maybe mumbled inaudibly, and melted back into the crowd.

Ena gasped, a strange knot forming in her chest.

She wasn't sure how to feel.

On the one hand, it was Jason's turn. The kid had tried to cut in. Wasn't that just him getting what he deserved? But Jason's ease, his certainty, the sheer physicality of it all unsettled her. She could see why Tara might not trust him.

And yet, at the same time, this was her dad.

This was the same person who, in her world, never pushed, never shoved, never threw his weight around, who was always quick to make a bad joke to make others feel better.

Ena turned away, her thoughts still tangled in the shove, in Jason's ease with power. Then she spotted Mike. And just like that, the mood began to shift.

He was at *Rampage*, aggressively mashing the buttons, his face scrunched in concentration. A King Kong-like monster scaled pixelated skyscrapers, fists flying, smashing out windows while avoiding attacks from army helicopters and tanks. The game over screen flashed, and Mike let out a dramatic sigh before turning to Ena with a grin.

"Wanna play Skee-Ball?"

Ena hesitated for half a second, then nodded.

Mike led the way to the row of machines along the back wall, their wooden ramps gleaming under dim arcade lighting. The clank of rolling balls and the sharp ding of scoring shots filled the air. It smelled like popcorn, bubblegum, and a vaguely metallic odor like old quarters and static electricity.

Mike plunked in the quarters, and with a heavy clunk, the first set of balls rolled into the chute. He grabbed one and immediately hurled it too hard, sending it ricocheting off the backboard before it dropped straight into the lowest-scoring ring. He groaned.

Ena's trademark half-smile appeared as she picked up her own ball. With a practiced hand, she rolled it smoothly up the ramp, sinking it into the 50-point slot on her first try.

Mike's jaw dropped. "No way."

Ena just shrugged. "Boardwalk."

And for the first time since she had landed in 1986, a lightness lifted her spirits. The burden of time travel, of uncertainty, of everything pressing down on her just lifted, at least in this moment. It was just a game she knew. She and Mike rolling balls, collecting tickets, competing but not really keeping score. The simple rhythm of it, the feeling of being good at this silly game, the tiny rush of victory when she landed another perfect shot. Something normal gave Ena a small escape.

She let herself get lost in it.

When the last ball clunked, registering the final score, Ena looked down at the growing pile of prize tickets at her feet. Mike eyed them with thinly veiled jealousy.

"Hey, you paid for the game," she said, handing him the whole bundle.

Mike's face lit up. "Seriously?"

"Seriously."

He practically skipped to the prize counter, scanning the rows of cheap plastic toys, erasers shaped like sneakers, and candy that had probably been sitting there since the dawn of time. After some serious deliberation, he settled on a glow-in-the-dark bouncy ball and a pack of grape Bubble Yum that smelled so artificial it could probably be classified as a science experiment.

As he unwrapped the gum, he checked his wrist. His simple digital watch blinked back the time in blocky black numbers.

His eyes widened. "Uh-oh."

"What?" Ena asked.

"It's 5:46."

Panic jolted through them at the same time. Without a word, they took off, weaving through the crowd, dodging slow-moving shoppers and stroller-pushing moms. Mike somehow was able to go up the stairs three at a time; Ena struggled to keep up.

Brandon and Tara stood there, arms crossed, unimpressed.

"Right on time," Tara deadpanned.

Brandon sighed. "Let's go."

WONDROUS STORIES

Ena followed Tara, Brandon, and Mike through the front door, trailing just behind as they entered the living room. Fiona and Graeme sat in their deep, matching purple wingback chairs, mirroring each other in relaxed symmetry. Both held cut crystal tumblers, the golden liquid inside catching the dim light—whiskey. Next to Fiona, on the end table, a homemade ashtray from years ago cradled a few smashed cigarette butts, one still smoldering, its long ash threatening to drop. Their conversation was cut short as the kids entered.

"Did you kids enjoy the mall?" Fiona asked.

Tara groaned. "Time of my life," she said, dripping with sarcasm.

Brandon grunted, noncommittal, while Mike beamed, holding up a pack of gum and a glow-in-the-dark ball like a trophy. "Look what I won! Well, what Jennifer and I won. Did you know she's the Skee-Ball Queen? I've never seen anything like it!"

Graeme and Fiona chuckled softly, maybe with a touch of gratitude. Mike was still so exuberant, so unapologetically young. His older siblings had settled into mopey teenage indifference, but he was still just a kid. Fiona winked at Ena, that familiar, knowing wink Ena recognized instantly. It was so Fiona, that mix of mischief, warmth, and unwavering spirit. If anyone was unapologetically kid-like, it was Fiona.

Graeme stretched. "I don't know about the rest of you, but I'm famished."

He rose, making his way toward the kitchen. Everyone followed suit. The house smelled of Graeme's famous stew that had been simmering all day. It smelled like home. Ena had eaten it many times before, in her other life, and the precise mixture of secret spices sent a wave of comfort and disorientation crashing over her. Sitting at this table, eating this meal, surrounded by this family was all so achingly familiar, yet impossibly different. The feeling lingered, that strange push and pull between past and present, between belonging and being a stranger, between being home and oh so far away. And, frankly, she was getting tired of it.

Dinner unfolded in the unremarkable, everyday way family dinners do. Small talk, casual bickering, clinking silverware. But then, as they finished, Fiona turned to Ena. "Good news," she said, her voice warm but matter-of-fact. "Graeme and I think we found a couple of leads. A good friend down in Eugene is checking out a few places tomorrow. I'm sure your family and the whole commune must be worried sick by now."

Ena's stomach plummeted. They were still chasing the lie. Not only that, but they had also pulled someone else into it. More people were looking for a girl who didn't exist. Guilt burned in her chest. She wanted to come clean, to tell them everything, but who would believe her? The lie barely held together, but the truth—

The truth sounded outright delusional.

"Geez. Thanks, Gran—" she caught herself, her heart slamming, hoping they just thought she corrected herself from using a first name.

"Mr. Quinn. And Fiona. I really appreciate it. I'm sorry for all of this. You've been so kind, so generous. You've made me feel like one of the family."

If they only knew that I was family. Ena longed to be back home, but going home meant saying goodbye to Fiona again. She wasn't sure she could handle that.

After dinner, the kids washed up. Ena insisted on helping, forming an assembly line: Brandon washed, Tara rinsed, Ena dried, and Mike stacked. It was easy, rhythmic, a dance they all knew well, even her.

When the last dish was put away, Fiona clapped her hands together. "A family that sings together, stays together," she declared. "It's family song night!"

Tara and Brandon groaned. Mike chittered excitedly. Ena hesitated, lingering at the edge of the group, unsure if she was included, but no one told her otherwise. They filed into the living room, where Graeme sat at the grand piano. Next to it, a bookcase stood, lined with folders of sheet music and, perched atop one of the shelves, a beat-up old tweed flat cap. The rim was frayed and soft with years of wear.

Graeme pulled down the cap. "Alright, names in the hat. You know the drill."

Brandon's name was drawn first.

"So, what are we singing?" Graeme asked.

" 'Gardening at Night.' R.E.M.," Brandon said, a beat too eager, as if he were trying to impress.

Fiona grinned. "Good choice."

Tara muttered, "Poser," just loud enough for Brandon to hear but not their parents. Maybe Brandon heard, maybe not.

Graeme flipped through one of his organized binders, found the sheet music, and played. Brandon sang confidently, unabashed, fully hitting the notes. His voice was no longer just a kid's. It shifted, settling into a voice with the depth of someone older.

The next name.

"Oh, look, Fiona and me," Graeme announced. "What's your fancy?"

" 'You're All I Need to Get By,' " Fiona said. Graeme nodded and began to play.

Ena was struck by the beauty of Fiona's voice. She had always known Fiona could sing, but years of smoking had roughened her voice in Ena's time. This younger version of Fiona had a clarity, a power, that hit somewhere deep. Graeme's voice was familiar, good, but against this stronger version of Fiona failed to measure up.

When Tara's name was drawn, she chose "Landslide." Graeme's fingers hesitated on the keys. Ena knew he loved that song, and his daughter. She could see he was grateful for this moment with her. Tara sang, unaware of how deeply the lyrics resonated with her father.

Mike, unsurprisingly, chose Van Halen's "Jump." Tara and Brandon shared an exasperated glance—because, of course, he would. Oblivious to their judgment, Mike launched into the song with full-throated enthusiasm, his voice surprisingly strong and on-key for an eleven-year-old. He didn't just sing, he performed, nailing the rhythm, the energy, and even the attitude, punctuating it all with theatrical air guitar. By the end, his infectious energy had won them over, and the entire family was bouncing along with the song.

Finally, Fiona reached into the hat. It was empty. She turned to Ena. "No song for you, Jennifer?"

Ena hesitated. "Oh, I just—I didn't know. I mean, I didn't think…"

Fiona gave her a knowing look. "When you're here, you're family. So, what's your song?"

Before Ena could stop herself, she blurted, " 'Wondrous Stories.' By Yes."

Fiona's brows lifted in surprise. She snuck a quick peek at Graeme, then back to Ena.

"Huh. Not the song I would've guessed from such a progressive Replacements fan." A small nod of approval. "Quite the range."

Graeme began to play, and Ena sang. Her voice wove through the dreamy, intricate melody, a song of stories, mystery, and journeys into the unknown. As she sang, she drifted through the lyrics, finding a calmness that was grounded in the familiar. Finally. Why had she picked this? She didn't know. But it made a difference.

Fiona looked at her kids, joy bright on her face, as if she were capturing the moment like a photograph in her mind, tucking it away to keep forever. "Thank you for indulging an old woman."

Ena gasped, Fiona's words stabbing her like a blade. The last time she heard those words was the last family sing-along Fiona ever had.

The love pressed in. But the loss hit harder. She tried to stifle a sob. It stung.

She wanted to tell Fiona the truth. She wanted to tell her to stop smoking. She wanted more time. And then, it hit her. She had more time. This was a gift.

She took a breath before asking, "Fiona? I'd love to hear the story about how you started your magazine."

THESE ARE THE DAYS

Fiona appeared to be momentarily caught off guard. She glanced at Graeme, sharing their special knowing look, then turned back to Ena, curiosity flickering in her eyes. Ena worried she might have overstepped.

"The kids have heard this story a hundred times," she said, taking a beat to look at her brood; each in their own way letting Fiona know she was right. A bemused smile tugged at Fiona's lips. "Let's leave them to it and go to the study."

Graeme hummed in some unspoken agreement, a quiet smile crossing his face as he stood to join them. "Hard to believe how it all started."

Ena followed them as they made their way to the study, trailing a few steps behind. The other kids drifted out of the living room to move back to their own priorities: homework, video games, phone calls.

Fiona pushed open the door, and the scent of old paper, ink, and lingering cigarette smoke met Ena like a memory. The room was lived-in, layered with history. Fiona walked over to the record rack, flipping through familiar worn sleeves before sliding out an LP.

"Ah. This feels right." She set the needle down, and soon, the room filled with the crisp, driving chords of Martha and the Muffins' "Echo Beach."

Graeme chuckled, an amused look passing between them. "Never get sick of that one, eh?"

Fiona laughed gently. "And I never will."

She and Graeme took their places on the bay window bench, their old routine, as natural as breathing. Ena hesitated for a moment, then settled into the armchair across from them. Graeme's fingers laced through Fiona's, just like they had in the hospital. The same quiet devotion, the same certainty. Only now, Fiona wasn't slipping away. Now, she was here, warm and alive, laughing with him.

Fiona leaned back, swirling her whiskey. "The story of *True Notes* begins years before the magazine. It was 1966. I was freelancing, hustling for any music column I could get, and I was supposed to be meeting someone for an interview at a bar in downtown Portland. And in the corner of that bar, a devastatingly handsome young man was at the piano."

Graeme grinned. "And I saw the most beautiful woman walk in." He paused, letting the silence hang for a beat, and then added, "And right behind her, Fiona."

Fiona gasped in mock outrage, swatting his knee as he laughed. Ena found herself smiling, caught up in the rhythm of their story.

"Anyway," Fiona continued, "I was waiting at the bar, and my interviewee never showed. Meanwhile, this one," she motioned to Graeme, "was watching me like a lovesick puppy."

Graeme sighed dramatically. "Not true."

"Oh, it was true. And then, he changed the song. Right there at the piano. And I knew, just knew, that he was playing it for me."

Ena leaned forward slightly. "What song?"

Graeme smiled. " 'My Girl' by the Temptations. I figured if it didn't catch her attention, nothing would."

Fiona's expression softened. "And it did."

"She could have left that bar. She could have gone home. She could have done a thousand other things. Instead, as I finished the song, she walked over to the piano and asked, "Do you know 'Can't Help Thinking About Me?' I launched into it without a second thought. And before I knew it, Fiona was singing. Not softly, not just to me, but to the whole damn bar."

Ena could see it so clearly, the audacity, the way Fiona would have commanded the room.

Fiona shrugged. "What? It is a good song."

"From that point on, it was game over," Graeme said simply. "A year later, we were married."

Fiona nodded.

"And somehow," Graeme continued, "she still made time to run circles around the music industry."

Fiona set her glass down, rubbing her hands together as if shaking loose the nostalgia. "I kept freelancing, Graeme had sold a couple of inventions, and life was falling into place."

Graeme smiled knowingly. "Which, if you know Fiona, meant she was about to turn it all on its head."

Ena watched as Fiona crossed the room to the framed first issue of *True Notes*—July 1976.

"I had a voice, a following, but no one was interested in hiring a woman music journalist full-time. Not without a degree. Not when I was more interested in lifting up bands that weren't getting airplay." She turned back to Graeme, with a wink and a nod. "So, I told this one, 'I think I'm going to start a magazine.' "

Graeme spread his hands. "And what could I say? Fiona was never one to ask for permission."

Fiona tapped the glass over the framed issue. "We started this with next to nothing. Graeme did the cover art. I wrote every blasted article. Our 'distribution' was laughable, but a few local music stores agreed to carry it. It was slow, there were lean years, but we fought for it. And by '79, we had national distribution."

Ena let her eyes drift over the punk chopping down a cherry tree with a guitar. The image spoke of rebellion even more now that she knew its origins. Ena took in the framed magazine, the stacks of records, the easy way Fiona and Graeme played with their stories. She had never thought of them like this before. As *people* before they were grandparents, before they were even parents.

And suddenly, Ena was struck by a wave of grief. Of loss. All over again.

Because she knew how this story ended.

In 2019, Fiona would be gone. Graeme would sit in this same house feeling lost without her. But right now? Right now, they were here. Younger and very much alive. And Ena was here, too.

She pushed down the lump in her throat and forced herself to speak. "Fiona, if you could go back to that night in 1966, to the bar, would you change anything?"

Fiona cocked her head slightly, intrigued.

"Now that's an interesting question, Jennifer." Her gaze lingered on Ena for half a second, just long enough to be noticeable, before shifting to Graeme, her eyes sparkling, her smile wide. "Not one flipping thing! And not a single thing since."

Ena followed Fiona and Graeme out of the study, her mind still tangled in the meaning of their words. A bridge had been built tonight, not just to Fiona, but to Graeme too. As they reached the hallway, Fiona turned back, watching her for a beat longer than was casual.

"Goodnight, Jennifer," Fiona said, her voice softer now, her tone not quite readable.

Ena hesitated. "Goodnight, Fiona."

She wanted to say more. To tell her to quit smoking. To tell her how much this night meant. To tell her the truth.

But she didn't.

TIME AFTER TIME

Ena barely slept. Her mind churned with questions, circling unanswered. She rehearsed what she'd say if she managed to track down the physics professor from the article on the library's microfiche reader. Would he help her? Would he even believe her? What if she couldn't find him at all? The thought of leaving 1986 should have filled her with relief; she *wanted* to go home, back to her life, her friends, the certainty of her own time. But that meant saying goodbye to Fiona. Again. How could she do that?

And what about 2019? How much time had passed? Was her mother worried sick? How could she possibly explain where she'd been?

The questions tangled inside her as she stared at the ceiling waiting for Tara's alarm to go off.

After Ena and Tara got ready for the day, Ena followed Tara downstairs, the smell of butter and eggs cutting through her haze.

Brandon stood at the stove, an omelet sizzling in the pan. He called out over his shoulder at Graeme. "Hey, Dad, what do you think if I add—" He grabbed a jar from the counter. "—a little peanut butter?"

Graeme hesitated, brow furrowing. "Peanut butter? In an omelet?"

Brandon shrugged. "It's rich, it's a little sweet, but it's got protein. Why not?"

Graeme considered. "Well, Brandon, I'm not sure that's the choice *I* would make, but that's the beauty of the experiment. If it's terrible, we'll have learned. If it's wonderful, we'll also have learned something. Either way, I call that a win-win."

Brandon grinned and swirled a spoonful into the egg creation. "Only one way to find out."

Ena smiled. She knew how this story ended. Years from now, in a cramped LA food cart, Brandon's Thai-Peanut Omelet would draw crowds, the first step in Brandon's career as an elite chef. *Was this the moment of inspiration? The seed of invention?*

Brandon flipped the omelet onto a plate and cut it into portions, offering it around the table.

Tara wrinkled her nose, grabbing a cereal box from the counter. "Gag me with a spoon," she said, drawling in her best Valley Girl impression.

Mike barely acknowledged its existence, instead maintained total focus on his cereal. "No way, that looks nasty."

Brandon masked the sting of his siblings' disapproval with a shrug.

At the head of the table, Fiona sat with a lit cigarette in one hand, a black coffee in the other, eyes skimming a marked-up article for *True Notes*. She was lost in her own world, entirely unfazed by the breakfast theatrics. She held up her coffee. "Breakfast of champions."

Ena and Graeme each put a portion on their plates. Ena chewed, considering. Not terrible. A little too salty, but with a nuttiness that hinted at a flavor profile *almost* brilliant.

"Great experiment, Brandon," she said. "What do you think?"

Brandon frowned, tasting it again. "Not what I was hoping for. Edible, but…off. Too salty. Feels like something's missing."

Graeme nodded approvingly. Apparently proud of the thought process, if not the actual omelet. "That's how you figure it out."

Brandon was clearly seeking approval from his father, and Graeme gave it in way that was both supportive and honest. Ena tucked the moment away, warmth spreading throughout her. She'd always loved Graeme, but she was starting to *understand* him. The understated way he showed up, again and again, and not just for Fiona, not just for his kids, but for their ideas, their wild dreams. He had unwaveringly backed Fiona as she built *True Notes*, even when it must have seemed impossible. And now, he was doing the same for Brandon, encouraging him to trust his instincts, to take risks, to create. Maybe this was his true superpower: believing in the people around him and what they could accomplish. Graeme had done it for Ena, too. He'd backed her completely when she hatched the idea for Skyler's Korakama. Never taking over, just offering quiet nudges and giving her and Piney the space to create on their own.

After breakfast, Tara and Ena walked to school, their footsteps falling into an easy rhythm. But as they neared an intersection, Ena slowed, her steps faltering. Her heart was racing, but she wasn't sure why. It wasn't fear exactly, or sadness, or even excitement. It was all of it tangled together, too big to name.

She turned to Tara. "I have an idea that might help me get home," she said, keeping her voice even. "I need to talk to someone. Our commune sells vegetables to the same vendor; maybe they can help me." A careful mix of truth and lies. She *did* need to see someone who might get her home. But not a vegetable vendor. A physics professor.

Dr. Docks.

Ena studied Tara's reaction. It was hard to read, but she guessed it was a mix of relief and something else. Relief because Ena had complicated things yesterday, drawing unwanted attention in class. But maybe disappointment too. As far as Ena could tell, she was the only one who'd treated Tara without an angle. Jason had been friendly, sure, but Tara clearly didn't trust it. With *Jennifer*, though. Maybe Tara felt safe, at least from the constant judgment of her classmates.

"Makes sense," Tara said finally. She pulled a battered spiral notebook from her backpack, its wire binding crushed in places from rough handling. Scribbling down a phone number, she tore the corner of the page and handed it to Ena. "If you find a way home, could you at least call before you leave? So my mom and dad don't freak out?"

Ena took the scrap of paper, her fingers curling around it. The gesture meant more than it should have. It wasn't just about Tara's parents. It felt like a small statement of friendship. Like Tara wanted to know Jennifer would be okay. Ena tucked it into her back pocket.

"Good luck," Tara added, shifting her weight, unsure what more to say.

"Thanks."

Ena swallowed hard. She *should* be relieved to leave, but instead, a knot tightened in her chest.

"Sorry I was such a pain," Ena added, her words came out awkward, far too small for everything she wanted to say.

Tara snorted. "It's fine. I guess you weren't *that* bad." She gave Ena a small shoulder-to-shoulder shove, casual but intentional.

Ena smiled, a little stunned. Maybe she'd gotten closer to 'friend' than she thought.

♪ ♫ ♪

Ena arrived at the City of Portland University, a feat in itself without Google Maps to guide her. She was grateful for Portland's simple grid layout, but an hour-long walk still left her a little tired.

She'd been on college campuses before, more than most thirteen-year-olds. Her dad had taken her along plenty of times in Boston and Portland back in her time, letting her explore libraries and science buildings while he worked. But this campus was a distorted version of the one she knew.

Students rushed past, books haphazardly tucked under their arms as they made their way to class. A group played hacky sack near a bench, their laughter mixing with the steady *thump* of the beanbag. Others leaned against railings, cigarettes dangling from their fingers, their conversations punctuated by lazy plumes of smoke. Ena still wasn't used to how much people smoked here. The smell clung to the air, to their clothes, to everything.

Once on campus, she realized she had no idea where to go. She stopped a passing student, probably in her early twenties, wearing faded jeans and a striped T-shirt under a light blue Members Only windbreaker, large hexagonal glasses perched on her nose.

"Know where the physics department is?" Ena asked.

The woman gave her a once-over, a hint of amusement in her expression. "A bit young to be a college student, huh?" She let out a small chuckle but pointed across the quad. "It's in that building there."

Ena followed her gesture to an imposing, Brutalist structure, a fortress of dark glass and raw concrete. It loomed over the sidewalk, squat and unwelcoming, as if someone had debated putting "UNINVITED" over the entrance instead of the university's name.

Inside, the air smelled of old books, burnt coffee, and a faint hint of floor polish. A bank of elevators stood to her right, and between them, a large black directory board with rows of plastic white letters listing names and room numbers.

She scanned the board, her pulse picking up.

Dr. P. Docks — Room 223.

Ena made her way up to the second floor, her heart rate quickening. She'd spoken to professors, but never without her dad, and never on a mission this important. She silently rehearsed her questions, trying to sound older, smarter. She was desperate to be taken seriously.

She wandered down the hallway. 219…221…223.

The plaque under the number read: *Dr. Parisa Docks.*

The door was slightly ajar.

Her hand hovered near the doorframe. Her mouth was dry. She reminded herself to breathe. This was ridiculous; it was just a person. Just a professor. *Fiona would never let her fear keep her from doing what needed to be done.* But what if this was her only way home?

Ena knocked, tentatively.

"Come in."

She pushed the door open and stepped inside. Behind the desk was a woman, early 30s, long black hair pulled into a sleek ponytail, typing at a clunky desktop computer. Ena had to shake off her expectations. She'd imagined someone completely different: a middle-aged man in a dull brown suit with a receding hairline and zero personality.

But Dr. Docks wore an emerald-green blazer, sleeves casually rolled to the elbows, revealing a tattoo on her left wrist: a small, ornate hourglass inked in precise detail.

It caught Ena off guard. The tattoo seemed out of place, almost rebellious. She hadn't seen many tattoos in 1986, especially not on women, and definitely not on a professor. The room smelled faintly of lavender. Ena stared at the small, gold-framed poster behind the desk, the words etched in bold letters: *Time waits for no one.*

Dr. Docks finished typing, then turned toward Ena. She raised an eyebrow at the sight of a thirteen-year-old standing in her office.

"Well, hello," she said. "Can I help you find someone?"

"I…I think I'm looking for you. Are you Dr. Docks? I read your article on the theoretical possibilities of time travel. I'm doing a research project for school."

Dr. Docks leaned back in her chair, studying Ena. She glanced at the institutional wall clock, its second hand ticking like a soft metronome. "Shouldn't you be in school right now?"

"Parent-teacher conferences," Ena lied, hoping it wouldn't be checked.

Dr. Docks scoffed, seemingly unconvinced, but curiosity softened her skepticism. A thirteen-year-old asking about time travel theories? That didn't happen every day.

"It sounds like you know who I am, and who might you be?" Dr. Docks asked.

"I'm…en…Jennifer Edison."

"Alright, Jennifer." she said, intrigued. "Let's hear your questions."

Ena's pulse raced, but she dove in. "Sorry if I got your article wrong, but in it, you suggested that if an advanced civilization could lock one end of a wormhole to a specific point in time, anything entering the wormhole would exit at that fixed time and place. Is that right?"

Dr. Docks sat up straighter, her eyes narrowing. Apparently, Ena had caught her attention. The shift from amusement to interest was subtle, but Ena felt it.

"It's a possibility," she said, "theoretically."

"So, let's say someone gets pulled into that wormhole. How would they get back?" Ena asked, leaning forward.

Dr. Docks frowned slightly. "I'm afraid it's likely a one-way ticket."

Ena's stomach dropped, but she pressed on. "But could someone get back if there was another wormhole locked to the place they left?"

Dr. Docks considered. "I suppose that's possible."

Ena's mind raced ahead. "Okay. So, if someone created a wormhole, how would they lock it to a specific point in time and space?"

Docks put her finger to her lips in thought, the first hint of a smile curling at the corner of her mouth. "That's the hard part. We'd need to think about it in terms of information. Could you encode data, coordinates, a timestamp, into a waveform, something stable enough to anchor the wormhole's opening? It's speculative. Highly speculative."

"But if someone traveled through a wormhole, could they carry that kind of information with them? Something that would let them lock a new wormhole back to the first time and place?"

Dr. Docks tapped her fingers lightly on the desk. Judging by cock of her head and the grin on her face, she was impressed. "That's extremely speculative. But if we accept the rest of the theory? Then yes. That would be a reasonable hypothesis."

Ena's brain was spinning. Information. Waveforms. Anchors. Maybe, just maybe, there was a way back. She just needed something that tethered her to her life and time.

Dr. Docks checked the clock. "Speaking of time, I've got a class in five, but this has been most unexpected. And impressive. Seriously, most people your age aren't tossing around questions about anchoring wormholes to a time and place."

She grabbed her satchel and stood, giving Ena a playful wink. "If you crack the space-time continuum, be sure I get credit for the Nobel committee."

"Thank you, Dr. Docks," Ena said, relief and pride swelling together. She hadn't been dismissed. She had held her own. As Ena turned into the hallway, a voice called from behind her, brusque, male. "Hey, Para, got a sec?"

Dr. Docks appeared in the doorway. "Talk and walk, I'm running late."

Ena shook her head and smiled. *Dr. Para Docks. Wow. That's subtle, universe. Real subtle.*

Ena had a plan forming. *The Fin Whale tape didn't just bring me to the past. It brought me to the exact time and place where they were recording the song. Sounds a lot like what Dr. Docks said about coordinates. I have that tape that Mom and I made in the attic. Could that be enough to get me back to my own time?*

BETWEEN THE BARS

Ena walked back to the house, eyes wide to catch every detail of 1986 Portland. The orange, gray, and white boxy buses looked so different from modern buses. The buses' headlights and grilles gave them the expression of a grim-faced worker trudging through the day, belching thick puffs of black smoke from their exhaust pipes. The city had a grittiness that clung to everything: neon signs flashing above adult theaters, the mix of punks, preps, lumberjacks, and businesspeople all sharing the same sidewalks. Portland was a city in perpetual flux, shadows and hints of the place Ena would one day call home.

Sadness perched on Ena's shoulders like a great horned owl that wouldn't take flight, whispering everything she was about to lose. She wanted to go back to her time, to her family, to her real life, but she knew she would miss this.

This Portland. 1986.

She couldn't say she would miss the constant haze of cigarette smoke, the way it lingered in clothes and hair and seemed to have a presence everywhere, but even that pulled at her. Nostalgia? Connection to Fiona? Or the strange ache of having lived a time that was never meant to be hers? All of it, tangled together.

By the time she reached the house, Ena was trying to steel herself. She tapped into her mother's mode, the Tara she knew in her own time, all business, tackle the next step, get through. As she opened the backyard gate, she saw the glow from Graeme's workshop. Good. That meant the back door was almost certainly unlocked and Graeme was lost in one of his experiments, the house quiet. She would be alone.

Ena climbed the stairs to Tara's room and changed into her own jeans and Replacements shirt, slipping on the worn denim jacket she'd found in the attic. She remembered that she'd started borrowing young Tara's clothes before she ever arrived. The loop had always been there. Downstairs, she started the washing machine, dumping the bundle of borrowed clothes. As she flipped out the pink nightgown, she hesitated, thinking about the night in the bathroom when Tara had comforted her, when the passive-aggressive edge had softened into a hint of a familiar kindness. Not friendship, but a fragile truce. An understanding.

Ena wandered into Fiona's study. She let her fingertips drift along the walls, over the shelves and framed photos. This room was so very Fiona, capturing both the woman Ena had known and the younger version she had just begun to understand: firebrand, driven, and unwaveringly devoted to those she loved. Ena lingered in front of the first edition cover: a punk chopping down a cherry tree with a guitar. She'd never known Graeme was the artist. She'd never even known he could draw. Her mother's tough exterior suddenly made more sense. And Brandon's seemingly ridiculous omelet experiment that probably was the seed to his big success. Such a short time here, and already she had learned so much about all of them.

At Fiona's desk, Ena found a pen and a piece of paper. She couldn't win. Writing the note was wrong. Not writing one?

Worse. Ena wanted to choose her words perfectly, but "Jennifer" was a stranger. "Jennifer" could not possibly say what Ena wanted, yearned, to say.

> *Dear Quinn Family,*
> *If you are reading this, I found my way home.*
> *I can't thank you enough for your kindness. I was so scared when Fiona found me on the street. I didn't know what to do. I was LOST in a way that word had never meant to me before.*
> *Your family is special. Sharing these few days with you has been a gift. One I never could have asked for, and one I will carry with me throughout time.*
> *I want to tell you all what this meant to me, but I don't think there are words that could ever be right enough.*

Ena lingered, pen in hand. She wanted to sign her real name. She wanted them to know the truth. But what would Ena mean to them now? Her conversation with Dr. Docks lingered, a warning about time travel's unpredictability. She signed it: *Jennifer*

She folded the note and placed it on the kitchen table, her fingers hesitating just a beat before letting go. If this worked, if that was even the right word, this would be her final goodbye to Fiona. A truth wrapped in a lie.

She took another scrap of paper and scrawled a simpler message:

> *You inspire me—J*

She brought the second note upstairs and set it on top of the boombox in Tara's room. She stood there for a moment, taking it all in. The room of a girl becoming the woman who would one day be her mother. Ena had seen the pain Tara carried, the isolation, but also the strength. It humbled Ena in a way she hadn't expected. She saw her mother more clearly than ever before. *If I get back to my time*, Ena promised herself, *I'm going to go easier on her.*

In the bathroom, Ena picked up the red Hot Wheels toothbrush. She sighed. Tara's reluctant offering, her passive-aggressive gesture of control. No one was ever going to use the toothbrush. Ena slipped it into her jacket pocket, a keepsake.

Ena felt time pressing on her. She thought back to her conversation with Graeme and Byron. She needed to get back as soon as possible. Every second she spent here increased the risk of changing things.

Ena pulled out the tape she and her mom made. Her pulse quickened as the questions swirled. Would this work? What if it only half-worked, and she ended up lost? What if she got stuck here forever?

She closed her eyes and took a slow, steady breath. "What would Fiona do?"

She knew the answer. Fiona would try to get back. Face the consequences. Live her life.

Ena pulled out the Walkman and inserted the tape. She slipped the headphones over her ears, pressed play. Nothing. No whir of gears, no sound in the headphones, and no black dot.

Ena's heartbeat spiked from fast to something so wild even a death metal punk band couldn't keep up. This was her only hope. If this didn't work, she could really be stuck here.

She could imagine Skyler telling her to slow down her breath, close her eyes, and focus on what she could control. Ena did exactly that. Batteries. It's the most obvious, worth checking.

She headed to the kitchen, to the drawer where Graeme and Fiona kept the batteries. She hoped that's where they kept spare batteries in 1986. She slid open the drawer and saw the unmistakable packaging of batteries. She grabbed two AA batteries and raced back upstairs to the bathroom.

She popped the batteries in. Before loading the tape, she tested the Walkman. The gears whirred to life. Ena slipped the headphones back on, loaded the tape, and pressed play again.

Her voice and Tara's filled her ears. For a moment, Ena marveled at how unlikely this ticket home had been. A song, a moment of connection, a bit of luck, all colliding to give her this one chance. It struck her how easily it might never have come together.

The dot appeared. That same impossibly black, dime-sized dot.

Ena's breath caught. Fear clawed at her chest, but she pushed through it. She reached out and touched the dot.

It pulled her in.

This time, she was readier. Having a sense of what might happen next didn't make it any less strange, but it steadied her. She understood Skyler's word now.

Ineffable.

Here, time had no meaning. She sank into a sense of safety. Warmth. The music wasn't just sound; it was color, movement, waves that cradled her. Words failed her; the experience was beyond language, but the closest Ena could come was drawing the analogy of swimming in a warm rainbow ocean, each note wrapping around her like sunlight on water, beautiful and immersive, yet impossible to fully describe.

And then.

She was back. The light, the physicality, the sensation of reality hit her all at once. It hit harshly, jarring. Like being wrenched from a warm embrace and plunged into cold water. The air had edges. Time moved forward again. The safeness was gone, leaving only the ache of its absence. The contrast unsettled her, leaving her disoriented. Not just from the trip, but from the loss of that absolute security she had just lived.

The attic. The present.

She saw them. Tara and…her.

Another Ena.

The girl she had been, only minutes ago by this timeline. But Ena had grown. Different. She had seen her mother as a kid, had watched her build armor against a world that could be cruel. And now, here was Tara, vibrant, eyes closed, singing, so achingly present.

Ena had landed just behind them. She ducked behind a stack of boxes, heart pounding so hard she worried they might hear it over their singing.

She hadn't belonged in 1986. And now, seeing this, she did not fully belong here either. She was stretching across time, not fully belonging anywhere. Would she ever feel right again?

She had to stay hidden. She knew it instinctively, deeply, that she couldn't be seen. She had to trust this other Ena would follow the same steps, spill the bottle, scramble to catch it, so the path would hold. Allowing her to slip back into her life.

But what even was her life now?

She watched herself move through those actions half-remembered. The spill, the quick grab for the bottle before it shattered. Watching her own movements, fluid and instinctive, Ena saw it clearly, the same grace she had seen in young Jason, that morning he easily flipped the skateboard into his hand, just before his confidence cracked by Tara's sharp words.

She saw her father in herself. It was eerie. Unsettling. And, somehow, deeply reassuring.

As Ena watched herself descend the stairs to dry off the Walkman, she stayed still, waiting. Watching.

Tara lingered, her fingers brushing over the remnants of her youth. She picked up a pair of old jeans, worn thin with time, the left knee patched with a red-and-blue plaid iron-on. Ena held her breath as her mother traced the patch, a thoughtful crease forming between her brows.

What was she remembering?

The moment stretched, unsettling in its quiet presence. Did Tara recall handing over those jeans, tossing them carelessly to "Jennifer" all those years ago? Or was it just a fleeting, unremarkable memory for her—one of countless forgotten hand-me-downs?

Ena's awareness shifted subtly inside her. Seeing Tara here, in 2019, a woman so composed under fire, she suddenly understood, really *understood*, the battlefields her mother had walked to build that armor of composure. She had always known, in theory, that Tara had been a kid once, but this moment made it real. Made her *human*.

Ena waited until Tara turned away, then slipped toward the attic ladder, moving with quiet precision. As she reached the top, she feigned nonchalance, stepping up as if she were just returning.

"So, did it work?" Tara asked.

Ena froze.

"What?"

"The Walkman. Were you able to dry it? Does it still work?"

Ena masked her disorientation. "Oh, yeah. It works, but I think it's still a little off. Can I go talk to Granddad? See if he has any ideas about how to fix it?"

"Sure," Tara said, distracted. "I still have some sorting to do, but we're getting close to finishing this section."

Ena nodded and climbed down the ladder.

As her feet hit the floor, dizziness surged through her. The hallway wobbled, warped slightly at the edges. She was back. But back to what?

STRANGE MAGIC

Ena found Graeme in the living room, reading. The mustard-colored carpet was gone, replaced by hardwood floors that glowed with a subtle warmth she didn't remember. The matching wingback chairs, no longer purple but now a deep ochre, stood in their usual place, like sentinels from a different timeline. The garish patterned wallpaper had been replaced by neutral beige paint. The room felt both familiar and altered, like someone had rearranged her memories.

Graeme sat in his usual spot, so much like he had looked two nights ago, except those two nights were thirty-three years apart. His familiar mannerism, rubbing his chin as he read, hadn't changed, though his mustache was long gone.

Ena stood in the doorway, watching her granddad. She wasn't sure if she should tell him. If anyone could understand, it would be Graeme, but would he believe her? Time travel was, by definition, unbelievable. But it had happened. It was real.

And more than anything, she wanted to share it with someone who might believe her. Graeme felt like he might.

"Granddad?"

Graeme closed his book, his left index finger hooked over the edge to hold his place. "What can I do for you?"

Ena hesitated. "Um—I don't know how to say this, but…I just came back from 1986."

Graeme chuckled, shaking his head. "Oh, you mean going through the old things in the attic? That can take you back in time, I suppose."

"No." Ena shook her head and continued, "I mean I actually went back to 1986. I spent two days in this house with you, Fiona, Mike, Brandon, and Mom."

Graeme studied her, his amusement fading into more measured look. "Huh. You time-traveled?" His voice held the same even-keeled patience he always had with her, but there was a large measure of skepticism. "You sure you didn't hit your head up there?"

Ena pulled the Walkman from her pocket and held it up. "No, I traveled with this. I spilled something on it, some kind of liquid from one of the beakers in the attic. When I tried to clean it off and check if it still worked—poof! I was in 1986. In a recording studio, listening to the exact song I had been playing."

Graeme leaned forward, elbows on his knees. "Maybe you shocked yourself unconscious and had a vivid dream."

Deep creases formed on his forehead.

Maybe this was a mistake. Maybe I should have kept it to myself. Ena looked for a way to retreat, but no easy way to get out of this now.

"Ena, time travel doesn't exist. And even if it did, you don't just stumble into it by spilling some liquid on a Walkman." He gave her a soft, indulgent smile. "I do believe that you believe something happened. But sweetheart, there's got to be a logical explanation."

Ena's grip tightened on the Walkman. "Okay, then explain this."

She reached into her pocket and pulled out a red Hot Wheels toothbrush. "Mom gave this to me the first night I was there. In 1986. Fiona brought me in as one of her strays."

Graeme took the toothbrush, turning it over in his hands. His brow furrowed. "Hmm. Maybe you found it in an old box somewhere, and your brain just spun a story around it?"

Ena took back the toothbrush. "You would have known me as Jennifer Edison."

Graeme's eyes drifted to the ceiling in thought. "That name sounds vaguely familiar, but I don't recall where I heard it."

Ena's jaw clenched. "Then what about this?"

She pulled out a small, marbled triangle of pearlescent celluloid, the guitar pick she had never meant to steal. "I accidentally took this from the recording studio. It belonged to Eva Kinsella."

Graeme frowned. "Who's Eva Kinsella?"

The question hit her like a slap. She blinked. "Eva Kinsella. Lead singer of The Fin Whales. You know them. Fiona helped them get their big break."

Graeme's expression shifted. His concern deepened. "Sweetie, maybe we need to get you checked out. I don't recall Fiona ever helping a band called The Fin Whales."

Ena's stomach twisted. That wasn't possible.

She reached for her back pocket, certain the Fin Whales tape would be there. Her fingers met nothing. Her breath hitched. She checked the other pocket, then both again, panic rising.

The tape was gone. Ena's thoughts raced. Had she imagined it all? Was it just grief and music and Fiona's stories, stitched into some elaborate dream?

No. I still have the toothbrush and the guitar pick. Maybe the tape was just time travel can be messy or maybe I dropped it in the bathroom before coming back. I was there. I know it.

She took a breath, steadying herself. "Give me one more chance to prove it. Let's go to Fiona's study. If I can't convince you that there's a chance I really went back to 1986, then I'll drop it."

Graeme gave her a long, measured look. Ena knew that look. Graeme had his skeptical scientific face out in full force. She believed he was not convinced, but he was taking her seriously now.

He sighed, slowly lifting himself out of the chair. He placed a bookmark in his book and set it down on the side table. "Alright," he said, his patience noticeably thinning. "Let's get this over with."

They walked down the hallway to Fiona's study. Ena moved to Fiona's sound system and dropped the needle on "Echo Beach." That unmistakable guitar riff filled the room, sharp and nostalgic. Ena's heart pounded.

"For me, this was last night. For you, it was September of 1986. We had just finished the family singalong, and I asked Fiona how *True Notes* started. She brought you and me into this room. You both sat in the bay window. She put 'Echo Beach' on the record player." Ena pointed to the stereo.

Graeme closed his eyes, as if the music had tugged him backward in time.

"You told me about the night you met, how she dared you to play a David Bowie song at the bar where you were playing piano. How that challenge led to a whirlwind romance, to *True Notes*."

She moved to the framed first edition of *True Notes* on the wall. "And I learned *you* were the one who designed the cover. You drew it."

Graeme's expression shifted. He was no longer humoring her. He was listening.

"And," Ena pressed on, "like I said, you knew me as Jennifer Edison. That's the name I chose in 1986. The kids called me one of Fiona's 'strays.' "

Graeme's face went pale.

Ena could see it happening, the way his posture stiffened, the way his mind spun through old memories. His expression had morphed from patient indulgence to quiet doubt. Then, to a deeper reaction.

Recognition.

"I remember that night," he said, his voice quieter now. His eyes flicked to the bay window. "Oh! Now, I do remember Jennifer. Fiona was so taken with her. Said she had fire. Heart. And a presence we couldn't quite place."

His lips parted slightly as if piecing together a puzzle that had been long forgotten.

"Honestly, once she left, I don't think I ever thought much about her again. Until this very moment."

A long pause.

"There's no way you could know these things." Then he said, almost more to himself than to Ena, "It's not possible. It's simply not possible."

Another long pause.

"But if that's true, then time travel…" He trailed off, jaw tightening. "No. That's impossible. It breaks too many rules."

Graeme stood up, began pacing. His movements were agitated, unlike him.

"You must have found something in Fiona's journals."

"Granddad." Ena let out a frustrated breath. "Come on, do you really think I'd make a story like this up?"

Graeme closed his eyes again, the music stirring long-buried memories. "You're right, Ena. You would not make this up. I just can't reconcile the impossible story you are telling me. But this song, it takes me back to that night. Almost like I'm there. Everything you said was spot on."

Ena watched as the impossible settled into him. Slowly, reluctantly.

But it *was* possible.

Because it had happened.

Graeme's expression shifted. The warmth of a caring grandfather gave way to the sharp, analytical focus of a scientist.

"Alright, Ena," he said, his voice measured. "I'm not saying I'm fully convinced. But you've presented enough evidence that I can't just dismiss this outright."

He rubbed his chin in thought.

"For now," he said, "let's operate under the assumption that you *did* time travel. If that's true, how did you get back?"

Ena's throat tightened. "Granddad, that's the scariest part. I almost got stuck in 1986."

Graeme's brows lifted slightly, but he said nothing. He just listened.

"If Mom and I hadn't made this silly little recording right before I left…" Ena popped open the Walkman and pulled out the tape, the one with their impromptu family anthem. "This saved me."

She turned the cassette over in her hands before meeting Graeme's gaze. "When I played it, it brought me back to the attic. But when I got here, I wasn't *alone*."

Graeme narrowed his eyes.

"I saw myself," Ena said, her voice barely above a whisper. "I hid and watched as *I*, the *other* me, sang with Mom. I saw myself spill the liquid on the Walkman and head down the ladder just as I had done. And once Mom was alone, I acted like I was just coming back up the ladder."

Graeme stood a little straighter, his hand rubbing his chin, his gaze off in the distance.

She shook her head. "The other me had repeated my own steps *exactly*."

It was obvious to Ena that her granddad's scientific mind was already working through the implications. A loop. A closed cycle. Time travel. And she had barely escaped it.

Graeme let out a long exhale. "Oh boy. It couldn't be. Time travel can't exist."

He rubbed his chin, eyes narrowing in thought.

"It's all true, granddad."

"Your story is consistent, and the evidence you've presented is compelling. But I'm not ready to say I believe it fully. Yet I can't offer another explanation. A discovery of this magnitude, if true, comes with dangers we can't even begin to understand."

He met Ena's gaze.

"Tell me exactly what happened. Step by step," he said.

Ena nodded, steadying herself. "Okay. So, I was digging through some of Mom's old things in the attic, and I knocked over a beaker. I caught it before it hit the floor, but some of the liquid inside splashed onto the Walkman." She hesitated. "A lot of it."

Graeme stayed silent, listening.

"I went to the upstairs bathroom to dry it off and see if it still worked. I put in the tape, hit play, and this *thing* appeared. It was a black dot, about the size of a dime. Just *floating* right in front of me. And I touched it." She reached out like she was reliving it.

Graeme's brow furrowed.

"It was like I was being pulled and squeezed at the same time. It wasn't painful, but it was *weird*. Next thing I knew, I was in a recording studio, listening to the end of the song that had been playing." She shook her head, reliving the moment.

She offered a small, half-smile, aiming for levity, though her voice carried the sense of just how absurd it all sounded. "I hid under a couch for a while, then wandered outside, through town, and Fiona found me out front." Ena pointed to the street through the bay window. "And the rest, as they say, is *history.*"

Graeme was quiet for a long moment. Then, finally, he said, "Interesting. *Very* interesting."

His gaze was lost in thought for some time before he spoke again.

"The first thing we need to figure out is *exactly* what you spilled on the Walkman."

Ena's face brightened. "That's easy, I can show you."

Without hesitation, she led Graeme up to the attic.

At the top of the stairs, Tara was just finishing up the last of her sorting, dusting off her hands. "Perfect timing, Dad. Let me show you what we did." She gestured to four piles. "Keep, Donate, Toss, and Granddad Decides."

Graeme gave her an approving nod. "Great work, Tara. I'll go through the Decide pile later." Then, turning to Ena, he added, "She says her Walkman isn't working the way it should. I think she might have spilled something on it, and we're trying to figure out what."

While Graeme and Tara talked, Ena retraced her steps to where the beaker had fallen. She carefully picked it up, turning to Graeme with a steady gaze.

"Here," she said, holding it out.

Graeme took it, his face shifting from curiosity closer to alarm. His fingers tightened around the glass as he read the label: *Tachyon Solution.*

His expression darkened as he turned to Ena, keeping his voice steady, careful not to alarm Tara.

"I think," he said carefully, "we should take this to the workshop."

No One Is to Blame

Ena had never been in Graeme's workshop before. As Ena crossed the threshold, the lab was completely Graeme; every inch of space was optimized with ropes, levers, and pulleys designed for maximum efficiency. Tools of all kinds hung in designated spots, meticulously arranged yet clearly well-used. The room smelled of oiled machinery and a faint trace of sawdust, the scent of things built, fixed, and tinkered with over time.

Graeme let out a long sigh, somewhere between relief and apprehension. "Ena, I think you might be onto something here. I abandoned a project long ago. I thought it was impossible. I'd been chasing a version of time dilation, trying to squeeze more hours into a day. Not metaphorically. Literally. I tried to harness tachyons, particles that travel faster than the speed of light, backward through time. And they have imaginary mass."

Ena's forehead wrinkled. "Imaginary mass? What's that? Was it like Byron's imaginary friend we all had to pretend was real?"

Graeme chuckled. "Not exactly, but you're not completely wrong either. It's called imaginary mass because it is normal mass multiplied by the square root of negative one, an 'imaginary' number since it technically shouldn't exist. It's kind of like negative mass, but even weirder, and definitely more dangerous. Sort of like how Byron's imaginary friend wasn't real but still managed to shape his world and experiences."

Ena's nose crinkled. This made no sense to her. "Okay," she said, clearly unconvinced.

Graeme smiled. "Don't worry if it doesn't click yet. The key part is that the tachyon solution might explain part of time travel. But what it doesn't explain is how you ended up in specific times and places."

Graeme wheeled out a large whiteboard and made three columns: *Observations*, *Hypotheses*, *Evidence*.

Under observations, Graeme wrote: *Traveled to 1986 – Fin Whales Tape, Traveled back to 2019 – Ena & Tara Tape.*

It was Ena's turn to grin knowingly. "When I was in 1986, I did some research. I had to use a microfish—"

"Microfiche," Graeme said, amused.

"Whatever. Google before they had Google. Anyway, I found this article by a local professor. I tracked her down, and she said if time travel was even possible, the bigger problem would be controlling where and when you arrive. She believed" —Ena made air quotes—"encoded data could fix an exit point in time and space, but honestly, she seemed to think it was all impossible."

Ena shook her head, and Graeme gazed at her thoughtfully.

"At first, I didn't really get it. I mean, how could data have anything to do with time travel?"

She shook the Walkman in her hand, gripping it tighter. "But then I remembered watching Tara saving programs on cassette with her Commodore-64. I never thought of tapes holding anything but music. And then I thought maybe music was more like data. Dr. Docks mentioned waveforms, and I thought about sound waves. And well, I just kind of put them together. Music is sound waves, tapes held data. Well, maybe that was good enough to create a way home. It was my only hope."

Graeme's face softened with nostalgia. "That's really impressive, Ena."

Ena pressed on, feeling the energy of her own revelation. "The first time I time-traveled, I had no idea what happened. But having seen Tara use those tapes, it started coming together. It started making sense. Then I thought, Mom and I had recorded that song in the here and now. Couldn't that create the path home? And I tried it. I was really afraid that it wouldn't work or would leave me lost in the nothingness in between, but it did work."

"Ena," Graeme shook his head, equal parts astonished and moved. "What you did? That wasn't just brave. That was brilliant."

After a long pause considering what may have been, Graeme snapped back into scientist mode. "That could be our first real hypothesis: the tape somehow carries the coordinates that lock in the exit point."

Ena added, "Yeah, and I guess our other hypothesis is I traveled by wormholes."

Graeme's brow furrowed, his mind working through it.

"Alright," he said, voice measured. "Let's see if we can test these hypotheses. You said when you played a tape on the Walkman, a dime-sized black dot appeared, but nothing happened until you touched it?" Ena nodded.

"Do you have a tape with you?"

"Yeah. The song I made with Mom is still in the Walkman. I can rewind it if you want."

Graeme nodded. "Alright. But listen to me carefully. Once it starts playing, neither one of us touches anything."

Ena nodded her acknowledgment and rewound the tape, pressed play, and held the Walkman steady in her hands.

Within seconds, a black dot flickered into existence in front of her.

Graeme's jaw dropped. His hands gripped the workbench like he needed to ground himself in reality. "I think you can stop the tape now."

Ena hit the stop button. The dot vanished. Graeme whistled softly, running a hand through his hair. His voice, when he spoke, was thick with a tone between awe and terror. "Well, this is the most unexpected thing."

He paused, his brow furrowing, then met her eyes. "Ena, I think you were close. That looked like a micro black hole."

Graeme went to the whiteboard and under *wormhole* added *black hole / white hole*.

"What's a white hole?" Ena asked.

"A black hole pulls everything in, nothing escapes, not even light. A white hole is the opposite. It pushes everything out, and nothing can go in. Some scientists think every black hole is connected to a white hole somewhere else. Everything that gets pulled in might come out again, just in a completely different place."

Graeme wrote under the hypothesis: *Tape is the time travel operant.*

"Let's test this hypothesis," Graeme said and pulled out an old tape recorder from one of the drawers. He put the same tape into a different tape player. Nada. Graeme crossed out that hypothesis.

Graeme and Ena spent the next hour creating and testing hypotheses and filling the whiteboard. Eventually, Ena wrote the last things on the whiteboard.

Rules governing time travel (as we understand):
1)   The specific tachyon-infused Walkman facilitates time travel
2)   The cassette sets the time and place for the exit 'white hole'
3)   Time traveler must contact the micro black hole to enter
4)   Black hole disappears if music stops or time traveler enters
with the Walkman

She stood back from the board for a moment and then wrote down a question: *Is the Walkman permanently capable of time travel, or will it wear out?*

Graeme let out a long, slow exhale, rubbing his jaw. "You didn't just survive time travel. You solved it."

Ena beamed. She had been fully absorbed in working with Graeme, and to hear those words from her grandfather was like winning a gold medal.

"Do you remember the professor's name?" Graeme asked.

"Dr. Para Docks."

An ambiguous look flickered across Graeme's face, recognition, maybe even concern. It was gone in an instant, replaced by a neutral expression.

Ena caught it. "Do you know her, Granddad?"

Graeme hesitated just long enough to make her suspicious. "In passing. She's a brilliant scientist." He left it at that, but Ena sensed there was more he wasn't saying.

Ena wanted to press him, but he steered the conversation back. "Well, we have a working theory. The evidence is lining up."

He inhaled deeply, steadying himself before continuing.

"Experimenting with actual time travel scares me beyond words. I can think of nothing more dangerous. We need to proceed with extreme caution."

Ena turned to Graeme, "So our working theory is 'You got tachyons on my Walkman'?"

Graeme laughed and replied, "No, you got Walkman on my tachyons."

Ena laughed. "Great. Now I suddenly have a sugar craving."

Graeme's smile lingered for only a moment before fading. His posture straightened, and his tone shifted, the importance of their conversation settling back in.

Her breath caught.

"Ena, you are the first-time explorer." Graeme's expression softened, his voice going quiet, almost unsteady. "I am just so incredibly grateful you made it back to us. That you were smart enough, and lucky enough."

He exhaled sharply, like he had been holding his breath for days, and pulled Ena into a tight embrace. She wasn't expecting it, and for a second, she just stood there, stiff. But then a mix of feelings inside her cracked. She had made it back.

But she almost hadn't. The memory rushed in. Standing in 1986, heart pounding, unsure if the Walkman would work, if she'd ever make it back. And then the in-between. Safe but unmoored. What if she had gotten stuck there? Her breath caught as she squeezed Graeme back, gripping his shirt like an anchor.

When he finally pulled away, his eyes were glassy, his hands still resting on her shoulders as if afraid to let go.

His voice, now steadier but heavy with finality, left no room for argument. "This is the most dangerous discovery I have ever encountered. We tell no one. We use it *never*. And I mean tell no one, Ena. Not a soul outside this room."

Ena shivered. For the first time, the full magnitude of what had happened settled over her. Not just the adventure, not just the thrill of discovery, but the terrifying *almost* of it all. She had nearly been lost. Not lost in the way people say when they take a wrong turn or misplace their keys. *Truly* lost. Stuck in another time, or worse, suspended in that strange, swirling space, colorful, endless, but untethered from anything real. No time, no direction, no guarantees. If that had happened, no one could have saved her. Not Graeme. Not her parents. Not anyone. She would have just—

Disappeared.

She had to reach out to the table to steady herself before asking, "So, what now, Granddad?"

Graeme stared at the floor, his hand moving to his chin in that familiar way he did when he was deep in thought. When he finally spoke, his voice was quiet but firm. "Ena, I have to be honest. I can't have this here."

He let out a slow breath and looked lost in thought before he spoke again.

"I want to experiment. I want to understand it. Heck, I want to see Fiona and tell her to stop smoking. I know it's too dangerous, but I don't know if I'm strong enough to say no."

He lifted his gaze to meet hers. She hadn't thought about that. She was suddenly feeling the weight of it all.

"Will you swear to me, Ena? Swear that you won't use this again? That you'll put the Walkman and the tachyon solution somewhere no one can ever find it? We got lucky once. We can't risk it again."

Ena stared at him, her understanding of Graeme tilting into new territory. Graeme admitting weakness, deferring to her, trusting her to be the stronger one, was unexpected and empowering.

She took a slow breath, her fingers tracing the edges of the Walkman. It felt heavier now, not just an object but a doorway to the *impossibly possible*, and she was about to lock it away forever. A quiet sense of loss settled over her.

But she knew what had to be done.

"I know exactly where to put it." She met Graeme's eyes, steady and sure. "I promise I won't use it. I know how close I came to being lost, and I don't want that again. Like, ever."

Graeme let out a relieved exhale, his shoulders sagging slightly. He gently draped an arm over Ena's shoulders, his touch warm and steady.

As they stepped away, Ena stole a quick look back at the workshop, so completely *him*. Order designed to bend reality. A place where ideas had been tested, where more had failed than succeeded. And yet, he was willing to bury what might be his greatest discovery, well, *partially* his.

Graeme gave her a small squeeze, then guided her out of the workshop and back toward the house. "I'm so proud of you," he whispered, his voice low but full. "You did something I never thought possible."

All We Ever Knew

Graeme and Ena stepped into the kitchen. The scent of freshly brewed tea filled the air. Tara sat at the table, fingers curled around a steaming mug, gazing into it as if it held answers.

"I made tea," she said. "Dad? Ena?" She poured two cups before either could answer.

Graeme accepted his with a grateful nod. Tara brushed dust off her jeans and rolled her shoulders. "We got a good amount done today, but there's still a lot left in the attic. Maybe we can bring Jason and Byron over tomorrow and knock out more. If you're up for it, Dad, you could make your famous stew. We'll do a family dinner."

A wistful smile flickered across Graeme's face. "That sounds wonderful."

"Good. That's settled, then." Tara tapped a knuckle against the table. "Before we're done, we need trash bags to bundle up the Toss and Donate piles. Ena, can you grab the box of bags? We can do a Goodwill run on our way home."

Graeme sipped his tea. "You need a milk crate for the books you're keeping?"

Tara added, her tone quickening slightly, "O! Ena, Graeme, find that too."

Ena hesitated. The words rang a little weird. "I think there's some in Fiona's office," she said finally, setting her tea aside. "I'll check."

"Thanks, honey." Tara nodded agreement.

Ena slipped out of the kitchen, heading toward Fiona's study.

The last time she had been here alone was when she left her note for the family, the note from Jennifer. Had they ever talked about it? Or had it just become one more inexplicable mystery, consumed by time?

She stood at the doorway for a moment, inhaling the scent of old paper and wood polish. This time, she wasn't sneaking or scrambling to prove she wasn't crazy. This time, she could take it in.

Her eyes landed on the bay window bench.

A pulse of memory hit, Fiona's foot nudging the baseboard, the soft click of a hidden compartment unlocking.

Her breath quickened.

Could the bootleg cassette tapes still be there?

Heart pounding, Ena moved toward the bench and lifted the blankets and boxes stacked neatly inside. She pressed her foot against the baseboard, just as Fiona had.

Nothing.

A hollow disappointment sank into her gut. *No. That isn't right.* Fiona wouldn't have just gotten rid of them. Those tapes were history, her story. She wouldn't have tossed them.

Ena adjusted her stance and tapped a little higher, a little harder.

This time, a faint creak.

Her pulse spiked. The mechanism was stiff, years of disuse making it sluggish. She wedged her fingers beneath the compartment's edge, gritting her teeth as she tugged.

It gave way. A hidden world unfolded before her. Ena's heart raced with excitement. An opportunity to connect with Fiona she had never imagined until today.

The stash had grown to a vast collection of cassettes, meticulously labeled, chronicling a lifetime of music no one else had.

At the very top, nestled on top of the cases, was a sealed envelope.

Ena froze.

Fiona's handwriting.

Her name scrawled in big, confident letters: *Ena.*

A message meant for her.

Her hands trembled as she picked up the envelope, tracing the ink. How? Why? How could Fiona have known she would find this?

Anxiety. Fear. Hope. Joy. The emotions rolled over her, too tangled to sort.

Fiona's final words.

She sank onto the floor, back against the bench, the letter resting in her lap. Carefully, she unfolded it.

> *December 4, 2018*
> *Ena (or should I say Jennifer),*

What the what? She knew. How? Graeme had no idea. She never said a word, not to me, not to Graeme, not to anyone.

> *I imagine you might be surprised. Let me answer your first question. I was suspicious then, but I wasn't certain until this fall, when we spent so much time together.*
> *My dear, I cherished those moments. And it became so clear, the Jennifer who visited in 1986 and the Ena I knew in 2018 were one and the same. And the time of your trip to 1986 is imminent.*
> *So, let's set some rules:*

Rule 1: DO NOT TIME TRAVEL – EVER.
(Because if I say it twice, it'll work, right?)
Rule 2: If you do time travel (seriously, don't), you <u>can't</u>
tell me anything about the future. Nothing. Nada. Zilcho.
Rule 3: If we meet in the past, never tell me your real
name. That's for your parents to decide. I love your name,
and I'd hate to think that knowing it could in itself alter it.
Jennifer Edison will do just fine. (By the way, your dad is
Ed Edison. Guess you were under Pressure. Maybe Queen
had it right.)

I am entrusting these bootleg cassettes to you. Guard
them. Protect them. Never sell them. Don't digitize them,
don't upload them.

I know I shouldn't have them, but they are our secret.
Our history.

Baby-girl, I love you to the moon and back. You are
smart, wise, strong, and loyal. I admire you and the woman
you are becoming.
—Fiona

Ena pressed the letter to her chest, her breath unsteady. Fiona knew. She had always known. Carefully, she folded the note and tucked it back into the envelope. The cassettes were a treasure: rare, irreplaceable pieces of music history. But compared to this? They were nothing.

Her mind drifted back to baking Christmas cookies. Fiona's eyes closed, remembering, "Echo Beach" playing softly in the background. That offhand comment about the song taking her somewhere. Could that somewhere have been the night in her study in 1986, talking to a stranger who wasn't really a stranger at all?

It struck with a quiet finality, the kind that rewrites what you thought you knew. Fiona had carried this secret for years, quietly, fiercely, without ever letting a hint slip. It was so completely Fiona. And yet, it made Ena ache, like she was losing her all over again, like discovering a new piece of Fiona just in time to have it vanish. Grief didn't wait its turn. It rushed in sideways, unexpected.

Ena wiped a tear from her cheek. The ache was sharp; she wanted to talk to Fiona. To thank her. To ask her everything. But she couldn't. And that impossibility let loose another wave of loss crashing into her again.

Fiona had given the bootleg cassettes to her. But she had also warned her to keep them secret. How was she supposed to get them out of the house without anyone noticing?

Her gaze flicked to the hidden compartment, the tapes still nestled inside. For now, they were safe. She would figure out the next step later. Right now, she had to get back to her mom. She replaced the blankets, smoothing them out. In the corner of the office, she spotted the empty milk crates and grabbed one. With one last glance at the hidden compartment, she left the office.

Back to Tara. Back to the rest of the day. Back to a world where Fiona was gone. Yet, somehow, Ena felt both the sting of loss and an even deeper closeness to her grandmother. They now shared secrets of time travel and bootleg cassettes, of things that no one else could ever fully understand.

Ena and Tara headed back up to the attic to finish the day's work. They filled bags with things to donate and toss, while Ena grabbed the milk crate and packed up the books Tara was holding onto. As she worked, her eyes drifted to the cassette case she had insisted on keeping earlier this morning.

Earlier. The word was not exactly right. Squeezed between this morning and now, she had lived two full days in 1986. The thought made her dizzy.

A plan started to form—the cassette case, a smuggler, and bootlegger. Tomorrow, she would hide Tara's cassette case in the bench, and when the time was right, she'd load Fiona's tapes to smuggle them to her bedroom.

Ena helped Tara pack up the minivan. A silver minivan.

Wait. When did we get a silver minivan?

Her stomach twisted. Their van was blue. It was blue that morning.

The realization hit her like a jolt of static electricity. A shift. A tiny, seemingly insignificant change, but a change nonetheless. Her time travel had left a mark.

Small. Insignificant. But real.

Ena steadied herself, forcing herself to appear unfazed. *No one can know.* Graeme's warning echoed in her mind. *Not Mom. Not Dad. No one.*

She kept quiet as they drove, her thoughts racing. If the color of the van had changed, what else might be different?

After dropping off the donations, they returned home. Ena took her bounty upstairs, her mom's old cassettes and the battered boom box to play them on. But as soon as she stepped into her room, things were wrong.

Her gaze snapped to the wall.

Where her *The Fin Whales* poster had once hung, there was now a *Cranberries* poster.

Her breath hitched. *No. That doesn't make sense.* She loved The Fin Whales. They were her favorite band. The Cranberries were great, sure, but they weren't *her* band.

Ena felt rocked, what she believed to be constants were changing under her feet. These were little things. Trivial things. But what if there were more? *What if it didn't stop at posters and minivans? What about Skyler, Piney, Byron? Were they still safe?*

She grabbed her phone and opened the group chat.

ENA: *Hey Guys, what's up?*

SKYLER: *The Sky, my mood, Sound logic's outlook. U?*

PINEY: *E, not ur usual text, you ok?*

ENA: *Yep am now. Been a weekend.*

Ena put the phone down, relieved. What a day, if that was even the right word. Secrets with Graeme. Secrets with Fiona. And now, the biggest one yet, Fiona had known. Somehow, she had always known. But Ena couldn't tell anyone. She would have to carry it alone. She would have to lie, if only by omission, to her parents, her friends, even Graeme.

Was it worth it? Would she trade the burden of these secrets for never having gone to 1986 at all?

She didn't know. She wasn't sure she was strong enough to carry this burden.

But for now, she had no choice.

In My Life

Ena slept deeply, exhaustion pressing her into a dreamless darkness. She was yanked from it by her mother's sharp voice. "Ena, get up. Get dressed. We're leaving in ten minutes."

She groaned, rolling over to check her phone—9:50. She'd slept nearly thirteen hours.

Panic jolted her upright. She scrambled into a sweatshirt and old jeans, brushed her teeth in record time, and jogged downstairs. The family was waiting for her.

They all headed to the silver minivan. Silver still wasn't right to her.

Byron hopped into the backseat ahead of her, slouching in his bucket seat, his expression unreadable. Ena slid in after him, glancing his way, just a flicker of a look.

And then she froze.

His eyes were green.

Her stomach tightened.

No. That wasn't right. Byron's eyes had always been brown. Deep brown. Like Jason's.

But now they were undeniably green. A bright, striking green.

The change itself seemed insignificant. Just pigment. A few strands of DNA expressing differently. But what did that mean for him?

Would people see him differently? Would it change who noticed him? Who liked him? How teachers treated him? It was such a small thing, but life was made of small things, tiny dominoes knocking into each other, altering the course of everything that followed.

And she had done this.

A slow, creeping unease settled deep into her bones.

It had been her.

She hadn't meant to. She hadn't even known she could. But she had. Her time in 1986—things she had done, something she had changed, maybe just her presence—had rippled forward and rewritten this one tiny thing.

And if Byron's eyes had changed, what else had?

She hadn't realized she was staring until Byron exclaimed, "Hey, weirdo, quit staring and just get in."

Her pulse stumbled. She forced herself to smirk. "Dufus, there's nothing to stare at. Don't flatter yourself."

Byron rolled his *green* eyes and turned away.

Ena swallowed and stared straight ahead as Jason pulled the van onto the street.

Outside, the world looked the same.

But Byron's eyes weren't.

And that meant she had rewritten history somehow. She couldn't undo it.

♪ ♫ ♪

The day blurred into dust and decisions. The attic was full of history, boxed up and waiting to be sorted, heavy with memories. At one point, Tara reached for one of Fiona's boxes, but Graeme's hand landed gently on her arm.

245

"I don't think I'm ready for that just yet."

Tara paused, reading the tension in her father's face. Her voice softened. "Of course, Dad. You know me, I get too mechanical. Just tackle the things in front of me."

Graeme gave her a small nod, gratitude unspoken but understood.

They worked until fatigue settled over them like the dust in the air. Tara clapped her hands together, shaking loose dust from her palms. "I think this is a great stopping point. What do you think, Dad?"

Graeme surveyed the half-empty attic, and Ena could read a mix of relief and loss settling in his eyes. Fiona. Pieces of their children's histories long buried.

"I reckon this is as good a place to stop as any," he said, his gaze drifting over the past, once buried, now unearthed. "Dinner's probably getting close to ready. Let's clean up a little and serve up some supper."

The family gathered around the dining room table, the rich, savory aroma of Graeme's stew mingling with the warmth of freshly baked soda bread. The scent wrapped around Ena like a familiar embrace, momentarily soothing her. It felt good, needed, to be with her family in this moment. She let herself settle into the feeling, taking in the scene around her. Her time travel dalliance hadn't touched her family, well, except for Byron's eye color.

Byron laid out the plates, the slight clank marking each placement. As Ena looked around the table, her throat tightened. There was no plate in front of Fiona's seat. The space was empty, as empty as the chair that would never again hold her grandmother. A sharp tug of grief pulled at Ena's heart, the unwelcome reminder pressing in. Loss layered upon loss. Frustration and anger threatened to bubble over, but she forced them down.

She forced herself to sit, shifting her focus. She shifted her gaze from Graeme to her mother, noting their identical smiles. That smile, she had barely seen it on young Tara's face in 1986. And Jason, his movements still held the echoes of the effortless grace she had seen in him as a boy. He slid into his chair with practiced ease, but now there was a difference, a slight hesitation, a quiet reminder that time had reshaped him. Her parents were now older than Fiona and Graeme had been in 1986. That realization sent a wave of unease through her, the inevitability of it all. Graeme, who had once been a man in his early forties, was now unquestionably old. His movements were more careful, his strength beginning to wane.

It was too much. Too much to hold in, too much to process. The air, thick with her memories, made it hard to breathe.

Ena pushed back her chair abruptly. "I—I just need to…need a moment," she stammered, not waiting for a response as she hurried away from the table. Her heart pounded in her chest as she moved through the house, barely keeping herself together.

She found herself in Fiona's study before she even realized her feet had carried her there. The familiar space welcomed her, a sanctuary. She sat at Fiona's desk, gripping its edges as she let out a shaky breath.

Speaking to the air, to Fiona, to nothing, she whispered, "This is so much. I miss you so much."

Tears slipped down her cheeks as she drank in the familiar study. The memories here were still fresh, still vibrant. She smiled through the tears, letting the thought settle. She had been given a gift so rare, so impossible: more time. Fiona had trusted her, had let her in, had shared her secrets. The hidden stash of bootleg tapes was a piece of herself, a gift.

And so was this. Right now.

Time with Graeme. Time with Mom. Dad. Even Byron.

She shouldn't be here, alone in her grief, when the very thing she was mourning was still present in so many ways. Time would keep marching forward, with or without her.

She might as well enjoy the ride.

That's what Fiona would do.

Ena inhaled deeply, drawing strength from Fiona's presence in every nook of this room. Her eyes landed on the framed first edition of Fiona's magazine. With quiet reverence, she kissed her fingertips and pressed them against the glass. "To the moon and back," she whispered.

She returned to the dinner table, sliding into her seat with renewed steadiness. The loss she felt in the room hadn't lifted, but it had shifted. It was no longer just grief. It was gratitude, love, family held in a moment. A moment that couldn't be repeated.

Tara met her eyes, understanding reflected in her gaze. "Ena, you doing okay?"

"Yeah, Mom. I just needed a moment." Ena turned to Graeme. "Thank you for dinner, Granddad."

Graeme gave a small, knowing nod. No words needed.

Jason leaned back with a sly grin. "You know, Graeme, this is delicious. I'd go so far as to say stew-pendous."

A groan rippled around the table. "Dad, no," Byron exclaimed.

Graeme chuckled. "Jason, I regret every time I encouraged you to speak."

Laughter bubbled up from Ena, unfiltered and free. It was a laugh well-earned, carrying the ghost of grief and the comfort of family.

EVERYTHING HAS CHANGED

Ena's day at school was like watching TV in 8K compared to the fuzzy, static-riddled picture of 1980s television she had seen just a few days ago. Everything was sharper, more vivid, too vivid. She moved through the day hypervigilant, scanning her surroundings, trying to determine what had changed. Ena's muscles coiled, a tight knot of fear and dread winding through her as she braced herself for what she might uncover.

As she passed the trophy case on her way to English class, her stomach twisted. Were all those trophies always there? Especially that big one in the back? Doubt crept in, making her feel adrift in a reality that wasn't quite right. But unlike the eerie safety she had experienced in the in-between moments of time travel, this was unnerving, disorienting. Her nerves were raw.

Then she spotted Piney and Skyler talking in front of their lockers. A wave of relief crashed over her. They were just as she remembered. Same expressions, same warmth. Her friends, unchanged, eager and happy to see her.

"Hey, youse!" Ena called out in an exaggerated Boston accent, forcing her voice to sound light, normal. Then her eyes landed on Piney's messenger bag. It was similar to the one she remembered, but the flap was blue denim, not black, and instead of the *404: Not Found* patch, there was an embroidered pixelated raccoon with the words *Data Bandit*.

"Sweet new bag, Piney," Ena said, keeping her tone casual.

Piney gave her a weird look. "Um, thanks? But this is the same bag I've had all year. You okay?"

Boom. It hit Ena again like a sneaker wave, another change. Unexpected. Insignificant, yet completely shattering.

"Oh, yeah. Must have been the light," Ena said quickly, scrambling for an explanation. "The blue flap looked black when I was walking up. I'm such a dummy."

Skyler tilted their head, studying her with that deep, thoughtful, investigative stare. They didn't say anything, but Ena could see their skepticism. Like they could sense she wasn't telling the full truth.

The three of them continued walking down the hall, while Ena's heart pounded in her chest. She was seeing her familiar school with new eyes. And she wasn't sure she liked what she was seeing. Her gaze caught Madison up ahead, laughing with a pack of friends. She looked unchanged. Same perfect hair. Same too-loud voice. Same self-assured walk that carved through the crowd like she owned it.

Later in the morning, when she got to history class, Ena took her normal seat; at least, she hoped it was her normal seat. No one said anything. Relief flooded her, and her shoulders relaxed slightly. At least this wasn't different.

She scanned the room, eyes flicking across familiar desks, walls, and windows. But now, every detail seemed sharper, as if she were seeing them for the first time. How much had she overlooked before? And how much had actually changed?

Then her gaze landed at the front of the room, and the all-too-familiar acknowledgment of yet another thing being different hit her like a punch to the gut.

The poster.

It had always been there. It had always said, "Those who fail to learn history are condemned to repeat it." A staple of every history classroom.

But now. Now, it was a picture of Einstein with the words: "Education is not the learning of facts but the training of the mind to think."

Ena's stomach twisted. Maybe it wasn't a big deal. Maybe the teacher just swapped it out. But the all-too-familiar unease settled deep in her bones. She looked at her classmates, none seemed to notice or care.

It was another change.

Then her eyes landed on Mr. Dickerson. He was no longer clean-shaven, he had a well-groomed but bushy goatee hanging from his chin, almost like a billy goat. Ena started feeling a level of frustration reaching new heights, she made tight fists, her knuckles white with the tension. She was beginning to feel like she was on a terrible amusement ride with no way off. How could so many things be different? There was no way Mr. Dickerson grew a goatee like that in a weekend. She was only in 1986 for two days, why so many differences?

The day dragged on, tension coiled tight in her body, never easing. When teachers called on her, she responded abruptly, curtly. Everything everyone talked about seemed insignificant as Ena continued to observe little things that were different and so many details she now noticed, unsure if they were different or not. Ena wanted this to end, she wanted to be home, in her room, insulated from the inundation of these details. It was so much, it was so close to too much.

Finally, lunch arrived.

To Ena's relief, they took their normal table. Skyler looked at Ena, in their quiet, thoughtful way, and asked, "Ena, what is wrong? Don't say nothing. We know something is wrong."

Tension rose in Ena. She had promised. She had sworn to Graeme that she would tell no one. But how can she bear this alone? This is Piney and Skyler two people she trusted more than any other. Skyler was the smartest person she knew, had ever known. They would be able to understand.

Her eyes brimmed as she faced Skyler and Piney. "I want to tell you, but I can't. I swore I wouldn't."

"You know that is usually a bad sign when someone swears you to secrecy," replied Piney.

"No, no, it's not like that; it's not cringy at all. It's just insane. You wouldn't believe anyway. It's crazy unbelievable, it's got me off balance. I shouldn't talk about it anyway. Trust me though, it's not bad. Just really not believable."

"You can trust us, Ena. We can help. You are so obviously going to break under this burden." Skyler's eyes and facial expression were full of empathy and care. It was the last domino to fall that broke Ena's resolve.

"You are not going to believe this. I am still having problems believing it myself. My weekend was longer than yours, way longer. I time-traveled to 1986 and spent two days trying to figure out how to get back."

Piney let out a sharp chuckle, loud enough to turn a few heads at nearby tables. She shook her head, crossing her arms. "Okay, Ena, you had me. If you don't want to tell us what's wrong, fine. That's your choice." Frustration edged her voice, the sting of being shut out clear in her eyes.

"Piney, I swear on everything I care about, on my guitar. I was in 1986. Things are different here…now. You know this morning when I said something about your messenger bag? It is different. It used to be brown and black, and your patch used to say *404: Not Found.* I don't get it. Why would that change? Why are so many things different? So many other things just feel off."

"Okay, we have to think through this," Skyler said, taking the lead. "Ena, explain how. It's not like you have a time machine parked in your driveway."

Ena studied Skyler's face. She felt a mixture of relief and frustration—relief that Skyler wasn't dismissing her but frustration that they were not fully believing her. "My granddad and I sort of figured it out like this. I accidentally spilled tachyons, don't even ask, on a Walkman. I had found it in the attic we were cleaning out. When I played a tape, I went back to 1986. I was literally in the recording studio where the band made their album. Eventually, I got back to the here and now by playing a goofy tape my mom and I had made in the attic. But I spent two full days with my grandparents with my mom and uncles as kids, in 1986. It sounds fake, but it happened."

Skyler became deeply thoughtful, not convinced but, in Skyler's particular way, very open to the idea that Ena might be telling the truth. "Huh, you convinced your grandfather that you time-traveled? That's impressive. What was the tape you listened to that sent you to 1986?"

"Oh, it was The Fin Whales. What's so weird, my Fin Whales poster was gone when I came back, replaced by The Cranberries. So weird. My granddad did not even remember them and Fiona was so pivotal in helping them make it."

"The who?" Piney asked.

"No, not The Who. The Fin Whales," Ena said, her brow knotting in frustration. "You know they're my favorite band of all time."

Skyler, exuding calmness, asked, "What did you do in the studio?"

Ena thought back. "Not much. Mainly hid under this kind of gross orange couch. When they went to lunch, I walked around the studio, but I still thought I was dreaming. I had no clue what happened. Once they came back, I dove back under the couch. No one ever saw me. I spoke to no one."

Skyler frowned. "Hmm, did you touch anything?"

Ena thought back. "I picked up Eva Kinsella's guitar pick, but they came back before I could put it back down."

Piney asked, "Who is Eva Kinsella?"

"Lead singer of The Fin Whales. I can't understand why you don't remember this. It's really freaking me out."

Skyler's eyes brightened with the dawning of understanding. "And the butterfly flapped its wings."

Ena frowned. "What does that even mean?"

Skyler leaned in, calm but intense. "It means you changed something. You took the guitar pick. That tiny change might've set off a whole chain reaction. If you hadn't been there, the pick would've stayed. No disruption. But because you *were* there and the pick *wasn't*, well, that might've been just enough to shift everything. The Fin Whales didn't make it. They fell off the edge."

A shiver went up Ena's spine. "Because of a *pick*?"

"Because of a moment," Skyler said. "Sometimes that's all it takes."

"No, that can't be." Ena shook her head violently. "They were too good to be obscure."

She turned to Piney, desperation creeping into her voice. "Piney, you can find them. Check Spotify. Check socials. Please, just show me they existed."

Piney didn't hesitate, already pulling out her laptop, fingers flying over the keys. The glow of the screen reflected off her glasses as she searched, brows furrowing deeper the longer she typed.

What felt like minutes stretched. Ena's breath was trapped in her chest. Ena watched Piney type away, silently bargaining with the universe. If Piney found them, maybe this wasn't real. Maybe she hadn't broken the world.

Finally, Piney shook her head and said, her voice flat, "Not on Spotify. Nothing on socials. No Wikipedia. No old reviews. If I can't find them, they might as well have never existed."

Ena's stomach plummeted.

This can't be real.

She had spent hours listening to their songs, their lyrics carving into her soul, leaving echoes she could still hear. The music that had once been a part of her life was now just, silence. As if it had never been there at all.

But it had been.

She remembered. And that meant other people should have too. Millions had loved them. Their music had been woven into the fabric of people's lives, their songs the soundtrack to countless moments. And now, all of it was gone. Not just a band, but an entire legacy. The fans who had once filled arenas, the people who had been moved by their lyrics, the cultural ripple effect they had left behind. It had all been stolen.

And all because of her.

A single missing guitar pick, a stupid, thoughtless action, had been enough to shift them from rising legends to total obscurity. Had she at least saved them from that awful, fatal crash? She could only hope, but she had no way of knowing. Had she traded one tragedy for another?

This was so unfair. She never meant to erase them.

The bell rang. Lunch was over. Ena had barely touched her food, but that was okay, she hadn't felt like eating. Crestfallen, she trudged to mandatory outdoor time, her feet dragging, every step an effort.

As they headed outside, Skyler opened their backpack and handed her a black-and-white notebook. "Ena, you know things are different. What if you wrote down all the changes you notice?"

Ena turned the notebook in her hands. The idea of writing things down made everything feel all the more real. Like writing 'The Fin Whales gone' would carry even more weight.

"You're probably right." She bit her lip, then said, "I don't know why it feels worse to write things down."

The day passed in a haze. Teachers droned on, their voices blending into a dull hum, unnoticed and unheeded. Notes were scribbled on whiteboards, equations solved, history dissected, but none of it touched her. She tried to focus on the whiteboards, on the teachers, but the words may as well have been hieroglyphs, indecipherable, meaningless. Her thoughts dragged her back, relentless, pulling her deeper into the turmoil.

Guilt, anger, denial, frustration, each emotion took its turn, clashing and colliding inside her. She had made a ripple in time, a change so small that expanded to an effect so devastating. But if The Fin Whales never made it big, how could she remember them? How could she still hear their songs in her head, still see those moments with Fiona so clearly? She could hear Fiona's voice, enthusiastic and knowing, breaking down the magic of each song, explaining how she had helped them get their first break, how she had believed in them before anyone else did. Fiona had been part of their rise, their success. And yet now, that history was erased. Had it ever truly happened?

Was her memory lying to her? Had it really happened? Could she exist in both versions of the world? One where The Fin Whales had soared and another where they had sunk before they could rise?

Questions without answers. Questions she didn't want answers to.

This was harder than being in 1986. Back then, at least, she had been fighting to get home. Now? Now she wasn't sure where home even was.

SHAKE IT OUT

Once school finally ended, Ena, Piney, and Skyler found each other by the lockers.

"Are we still practicing today at your place, Piney?" Skyler asked, adjusting the straps of their overstuffed backpack.

"Definitely," Piney responded, then looked over at Ena. "You up for it?"

Ena barely registered the question at first, still shaken, thoughts tumbling over each other like sneakers in a dryer. "Sure. Sounds good."

Piney raised an eyebrow. "With that much enthusiasm, we might as well change our name to The Sloths." She cracked a small smile and gave Ena a gentle shoulder-to-shoulder shove, not pushing too hard, just enough to connect.

Ena exhaled, rubbing her temples. "I think practice is exactly what I need. I'll be better."

"You better be," Piney teased. "Otherwise, I'm making you play the recorder."

"Rude," Ena said, the smallest trace of a smile breaking through.

"Let's swing by the music room so I can grab my guitar," Ena added, rolling her shoulders as if preparing to shake off the challenges of the day. She could feel her fingers longing to work the chords. At least she had not erased her ability to play guitar.

♪ ♫ ♪

The scent of the music room hit Ena the moment she stepped inside, a sharp mix of brass polish, warm and rich aged wood, and the faint, stale tang of saliva-dampened reeds and spit valve drippings. It was familiar, grounding in its own way.

She walked over to where her sky-blue guitar case rested near the back wall, next to the row of orchestra instruments. Swinging it over one shoulder, the padded straps fit snugly, as familiar as the weight of the guitar itself. The whole thing felt like an extension of her, and right now, that brought a quiet comfort.

The blue had softened like well-worn jeans, shaped by use but never neglected. A newly sewn patch of a woman holding a lantern stood out on the front pocket. Near the bottom seam, faint Sharpie doodles bled into the fabric, a crooked star, a bass clef, and Piney's scrawled handwriting that read: *Rock god (approval pending).*

Ena adjusted the straps with a practiced tug, flipping the case onto her back. Solid. Dependable. A constant in a world that suddenly had become unstable. Her guitar would always feel the same beneath her fingers, always sound the same when she played it.

That, at least, was a comfort.

The trio walked the relatively short distance to Piney's house, the rhythmic sound of their footsteps filling the spaces where words didn't.

At an intersection, a car blew through the marked crosswalk without even slowing.

"Jerk!" Ena shouted, throwing up a less-than-polite hand gesture. "That guy could have killed us. Irreversible."

Skyler, in their usual calm, measured tone, said, "They are we. Impulse doesn't make intent."

Ena groaned. "Skyler, sometimes…" She trailed off, unable to finish the thought. Everything about today felt too tangled, too impossible to sort out. Couldn't she just exist for a second without some existential revelation?

Piney, sensing the tension, cut in. "You're both wrong. That was definitely an alien in a human suit who doesn't know how to drive yet."

Skyler tilted their head in mock consideration. "Hmmm. Plausible."

It was just enough to break the moment, to let Ena breathe again.

Piney's step-grandmother was home when they arrived, standing in the kitchen as they shuffled in.

"Good afternoon, darlings," she greeted warmly. "Would you like a snack?"

"No thanks, Grams," Piney said over her shoulder, already making a beeline for the garage. "We gotta practice."

"Uh-uh. Sweet thing, you might not have time for a snack, but you definitely have time to give your grandmother some love."

Piney halted mid-step, sighed theatrically, then turned around and wrapped her arms around her grandmother's waist in a tight hug. "Sorry, Grams."

Ena watched, and it hit like a dart to the chest.

How many times had she failed to give Fiona "some love" before it was too late? How much would she give for just one more hug?

Piney's step-grandmother, Josephine, turned to the others. "Ena, Skyler, how are you two?"

Skyler, without missing a beat, said, "Everything's relative, but better than I deserve."

Ena half-laughed. "Doing okay. Thanks, Josephine."

"Good. Now, you kids are released. Go make some noise."

They didn't need to be told twice.

Ena followed Piney and Skyler toward the garage, her guitar case firm against her back. For the first time since school let out, hope sprang up. Like maybe, just maybe, she could shake the day off. At least for a little while.

The trio entered the detached garage, which had long since abandoned its intended purpose of housing a car. Storage containers lined the walls, neatly labeled. A pegboard by the garage door held gardening tools arranged with perfect precision.

Taking up one corner was Skyler's Korakama. Skyler had been adding to it since the big relieve. It now looked like a metal octopus had crashed into a plumbing van, but the sounds it produced were undeniably incredible.

Piney's synthesizer was set up next to Skyler's rig, its cross-legged stand sporting a sticker that read: *Powered by Women*. A tripod with a camera faced the setup, ready to capture their session.

"Where do you want to start today?" Skyler asked.

" 'Destroy Everything You Touch,' " Piney suggested.

"Good enough for me. You, Ena?"

Ena hesitated but nodded. "Sure. Sounds good."

Piney settled at the synthesizer. Skyler took position behind their invention. Ena pulled her guitar from its case, slinging it over her shoulder, and adjusting the strap. She strummed a few test chords, ensuring it was in tune.

Piney checked in with Skyler, then Ena. "Ready?"

Ena and Skyler nodded. Piney clicked the remote for the camera.

"A one, a two…" Skyler said emphatically.

The music started, Piney's synthesizer pulsed, and Skyler's percussion locked in perfectly. Ena opened her mouth to sing, late, flat.

They stopped.

"Sorry, guys. Let's try again."

"From the top," Piney said, frustration creeping into her tone.

They restarted. Ena overcorrected, this time too sharp, too rushed.

"Ena! Come on, get your head in the game," Piney snapped, pushing back from her synth with a huff.

Skyler was more patient. "It's okay, Ena. No one's peak every day. If today's off, there's always tomorrow."

Ena dropped her hands to her sides, her guitar pick clenched in her palm. "I'm trying, okay? But I can't get out of my head." She dropped her hands to her sides, shoulders tense. "I feel like I actually do destroy everything I touch. I mean, how did I erase my favorite band? It's messed up."

Silence.

Piney, ever blunt, leaned back against her keyboard. "Sorry, Ena, but you did. It's spilled milk. You're just gonna have to get over it."

Skyler shot Piney a look before turning to Ena. "Let's take a few deep breaths together. Close your eyes."

Ena sighed but closed her eyes.

"Breathe in the life-giving oxygen," Skyler intoned. "Clean. Refreshing. Now breathe out the carbon dioxide. Let it carry the toxins in your thoughts, the heaviness in your body."

They repeated the breathing cycle a few times.

Ena wasn't sure if she felt better. But she did feel a little less like she was spiraling.

Piney, unimpressed, crossed her arms. "So, are we practicing or are we doing interpretive yoga?"

Skyler ignored the jab. Instead, they stayed with Ena. "Now that you've let go of a little of that negativity, do me another favor. Close your eyes again and just answer my questions."

Ena hesitated. She wasn't sure she liked being at the center of Skyler's focus. But she trusted them.

She closed her eyes again.

"Okay," Skyler began, voice softer now. "We know The Fin Whales never made it big. We know you feel guilty about that. Given where we are now, what does your body tell you to do?"

Ena focused her thoughts. "I want to make it right somehow."

"Great. You want to make it right. Tell us what that's like, in your own words."

A pause.

"I need to try to make things right, but I don't know how."

"To whom?"

Ena's eyes shot open as the answer hit her like a jolt of electricity.

"Eva Kinsella."

The realization wrapped around her like a warm blanket. This was it. The thing she needed. The thing she could do.

Skyler gave a knowing nod. "Well, there's your answer."

Ena thought a moment. "But how? I don't even know where she is. Or if she's even alive."

Piney stretched her arms behind her head. "Well, lucky for you, we're very good at finding things."

Ena furrowed her brow. "Wait, we?"

Piney scoffed. "Obviously, we. You think we're gonna let you have all the fun and go full detective mode on your own?"

Guilt twisted within her. Breaking her promise to Graeme had been awful, but not telling them? Now that seemed unthinkable.

Skyler grinned. "We have a mission. We have a way forward. And we're with you every step of the way."

Ena exhaled, the tightness in her chest finally easing. Her friends were with her.

For the first time since realizing what she had done to The Fin Whales, she wasn't alone. And maybe, just maybe, she could make peace with it.

IN BETWEEN DAYS

The rest of Ena's afternoon passed like any other: homework, texting with Piney and Skyler, and working her way through Hendrix's 'Little Wing,' coaxing out its ghostly bends and fluttering double-stops. Her parents came home from work, her dad arriving last with Du's Teriyaki in hand. The smell of grilled chicken and yakisoba noodles drifted up to her room, announcing dinner before he even had to call her down.

They gathered around the table, plates piled high with noodles, rice, and sweet, smoky teriyaki chicken. Du's had been one of their favorite finds since moving to Portland. It was comfort food. Ena hadn't realized how hungry she was until she started eating, barely registering the usual dinnertime chatter.

When she finally looked up, she studied her parents. She could still see the shadows of the two eighth-graders she'd met in 1986. But this time, her mom wasn't just Mom. She was Tara, the kid who had been teased, who had built herself up, who had figured out how to be strong. And somehow, through all of it, she had become this: the kind of person who would understand things Ena once thought she never could.

Warmth spread in Ena's chest, quiet but certain. She had always loved her mom, but this was different. A deeper kind of knowing. The distance between them was shrinking. *Maybe, just maybe, Mom understands more than I realized.*

Tara noticed.

"Everything okay, Ena?"

Ena, caught, a deer in headlights. "Sure, Mom. Everything's fine."

Tara wasn't buying it. "Unconvincing. What's up?"

Ena hesitated. How do you tell someone you've met their thirteen-year-old self? She grasped for a truth, albeit not the whole truth. "I guess I was just, feeling lucky. To have you and Dad as parents."

Jason joked, "Hey Tara, do we have a thermometer handy? Might need to check Ena's temperature."

"You know what, Dad? I take it back."

"That's the Ena I know, and love." Jason grinned.

Tara's gaze lingered a beat too long making, Ena think she was aware there was more. But Tara did not press.

Byron made a face at Ena. "Weirdo." Then he added to the rest of the family, "I love Du's chicken; it's so good."

Jason, ever the dad, saw his moment. "Why did the chicken go to the séance?"

Ena rolled her eyes into another dimension.

Byron took the bait. "I dunno, why?"

"To get to the other side!"

The family groaned in unison. Ena let the joke wash over her, secretly grateful for her dad's ability to keep things normal. Well, normal-ish.

She scraped her plate clean. "Can I go play Minecraft?"

"After you clear the table. And homework's done?" Jason asked.

"Already finished." Ena hastily grabbed plates, dumping them in the sink before anyone could question her.

Time to escape into the game.

Ena logged into Minecraft and hopped onto Discord, where Piney and Skyler were already chatting. She joined them in-game at the rock arena they'd been building for weeks, a chaotic fusion of their styles.

Futuristic columns shaped like rocket ships supported a roof designed to amplify and direct sound. At the center, a rotating stage spun like a giant vinyl record, its blue center emblazoned with a peace symbol. Surrounding it, four towering speakers embodied the elements—cloud, flame, wave, and globe—giving their stage the power of wind, fire, water, and earth.

"Hey Piney! Hey Skyler!" Ena spoke into her gaming headset.

Piney's voice crackled through: "Hey, girl! What's up?"

"Hi, Ena!" Skyler added brightly.

"So, what's the plan for tonight?" Ena asked.

"We are building Skyler's pipe monstrosity," Piney replied, exasperation creeping into her voice.

"Your monster, my dream," Skyler corrected. "We're creating the ultimate musical instrument Korakama by an order of magnitude, The Pipe Dream."

Piney scoffed. "Perfectly named."

They all laughed.

"E," Piney said, switching gears. "I've been thinking about your problem."

Before Ena could respond, a meme popped up in the Discord chat:

> *Ena: 'I am going to find Eva Kinsella.'*
> *Ena after searching Insta:*
> *(Image of Tired SpongeBob, cheeks puffed, wheezing.)*

"Burn," Skyler said and chuckled.

Ena grinned, shaking her head. "How do you expect a child from 1986 to keep up with all this newfangled technology?"

"Seriously though," Piney cut in, getting back on track. "Let's come up with a real plan. I can start writing a bot to scrape socials and flag any promising matches to help us find Eva, but I need to know more about her to filter out the bad matches."

"That'd be amazing," Ena admitted. "I tried Insta, but your meme hit closer to home than I'd like to admit. There were a few Eva Kinsellas, but none were the right one. I thought it'd be easy."

"What do we actually know about her?"

Ena sighed, thinking. "She was 24 in 1986. She recorded in Portland. She played guitar and sang lead."

"That's something," Piney mused.

"Anything else?"

"Her bandmates were Georgia Zeit and Liz Betts, but that's all I've got."

Skyler's voice lifted, curious. "Liz Betts? That sounds like a stage name."

"Oops," Skyler added suddenly.

A hiss and spark echoed through the game as a column on the arena's edge flickered with a faint scorch mark.

Piney groaned. "Did you just set fire to one of our rocket columns?"

"Honestly, looks kind of epic," Ena added.

"There's a thin line between genius and accident," Skyler said with theatrical wisdom.

"You know what, Ena?" Piney said. "You're right. Low-key fire."

Back in 1986, Ena had missed this—how easily the three of them clicked, how natural it felt to fall into rhythm again.

"Okay, back to detective-ing," Piney said, pulling up another screen. "We're looking for a woman in her late 50s, was in a band in the '80s, played guitar, sang lead. Could be worse. We're not searching for a Jennifer Smith."

Ena laughed, leaning back in her chair. "Funny thing about that, I had to make up a name in 1986 when I ran into Fiona. I went with Jennifer…Jennifer Edison."

Skyler perked up. "Wait, tell us more about your trip back."

Ena hesitated. "It was so weird. Kids were still kids, but their parents let them run wild. Googling was card catalogs and microfiche, slow and clunky. Seeing my mom as a kid. That broke my brain. I always knew my parents were once our age, but this was real."

"And TV?" Piney prompted.

Ena snorted. "Old. Grainy. Hilariously bad, but hey, MTV was actually music television. But the '80s were crazy—blaring boom boxes, people answering the phone without knowing who was calling, people walking around with no screens. It looked normal, but off. Like I was watching it through a warped lens. The cars were so boxy and bright, riddled with bumper stickers. Seeing it for real, not like a movie, was wild."

Skyler leaned in. "What about the actual time travel part? Like in between here and there?"

"Going back to 1986? Total surprise." She faltered and then continued, "But when I came back, I tried to be more aware. And, Skyler?"

Her words stumbled for a moment.

"I think I finally get your word 'ineffable.' I felt safe, but out of time. Talking about how long I was 'in between' doesn't even make sense. It was beautiful, strange, and completely indescribable."

A beat of silence stretched between them.

Finally, Piney broke it. "Alright, I'll start running the bot. We'll get some leads on Eva soon."

Ena yawned. "Kids, I am totally spent, I need to log off."

"Don't let the time paradoxes bite," Skyler said.

"Night, losers," Ena teased.

"Later, E."

Ena logged off, the pixelated world vanishing, leaving only her darkened screen and the lingering hum of possibility.

SOMEBODY'S FOOL

The rest of the week dragged on. Piney had set her bot loose, scraping social media, old forum archives, and obscure listing sites for any trace of Eva Kinsella. Every morning, Ena asked for updates, but Piney remained frustratingly cryptic. "It's doing its thing," was all she would say.

Ena wanted action, not waiting.

On Saturday morning, she was absentmindedly strumming her guitar on her bed when her phone chimed.

PINEY: *Kaboom! We got her. Eva Kinsella. Portland. Meet at my place in 30 minutes!*

Ena jolted upright, almost launching her guitar.

ENA: *You found her! Leaving now!*

SKYLER: *On my way.*

Thirty minutes later, they were packed into Piney's bedroom, the air electric with anticipation. Piney's desk was its usual controlled chaos—scattered peripherals, jotted-down notes, a couple of empty soda cans—but all eyes were on the massive, curved monitor in front of them. Three windows stretched across the screen.

On the right, Piney's dark mode text editor, multicolored Python code scrolling.

On the left, a Google Map with a pin dropped at a Portland address.

In the center, a Myspace profile.

There she was: Eva Kinsella. Older. Different.

Ena squinted at the too-wide, too-fake smile staring back at her. Her oversized dreamcatcher earrings dangled in a profile picture taken at an awkward angle. Her glasses were bright blue horn-rims, rhinestones glittering in the corners. A mess of necklaces, some wooden, some colorful, draped over her chest. The largest piece was a half-moon jade pendant, absurdly oversized. A pink stone embedded in silver popped out of the side of her right nostril.

This was supposed to be Eva Kinsella?

Ena asked Piney, "Are you sure?"

Piney's fingers flew across the keyboard. "Trust the bot. Every data point led here. This has to be Eva Kinsella, lead singer of The Fin Whales."

Ena stared at the screen again, a gnawing unease creeping over her.

Piney pointed to the Google Map. "And that, my friends, is where she lives. Montavilla. Just a quick bus ride. Could be a today thing."

Ena gulped. Fear crept in, was she really willing to face Eva and tell her what she took from her? Her hands were clammy, her heart outpacing a rabbit's. But it was like she heard Fiona whisper: *Tomorrow's just an excuse, handle it today.*

"No time like now. I guess I should head off to the bus stop." Ena said it like a prisoner going in front of the judge for sentencing.

"Girl," Piney said, "Why do always try to make this a you-thing? We're going with."

"For real?"

"Of course, just look at her," Skyler added. "How could we not want to meet her? It could be the most fascinating thing that happens this year, at least for me and Piney."

They made their way through town and dropped down from the bus in the Montavilla neighborhood. As they walked towards Eva's address, they passed a hodgepodge of houses, some falling into disrepair, others gentrified, and some brand-new houses sticking out like sore thumbs against the century-old houses surrounding them.

They got to Eva's block.

One house stood out from all the others. A blinding, mustard-yellow house loomed over the block, its obnoxious orange trim so bright it practically required sunglasses. Deep teal gutters clashed violently, as if the house itself had been decorated on a dare.

In front of the house was a rainbow-colored toy horse tethered to century-old hitching ring cemented into the curb.

It felt like electricity wound through Ena's body. Was it hope or instinct warning her? The deeper they waded through the overgrown yard, the stronger the feeling became. This did not feel quite right. Two possibilities ping-ponged in her brain. Her Eva, her hero, could not be this person, and what if Ena was responsible for sending Eva down this path.

They climbed the porch steps. The wood creaked like it was rethinking its structural integrity. Paint peeled from the door frame. Ena knocked.

A deep, rumbling bark answered from inside, loud but not unfriendly.

The door swung open. There she was. Eva Kinsella.

The woman from the Myspace profile, blue rhinestone glasses glinting, necklaces jangling, half-moon pendant knocking against her chest. Her dreamcatcher earrings had been swapped for oversized dangling ice cream cones. Bracelets clattered like wind chimes as she gestured toward them.

"Yes, my dears, how can I help you?" she crooned, her voice teetering just below a crow's screech.

Ena stood frozen until Piney nudged her from behind. Reluctantly, she said, "Um, we're looking for Eva Kinsella, lead singer—"

"Oh! Fans!" Eva clapped her hands. "I knew my music would speak to the younger generations! Yes, yes, come in."

There was no choice. They were ushered inside.

A huge rust-colored dog greeted them, jowls sagging, eyes droopy with exhaustion. His tail thumped against the wall. Ena couldn't tell if he was happy to see them or begging to be saved.

Eva waved dismissively. "Don't mind Jupiter, he's just a love monster."

They stepped into the living room, or what passed for one.

Furniture jammed against walls with no logic. The sofa was buried under a mountain of mismatched pillows. Paintings—crooked, clashing, chaotic—covered every inch of wall space. Jupiter flopped down, taking up half the room.

Eva sank into a rattan wingback chair and motioned to the couch.

The trio eyed the dog-hair-covered pillows. They nudged them aside, revealing a pea-soup green velvet couch, worn threadbare by time and, most likely, Jupiter. They squeezed in.

Ena's skin prickled. This was wrong. So, so wrong.

Eva beamed. "So, what can I do for my fans? Are you here for a school project? Interviewing local legends?"

"Something like that," Ena said carefully. "I wanted to find you to—"

Eva sprang to her feet. "Ask me to sing for you? Of course, of course! I would love to!"

She hummed, then shook out her arms, her shoulders, her whole body.

Then she sang.

It sounded like bad Mongolian throat singing in a blender with a dying frog.

Jupiter groaned, shoving his head under his paws.

Eva kept going.

"Moon my master, Sun my sister."

Five minutes. Five whole minutes of sonic agony.

By the end, Ena's suspicions were all but dead and buried.

Eva paused, expectant.

"I…didn't know sound could do that," Skyler managed.

"Yeah, thanks for the song," Ena said weakly. This was her final test. "I wanted to talk about your days in The Fin Whales."

A slight wave of confusion crossed Eva's face. "Oh! Yes, yes. The Fin Whales. Resplendent days. What would you like to know, dear?"

Ena narrowed her eyes. "Do you keep in touch with your bandmates? What happened to Sam Natha?"

Piney and Skyler exchanged uncertain looks. Ena knew why. There never was a Sam Natha. Liz Betts, sure, but no Sam Natha.

"Oh my, yes." Eva's head tipped back, eyes flicking toward the ceiling. "Sam Natha. He was so dear."

A pause, just a beat too long.

"Such a tragedy." She wrung her hands dramatically, glancing away. "He died in a skydiving accident."

Ena forced a solemn nod. "That's…too bad." And just like that, her last doubt evaporated. This wasn't her Eva. Not even close.

Skyler caught on. "Jennifer," they said with pointed emphasis, catching Ena's cue. "I think we're gonna be late. Our parents need us in ten minutes."

Eva pouted. "So soon? Are you sure you don't want another song?"

"No, we gotta go." Piney shot a little too empathetically. Eva looked like she had been physically stung.

"Yeah, sorry," Skyler added, smoothing it over. "That was truly like nothing I've ever heard before."

They scrambled for the door before Eva could trap them again.

Once out of sight, they collapsed, wheezing with laughter. Piney croaked out a mimic of Eva's singing, sending them spiraling into another fit.

Ena wiped away tears, her sides aching. For a moment, tension lifted, like she'd dodged a bullet.

"Trust the bot, she said." Ena shook her head, still catching her breath. "This is the Eva Kinsella, lead singer of The Fin Whales, she said."

Piney groaned, rubbing her temples. "Okay, okay. This will be harder than I thought. If she's not even on MySpace, much less anything from this decade, we'll have to go deeper."

The relief faded, replaced by the need to refocus. This wasn't over. Not even close.

She felt that the universe was mocking her, but she made herself say it: "Yeah. We will."

TALK TALK

On Monday morning, Ena and Piney leaned against Piney's locker, chatting. Then Madison passed by.

Madison's glare struck Ena deeply. It was raw, ugly.

She had seen that look before, Tara's sneer, the one reserved for Carrie and Eileen back in 1986. Recognition hit like a sucker punch. The same look.

Like cold water rushing over her, stealing her breath. Guilt. Shame. *Had she really been as bad as Carrie and Eileen?*

Madison had earned what she got, hadn't she? Queen Bee. Untouchable. But that look, pain and anger, tangled together, was not what Ena had expected from Madison.

Ena had put that look there. She had earned it.

She gasped, caught off guard by the guilt. Fiona would tell her to face it head-on. *No excuses, No dodging.*

She prepared herself and then told Piney, "Hey, I gotta do something."

Before she could second-guess herself, she turned and called out, "Madison! Madison, wait."

Madison stopped but didn't turn right away. Her shoulders tightened slightly, betraying a brief flash of hesitation, like she was bracing herself for another blow. When she finally faced Ena, her eyes darted briefly to the surrounding crowd before her voice hardened with practiced contempt. "What?" Slow, deliberate. A challenge wrapped in a sneer, but beneath it, a flicker of fear?

Ena's confidence, shaky at best, wobbled. Too late now.

"Hey, can I talk to you? In private?"

Madison rolled her eyes, exasperated. "Look, Ena, you should learn when to walk away."

Around them, kids started to take notice. Another round of Madison vs. Ena. Except this time, Ena wasn't here to win.

She took a breath, steadying the tremble in her chest. *You can do this.*

"Madison…" She hesitated. Madison's gaze sharpened. She had her attention now. And unfortunately, everyone else's too.

Ena gulped. *Fiona would be proud of me right now.* The thought steadied her.

"I'm sorry," she said. Loud enough to be heard, quiet enough to mean it. "I shouldn't have pranked you during your speech last fall."

Madison's eyes narrowed. "No. No, you shouldn't have." The bite was still there, but there was a hesitation. Suspicion. Uncertainty.

Ena continued. "I really mean it. I am sorry."

A beat of silence. Then Madison's expression shifted slightly, not quite trust, not quite forgiveness, but possibly the tiniest suggestion of warmth. A hint of understanding. Maybe even the tiniest bit of respect.

Madison turned to leave, shoulders squared, but her steps weren't as sharp as before. The watching crowd, disappointed by the lack of spectacle, drifted back to their own lives.

Only then did Ena realize Skyler had been among them.

They were smiling, not gloating, not teasing. Just deep, knowing approval.

"When we hurt others, we hurt ourselves." Skyler repeated their mantra, "But when we make things right, we make peace with ourselves."

Ena's knees wobbled. It was always easy to rely on quick wit. But to be so visibly vulnerable, that had shaken her to her core.

Skyler stepped closer. "You know Fiona would be giving you a standing O right now."

Ena tried to steady herself. Skyler was right, but it didn't feel right. Not yet. She groaned. "Then why do I feel so weak?"

Skyler's voice was quiet but certain. "Because real strength never feels like strength at first."

They let that hang, then added with a small, knowing smile, "Time has a way of making things clearer."

Ena breathed deeply, rolling her shoulders as if physically shaking off the stress of the moment. Madison was gone. The crowd was gone.

But the unease still lingered.

Piney blew out a breath. "Well. That. Was. Brave."

She didn't sound mocking, but she didn't exactly sound approving either.

Ena watched her, waiting for more. Piney just adjusted her bag. "We still got class to go to."

Skyler gave Ena one last unreadable nod before turning to follow. Ena fell in step with them, but her thoughts were still trailing in the opposite direction.

♪ ♫ ♪

During their study period, Ena, Piney, and Skyler reconvened in the library, hunched around a heavy oak table.

"Okay," Piney said, tapping her fingers against her laptop. "As fun as it was meeting that *Eva Kinsella,* we gotta refocus and find the real one."

She flexed her fingers over the keyboard. "Obvs, social media isn't enough. I need to go deeper. I'll set loose some bots, real deep. Long-forgotten bulletin boards, old databases, obscure archives. If she left any trace, I'll find her."

Ena hesitated, then nodded. "Yeah, do that. But—" she flicked her eyes to Skyler, then back at Piney. "We should also go old-school. Paper. Magazines. Fiona might've mentioned them in *True Notes.*"

Piney stopped mid-keystroke, then slowly looked up at Ena, almost offended. "Analog? You've got to be kidding me."

"I'm serious," Ena said, leaning forward. "I was there. 1986. You have no idea how simple things were. Even computers; my mom's ski game was just a bunch of letters on a screen."

She gestured toward Piney's laptop. "Trying to find The Fin Whales digitally might be like searching Spotify for 'Old Town Road' by typing *that horsey song.*"

Piney scoffed. "Wow. Rude. My bots have precision."

"Sure," Ena said with a half-smile, her right dimple appearing. "But our target still eludes us."

Skyler, who had been quietly observing, finally spoke up. "If either of you finds her, we win."

Ena leaned back, exhaling. "You're right. Doesn't matter how, just gotta do it. Granddad has all of Fiona's back issues, we'll start there."

Piney raised an eyebrow. "And what exactly is our excuse for digging through decades-old zines? 'Oh hey, Graeme, mind if we time travel through your attic, again?' "

Ena winced. "Yeah. No. He made me swear not to tell anyone about this. No one."

Skyler tapped a pencil against the table, thinking. "What if we say we have a music assignment to research the roots of one of our favorite bands?"

Piney considered, then nodded. "Plausible enough."

Ena smiled. "Then let's get to work. Piney, launch those bots. If they don't turn up anything in the next couple days, we'll hit my Granddad's and dig through *True Notes* ourselves. I'll text the deets once I clear it with him."

After two days of failed bot searches, Ena, Skyler, and Piney clambered up Graeme's front steps, ready to go analog.

The afternoon was cool, the porch wood creaking under their sneakers. Piney adjusted her bag, clearly still convinced her bots had just needed more time.

"Okay," she said doubtfully, eyeing the house. "Let's see if dead trees have more to offer than my entire digital arsenal."

Ena rolled her eyes with a soft laugh, then knocked on the door. Time to find out.

After a moment, Graeme opened the door. "So, Ena tells me you want to go through some old back issues of Fiona's *True Notes*? School project, eh?" His voice was light but layered with slight skepticism.

Ena nodded. "Yep, Ms. Calla told us to try to trace the roots of one of our favorite bands. I really need a good grade on this project, so we wanted to go deep."

Graeme nodded clearly not fully sold.

"We're researching CHVRCHES, they have big influences from the '80s," Skyler added.

"Well come in," Graeme said, his face betraying him, not fully convinced but not going to push the issue. "Ena, you know where Fiona's study is, you'll find her back issues there."

Ena led the way to Fiona's study. She put her hand on the doorknob, ready to open it. So much history was held behind this door, recent and in 1986. Fiona had been here, guiding her. She took a breath, turned the knob, and stepped inside.

Piney beelined for the bench by the bay window, already typing, determined to prove digital would win.

Ena moved toward Fiona's vinyl collection, music to fill the silence while they worked. Ena loved vinyl records, the smell, the weight in her fingers, the ridiculously large size, but a permanence missing from the digital realm. She slid Simple Minds' album *New Gold Dream (81–82–83–84)* from its sleeve, set the needle, and let "Someone Somewhere in Summertime" drift through the room.

Skyler had made their way over to the back issues of *True Notes*. They ran a careful hand over the aged covers, the paper yellowed, edges soft with time. "We should start with 1984 through early '86," they said, pulling out a stack and crouching on the floor. They handled the magazines gently, as if too much pressure might turn them to dust. Skyler handed a magazine to Ena.

The pages, once crisp, were now delicate, thinned by time. The ink, fading in places, whispered the inevitable truth of analog, everything physical breaks down. History pressed between Ena's fingertips. A quiet reminder: some things survive, but only if you're lucky enough to find them before they're gone.

Skyler made two neat piles.

Ena settled across from them. "I'll take this one."

Piney, still typing, said, "Let's see who finds the first clue."

They read; they searched. Eventually, the needle lifted from the turntable, Side A complete.

Skyler groaned. "I swear, I've read fifty thousand words about bands I've never heard of."

Ena flipped another page. "Samesies."

Still nothing. Frustration in the room was mounting. Piney's forehead furrowed in concentration. Piles of magazines yet to be searched through dwindled, while piles of searched magazines grew, leading to nothing. Ena sighed deeply, picked herself up from the floor, and flipped over the album to the B-side.

Skyler suddenly snorted. "I can't get over some of these ads. Listen to this."

They read aloud: *"GET THE HOTTEST UNDER-GROUND TAPES! Mail $3.99 + $6.95 S&H for your choice of rare demo cassettes! Choose from: The Germs, Redd Kross, or an exclusive compilation from the L.A. scene! Allow 4-6 weeks for delivery. No C.O.D. orders."*

Skyler shook their head. "Four to six weeks? My mom loses it if Prime takes two days, and she actually lived through this." They tapped the ad for emphasis.

Piney raised an eyebrow and said, "Can you imagine mailing cash to some rando and just hoping something shows up a month later?"

Ena raised an eyebrow. "The original Kickstarter, with no guarantees."

A small moment of laughter cut the tension just enough.

The search continued. Ena was going through an issue from early 1985. She flipped to the next page, and her breath hitched.

A column titled "Sounds to Watch."

She read silently. "The Fin Whales are finding their footing; moody, textured sound with bite. Lead singer, Eva Kinsella, brings a powerful and unique voice. A few college stations have already caught on. Expect more to come."

She sat up straight. "Boom. There they are. I found them." She re-read the short blurb aloud.

Skyler leaned in, reading over her shoulder.

"Well, there you go. Analog: one, digital: zero," Piney said, defiance lingering in her voice, fingers flying over her keyboard. She didn't look up, but the edge in her voice gave her away. "So, now what? We wait for a telegram?"

Ena's enthusiasm wavered. Piney was right. This didn't actually get them anywhere.

Skyler tapped their index finger against their lips. "It's not just a mention, it's a lead. If they got college radio play, we may be able to trace it."

Ena nodded. "They were based in Portland, so they almost certainly would've been played on a local station."

Piney's eyes lit up. "You know, I did find something earlier. The City of Portland University had one of the best indie shows in the '80s. If The Fin Whales got airplay, it would've been there. Ena, your dad teaches there, right?"

A beat of silence.

Skyler grinned. "Okay. That's something."

Ena's energy returned. "*If* they *did* get airtime on that show, what's our next move?"

"I can search their databases. Maybe there's something in their archives," Piney offered.

Ena scratched her temple. "Maybe, but databases already failed us. Should we stick to analog? Actually go to the station?"

Piney smirked. "And say what, 'Hey, my friend erased a band from music history while time traveling, mind if we flip through your files to see if we can find them?' "

Skyler considered. "Obviously not that approach, but Ena's right. Digital hit a dead end. It's a long shot, but maybe we have to sneak in and look for ourselves."

Ena's eyes lit up. A challenge. A little mischief. "We could at least scout it. Make up some excuse to meet my dad there."

Piney's grin widened. "Sneaking into a radio station? Yeah. I could be into that."

PENDANT

It crept up on Ena, unexpected, almost forgotten.

Fourteen. Her birthday.

A day that was supposed to feel bigger. Different.

Instead, it just…was.

Maybe she would have cared more before. Before Fiona was gone. Before she had a problem only a time traveler could face. She wanted to feel excited, the way she used to on birthdays. But life had shifted.

Fiona's absence still ached in her chest. The secret she'd left behind, her strange legacy, had quietly reshaped Ena's world. She and her friends were chasing the impossible, and it made this milestone feel small.

Fourteen was supposed to mean more. And maybe it did. Just not in the way she expected.

But the truth was, the meaning of it barely registered. The house looked the same. The afternoon light hit the stairs at the same slant. Nothing had changed. And yet, everything had.

Ena opened the front door. "Lightning Crashes" blasted from the kitchen. Dad's '90s grunge phase, alive and well.

"Welcome home, Birthday Girl!" Jason's voice rang out over the music.

Ena followed the sound, stepping into what could only be described as a flour-based crime scene. It coated the counters, the floor, and, somehow, Jason himself. The maroon stand mixer sat at the epicenter, looking suspiciously like it had detonated.

Ena took in the scene like a detective on TV, her eyes sweeping the devastation. "Hey…Dad. You okay? Did a bomb explode in here or something?"

Jason grinned through the flour streaked across his face. "Just baking a cake."

"You do know the flour is supposed to go in the cake, right?" Ena asked, squinting at him. "Not the entire kitchen?"

Jason struck a dramatic pose, sending another puff of flour into the air. "Challenge accepted. Birthday cake for the ages coming up." He dusted off his hands, only making it worse.

"Well, I got homework to do," Ena said, unconvinced, as she turned to head upstairs to her bedroom.

Soon Ena lost track of time, buried in math problems and half-finished essays.

"Dinner's almost ready!" Tara's voice floated up from downstairs.

Ena froze. Dinner. Mom made dinner.

At a normal time?

It had been so long since Tara had come home early enough to cook. Most nights, Jason threw together simple meals: grilled cheese, pasta, the occasional takeout while Tara's job kept her buried.

The scent hit first. Saffron, garlic, the briny warmth of seafood.

Ena slowed, stepping into the kitchen, her breath catching.

Fiona's paella.

She hadn't even realized how much she missed it until now.

Graeme stood near the stove, a large wooden spoon at his lips, nodding appreciatively. "Mmm. That's so good. Your mom would be proud," he said, his voice thick with more than just approval.

Ena's eyes flicked to the pan on the stove, the golden rice, the prawns, the clams, the unmistakable curl of calamari.

Ena took in the scene. This wasn't just any dinner. This was a memory made real.

Her mom had reached out, not just with food, but with intention. It felt as if Tara was welcoming Ena into a new part of life, a life where they were more equal.

In that moment, Ena sensed the shift: the quiet ache of losing a part of her she could never regain, and the surprising warmth of being accepted as becoming more.

She barely had time to process it before Tara turned to her with a warm smile. "Happy birthday, Ena. Fourteen is impressive."

"Happy birthday," Graeme echoed, setting the spoon down. "You're growing up so fast."

Tara told Byron, "Set the table. Use the good plates."

Byron opened his mouth to protest, but Tara had already leveled him with *the look*. The "Not a debate, protest at your own risk" face.

With a dramatic sigh, Byron grabbed the plates and trudged to the table, muttering under his breath.

Tara pulled down a large serving dish, tilting the pan over it. The rice tumbled out in a cascade of deep yellow, streaked with saffron, studded with seafood, a perfect replica of Fiona's paella.

Jason picked up the serving dish as everyone settled into their seats, standing beside Ena as she scooped paella onto her plate. The moment she inhaled, the scent pulled her back in time to the first time she ever had Fiona's famous paella. She had loved it.

Fiona had made it to her birthday after all, at least in a small way. Tara had done this. She had brought Fiona to the table for Ena.

Ena felt the depth of that love down to her core.

Jason continued serving, each person piling generous portions onto their plates until he reached Byron.

Byron eyed the dish with deep suspicion. "That looks nasty. Can't I just have a peanut butter sandwich?"

Jason sighed, forehead wrinkling. "Buddy, your mom worked hard on this. You gotta try it."

Byron crossed his arms. "But it smells weird. And it looks weird."

Jason's patience thinned. "Here's the deal. You eat what's on your plate, and you get dessert. Or you sit here with an empty plate and no dessert. Your call."

Byron weighed his options. "What's for dessert?"

Jason arched an eyebrow. "Cake."

Byron let out a long, suffering sigh and took the tiniest spoonful of rice possible.

Jason shook his head. "Not quite, my friend." He scooped a proper portion including at least one prawn and a piece of calamari onto Byron's plate.

Byron glared at his food like it had personally insulted him.

Jason leaned in. "All of it or no cake." The discussion was over.

Graeme winked at Jason. "Well, I guess Byron just isn't ready for something so grown-up."

Byron scowled but started shoveling food into his mouth, washing down every bite with dramatic gulps of water.

Tara's paella was fantastic. Ena loved it so much she had seconds. Jason and Graeme both praised the chef, and soon, the once-overflowing serving dish was nearly empty.

As plates were scraped clean, Graeme stood up. "Let me clear the table."

He gathered dishes and carried them to the sink. But when he returned, he placed a small package, carefully wrapped in plain, pale blue paper, on the table in front of Ena.

"A little gift for the birthday girl."

Ena stared at it for a moment before meeting Graeme's eyes.

"Go ahead," he encouraged. "Open it."

The wrapping was too neatly done to just tear into, so she slipped her finger under the tape, carefully lifting the paper.

A small velveteen box slid into her hands.

Ena flipped it open. Her breath hitched.

Inside lay a delicate gold chain, a small eighth-note pendant, no bigger than her fingertip.

For a moment, she thought it was new, a replica. But then, her fingers found the barely noticeable scar in the chain. The spot Graeme had mended years ago, refusing to let it go when it had broken.

This was Fiona's.

A long moment passed. Ena stared at it, traced the chain, felt its history resting in her palm as she held the pendant. Her fingers lingered on the note. It was delicate. Light in her hands. But the weight it carried in her heart was immeasurable.

A piece of Fiona, real and worn and loved, would now always be with her. Around her neck. Close to her heart.

Ena knew it; a torch had been passed. And with it, an unstated expectation to live up to Fiona's legacy, to be worthy of not only the necklace, but all that came with it.

Graeme smiled softly. "She wanted you to have it."

Ena gazed up at him, her eyes welling with tears of gratitude as she nodded.

"May I?" Graeme asked, gesturing to the necklace.

Ena wordlessly handed him the chain and bent her head forward. His fingers were steady as he clasped it around her neck.

The moment it rested against her skin, it felt right, as if it had always been hers.

Ena stood up and hugged him so tightly Graeme could barely breathe.

"Thank you," she whispered into his chest. It was all she could manage.

When she pulled back, she looked around the table. Her family.

She touched the pendant gently. "I will wear it always."

It was more than a statement. It was a promise.

Tara and Jason watched their daughter, their teenage daughter, their faces washed with love, with pride. The moment stretched, held in time.

Then Jason clapped his hands together. "Well! Who's ready for cake?"

"Me! Me! Me!" Byron shot his hand into the air.

Jason disappeared into the kitchen, re-emerging moments later carrying a slightly lopsided cake, its white frosting uneven, the strokes of the icing knife clearly visible. In places, the dark chocolate cake peeked through where the icing was too thin.

Fourteen glowing candles flickered atop it.

Jason beamed with pride as he started singing. The rest of the family joined in.

When the song ended, Jason grinned. "Make a wish."

Ena closed her eyes.

Find the real Eva.

The thought flashed through her mind as she exhaled, extinguishing all fourteen candles in one steady breath.

Jason cut into the cake and passed slices around the table.

The first bite was perfect. Deep, rich chocolate, moist and dense, balanced by sweet vanilla frosting.

Graeme nodded appreciatively. "What it lacks in aesthetics, it makes up for in flavor."

Jason chuckled. "I have always been function over form."

Ena smiled, looking at the people around her. Her family had made such an effort tonight.

Ever since coming back from 1986, she had seen them differently. She could not untangle the kids they had been—Jason, his confidence cracked by Tara's sharp words; Tara, lost in her own social struggles and loneliness. And now? Now they were parents. Her parents. Somehow.

She knew them in a way she never expected. She saw more of their flaws, but they were more human. And she loved them even more for it.

Her eyes moved between her parents. "Thank you for such a great dinner and cake."

Turning to Graeme, she held up the eighth-note pendant between her fingers.

"And thank you for this. I love it."

SUSPICIOUS MINDS

The day marked exactly six weeks since Fiona passed.

Ena carried the loss with her as she walked beneath a canopy of new leaves with Skyler and Piney. Sunlight filtered down through the branches, dappling the sidewalk, creating pools of warmth against lingering shadows. Birds fluttered busily from tree to tree, twigs in their beaks, crafting nests with quiet determination. Above them, the thickening green leaves created a lush ceiling, and Ena imagined the fresh burst of oxygen cascading down around her. The air carried the rich, damp scent of freshly cut grass mingled with the sweet perfume of lilacs and rhododendrons, their blossoms a vibrant springtime firework display against the backdrop of campus buildings as they approached City of Portland University and its radio station.

It was hard to comprehend that six weeks had already passed since that day at the hospital. Six weeks moved like a paradox, both impossibly long and painfully brief. Normal time, Ena realized, can be almost as strange and slippery as time travel.

Beside her, Piney and Skyler had fallen into an animated debate about their ongoing Minecraft Rock Arena project. Piney was enthusiastic about creating VIP sky boxes inspired by the sleek, futuristic design of Wakanda from the Black Panther movie, while Skyler countered that since they were sky boxes, they should embody the airy and ethereal, like floating islands or glass structures in the clouds.

"What do you think, Ena?" Skyler asked.

"Huh?"

"Should our stadium sky boxes be Black Panther-inspired or more ethereal?" Piney clarified.

Ena considered it for a moment. "What if we combined them? Maybe sleek, Wakandan architecture suspended in glass or crystal-like structures floating above the arena?"

"That could actually work," Skyler and Piney said in unison.

"Jinx, you owe me a coke," Piney blurted, grinning.

Before they could dive deeper into their ideas, an assertive voice cut through the air: "Jennifer? Jennifer Edison?"

Ena stiffened, looking up quickly. An older woman stood there, her sharp gaze fixed firmly on Ena, gray hair drawn tightly back into an unforgiving ponytail. Recognition flooded Ena as the woman reached up and brushed a hand along her hairline, revealing the familiar hourglass tattoo. This was Dr. Docks, thirty-three years older.

Behind Dr. Docks hovered a younger man, his eyes unsettlingly sharp, giving Ena the uncomfortable sensation of being seen straight through. He stood rigid, poised like a predator ready to spring.

"Sorry, I think you have the wrong person," Ena managed, her heart suddenly racing. She needed to end this quickly; Dr. Docks could not figure out who she was.

"Hmm, perhaps," Dr. Docks mused, her eyes narrowing slightly. "But I never forget a face, especially one who impresses me. Could your mother perhaps be named Jennifer?"

Ena forced a calm smile, hoping her nervousness wasn't obvious. "Sorry, just a doppelganger, I guess. No Jennifers in my family."

"Interesting," Dr. Docks responded slowly, clearly skeptical. "May I ask what you three are doing here, then?"

"Yeah, my dad works here," Ena replied quickly. "Dr. Baker, in geology. We were just waiting to catch a ride home with him after his class."

Dr. Docks appeared unconvinced. The assistant intervened smoothly, a note of suspicion hidden beneath helpfulness. "Well, geology would actually be in the opposite direction," he said and gestured diagonally behind them, northwest. "Just thought you'd like to know."

"Yep, thanks," Ena replied firmly. "We just had some extra time, so we thought we'd walk around campus."

Dr. Docks gave a tight smile, her gaze lingering a second too long before moving on. As she walked away, she leaned slightly toward the assistant, murmuring inaudibly but urgently. The assistant's posture stiffened; he glanced back sharply, his eyes narrowing into a deliberate stare at Ena. An involuntary shiver ran through her. She had managed to deflect suspicion this time. Ena had won this round, but the assistant's lingering glance hinted that the game was far from over. The encounter left her deeply unsettled; she sensed that Dr. Docks and her assistant had just made a move, and next time, Ena might not be able to slip away quite so easily. She thought of Graeme's reaction to Dr. Docks's name. Ena didn't know what game they were playing, but she knew one thing for sure, she couldn't afford to lose.

"Woot! Woot! Ena for the win!" Piney said with exaggerated confidence, punching the air playfully. "That was intense. Seriously, WHO was that?"

"That was Dr. Docks," Ena replied softly, her eyes still following the distant figures. "She actually helped me figure out how to get back to 2019. Honestly, I'm not sure that was a win."

Skyler shuddered slightly. "I don't know about you two, but something about that guy creeped me out. Can't quite put my finger on why, but definitely creepy."

"Major cringe," Piney agreed.

Ena took a breath, shaking off the unease still lingering. "Okay, focus. We came here for a reason, not to talk about weirdos. That building, pretty sure the radio station is in there." she said, pointing to an old, blocky cement structure about a block and a half ahead.

Piney raised an eyebrow, clearly unimpressed by the building's blandness. "Looks like a noob's Minecraft build."

As they approached the building, uncertainty grew within the group. "Um, guys," Skyler began tentatively, "have any of us ever scouted a radio station before, or anything, really? Do we even know what we're doing?"

Reality settled over them heavily. Excitement had carried them this far, but now that they were standing there, the plan, or lack thereof, was suddenly inadequate. The imposing, stark building loomed before them like a medieval fortress protecting secrets hidden deep within.

"This has to be the building," Ena murmured nervously, stating aloud what they were all thinking. "Bigger than I thought. We have to go inside if we have any hope finding the radio station."

They found the building's entrance and stepped into a space that instantly evoked an institutional aura. Scuffed linoleum flooring marked by countless footsteps stretched beneath harsh fluorescent lights, one bulb flickering intermittently and signaling its impending end. A long corridor lined with evenly spaced doorways ran to their left and right, while directly ahead, a wide stairwell beckoned, its stairs worn, chipped, and splitting into two paths, ascending and descending. The building wasn't dilapidated exactly, but it was weary and overlooked, desperately in need of care. No helpful directory or bulletin board greeted them.

"Start from the bottom?" Piney's voice echoed louder than intended.

"Good a place as any," Ena replied, barely above a whisper.

Descending the stairs, they spotted a peeling poster on the stairwell landing, a faded advertisement for a winter concert long past. Encouraged, they quickened their pace. Reaching the basement level, a trail of flyers and hand-drawn signs lined the walls, announcing various bands, radio shows, and concerts. Some were polished and professional; others seemed hastily scribbled on colored paper.

At last, they found it, a modest, black sign with white etched letters: *KCPU - City of Portland University Radio.* Beside it was a large glass window, behind which lay a web of tangled cables, stacks of CDs, and an array of audio equipment. A young woman with bright red hair, a nose ring, and tattoo-covered arms spoke animatedly into a microphone, pausing suddenly to cast a puzzled glance at the three teenagers standing awkwardly outside.

Panicked, Ena, Skyler, and Piney spun around, hurried back up the stairwell, and burst through the doors into fresh air and freedom.

Piney leaned over, trying to catch her breath. "Well, frontal attack is definitely out."

"For sure. Total no-go," Skyler agreed.

Ena squared her shoulders, determination flickering back into her eyes. "We're not giving up yet. Let's circle the building. There might be another way in."

Exploring further, they found an exterior stairwell partially hidden by a dumpster, descending to a basement door.

"You two stand guard. Whistle if anyone gets close," Ena instructed.

Descending carefully, Ena reached the cement landing and tugged at the door handle. Locked tight. She pushed her fingers through her hair, frustration building as she searched for another option. Her eyes drifted upward, drawn toward a small window, hinged at the top and slightly ajar at the bottom. It seemed impossibly small and just out of reach. If anyone could fit through the window, it could only be Skyler.

Fiona's voice echoed in Ena's mind, clear as if she'd stood beside her: *The windows you barely notice, cracked open just enough to squeeze through…those lead to the experiences that shape you.*

Lately, everything reminded her of Fiona's wisdom and boldness. Ena's chest tightened sharply as the familiar ache of loss welled up, mingling with a fierce longing for additional guidance she could no longer receive.

Returning quickly to Piney and Skyler, Ena shared her discovery. The trio carefully descended together to inspect the window more closely. It seemed perfectly positioned, potentially leading right into the radio station's back rooms.

"Skyler," Ena said hopefully, "do you think you could reach it if Piney and I boosted you up?"

Skyler hesitated. "Uh, not loving this."

The trio stared up at the small window. To Ena, it suddenly became more than just a window in an old building; it was a threshold. If they crossed it, their lives would split into a clear before and after: before breaking into a radio station, and after. Even turning back now meant making a choice, a choice between playing it safe or stepping boldly into the unknown.

Piney raised an eyebrow, playfully challenging. "Time to show us what you've got."

"Just a quick check," Ena assured Skyler. "Not going inside, just seeing if it's possible. Piney and I will brace against the wall and boost you up."

Skyler sighed, reluctantly nodding. "Well, neither of you will let me live it down otherwise."

Working together, Piney and Ena gave Skyler the needed boost. Standing precariously on their shoulders, Skyler reached the window, gently lifting it outward. It opened easily. Skyler peered inside cautiously, whispering down, "There's a bank of filing cabinets right below. I think I can slip through."

"Not now," Ena quickly replied. "Let's get you down. We need to get over to my dad's office. We'll come back after dark."

As they ascended the stairs again, Piney and Ena brushed dust from their shoulders left by Skyler's shoes. Checking the time on her phone anxiously, Ena sighed, "Okay, let's go. We're going to be late if we don't hurry."

As they walked quickly toward Jason's office, Ena's heart was still thumping from their near-discovery at the radio station and the unsettling encounter with Dr. Docks and her creepy assistant. Her worry lingered over Dr. Docks and the strange feeling that she was missing an important insight. She tried to push down her anxiety, grounding herself in the steady rhythm of footsteps against pavement and the reassuring familiarity of heading toward her dad. By the time they arrived at Jason's building, Ena had reclaimed some steadiness. She wasn't entirely settled, however, as her mind began to shift toward what lay ahead.

Inside Jason's office, Ena's eyes immediately settled on a polished wooden display mounted neatly on the wall, holding nine rocks arranged carefully in a three-by-three grid behind clear glass. Her gaze fixated on the centerpiece, a seemingly ordinary stone with a distinctive, lopsided heart shape. It was meticulously polished now, completely free of the dirt and dust it had carried the last time she'd seen it.

"That's the rock," Ena whispered under her breath. It was unmistakably the same stone Tara had handed to Jason years earlier, dismissively taunting, "Rocks are for jocks." What had started as an insult had somehow transformed into a prize Jason chose to highlight, even treasure.

Jason noticed Ena's stare and chuckled softly, approaching her side. "Funny, isn't it? I probably owe my entire career as a geologist to that rock. It was the first time I'd ever really looked at a stone and wondered, truly wondered, about the journey it took, the millions of years, the countless miles, just to end up in my hand at exactly that moment."

Ena raised an eyebrow skeptically. That might be true, but it wasn't the whole truth. She knew it, and judging by the flush creeping into Jason's cheeks, he knew it too. Questions tumbled through her mind in quick succession. Had this rock always been important, or was this another ripple she had unknowingly caused? Her parents hadn't even dated until well after high school. Why had Jason held onto this particular stone all these years?

That small stone had launched her dad's career, and a guitar pick carelessly taken had erased her favorite band from history. Such tiny, seemingly insignificant moments could carry profound consequences. Skyler's words echoed clearly in Ena's mind: "And the butterfly flapped its wings." The truth of that metaphor settled deep inside her, both heavy and comforting. She couldn't quite name the feeling, but she recognized it— solid, grounding, reassuring, like the familiar pressure of her guitar strapped securely across her back.

Jason cleared his throat, breaking her concentration. "Well, we better get going," he said, glancing toward Piney and Skyler.

Pulled back to the present, Ena turned toward the door, but paused at the threshold, stealing one last look at the polished display behind her. Instead of feeling unsettled, she found comfort in knowing the rock had become meaningful.

Jason gently closed and locked the door to his office, and they made their way to the car for the trip home.

RADIO GA GA

Saturday night, the trio gathered at Skyler's house for a sleepover. Their group chat had been buzzing since they scouted the radio station, mapping out every step of what they'd dubbed *Operation Radio Free Eva.*

Skyler's house was closest to the MAX light rail station, and more importantly, Skyler's basement had a window just big enough to slip through. They'd studied the transit schedule. It was going to be tight. Skyler's parents were usually asleep by 10:00 p.m. The last MAX back left at 12:30 a.m. If all went according to plan, they'd be at the radio station by 11:15.

They unrolled their sleeping bags and booted up Minecraft, picking at their ethereal, Wakandan-inspired skyboxes for their rock arena. But the usual flow of creativity wasn't there. The air was thick, heavy. Piney's quips were sharper, clipped like little darts. They weren't really building; they were stalling.

No one said it directly, but Ena knew the same questions lingered in all their minds.

Are we really doing this?

Can we actually pull it off?

What if we get caught?

And what does it mean about us if we don't do it?

Ten o'clock. Skyler crept upstairs under the pretense of getting water. They returned a minute later, standing at the top of the basement stairs like an executioner delivering the final verdict.

"They're out like *fake Eva* in the first round of a talent show," they said.

Piney laughed. "Then we've got nothing to worry about."

"Agreed," Ena said and hoped that was true.

That was it. Game on. They took turns slipping into the bathroom, changing into their darkest clothes.

Ena emerged last. Black Chuck Taylors. Looking at it now, the white rubber seemed to glow in the dim light. Black jeans. A dark navy sweatshirt. Her brother's "borrowed" Steelers knit cap.

Skyler, on the other hand, had gone for stealth-meets-flow. A loose black tunic, the intricate embroidery lost in the shadows. Black sweatpants. Dark brown hiking boots, practical, if not exactly subtle.

And then there was Piney. All black, head to toe. Shoes that looked suspiciously like they'd been spray-painted last minute. A black bandana covering the bottom half of her face.

Ena raised an eyebrow. "Hmm. Suspicious much?"

"Not gonna gamble, full invisibility cloak," Piney said, voice muffled behind the fabric, "I'll ditch the outlaw mask at the MAX station."

For a moment, they just stood there, taking each other in, feeling the significance of what they were about to do.

Then Piney squared her shoulders. "*Operation Radio Free Eva* is a go."

A trio of sharp nods. Although their confidence didn't entirely feel settled in place.

Skyler slid the window open.

One by one, they vanished into the cool, dark night.

They moved quickly but quietly, sticking to the edges of the sidewalk, every sound amplified in the midnight hush. The scuff of a sneaker, the snap of a twig, the whisper of fabric against an overgrown hedge, each noise thundered in the silence, as if it could wake the entire neighborhood.

Every rustling leaf, every distant car engine morphed into phantom pursuers. At any second, they expected to hear a sharp voice demanding they stop, but it never came. Their paranoia was a pulse in their ears, quick and relentless.

By the time they reached the MAX station, their hearts hammered against their ribs, but no sirens wailed, no floodlights pinned them in place. They had made it. Undiscovered.

A young guy leaned against the railing, hands resting lazily on the handlebars of a beat-up old bike. He glanced at them, expression blank, then looked away, uninterested.

Maybe not everyone was out to catch them.

A faint vibration ran through the concrete as the MAX train approached, its headlights cutting through the dark like a searchlight. The doors hissed open, spilling bright artificial light onto the platform.

They stepped inside, and suddenly their dark, carefully chosen outfits practically shouted mischief under the fluorescents. In the dim streets, they had moved like shadows melting into shadows, but now, under the MAX car's unforgiving fluorescent glare, they might as well have been wearing neon signs that said, *UP TO NO GOOD.*

They moved quickly, clambering up the few steps toward the raised back of the train car. The few scattered passengers barely looked up, a man in headphones scrolling on his phone, a woman with her head against the window, half-asleep.

Except for one older woman. She scanned them over the top of her book, eyes flicking from Piney's all-black getup to Skyler's flowing tunic to Ena's too warm Steelers knit cap. For a brief moment, her gaze lingered, curiosity flashing across her face. But without a word, she turned the page and went back to reading.

They arrived at their stop and hopped off the car. Piney immediately replaced the bandana over the bottom half of her face. Ena rolled her eyes.

Skyler checked their phone. Time was slipping away. They had to move.

The trio wove through campus, hugging the shadows cast by the looming buildings of City of Portland University. The campus was still, urban, quiet. A few dimly lit windows glowed in the night, professors grading papers, grad students grinding through projects, but almost no one walked the pathways.

Somewhere in the dark, two women's voices pierced the silence. Sharp. Shrill. An argument. A confrontation. None of their concern.

They reached the cement landing. The window was dark. Ena stared up at it. This is it. Time was about to fracture. Before and after breaking into a radio station. This was illegal, highly illegal. No sugarcoating it. But they weren't acting out of malice or greed. They needed answers. And there were no other options left. Ena's mind raced, justifying, second-guessing, looping through the ethics of it all. And then there were Piney and Skyler. She had asked so much of them. And still, they were here. At her side.

She turned to Skyler. "You don't have to do this."

Skyler tapped the side of their headlamp as they switched it on. "It's Schrödinger's cat. Time to open the box and see what we find."

"Make sure you switch that thing to red light." Piney's voice was sharp, urgent.

Skyler flipped the setting. A dim red glow bathed their faces.

Piney and Ena exchanged a glance as they pressed their bodies against the wall, lacing their fingers together for the boost. Skyler stepped into their grip, pushed up, caught the ledge. Just like during yesterday's scouting run. But this time, they had to commit. A final push, and Skyler slid through the window.

It was all quiet until Ena and Piney's phones chimed.

SKYLER: *Is this what I think it is?*

Skyler had sent them a snapshot of a sliver of plastic, wedged tight against the door. A thin wire snaked up the wall, feeding into a box. An alarm.

Ena's body tensed. Piney gave her a calming glance and then typed back to Skyler:

PINEY: *Yep! Ancient tech. Magnetic.*

SKYLER: *So the circuit has to remain intact.*

PINEY: *You need steel thin enough to slip between the contacts and hold the circuit. Anything that could bridge the gap.*

SKYLER: *A metal file divider?*

PINEY: *Too light.*

ENA: *What about the bar on the ground?*

PINEY: *Aluminum. Useless.*

SKYLER: *There's a dusty box here with a row of thin plastic squares, standing upright, back-to-back like dominoes. Strange.*

ENA: *Floppy disks. I saw them back in 1986 at school.*

"You went to school back in 1986?" Piney asked her.

SKYLER: *They are rigid plastic, not even floppy. Why were they called that?*

ENA: *There should be a metal slider on each. See if you can pry the slider off the casing, bending one end just enough to wedge it between the sensor and the door.*

SKYLER: *Okay. Here goes. Get ready to run if the alarm goes off.*
PINEY: *You got this, Skyler.*
SKYLER: *A red light is blinking. Maybe it has always been blinking?*
PINEY: *Just do it.*

The door opened a crack. Ena and Piney ran over to it and slipped inside, their breaths held tight in their chests.

Skyler grinned. "Welcome to my humble abode."

Piney and Ena flipped on their headlamps, the dim red glow casting long shadows across the storage room.

The task ahead loomed impossibly large, pressing heavily on Ena's shoulders. The narrow space was lined with old green metal filing cabinets and gray industrial shelves, a graveyard of forgotten records. Somewhere inside, buried in a sea of aging paper and dust, was the answer. The key to finding the real Eva Kinsella.

It was an overwhelming haystack, and they were looking for a very small needle.

Ena checked her phone. Time was against them. Their plan hadn't accounted for the alarm, and now they had ten fewer minutes than they had allotted.

"I have zero patience for the slow, messy analog world," Piney said, voice laced with frustration. "Here's to hoping they kept thirty-five-year-old files. Somewhere."

Ena nodded, her voice barely audible. "Hoping. Yeah."

Skyler cut in before the impossibility of the task settled in. "When in doubt, just act. We each take a section. If we find anything promising, we regroup."

They split up, their fear of getting caught momentarily forgotten, the illicitness of their actions fading into the background. Right now, there was only the search.

Piney yanked open a file cabinet drawer. "People actually lived like this?" she whispered, flipping through thick folders. "Paper files? No search function? This is barbaric."

Handwritten labels, scrawled in fading ink, blurred past her fingers. Too recent. She gently closed the drawer and moved on.

Skyler scanned old cassette tapes, then looked at a box of reel-to-reel tapes. "These look like old films, but the reels are too thin." Skyler's optimism faded. "This is insane. Like trying to spot a subatomic particle with a telescope."

Ena moved toward a dark corner, her red light barely illuminating the cabinets. The paint on the bottom corners had been scraped away from years of moving, rust creeping in where the metal had been exposed. She tugged open a drawer, a damp, musty scent curling out, old paper losing its fight against time.

Ena pulled out a file. A playlist from 1977.

"Hey, I think we need to be looking over here," she called. "There's some ancient stuff here."

They refocused, targeting the cabinets near Ena's discovery. Within minutes, they narrowed the search down to two drawers filled with records from the early '80s.

Ena's hand hovered over an unmarked folder. It was thicker, heavier than the rest. She slid it out, felt the weight shift unevenly inside.

She opened it.

Inside was a cassette tape, wrapped in a folded sheet of paper. Ena turned the tape over, her breath catching.

A handwritten label stared back at her: *THE FIN WHALES*.

She unfolded the paper. The handwriting was meticulous, neat but with a personal touch:

Hope you give our demo a spin.
Thanks for listening.
—The Fin Whales
Aoife Kinsella – Lead/Guitar
Georgia Zeit – Drums
Elizabeth Brzeczyszczykiewicz – Bass/Vocals

Ena froze. Her breath caught in mid-inhale. "I found it!" The words were too loud, too fast. For a second, she forgot they weren't supposed to be here.

Piney and Skyler whipped around.

"Huh," Ena said, grinning. "Skyler, you were right. Liz Betts was a stage name. And I totally get why." She ran a finger under the last name. "But so was Eva's."

She pointed to the name Aoife Kinsella as Piney and Skyler sidled up to her, their red lights on the letter. "Any idea how to pronounce this?" she asked them.

"Ow-ee-fay," Piney guessed.

"Hmmm. Maybe ah-oy-fee?" Skyler said.

Ena cocked her head. "I think it's more like…ah-oo-fuh?"

"Kids," Piney cut in, "I'd love to spend time debating pronunciation, but we need to go. Like, five minutes ago."

Piney's urgency snapped them back. No time to reflect, just get out. Ena snapped a picture of the tape and note and quickly returned them to their place in the cabinet.

They moved toward the door. Skyler spotted the floppy disk missing its metal slider, still sitting on the shelf. They snatched it, slipping it into a pocket. "No trace left behind."

Skyler held the shim in place as Ena and Piney slipped through the door, stepping back into the night.

Skyler was nearly through when—*clink*. The shim slipped and bounced off the cement. Once. Twice. A frozen second of silence, and then the alarm screamed.

Piney snatched up the shim. "Run!"

They bolted. Up the stairs, feet pounding, lungs burning.

They didn't stop until they reached the edge of campus.

A blue flashing light cut through the night, a campus security golf cart speeding in the direction of the alarm.

They threw themselves behind a thick bush, pressing low to the ground, watching as the cart rushed past.

A pause.

They waited for what felt like an eternity. When the coast was clear, they stood, brushing dirt off their knees. They had done it.

Now, they just had to catch the MAX.

They turned the corner, jogging toward the station, just in time to see the red taillights of the final train disappearing down the tracks.

A deep, frustrated exhale rushed from Piney's lips. "Aw, man! Guess we're hoofing it back to Skyler's."

Skyler adjusted their tunic. "Walk we must, walk we will."

With no other option, they set off.

None of them had ever been out like this, walking the streets of downtown Portland after midnight.

As cities go, Portland isn't dangerous, but at this hour, it carried an unspoken threat. The buildings loomed larger. The deep shadows stretched wider. Even on a Saturday night, some streets were eerily quiet, while others held clusters of noise of drunken laughter floating out of a bar, the distant wail of a siren.

People slept in doorways, curled under blankets against the chill. The trio kept moving, not wanting to linger too long anywhere. The thrill of their success had dulled, replaced with a feeling heavier, quieter.

Piney broke the silence first, her voice half-triumphant, half-determined. "I knew it. I knew my bots weren't failing me. We just had bad intel. I can relaunch them on—" She hesitated, unwilling to even attempt the pronunciation. "Uh, the new name."

A rush of exhilaration grew in Ena. For the first time in what seemed like forever, hope wasn't just an idea, it was real.

"It's a fresh start!" She practically bounced as she walked, weeks of frustration, dead ends, and doubt finally paying off. It was as if a mocking monkey had sat on her shoulder all this time, whispering, "Might as well be searching for a unicorn." But now? That monkey had jumped off her shoulder and scampered away. A weight lifted. Ena felt physically lighter.

Skyler let out a laugh, a little too loud for the quiet street. "I can't believe it. We actually did it. We broke into a radio station. Never in a million years did I think I, we, were capable of that. I feel amazing." They shook their head, grinning.

The words hung in the air.

Ena's footsteps slowed. The night seemed to close in a little tighter.

She came to a dead stop and looked at Skyler and Piney. "Yeah. But we didn't just break rules tonight. We broke laws. We actually committed a crime. Does that make us—"

"Criminals?" Piney finished her sentence.

Skyler turned the thought over and shrugged. "Who did we hurt? We didn't take anything. We didn't destroy anything. We didn't harm anyone. Is that criminal?"

Piney let out a huff and smiled, casually flipping a small piece of metal between her fingers. "Well," she gave Skyler a gentle shoulder check, "we didn't take much."

Piney held up the bent metal slider from the floppy disk.

Skyler slowed. They reached into their pocket and pulled out the actual disk.

It became real.

Before, it had just been a break-in. A search. A mission. Now, with evidence in their hands, there was no denying it. Breaking and entering. Theft.

Skyler turned the disk over. They stopped walking and glanced up at them. Ena and Piney turned around to look at them, obviously rolling the reality of it in their mind.

Piney snorted. "Skyler's having a moral dilemma. Mark the date."

They kept walking. The night stretched long and uncertain ahead of them.

Eventually, Skyler spoke again. "It's history now, our history. Whatever it is, whatever it means, we can't pretend we're the same people we were this morning."

The words settled in. None of them were the same.

The burden of it hung heavy from Ena's shoulders. It was because of her.

Her quest.

Her mistake.

It hung like a heavy chain, cold and unshakable. It was a silent reminder that she was the reason they were walking through the city in the middle of the night, changed forever.

The guilt cracked through her resolve.

"I'm sorry," Ena blurted out. "I never should've asked you to help."

Piney stopped mid-step, reached out for Ena's arm, and turned her to face her. "Umm, no. We volunteered, remember? No need to get all drama queen on us."

Skyler nodded. "We chose this, Ena."

Ena closed her eyes and smiled. The guilt wasn't gone, but somehow, it felt lighter. A burden shared.

She forced a half-smile and dropped into her exaggerated Boston accent. "Well, no one could ask for bettah friends. Youse rocks."

That finally cracked the tension.

Piney snorted. Skyler shook their head.

And for the first time since the night began, they laughed. Genuine, relieved, exhausted laughter.

The streets of Portland stretched ahead. The streets hadn't changed, but the city for them would never be the same.

THE TRUTH

The morning after the sleepover, Ena woke up with feelings tumbling through her like clothes in a dryer, spinning, colliding, impossible to sort. Relief, because they had pulled it off. They had a name. But guilt too, guilt for what she had asked her friends to do, for breaking rules and even laws, and most of all, for breaking Graeme's trust. That last one weighed heaviest, pressing into her chest like a stone.

She was tired of feeling this way. Tired of lying, of keeping secrets, of breaking confidences. A part of her wished she had never found that Walkman, never traveled to 1986. Life would be simpler. Easier. But then she thought of Jason's rock, of Tara's struggles, of seeing Fiona one more time, younger, vibrant, alive. Would she really trade that?

Ena sat up in her sleeping bag, rubbing her eyes. Skyler and Piney were still groggy but starting to stir. As she looked at them, warmth spread through her. They had been there for her, more than she could have ever asked for. She thought back to Fiona's advice before the first day of school, about not just walking the easy path, and she understood it now. It really did make all the difference.

"Morning, sleepyheads," Ena said, stretching. "I need to talk to my Granddad today. He swore me to secrecy, and I broke it. I need to come clean."

Skyler perked up, eyes flashing with interest. "Mind if I tag along? There's something that's been bugging me, and I'd love to hear Graeme's take on it."

With a wave of relief, Ena responded, "Yeah, of course. I'd rather not go alone."

She turned to Piney. "You in?"

Piney groaned, rubbing her face. "I have bots to rewrite and relaunch at our new target, plus a mountain of chores. My moms are already on my case."

"Bummer," Ena said and turned back to Skyler. "Can you swing by my house around one? We'll head over together."

"Works for me," Skyler said with a nod.

With that settled, Ena felt a little lighter. She wasn't sure how this conversation with Graeme would go, but at least she wouldn't be facing it alone.

♪ ♫ ♪

Skyler and Ena stood at the base of Graeme's front porch, looking up. Today, it seemed bigger. More imposing. A threshold between safety and reckoning.

Ena took a beat to focus and stepped forward, Skyler right behind her. They climbed the steps, the wood creaking beneath them, and knocked. The sound seemed to echo longer than usual. After a long moment of silence, Ena shifted on her feet. "Maybe he's in his workshop."

Without another word, they made their way around the side of the house to the back gate. As Ena pushed it open, a strange sense of déjà vu washed over her. The last time she had used this gate, she had been on the verge of leaving 1986.

The soft glow from the workshop window signaled Graeme's presence. Ena hesitated, then gently turned the knob. The door creaked as she peeked inside, her voice barely above a whisper. "Granddad?"

Graeme glanced up from his workbench and grinned. "Ena? How's my favorite time traveler?"

Ena stepped inside, Skyler a half-step behind her.

Graeme's grin faltered. His face flushed as he stammered, "Er, just a little inside joke." He cleared his throat, clearly trying to recover.

An urgency rose in Ena's chest. There was no easing into this. No building up to the moment. The words rushed out before she could stop them. "That's actually what I wanted to talk to you about." A sharp inhale. "I told Skyler and Piney. They know."

Graeme's smile vanished. His eyes darkened, and a frown carved deep lines into his face. Ena had never seen that expression from him before, not like this. It sent a chill down her spine.

"Ena," he said, his voice quiet but firm. "You swore. I told you it was dangerous to tell anyone." He was so focused on her, it was as if Skyler had disappeared from the room entirely.

Ena's breath hitched. "Granddad, I am sorry. Truly. But—" She held up her notebook. "There were too many things that didn't add up. Piney and Skyler are too smart. They knew something was off."

Graeme's jaw tensed, but his gaze flicked to the notebook. Some of the anger drained from his face, replaced by a different look. Concern, maybe.

"Ena, this is serious," he said, his voice lower now. "This is really dangerous. I trusted you and—"

"I know," Ena said, her voice wavering. She struggled for the right words, her thoughts colliding. "I broke that trust. I get it, and I hate that I did. I really, really do."

She clenched the notebook tighter. Her granddad did not alter his sharp gaze.

"But it was all too much. I couldn't keep lying to them. Not to Piney and Skyler. Not when everything was spiraling. And you know what?" Her voice steadied. "They didn't freak. They showed up for me. For everything. There was no right choice, but telling them was the best choice."

She lifted the notebook again, as if to prove her point.

Graeme looked at her, then at the notebook, his expression shifting. His sharp, stern gaze softening into a more thoughtful expression. His voice changed too, moving from disappointed grandfather to intrigued scientist. "What do you mean, 'For everything'?"

Ena handed him the notebook, its pages filled with frantic scribbles, half-formed theories, and frantic attempts to piece everything together.

Graeme read in silence. Ena watched his face shift, eyebrows knitting together, jaw tightening, a slow exhale through his nose. The seriousness of everything she had written settled onto him. It was a lot to ask of anyone to carry alone, much less a fourteen-year-old.

After a long pause, he shut the notebook gently and met her eyes. "I wish you had come to me earlier," he admitted. His voice was quieter now, regretful. "This is a lot. I can see how much it's been weighing on you. I hadn't really thought about how many questions you'd have, how much uncertainty there would be. I guess I owe you an apology too. I asked too much."

Ena startled, caught off guard. She hadn't expected that.

Graeme peered at Skyler, acknowledging them for the first time. His lips quirked up just slightly.

Returning his gaze to Ena. "So, brown-eyed Byron? I can't even imagine it."

Ena let out a little chuckle, "I am still not used to green-eyed Byron."

The tension in the room cracked, just a little. The air wasn't quite so heavy.

For the first time since knocking on the door, Ena relaxed a little.

"Granddad, you saw that I 'erased' my favorite band from music history. I feel terrible about it. We've been trying to track down the lead singer. It proved a little difficult, but we finally have her real name."

Ena flipped open her notebook to last night's discovery, carefully pronouncing each letter. "A-O-I-F-E. Any chance you know how to say this?"

"Ee-Fa," Graeme said without hesitation. "What a beautiful Irish name. It means radiance."

Ena cringed, recalling how she, Skyler, and Piney had butchered the pronunciation the night before. But understanding dawned, Eva Kinsella had chosen her stage name as a simplification of her real one.

Graeme leaned back, curious. "So, why are you trying to track her down?"

Ena hesitated, then took a breath. "They were supposed to be huge, one of my favorite bands. But when I went back to 1986, I accidentally took her lucky guitar pick, the one I showed you. And that was it. Feels meaningless, but it was the difference between making it or not. I feel like I have to find Aoife."

She paused, the name still feeling foreign on her tongue.

"And I have to tell her what happened. Nothing I can do about it, but she should at least know. I feel so guilty. So responsible. I need to try to make it right. Whatever that means."

Graeme's smile broadened, a look of admiration in his eyes. "Wow, Ena. That's really big of you. But you realize you can't tell her without revealing time travel."

Ena let out a heavy sigh. "I hadn't really thought about that yet, but deep inside me, I know I have to do this. I took fame from her, and she should know."

Graeme studied her for a long moment. "Ena, I can't say I'm fully on board. But I also didn't trust your instinct about telling Piney and Skyler, and maybe I should have. So, if you feel you must, I'll support you. Just promise me something."

Ena nodded in agreement, waiting.

"Up until the very last second, listen to your instincts. If it doesn't feel right, you don't have to tell her anything. If she doesn't believe you, you don't have to press. These are tough choices, and once you say it, you can't unsay it."

The importance of his words landed on Ena, yet another task added to the growing list.

Skyler cleared their throat. "Mr. Quinn, something's been bugging me. Ena saw another Ena for the brief time their times overlapped. So—"

Ena gasped. She knew exactly what Skyler was about to ask. She hadn't thought about that. "What happened to the other Ena?"

Graeme scratched his chin. "Hmm, now that's a difficult question. What are your thoughts, Skyler?"

Skyler, so much smaller than Graeme, still commanded his full attention. He treated them as an equal, and it showed.

"Well, I can think of three possibilities," Skyler said. "One: infinite multiverse. Ena's double jumped to a different universe. Two: they created a time loop, and when that Ena time-traveled, the loop closed, reconverging into one Ena. Or three: that the other Ena simply ceased to exist."

"Wait! What? I might have killed that other Ena." The words hung heavy in the air. Frustration welled up. She did not particularly care for a scientific discussion about herself. She had been so focused on finding Aoife since she returned that she had nearly forgotten about the "other Ena." How much more bad news was she supposed to take?

"Not killed," Graeme jumped in quickly, protective. "Not at all. Ceasing to exist is just another way of looking at the reconvergence theory."

"Or—" Skyler offered, "—the other Ena was reabsorbed by the universe, her energy becoming part of something greater."

Skyler tapped their fingers on the workbench, deep in thought.

"But," they continued, "the reconvergence theory has a hole. If the other Ena never knew The Fin Whales, since they never made it big in this timeline, then she wouldn't have listened to the same tape and gone back to 1986. Which means the guitar pick was never taken. Which means the band should have made it. And that's a paradox."

Graeme let out a low whistle. "Woof. Yeah, that's not an easy one."

"I think we've got a full-blown Spidey-Verse situation here," Skyler said, deadpan, looking at Ena. "Maybe your other self didn't disappear, maybe she just jumped into another timeline, living a totally different life right now." They paused, then smiled and said, "Maybe she's got cooler hair."

Graeme chuckled. "It's a strong theory. But if that's true, it opens up a whole other set of questions."

Ena watched them, seeing that neither was anywhere near finished with their debate. She knew they weren't going to find a definitive answer, and frankly, she couldn't handle debating her own existence right now. Maybe she'd think about it more, later. For now, she'd settle for the multiverse explanation. She could have stayed and argued her case. She had thoughts on all of it, but she had more important things to do. Another secret she was sworn to keep. And this one she had no intention of breaking.

"Okay, may let you two debate the mysteries of the universe or multiverse? Without me? There's something I need to do."

Graeme waved her off. "Of course."

As she slipped away, she heard him say to Skyler, "The concept of infinity makes sense, but the reality of infinity really doesn't. Most of the time, when infinity comes up in science, it just signals the boundary of our understanding."

Ena shook her head as she walked away, relieved to have escaped before her brain exploded. Skyler and Graeme together could be too much.

She made her way to Fiona's study, her chest tightening as she stepped inside. The last time she had been here, she had hidden her mom's cassette carrier in the hidden compartment in the bay window bench. Now, she opened it and carefully began filling it with tapes from Fiona's stash.

Her fingers hovered over a The Replacements cassette. She lingered, tracing its spine. She could almost hear Fiona's voice, almost see her sliding the tape into the stereo, the familiar click as it locked into place. Then, the music, Westerberg's voice rising, crackling just slightly from the worn tape.

Ena remembered the elation of that night, the way Fiona had smiled conspiratorially before pulling out the first bootleg and saying, "You have to keep this a secret." That was the moment she had been let in, welcomed into Fiona's hidden world.

Ena wondered about that night. How much had Fiona really known? What more would she tell her now, if she could? The thought struck her out of nowhere, a sharp pang of loss cutting through her. She would never have those answers. Never have those conversations. Never share another moment.

The grief hit her, just as raw as before. *Would I ever stop feeling this way?*

She blinked away tears and kept filling the case. Over a hundred illicit tapes. Soundwaves captured. Moments in time, stolen but preserved. She thought about how history itself, capturing a moment, freezing it in place, was its own kind of time travel. And now, she was the protector of this history.

Ena returned to Graeme's workshop, finding Skyler and Graeme still deep in debate, their conversation now moving into other time travel paradoxes.

"I hate to break up the great debate," Ena said, "but we should probably get going."

Graeme's gaze flicked to the cassette case in her hand, one eyebrow raised.

"Oh, this?" Ena said casually. "Just one of Mom's things that I salvaged when we cleared the attic. I forgot to bring it home." It was half true; the most honest she could be in that moment.

Graeme checked his watch and offered his signature smile to Skyler. "I suppose you've humored an old man long enough."

He stood and reached out to shake Skyler's hand, a gesture of respect. Skyler, without hesitation, took his hand and met his gaze squarely. A silent exchange between equals, despite the decades between them.

"I'm sorry, Ena," he murmured. "I should have understood better. Should have seen how hard this was on you. Asking you to carry this alone wasn't fair."

Ena quivered, feeling completely seen. Completely loved. She held onto that feeling. "I'm sorry too. I should've come to you sooner. I love you, Granddad."

"Love you more."

RECOGNIZE

After Piney retargeted her bots, she texted Ena and Skyler.

PINEY: *Whoa. Way more Aoife Kinsellas than Eva Kinsellas. This is gonna take a minute.*

ENA: *You got this!*

SKYLER: *We'll find her.*

A few days later, they huddled in the school library. The trio had claimed a back corner table, their laptops open, but all eyes were locked on Piney's screen.

Huddled close, they scanned the search results.

"I filtered out the obvious wrong ages and scored the rest: connections to Portland, music, that kind of thing." Piney tapped through the list. "No perfect matches, but we've got a few solid contenders."

She leaned back, cracked her knuckles, and clicked open the first profile.

"Wow," Madison said, coming up behind them. She hovered at the edge of their table, arms crossed, scanning Piney's laptop screen. "Your descent continues. Stalking old ladies now?"

Piney sighed, finally looking up. "Wild. You went out of your way to stalk the stalkers. What does that say about you? Risking your Snap score just to keep tabs on us?"

Madison seemed to be pretending not to hear and drifted toward a nearby bookshelf.

Skyler, noting the section she wandered into, tilted their head. "Huh. Never pegged Madison as an animal husbandry enthusiast."

They watched casually, but Ena wasn't amused.

"We have more important things." Ena said, her voice holding an edge, frustration creeping in.

The trio refocused on the screen.

Aoife Kinsella.

Music teacher, Bend, Oregon.

Ena studied the picture. It didn't feel right. But it didn't feel wrong either. Not like Fake Eva.

"A definite maybe," Ena said.

They cycled through more candidates—women in their late 50s, their faces reshaped by decades Ena hadn't lived, their lives rewritten by time.

Ena's conviction wavered. Was this just a fool's errand?

Skyler and Ena, halfhearted now, toggled through Instagram and Facebook profiles, their searches slowing as doubt crept in.

But then Piney pulled up the next candidate.

A mature woman. Sleek, her sharp features softened slightly by time. Salt-and-pepper hair (more salt than pepper), shoulder-length. A navy blazer. Striking blue eyes.

Ena's breath caught. The eyes. That directness, that intensity.

Familiar. Her heart lurched, caught between hope and fear.

In the blurred background, an acoustic guitar rested against the wall. Above it, a poster of piano keys with bold lettering: BridgeResonance, barely readable.

"I don't know for sure," Ena murmured, voice quieter now. "But I have a feeling about this one."

"This one," Piney said, scanning her files. "Not much of a social presence. Looks like the bots found her on TechCrunch. CEO of a company called BridgeResonance."

Ena quickly typed it on her laptop, pulling up the website.

And somehow, Madison was back.

Book in hand: *The Complete Guide to Alpaca Milking and Cheese Making.*

Piney eyed the book like it personally offended her. "I think we found your first customer." She shared a knowing look with Skyler and Ena, "She lives in Montavilla."

Skyler and Ena stifled their laughter.

Madison rolled her eyes, hugging the book to her chest. "BridgeResonance? So, you're finally getting music lessons?"

Ena didn't bother responding. She was locked onto the screen.

Madison didn't speak, but her eyes flicked to the screen. Then to Ena, intent and focused. Ena watched her for a moment out of the corner of her eye as Madison shifted her gaze to Skyler and Piney, working together like a well-oiled machine. Madison's expression shifted, unreadable. She hesitated a moment longer than necessary before returning her book to the shelf.

BridgeResonance.

Music: Everyone, Everywhere.

Ena clicked on the "About Us" tab.

BridgeResonance focused on increasing music education and access through software products. Established in 1999. Seattle, Washington.

Ena's pulse picked up.

She navigated to the "Contact Us" tab.

A simple web form.

No email. No phone number. No easy way in.

Ena started typing anyway.

Piney scoffed. "You might as well shout into the void. Those forms never go anywhere."

Ena sighed. "Do you have a better suggestion?"

Piney grinned like a shark. "Better suggestion? You do know me, right? Give me ten minutes."

Her fingers danced across the keyboard.

Ena, half-listening, kept clicking through the website. She was trying to convince herself. Trying to believe they had found her.

Her mind spun. *How do I even start this conversation?*

This Aoife, she was on a completely different path. A path Ena had rewritten.

How could she explain? Would she believe her? Would she even answer?

Ena was a paper boat in a too-rough patch of creek water. No control, just adrift, waiting for the current to decide.

Then—

"And the winner is…Piney!" Piney threw her hands in the air like a victorious boxer. "Here's Aoife's email."

Ena's Skype messenger popped up with the address.

Skyler high-fived Piney.

Ena took a deep breath and wrote her email.

> *Subject: Interview Request for School Project*
> *Dear Ms. Kinsella,*
> *My name is Ena Quinn-Baker, and I'm in eighth grade.*
> *I'm working on a school project about inspiring women in business. I came across BridgeResonance and was really*

drawn to its mission. I love music, and I think it's amazing
that you're working to make it more accessible to everyone.
I'd love the chance to interview you and learn more about
your journey. If could chat with me, it would mean a lot. I
can do whatever works for you. It would mean a lot.
Thank you for your time, and I hope to hear from you soon!
Best,
Ena Quinn-Baker

Piney and Skyler read over Ena's email.

"Looks good enough to send," Piney said, pushing back from the screen.

Ena took a deep breath. Her finger hovered over the trackpad. "Once I send this, there's no turning back."

Piney and Skyler gave her an encouraging nod.

She clicked *Send.*

The email disappeared into the ether.

Now, all she could do was wait.

♪ ♫ ♪

The weekend passed. Nothing.

Sunday night, Ena texted Piney and Skyler.

ENA: *Nothing yet.*

PINEY: *Bring your laptop to school tomorrow.*

SKYLER: *Maybe she saw it and chose not to respond. Silence is also an answer.*

ENA: *Not helpful, Skyler.*

PINEY: *Just bring your laptop. It ain't over.*

♪ ♫ ♪

Monday morning, before classes started, Piney worked on Ena's laptop for a few minutes.

"Okay, I've got good news and bad news."

Ena snapped to attention.

"Good news. She opened your email. Twice."

"Bad news?" Ena braced herself.

Piney shut the laptop. "No reply."

Ena snatched it back and immediately started typing, her frustration clear in every loud keystroke.

Skyler watched her quietly for a moment. Then, in a calm voice, they said: "This is not the time. This is not the way. Give her today. She might still reply."

Ena stopped.

The words were exactly what she needed to hear.

Her mom's advice surfaced in her mind, too. *Never send an email when you're upset. Step away, come back to it later.* She shut the laptop.

♪ ♫ ♪

That evening, Ena put on her headsets and signed onto Discord. There the three friends worked on their Minecraft stadium until Piney interrupted. "The suspense is killing me! Anything yet?"

Ena barked into her headsets, "UGH. NO!"

Skyler said, "We can craft another message together. She opened your email TWICE. She's interested. We just need that final push."

Ena thought a moment. "Fiona was involved in helping The Fin Whales in the '80s. Maybe Aoife knew my grandmother? Maybe we play that angle?"

"Now that's something," Piney said, her clap booming through Ena's headsets. "If Fiona wrote about The Fin Whales, that might be too tempting to ignore."

Ena typed a draft and dropped it into their Discord chat.

Subject: Interview Request for School Project – Follow-Up
Dear Ms. Kinsella,
I know you're probably super busy, and I really appreciate you even reading this. I just wanted to follow up and explain a little more about why I'm reaching out.
My grandmother was Fiona Quinn, I think she might've known you when you were the lead singer of The Fin Whales. She mentioned the band in her Sounds to Watch column in True Notes.
I'd love the chance to talk with you.
Thanks again for your time, and I hope to hear from you!
Best,
Ena Quinn-Baker

"That's perfect," Skyler said over her headphones.

Ena dropped it into her email and hit send.

Not five minutes later, the reply came.

From: Aoife Kinsella
Fiona. I have not heard that name in so long.
Friday. BridgeResonance offices. 12:30. You have 30 minutes.
– Aoife Kinsella

Ena stared at the screen, her breath slow and controlled.

They had done it.

They had found her.

Not a miracle, not a fluke, just three kids, determined, sifting through a haystack until they found the needle.

And now, Ena had to face Aoife. In person. Her nerves tingled. Relief, because the search was over. Terror, because this was real now. She had to explain herself. Gratitude, because she hadn't done this alone.

Her fingers hovered over the keyboard, unsteady with hesitation. She was stuck on one realization, a feeling so overwhelming it nearly short-circuited her.

She would have never gotten here without them.

Skyler, who saw connections in ways no one else did.

Piney, who never backed down from a challenge.

Neither of them had anything to gain from this search, yet they had been there for her every step, every frustrating dead end, every insane possibility.

Not for the thrill. Not for some payoff. Just for her.

She was exposed by it, cracked open by the power, the meaning of their loyalty.

All those feelings collided, overwhelming and impossible to categorize. She closed her eyes and breathed, looking for a center.

She clicked her tongue. "Looks like I'm going to Seattle on Friday." She hesitated, "Somehow."

Piney cracking her knuckles was audible through Ena's headphones. "Ena, do I have to say this again? We are with you every step."

Ena shook her head. "I can't ask you to skip school. You've already risked too much."

Skyler's voice was steady in her headset. "Who says you have to ask?"

"Skipping school isn't the problem," Piney said, her smile noticeable in her voice. "We won't miss a thing. And I'll make sure our parents won't even realize we are missing."

CRAZY TRAIN

The trio shifted from the possibility of meeting Aoife to the reality of it. This was happening.

Right there in Discord, Piney moved effortlessly into tactics: "Okay, how are we getting to Seattle?" she asked.

"I could ask my granddad to take us?" Ena offered.

Piney didn't miss a beat. "Hard pass. Six hours in a car? No way we dodge the radio station break-in conversation if he presses."

Ena conceded. "Yeah, you're right."

"Private plane?" Skyler offered dryly.

"Give me a few more years." Piney's confidence came through in her voice.

Skyler said, "Well, while we wait for Piney's private jet, the only real alternative is the train."

"Train?" Ena considered it. It sounded right. "Train works."

"How do we afford the train tickets?" Skyler asked.

"Already on it," Piney said. "Tight, but doable."

"How much?" Ena asked.

"Close to two hundred," Piney replied.

Ena hesitated. That number was bigger than she expected. "I've got sixty from my birthday."

"I've got it covered," Piney said without hesitation. "Been piling up some crypto, Zcash, flipped it to Bitcoin before it nose-dived. I guard it like a dragon with trust issues, but this is an emergency."

"You seriously weren't kidding about the private plane." Ena tried to keep it light, but she was still absorbing the fact that she couldn't actually afford this on her own.

Piney's voice came through, half-amused, half-self-aware. "When it comes to private jets, Piney doesn't joke."

Ena laughed, but it didn't shake the weird feeling gnawing at her. She hated owing people. But Piney was just doing this, like it wasn't a big deal.

"It's not much, but I have twenty," Skyler offered.

"Keep it," Ena said. "Piney, I swear I'll pay you back."

"Yeah, yeah. I'll load a debit card and buy the tickets tomorrow." Piney sounded dismissive but not unkind.

Ena tapped her fingers against her desk. "I'll give you my sixty tomorrow." She hadn't expected it to sting, but it did. If Fiona were here, she wouldn't even blink at buying the tickets. But she wasn't. And now Piney, who guarded her Bitcoin like a dragon hoarding treasure, was casually covering the gap like it was nothing.

"Thanks, Piney," Ena said. Her words did not stand up to Piney's sacrifice. Piney had stepped up through this whole journey, and here again, she came to the rescue. No words were enough. Ena wondered what she had done to deserve this. No answers seemed sufficient.

Piney exhaled through her nose, a short, knowing breath. "Ena, when are you going to realize? I got you."

♪ ♫ ♪

All week, Ena had wished Friday would just arrive, but when it finally did, she woke up after a night of tossing and turning, feeling like an invisible hand was holding her down, pinning her to the bed.

It was judgment day.

She'd dragged her friends into yet another high-stakes game—this time, skipping school, sneaking off all the way to Seattle. The gamble was real. If they got caught? She'd probably be grounded until freshman year of college.

With a sigh, Ena dragged herself out of bed, staring at her closet. What do you wear to interview a CEO of a music company? To face the woman whose life you accidentally rewrote? She couldn't raise suspicion at home. It had to be right. It had to say, "I'm confident, but not desperate." It had to.

An idea clicked. Fiona.

Ena hesitated, picturing her grandmother, how she could so easily pull off *I mean business* without ever looking like she tried. A leather jacket, the perfect band tee. Casual, but always intentional. Fiona never overdid it, but she never blended in either.

Ena stared at her reflection in the mirror. I'm about to tell someone I erased their past.

She investigated her closet again. The Blondie shirt? It could work. The tweed blazer she had found at a vintage shop? Ena slipped it on, adjusting the sleeves.

She stepped closer to the mirror. Turned to the side. Tugged the sleeves of the blazer. Not too formal. Not too forced. Ena knew she would get Fiona's stamp of approval.

She slipped the blazer off and sighed, folding it into her backpack. Here's hoping I don't regret this.

Ena headed downstairs, as ready as she was going to be to face the day.

Her mom was already at work. Her dad sat at the kitchen table, eyes locked on his phone, scrolling through emails.

"Morning, Ena." He barely looked up.

"Morning, Dad."

Byron, hunched over his Nintendo Switch, didn't even acknowledge her arrival.

So much for worrying about passing the family's scrutiny of my outfit.

"I have an early morning today. Piney and Skyler need to meet up before school to talk about Sound Logic," Ena said, keeping her tone as casual as possible.

"Okay. Have a good day, Ena. Love you." Jason responded automatically, still absorbed in his screen.

That was it. No second glance. No interrogation. For days, she had imagined this moment, bracing for suspicion, for questions, for the need to evade.

Ena grabbed a few protein bars from the cabinet and tossed them into her backpack. As Ena zipped it up, her phone vibrated. A message from Piney: *School calls successfully rerouted. We're ghosts.*

Of course, Piney handled it. Ena hadn't expected anything less.

Ena hopped on a TriMet bus, heading downtown toward Union Station. Her stomach still hadn't settled, her mind flipping between possibilities. Would Aoife recognize her name? Would she even care?

When she arrived, Skyler and Piney were already there, sitting on a bench in the waiting area of the train station.

"Hey, youse." Ena slipped into an exaggerated Boston accent, betraying her nerves.

Piney smirked. "Morning, sunshine."

"The adventure begins," Skyler mused. "Ready for the collapse of the Aoife duality into certainty?"

Ena gulped. Was she? "I guess. No time like the present."

The train arrived from the south, a deep hum rumbling ahead of it. They heard it before they saw it. When it lurched to a stop, Ena's heart did the same. The significance of everything, the risk, the unknown, the stakes, crashed over her like a wave.

They boarded, hovering a little too close to a grandmotherly woman, acting like she might be their chaperone. Their seats were tucked away at one end of the car. The train was almost deserted.

"I sent you screenshots of the train tickets," Piney said as they settled in. "Have them ready when they come around."

"Thanks, Piney." Ena pulled out her phone, making sure the screenshot was easy to access. She logged onto the WiFi, pulled up her playlist, and plugged in the headphone splitter.

The train started moving. "Fire with Fire" by Scissor Sisters kicked on as the trio shared earbuds, the rhythm matching the steady *clack-clack-clack* of the train rolling forward.

Not too long after, a conductor approached. After scanning their tickets, he paused, raising an eyebrow.

The conductor's gaze lingered too long. Sizing them up. "A little young to be traveling alone, aren't you?"

Skyler didn't blink. "My dad's in the next car. Buried in work. Didn't want us bugging him."

The conductor's expression didn't shift. A long pause.

Ena's pulse ticked up.

Then, finally, a grunt. A nod. He moved on.

Piney let out a slow breath. "Flawless execution."

Skyler tapped their temple. "Believability lies in specificity."

Ena's tension didn't ease completely, but at least one hurdle was down.

Somewhere along the ride, the WiFi cut out. The playlist stopped. The trio sat in silence for a moment, the absence of music making the world feel heavier.

Piney let her head rest against the window, watching the trees and buildings blur as they passed.

Then, softly, barely above the hum of the train, she started beatboxing.

"Tick, tick, tick." A rhythm, matching the pulse of the wheels on the tracks.

Skyler, wordless, dropped the food tray down from the seat in front of them, tapping out a beat with their fingers.

Ena closed her eyes, feeling the rhythm settle into her bones. The train, the movement, the uncertainty, it was all music.

She let her words flow, starting in spoken word:

> *Steel wheels hum, the rails don't lie,*
> *Windows flash like a film gone by.*
> *We don't know where we're going, but we're on the way,*
> *We tracked Aoife down, but what will she say?*

Skyler leaned into the beat, adding accents. Piney's bass notes sharpened. Ena rode the wave. She shifted into singing, eyes still closed, head tilted back, letting the music pull her forward:

> *The world ain't waiting, don't look back,*
> *Onward we go, gotta move like that.*
> *Fast train, lost name, the future arrives,*
> *Now and then, time collides.*

Skyler harmonized low. Piney dropped the tempo, letting the rhythm stretch.

Ena shifted again, falling into a space between rap and spoken word:

> *Clack-clack heartbeat, rolling in time,*
> *Piney on the kick, Skyler on the line.*
> *No map, no guide, just a name we chase,*
> *A ghost in the groove, just a breath to trace.*

Piney grinned, flipping the beat. Skyler synced up instantly. The shift built energy, lifting, lifting, lifting.

> Ena leaned into the singing again:
> *The world ain't waiting, don't look back,*
> *Onward we go, gotta move like that.*
> *Fast train, lost name, the future arrives,*
> *Now and then, time collides.*

She leaned back in her seat, letting the music settle back into the train, into the moment. She hummed the chorus under her breath, softer now. Piney echoed the last line. Skyler let the rhythm linger, fingertips still tapping as the song dissolved into the sound of the train itself. The moment didn't need words anymore. It just was.

"That was sick," Skyler said, voice full of awe.

"We should've recorded that and put it on YouTube," Piney added.

Ena shook her head, smiling. "Sometimes…I don't know. It feels right to just let the moment be." Adding a camera, a recording, she knew it would have changed it.

Skyler grinned. "Next stop, Sound Logic's first album."

Piney snorted. "What should we call our first song?"

Ena thought a moment and said, "I think 'Off the Rails' works."

Piney drummed her fingers on her knee, pretending to consider. "Mmm. Possibly. But…'Fast Train, Lost Name?' "

Skyler nodded sagely. "Deep. Symbolic. Absolutely pretentious enough for us."

Ena laughed. "Oh, definitely. We'll win 'Best Song Title That Sounds Like an Indie Movie' in no time."

Piney mimed writing it in the air with a fake pen. "Certified future classic."

They dissolved into laughter, loud, unfiltered, the kind that shakes off nerves without trying.

As it settled, Ena let her head rest against the seat, exhaling slowly. The train still rumbled beneath them, steady, forward.

But reality didn't wait. It never did.

Piney watched her for a beat, then nudged her foot. "So, fearless leader, what's the plan?"

"Huh?" Ena said, still caught in the echo of the music.

"Aoife. What are you going to say to her?" Piney pressed.

Ena looked at her hands in her lap and said, "Phewwww. I've run it through my head a million times, but it always feels wrong. I guess, I'll tell her the truth…and hope. Things have a way of working out for the best."

Piney immediately groaned. "Ugh. I hate that. It's BS."

Ena startled. The reaction was so strong, so immediate.

Piney continued, voice sharp. "Look at the heroin addict on the street, things don't just work out for the best."

Ena frowned, caught off guard by the heat in Piney's voice.

"We have to work. We have to push. Chips don't magically fall into neat little stacks. You have to make them."

Skyler, calm as ever, leaned into the discussion. "The universe ticks on, with or without us. It doesn't care if it 'works out' for us, what does that even mean. That's on us to figure out. It's what we do with the time we have that matters."

Ena thought for a moment. "But it's not all up to us. What about luck?"

Skyler took a moment. "Sure, random happens. Some things are out of our control. But to give up agency? To leave it all to the universe? That feels like wasting a chance."

Ena stared at Skyler, taking it in.

"Think about this whole journey," Skyler continued. "It was 'luck' that put you into 1986. But *you*, Ena, found a way back. We worked together to get here. Luck started it. But it was us, not luck, that got us right here, right now."

Ena sat with that. Her throwaway line had led to this, a conversation unexpected, a perspective she needed.

She nodded slowly. "You two are right. It might not work out for the best on its own."

"I'll deal with—" She corrected herself, her voice steadier. "*We'll* deal with the fallout."

The heavier-than-expected conversation settled over the trio. Each of them sat in quiet thought, the train rolling on beneath them.

Eventually, Skyler pulled out their notebook. "I want to get your words down before we lose them. That was strong. I really think it *could* be a Sound Logic original."

Ena watched as Skyler jotted down lyrics, giving shape to what had, just minutes ago, been nothing but an impulse, a feeling. Writing it down made it real.

She hesitated, then reached for her own notebook. It does help to write things down. Flipping open to a blank page, she let the pen move, ordering her thoughts on Aoife. Not just loose, tangled ideas spinning in her brain, but a plan.

Skyler and Piney fell into easy conversation, filling the space while giving Ena room to write.

Pages filled with ideas, options. As Ena wrote, thoughts floated to Fiona's boldness, her ability to take things head-on. *Could I be that bold?*

Before they knew it, the train was pulling into King Street Station in Seattle.

WHAT'S DONE IS DONE

The train eased to a stop at King Street Station, the end of their trip. As Ena stepped onto the platform and took in her first real look at Seattle. The skyline rose to the north, distant beyond the tangle of freeways. To the south, twin stadiums sprawled, vast and self-contained, leaving an unexpected sense of space around them.

It didn't loom large like she'd imagined. Instead, the noise hit her first.

The steady hum of traffic, the deep whoosh of cars speeding along I-5, the occasional wail of a siren in the distance. It didn't have the compact chaos of downtown Boston, but it carried its own kind of motion, faster and louder than Portland, yet somehow it was more spread out.

She barely had time to process it. Piney checked the time. "We should get moving."

Ena nodded, gripping the strap of her backpack a little tighter. The real city was waiting for them.

They followed the signs toward the Link light rail, making their way into the station. The train arrived with a soft hiss, sliding up to the platform quieter than any subway Ena had ever taken.

They boarded, standing near the doors as the train hummed to life.

At first, Seattle's skyline was visible through the windows, the clean, modern edges of glass buildings and the distant mountains peeking through gaps in the cityscape. But soon, the train dove underground, swallowing them into the tunnels.

The neon-green tunnel lights blurred past. Too quickly.

Just a few stops. Too soon. The train slowed. "Next stop, Westlake Station." The robotic voice echoed through the car as the train glided to a stop.

And then, the moment hit. They climbed the stairs, stepping out of the station and straight into the beating heart of Seattle.

The buildings soared, glass and steel boxing in the sky. The sidewalks overflowed with people, professionals moving with purpose, tourists pausing to take it all in, bike messengers slicing through traffic with expert precision.

Cars and buses clogged the city streets, and somewhere, a street musician strummed a guitar against the steady, pulsing rhythm of the city.

Ena paused, just for a second. Seattle definitely wasn't Portland; it was bigger, more electric. It wasn't Boston either; it was sleeker, less cramped, not quite as intense. For the three of them, Seattle was its own beast, unfamiliar, untamed, a new place that they had to learn to navigate.

Ena focused. No time to linger; Aoife did not seem the type to wait.

As they walked the few blocks to Aoife's building, Skyler mused as they walked, "You feel that? The energy here, it's not just movement. It's like…a pressure. Almost physical, like you could reach out and shape it."

Piney let out a quiet snort. "Skyler being Skyler," she mused, more fond than dismissive.

Ena didn't completely register the exchange. Her thoughts were tangled and looping. With every step, her heartbeat climbed, faster, heavier, hammering against her ribs. By the time the building came into view, Ena thought that her heart might just climb right out of her chest and run in the other direction.

The building loomed before them, towering, a silent giant standing guard. Glass and steel stretched toward the clouds. They all instinctively tilted their heads back, straining to see the top, but it just kept going.

Piney gave a sharp nod. "Now or never. Ena, we got this."

Ena tried to match her confidence. "Now or never." The words left her mouth, thin, unsteady.

When she started the journey of making things right with Aoife, it felt clear, doable. She had been sure of herself. But standing here now, doubts she had spent weeks trying to outrun crystallized into a feeling almost tangible. Heavy. Real.

Skyler, attuned to the shift, placed a steady hand on Ena's shoulder. Their voice was quiet, grounding. "Ena, Fiona would be proud of you. She'd tell you that you've come so far, and no matter what happens, you'll be fine. You are strong enough. Brave enough."

Piney didn't hesitate. "And you know what? We know you're strong enough and brave enough too."

She stated it as if it were a fact, so obvious that it seemed as if it might have been written in the air.

Ena inhaled deeply, exhaled slowly. Maybe she could believe it too.

"Now or never," Ena said more confidently. *Skyler is right. Fiona would be proud and would believe in me. Time for me to do the same.*

They stepped into the lobby, a space designed to impress, two stories tall, airy, open, a study in monochrome. Every surface a shade of white, except for the abstract paintings punctuating the walls like deliberate shocks of color.

To their right, cushioned leather seats lined the windows, a place for visitors who had time to linger. They didn't.

Ahead, the lobby narrowed into a sleek hallway flanked by two banks of elevators.

A large digital touchscreen display flickered under their fingertips as they searched for BridgeResonance.

Twenty-seventh floor.

As they moved toward the elevators, Ena pulled her blazer from her backpack, slipping it on. The cool fabric settled over her shoulders like armor.

She caught her reflection in the polished elevator doors. If she squinted, she could almost see Fiona standing there instead, leather jacket, band tee, unshakable confidence. Ena didn't have Fiona's certainty, but maybe, just maybe, she could borrow a little of it now.

She adjusted the blazer, making it right. Nodded. Stepped forward.

Skyler entered first, pressing floor twenty-seven. Piney and Ena followed, the doors sliding shut behind them. A soft chime. Then the tug of gravity.

The elevator surged upward, rising faster than seemed possible, like they were being pulled, not lifted.

Too fast.

Before Ena was ready, the doors slid open. Ena scanned the workspace. It was wide open, buzzing with quiet focus. Employees sat at long bench desks, headphones on, eyes locked on laptop screens, fingers flying over keyboards.

Beyond them, glass-walled meeting rooms framed animated debates. Employees sketched on whiteboards, layering ideas in bold, looping strokes.

To the right, a foosball table rattled, making a sharp clack as the ball struck the back of the goal. Loud laughter followed, a brief celebration before the game continued.

Near the kitchen, a cluster of employees balanced lunch containers on their laps, deep in discussion, ideas mixing with bites of food.

The office brimmed with life and activity. Purposeful. A space built for creating.

"May I help you?"

The voice was sharp, efficient, clipped with precision.

Ena's eyes landed on the reception desk, a simple white standing desk. The receptionist, a tall, lanky man with short red hair, oversized black glasses, and a blue gingham shirt buttoned to the top, watched them expectantly.

A tattoo peeked from his forearm: a treble clef overlaid on the cardinal directions, as if music itself were a compass.

Ena stepped up to the receptionist's desk. "We're here to see Aoife Kinsella?" It came out more like a question than a statement.

The receptionist arched an eyebrow. "Are you now? And you are?"

"Ena Quinn-Baker. Aoife said she'd meet with us at 12:30."

"Give me a minute." His voice was clipped, efficient. "Wait here."

The trio exchanged glances as the receptionist disappeared into the office. Ena fought to contain her nerves, resisting the urge to fidget. When he returned, he barely looked at them. "Aoife said okay, but she only has fifteen minutes."

Ena turned to Skyler and Piney. "I think I have to do this on my own."

Piney started to protest, but Ena shot her a look, a rare one, one that meant trust me.

Already moving, the receptionist said, "You two can wait over there." He motioned to the sleek, egg-shaped chairs in front of the desk, then turned sharply to Ena. "You, this way."

There was no mistaking his annoyance at having kids in the office. He led Ena past the open workspace, down a hallway lined with glass-walled offices, and stopped in front of a closed door. A sharp knock.

"I have your 12:30."

A voice, sharp, focused, floated from behind the door. "Let her in."

The receptionist opened the door, gestured Ena inside, and shut it behind her.

The point of no return. No turning back now.

Aoife's office was sleek, almost minimalist, with an edge of industrial efficiency. No clutter. No warmth. Just purpose.

To Ena's left, a glass conference table rested on chrome bass clefs, surrounded by black rolling chairs.

Straight ahead, a massive desk, clean except for a laptop, a Bluetooth keyboard, and a large monitor angled slightly away.

And Aoife.

Exactly like the pictures Ena had seen. Sharp. Controlled. Eyes that didn't miss a thing.

Behind her, against the far wall, stood a guitar on a stand. Above it, a framed BridgeResonance poster.

That familiarity, that proof this was real, settled Ena's pulse from a wild sprint to only slightly less out of control.

Aoife didn't look up as she gestured to the chair across from her. "One minute."

Ena sat. She tried to keep her hands still as Aoife finished typing, then she finally leaned back, assessing Ena with an unreadable expression.

"So. You want an interview?" Aoife's voice was direct, impatient. "Bad timing. We've had a few surprises today. I only have fifteen minutes."

The added time pressure twisted inside Ena. This was already slipping away from her.

"Well—" Ena paused. It felt like standing at the open door of a plane, hoping her parachute had been packed correctly. Too late to back out now, but there was no time. She was just going to have to blurt it out. "I actually need to tell you something."

Aoife let out a sharp sigh, already irritated. "Kid, I run a company. I don't have time for this."

Ena didn't argue. Instead, she reached into her pocket.

Pulled out the guitar pick. Set it on the desk between them.

Aoife's expression didn't change at first. Then, slowly, she picked it up, turning it over between her fingers. Her eyes narrowed. The faint, worn-down logo from an old music shop barely visible.

"Where did you get this?" The edge in her voice was different now. Not just annoyance, curiosity and intrigue.

Ena's confidence wavered. Aoife's presence was sharp and heavy, like standing under a spotlight with nowhere to hide.

"That's yours," Ena said. "I—I accidentally took it."

Aoife's eyes snapped to hers. "What do you mean, you accidentally took it?"

Ena said her next words slowly, each word chosen carefully. "I was there. I was in the recording studio. I'm the reason it was lost before you recorded 'Midnight Current.'"

Silence. Aoife set the pick down. Folded her arms. "Kid, either you're high or joking, either way, wasting my time."

Ena closed her eyes. Took a breath. Fiona's presence stirred inside her, the kind of quiet confidence Fiona would bring into a moment like this.

When she opened her eyes, her voice was steadier.

"Aoife," she said, looking directly into those intense blue eyes, "you have no idea what it took for me to get here. I had to ask so much of my friends just to sit in front of you. I know it sounds crazy. I know it's impossible. But it happens to be true."

The mood shifted.

Aoife studied her, not brushing her off, not dismissing her outright. Not yet.

She picked up the pick again, rolling it between her fingers.

"Okay." Her voice was wary but curious now. "Let's pretend, for a minute, that I believe you. How?"

"It's complicated," she said. "But I accidentally created a time machine. With a Walkman of all things. Long story."

Aoife raised an eyebrow.

Ena pressed on. "When I played your tape, I was transported back to the studio where you were recording it. You had just finished 'Fight, No Flight.' I hid under the orange pleather couch in the sound engineer's room."

Her voice was steady, but inside, her pulse pounded.

"You all went to lunch. I thought I was dreaming. I looked around, checked out the equipment, and then—" She took a deep breath. "I picked up your pick. Before I could put it back, I heard someone returning. I panicked. I hid again. The pick forgotten in my hand."

Aoife continued rolling the pick between her fingers. "You realize how ridiculous this sounds, right?" Her voice was even. Measured. "A kid time-traveled and stole my lucky pick, derailing my entire career? You're lucky I don't have security throw you out for wasting my time."

Ena stammered. "I know."

Silence stretched between them.

Aoife's expression didn't shift, but she wasn't dismissing Ena outright either.

After a long beat, she muttered, almost to herself, "This is absurd, but it's a little too detailed."

Without looking away, Aoife tapped a button on her keyboard. "Cancel my 12:45."

A crackle from the PC speaker. "Roger that."

Her eyes flicked up, sharp. "Okay, kid. You're a storyteller for sure, but how did you get a copy of our album?"

Ena drew on her inner strength to continue. "I was cleaning out my granddad's attic with my mom. I accidentally spilled a forgotten science experiment on the Walkman and wanted to check if it still worked. The Fin Whales were my favorite band, so I grabbed your cassette to test it. Well—" She shrugged, palms up. "It worked. Just not the way I expected."

Aoife frowned. "That doesn't really answer the question. We had a tiny run of that recording. We never caught on. We barely sold any copies. We weren't exactly a household name. So how the hell does a kid in 2019 even know we existed, let alone call us their favorite band?"

Ena knew what she had to say next. She didn't want to, but gravity pulled her anyway. You can fight it, but you can't win.

"That's the real reason I'm here." Her voice was quiet but firm. "I have to apologize to you. I didn't mean to, but somehow, taking that pick altered your destiny. Before I went to 1986, you had been a huge success."

Aoife let out a vocalization between a grunt and a laugh. "It was my lucky pick. I guess losing it could've thrown me off a little bit more than I'd like to admit."

Ena shook her head. "No. More than that. Your big pulse track, 'Midnight Current,' it was your big hit. It got radio play. My grandmother, Fiona, featured you on the front cover of *True Notes*. She thought you, Liz, and Georgia were really special. She helped you land some of your biggest early gigs."

"Kid, so because I was a little off on 'Midnight Current,' I'm supposed to believe that was the difference between making it or not?"

Ena gave a hopeless shrug.

Aoife sat back, processing.

"So, you're telling me…we could have made it? We were good enough?" The words came slow, deliberate, as if she was rolling them around in her mind. "And all it took was a missing guitar pick."

She paused. A hollow chuckle followed.

"Crazy to think the line between fame and obscurity could be that thin," Aoife said.

Ena couldn't tell what Aoife was thinking. Was she mad? Hurt? Relieved?

Then, quietly, almost too casually, Aoife asked, "So, in theory, if I had a cassette of our original recording, you could go back and fix this?" She held up the pick for emphasis.

Ena's stomach tightened. *This wasn't just a hypothetical, was it?*

She was hesitant but responded, "I swore to my Granddad I wouldn't time travel again." Her voice wavered. "But if you wanted me to—" She hesitated. "I guess I could try."

The air in the room changed. A heavy, uncertain silence stretched.

Aoife turned the pick over between her fingers, staring at it.

Then Ena spoke, carefully, measured. "But there's more."

Her hands clenched in her lap. "I don't know how to say this, but—" She shifted in her chair. "—that album was the only one you made."

"What?"

Ena clenched her hands in her lap. "The Fin Whales…well, one night, coming back from a concert in Big Sur, your bus went off a cliff in the rain. No one survived."

Aoife went still.

The pick that had been spinning idly between her fingers suddenly stopped.

"Wait. So you're telling me—" Her gaze flicked around the office, the company she built, the life she lived. Her voice dropped, became unreadable. "—we all died?"

Ena nodded. A long pause. Aoife took that in. She, Georgia, and Liz, all gone.

Her fingers stilled against the desk. Aoife looked out into the distance. "That's what would have happened?"

Aoife slightly shivered. Ena could imagine that familiar sensation crawling up Aoife's spine, that feeling between disbelief and the magnitude of the alternative reality. She had felt it too when she first realized the truth.

Then, with a slow, sharp exhale, Aoife seemed to recenter, grounding herself in the now. In the life she did have. "Wow. You know how to spin a story. Of course, there's no way for me to know if any of this is true." Once again, Aoife became unreadable.

Ena nodded again. "That's true." She took in the office, then met Aoife's gaze head-on. "But you built all of this. I imagine you know how to judge character. You'll have to decide if you believe me."

For the first time, Ena didn't feel like she was asking for permission to be believed. She was standing in her own truth, and that truth was enough.

Aoife studied her for a long moment. "I remember Fiona. And you're right, she tried to help us. I guess it wasn't to be."

She paused, gazing out the window again. Ena waited.

Aoife turned toward Ena, her words softening, just a little. "You remind me of her, you know. Coming in here, going toe to toe with me. I can't imagine too many kids, young adults, doing that."

She paused again, nostalgia in her eye. "Is Fiona still causing trouble the only way she can?"

Ena's breath caught. The words touched an exposed nerve.

Ena spoke, unsteady past the lump in her throat. "She passed away a couple of months ago." The words came out quieter than she intended. "In some strange way, that kicked this whole thing off. If she hadn't passed, my mom and I wouldn't have been in the attic. No time travel."

Mentioning Fiona's death made the loss feel sharp all over again.

Aoife was silent for a long beat. "I'm sorry for your loss," she said quietly. "She was a force of nature."

Her gaze flicked around her office. "In some strange way, I owe Fiona my life, this life."

Another pause. Then, in a softer voice, "Ena, it took real guts to show up here and tell me the truth."

She gave her a slow, reflective nod. "Even if you could go back in time and undo things…" Aoife's voice was steady, knowing. Her fingers drummed once on the desk, then stilled. "I think the life I've lived has been an amazing, rocky, wonderful ride."

She took a moment to reflect, a small, almost private smile tugging at the corner of her mouth. "And wouldn't trade it."

Ena nodded.

Aoife considered her. "It might be that I owe you."

Ena thought for a moment. "Maybe. But so many people loved your music, and I took that from them. I didn't just rob you, I robbed the world."

Aoife shook her head. "That's heavy. You've been carrying that, haven't you?"

Ena didn't answer. She didn't have to.

Aoife leaned forward. "Look, it's not like you robbed the world of a cure for cancer. You have to look at the other side of the coin." She gestured around her office. "I'm proud of the work we do here. We get thank-you letters all the time. People telling us we helped them learn to love music, to create music. If you stole some songs from the world, you also gave the world this."

Ena gasped. Since returning from 1986, Ena had been carrying guilt, responsibility for doing something bad, wrong. The guilt fluttered away. Aoife's words freed her from it.

"Aoife?" Ena hesitated. "I had looked up to you, and I felt the sting of taking something from you. But I also took that from Georgia and Liz. Shouldn't I talk to them?"

Aoife let out a long, thoughtful exhale. "That's a biggie."

She leaned back, considering.

"We gave ourselves until the end of '87 to make The Fin Whales sustainable. When it didn't happen, we all moved on. They've done amazing things. Maybe it's best to leave this between us."

Ena studied her. It felt like Aoife was letting her off the hook. And Ena was grateful. Graeme had warned her about talking too much about time travel. And after just going through it with Aoife, she had zero interest in an encore with Liz and Georgia.

She nodded. "Yeah. That's probably for the best."

Aoife's gaze sharpened. "Ena, we always need more sharp minds around here. Stay in touch."

Ena smiled. "You should meet my friend Piney. She's the computer genius. Without her and Skyler, we never would have found you."

Aoife nodded, amused. "Then maybe we should all talk sometime." She checked the clock. "Now, as much as I hate to say it, work calls."

Ena stood. Relief filled her, a lightness she hadn't felt in weeks.

She hesitated and then said, "My grandfather swore me to secrecy, so now I have to do the same."

Aoife raised an eyebrow. "Oh?"

Ena's signature half-smile appeared, mischief flashing in her eyes. Her right dimple deepened.

"This never happened." She winked. "But you already knew that."

Aoife chuckled and nodded. "Loud and clear."

UNBROKEN CHAIN

Aoife walked Ena back up to the reception desk, her expression still tinged with curiosity. She extended a hand with a wry smile. "Well, Ena, that was easily one of the most fascinating 'interviews' I've had in a long time."

Ena shook her hand, meeting her gaze. "Thanks for the...*time*," she said, punctuating it with a wink.

Skyler was curled up in their egg chair, legs folded beneath them, gazing out at the sweeping view of Mt. Rainier and Puget Sound, lost in thought. Nearby, Piney was deep in conversation with a young woman whose short, jet-black hair framed her angular features. A delicate chain connected the twin rings in her nostrils, arching over the bridge of her nose. The woman looked up as Aoife approached, then jerked her chin toward Piney.

"Boss, we hiring? We can't let this one slip through. She's got some sharp takes on where things are headed in our field."

Aoife chuckled, her eyes twinkling as she turned to Piney. "You must be Piney. Ena had great things to say about you. And we're always looking for sharp minds." She tapped a finger against her temple.

"I'll have my people talk to your people." Piney grin

Ena cleared her throat. "Well, we should get going. ʿ
you again."

"The pleasure was all mine." Aoife met Ena's eyes one la
time before turning back to the steady hum of work waiting for
her.

As the trio gathered their things, the receptionist, still
looking slightly starstruck, fumbled for words. "Uh, thank you
for visiting us today."

"Thanks," the three friends said in unison.

The elevator doors slid open, and they stepped inside. As
soon as they shut, Piney spun to Ena. "And? It seems like it must
have gone okay."

Ena closed her eyes for a second, then launched into a blow-
by-blow retelling of the conversation. She detailed how Aoife
had shifted from irritated skepticism to cautious curiosity, then,
finally, to something that looked a lot like acceptance. By the
time they reached the train station, Ena had relived every key
moment.

But as they settled into their seats for the ride back to
Portland, a shadow of doubt lingered. She let out a breath,
staring at her hands. "I still can't shake the feeling that I did
something wrong. That I broke something that shouldn't have
been broken."

Skyler, who had been quiet, turned to look at her, that
unnervingly deep, searching look only Skyler could give.
"Maybe," they said softly. "Or maybe you actually unbroke
something that should never have been broken."

Ena frowned, lifting an eyebrow.

Skyler leaned back against the seat, gaze flickering toward
the window. "Think about it. Aoife built a meaningful business.
She's helped people. The other two band members? She said

...t on to have solid careers. If they'd stayed on the path ...e, they all would have died young."

They turned back to Ena, gazing at her thoughtfully.

"It's impossible to say for sure," Skyler continued, "but it seems like this version of things tips the balance in our favor. It feels right. I think you might have rearranged the puzzle for the better."

Ena let Skyler's words settle in, turning them over in her mind.

She remembered Aoife's voice, firm with certainty: *Even given the choice, I wouldn't change my destiny.*

Maybe she hadn't broken anything after all. Maybe, without meaning to, she'd just shifted the game pieces around, and somehow, this version was better.

She exhaled, the tension in her shoulders loosening but not vanishing. There were still questions. There were still unknowns.

But maybe she could live with that. She turned to the window and watched the landscape blur past.

Piney stretched her legs out in front of her. "So, that's it? You're good with this?"

Ena hesitated. "I don't know about good, but I think I can live with it."

Piney pressed her lips together, weighing that answer. "Hmph."

Skyler tilted their head, studying Piney. "You don't agree?"

Piney shrugged. "I just keep thinking…Ena interfered with time. That can't be right, can it?"

Ena looked down at her hands. "I guess that's the thing, small actions can have big impacts. Who's to say what's 'right'? Look at Skyler, they took that disk from the radio station. Who knows what that might change? And they didn't even need time travel to do it."

A beat of silence passed before Piney gave Ena a sideways look. "Damn, Quinn-Baker. You look like you just finished a boss battle."

Ena let out a weak laugh. "That's exactly how I feel."

Piney grinned. "That's it. We're making 'Time Travelers Anonymous' a thing."

Skyler tapped their chin. "Rule 1: Don't steal from your favorite musician unless you're sure you won't erase them from history."

"Rule 2: If you break reality, you're in charge of fixing it," Piney added.

Ena yawned, stretching her arms over her head. "Rule 3…" She trailed off as her body sank deeper into the seat.

She didn't finish the thought.

The train rocked gently beneath them, the motion pulling her under. For the first time in weeks, she slept, deep and dreamless, all the way home.

♪ ♫ ♪

A few days later, Ena sat with Graeme on the front porch swing, sipping iced tea. The late afternoon air was warm, birds chirping in the distance.

"Granddad, can I ask you something?"

Graeme took a slow sip, then nodded. "Of course, Ena."

She hesitated, rolling the condensation on her glass between her fingers. "Every time I mentioned Dr. Docks, you got a look. There's more to the story, isn't there?"

Graeme set his glass on the porch railing. "Honestly, there's not much of a story. I've always had a good relationship with CPU, even taught a few classes here and there. Dr. Docks, she's brilliant, no doubt about that. But she's a dog with a bone when she wants something. Her ambition can cloud her judgment."

He shook his head.

"She was always quick to push herself to the front of the pack, making sure her name was the one people remembered. She's someone I've always kept at arm's length, just never felt like I could fully trust her."

Ena frowned, turning that over in her mind. She trusted her grandfather implicitly. He was a good judge of character. But Dr. Docks had been generous with her time and had helped her solve the puzzle of how to get back to 2019.

"People are complicated, I guess," she said finally.

Graeme chuckled. "Truer words." His eyes twinkled as he reached for his glass. "Oh, before I forget, a package came for you. Strange that it was sent here."

He pulled himself up off the swing and disappeared inside. A moment later, he returned, carrying a large cardboard box and setting it down in front of her.

Ena eyed the return address: BridgeResonance.

Her stomach did a small flip as she tore open the box.

On top was a handwritten note, resting against a CD case. She unfolded the note and read:

> *Ena,*
>
> *Thank you for the visit. It was illuminating.*
>
> *Here are some BridgeResonance hoodies for you and your friends.*
>
> *I thought you might like a copy of The Fin Whales recording.*
>
> **Note: This is NOT a cassette. ;) **
>
> *Do stay in touch.*
>
> *Best,*
>
> *Aoife Kinsella*
>
> *P.S. I only had Fiona's address, my assistant said it was still accurate. Hope this finds you.*

Ena let out a soft laugh, shaking her head.

Graeme raised an eyebrow. "Care to share?"

Ena held the note tightly. "We tracked down Aoife. I told her the whole story. And what could have been."

Graeme studied her for a moment, then nodded. "I'm really impressed, Ena. That was brave. Fiona would be proud of you, and so am I."

His words sank in, a stamp of approval from someone she loved. It settled deep, warm and steady.

Ena nodded, but her fingers still traced the edges of the CD case. Some questions had answers. Some didn't.

Ena flipped open the CD case and moved over to a little cabinet on the porch that housed an old CD player. She popped in the CD, and the defiant chords of "Fight, No Flight" broke the quiet spring afternoon. The song was loud and unapologetic, much like Fiona.

The pre-chorus echoed meanings, deep and earned:

> *They write the rules, we fight back*
> *We're lighting matches to their past*

Ena thought about Fiona and how she never accepted rules as a given. Creating *True Notes*, lifting up voices, and refusing to take the easy path. Fiona left inspiring footprints in the paths she had walked.

Reflecting on Tara, Ena saw how, in a very different way, her mother embodied that rebellious nature, quieter but no less challenging of the status quo. A bold leader in a place where women were not always welcomed, Tara never backed down; she didn't have to prove she belonged. She just *did*.

And Ena? She saw how that legacy lived in herself. She'd faced the impossible, learned to lean on friends, confronted her fears, and made it through. Maybe, just maybe she should avoid the '*lighting matches to their past*' in the future.

The chain held. And it moved forward with her.

A Sound Logic Journey continues in Book 2

Missing Notes

If you enjoyed *Keeping Time*, Ena's story continues in *Missing Notes*.

You'll meet Wanderers of Wonder, a band haunted by the past. Can time heal old wounds? Step into the story of a group that never made it out of the '90s and discover how their music still echoes into Ena's world.

Meanwhile, Sound Logic pushes forward on their own path, learning what it truly means to chase the spotlight. Friendships are tested as Ena struggles to balance promises and temptation, Piney wrestles with trust, and Skyler searches for meaning when the world feels like it's unraveling.

Fiona's voice still lingers, lighting the way when things go darkest. Original songs from Sound Logic and Wanderers of Wonder carry the story forward, blending lyrics and narrative into an unforgettable soundtrack.

Then comes a challenge no one could have imagined, a world suddenly brought to a halt. Stages go dark, possibilities vanish, and isolation opens doors that should have stayed shut.

Because in a world where music is memory, every note holds the power to change everything.

Coming Fall 2026

* 9 7 9 8 9 9 9 7 3 9 1 0 0 *